SECRETS

NADIA LEE

1

ANTHONY

I HIT THE NUMBER FOR IRIS AS I RUSH THROUGH THE corridor of aquariums. She doesn't pick up. Panic spikes my blood, drying my mouth.

Is she already with Sam? That motherfucker didn't go to the trouble of setting everything up like this just to hand a check over to Elizabeth's foundation.

I try to text, but my fingers are too clumsy. What I send has so many typos, I doubt Iris will understand a word.

No response.

Damn it.

I burst out of the restaurant. One of La Mer's valets says, "Your ticket, sir?"

I tunnel my fingers into my hair, ready to tear it out. I fucking *hate* valet parking. *Where's TJ?* Sometimes he just sits in the car if he thinks I won't be long, but sometimes he takes a break or has lunch. Shit.

Then I see the Cullinan pulling in. *Thank God.* The valet

reaches over to open the door, but I shove him out of the way, opening the door myself and jumping in.

TJ is already pulling away. "Where to?"

"Peacher & Son," I say, calling Sam's office with one hand and using the other to slam the door shut.

"Peacher & Son, Sam Peacher's office. How may I help you?" comes a pleasant female voice.

"Is Iris there?" I demand.

"I'm sorry, but who?"

Either she's playing dumb or she has no clue. "His niece. I know she went to see him."

"Oh. Mr. Peacher is taking the day off."

"So he's home?"

"I can't tell you that. If you'd like to lea—"

I hang up. This is so much worse. At least in the office, Sam couldn't do anything rash—too many witnesses.

But now... Iris could be anywhere. How the hell could I have been so careless? That bastard tried to browbeat her into leaving the country. Even packed a couple of Iris's bags, and would've dragged her to the airport and put her on a plane if I hadn't shown up. People who're willing to go that far don't just give up. They try again and again. How many times did he try to get Mother to invest with him until he succeeded?

Idiot. Should've known better. If anything happens to her, it'll be your fault.

I bite my lip until I taste blood.

"Not to Peacher & Son?" TJ says.

"No." *Iris, where are you?*

If I can't reach her in time... I press the heel of my palm against my brow. I can't even think about the possibility. It's too horrific. A text pings my phone, and I jump, praying it's Iris, telling me she's okay.

It's from Elizabeth. *Iris went to Sam's mansion.* She adds the address.

I recite it to TJ. "Go as fast as you can." To my shock, my voice is shaking—pleading. I quit pleading nine years ago when I realized nothing could bring her back.

Have to get there in time to stop Sam.

The SUV weaves through the Los Angeles traffic. Acid seems to drip into my veins with every second that ticks by. My nails dig into my palms. *I'm a fucking moron.* I should've hired an army of guards to keep Iris safe.

If anything happens to her, I'm going to rip Sam to pieces with my bare hands.

Finally, Sam's mansion comes into view. Gated, of course.

"What do you want to tell them?" TJ asks.

I squint at the fancy wrought iron. It's designed to look impressive, not provide actual security. "Nothing. Step on it and drive through."

TJ grunts.

The engine roars as the car accelerates. I brace myself. The SUV slams into the gates, breaking them. A corner of one of the gates hits the windshield, leaving a crack on the glass. TJ curses under his breath.

"Doesn't matter." A million Cullinans can't equal Iris.

The car comes to a screeching halt in front of the mansion. I jump out, then leap up the steps, ready to tear the building apart for her.

A tall toothpick of a butler raises a hand, his florid face alarmed. "Sir, I must ask you to—"

"Fuck off." I push him out of the way. "Iris!" I yell into the vast foyer. "*Iris!*"

"I'm calling the cops!" the man shrieks, his butler-ish dignity apparently forgotten.

I grab him by the back of his collar before he can run off. "*Where's Iris?*"

He bristles. "I'm not saying anything to you, you...criminal!"

I bare my teeth. "You want to do this the hard way?" I raise my fist, ready to beat the answer out of him if that's what it takes. I doubt Sam's butler is as tight-lipped as my parents' back in Tempérane.

"Ack!" He raises his palms in front of his face. "Not my nose!"

"*Where is she?*"

"By the pool in the back." He gestures with a shaky hand.

Shoving him out of the way, I run down the hall. Sam and Iris are visible through the closed French doors. Relief almost makes me stumble. She's still here. And she doesn't seem hurt, but...

They're sitting at the edge of the pool, him leaning back on his hands and her hunched over, a palm resting on one bent knee. Their feet are in the water, and Sam and Iris are both drenched. Son of a bitch. What the hell did he do?

Iris turns her head and says something to Sam. He stiffens, then shoves her hard into the water with both hands.

I see her reaction like a horror movie in slow motion. Panic and fear cloud her eyes. She flails, reaching for Sam, but her hands grasp nothing but air as she falls into the pool with a small splash.

What the fuck!

My heart racing, I pump my legs and arms faster. Sam stares at the surface, not moving. Not even blinking.

I burst through the doors and dive into the pool. Iris's hair clouds around her as she jerks her head this way and that. Small air bubbles escape her nose and mouth as she flails her arms and her legs, but she's sinking.

My blood runs cold. *She can't swim.*

I wrap an arm around her and pull her upward. She thrashes a bit, her movements weak. *Iris. It's me. Just a little longer. I'm taking you out of here.*

I repeat that in my head as though she can read my mind. I drag us out on the other side of the pool. I lay her on her back, then on her side, unsure what the hell I'm supposed to do to help her now that she's out of the water.

"Iris, are you all right? Talk to me, babe."

She gasps, then starts coughing violently, her whole body shaking. Did water get into her lungs?

Desperate to know how badly she's hurt, I run my hands over her. She's shivering badly, as though chilled to the bone. I don't feel anything broken, and she isn't crying out in pain. But what I'm doing is a crude check. She needs to see a doctor.

Finally, her coughing fit subsides, and she looks up at me, her gray eyes glassy. "Tony?" she whispers dazedly.

Thank God. Tears of relief spring to my eyes, and I blink them away as I pull her into my arms. "I'm right here, Iris. I'm right here."

I feel her small body tremble, and bitter self-recrimination spreads through me like poison. I screwed up. *Again.* One step too late. How long has Sam been pushing her into the water and dragging her back out, just to do it again? Nausea starts in my gut, leaving a sour tang in my mouth, but I hold it together. There's no time for weakness. Iris comes first. She always comes first.

"Tony..." She looks up at me, her pupils wide. Her lips are bloodless. Just hours ago, she told me, "Love you," with those sweet lips, her eyes bright and tender.

Oh, Iris, my heart.

"I..." She goes limp.

"Iris!" I put a shaking hand on her cheek. Why the hell is she so cold? And pale? *"Iris!"*

"What the hell are you doing here, Anthony?" Sam demands.

I glance in his direction. He's finally made it around to this side of the pool.

Underneath the anger are frayed nerves he's desperately trying to hide. His face is ashen, his hand clenched around a towel.

Murderous rage erupts in my chest. I want to beat the shit out of him for hurting Iris. I want to break him the way he tried to break her—shove his face into the water and hold it there, make him feel the terror of drowning.

But right now, Iris needs me.

I pick her up. She's too light, one of her arms dangling loosely. Swallowing my anger and panic, I start to walk past Sam.

He blocks my way. "She and I have unfinished business."

"Get out of my way!" I try to move around him again.

The asshole stays in front of me, his arms spread. "She's my niece!"

I bare my teeth, ready to rip him to pieces. I won't even have to put Iris down to kick this fat, red-faced moron's ass.

"Enough!" One sharp word cracks the air, the voice high-pitched and cold.

5

Coiled for action, I look up and see a pale Elizabeth standing at the French doors with her Russian hound.

Sam licks his lips. "Elizabeth."

"So. This is what the donation was really about."

They can hash out the money problem later. I start to walk away.

Elizabeth turns to me. "Tony—"

I don't bother to slow down. Elizabeth is a great actress, just like her brother. Her entire family, including her, thrives on drama—from sex tapes to crazy "marry for inheritance" gossip to over-the-top public declarations of love. I have no patience for any of it right now.

She follows. The Russian moves toward me, but she raises a hand to stop him. "Tony, please. Listen—"

"I'm done with you. If you wanted to get back at me, you should've taken a shot at *me*. You and your freaking family... I should've known better."

"I swear I didn't know!"

TJ is holding the door to the Cullinan open. "None of that matters," I say coolly. "Iris is hurt, so none of that matters." I deposit Iris on the back seat and get in after her.

"Now what?" TJ says the second he's behind the wheel.

"Home." I pull Iris tighter toward me. "Get Dr. Young to meet us there."

"Should send a driver. That woman drives like a slug."

Right. She's a brilliant doctor, but a stickler for rules and refuses to drive a mile over the speed limit. "Tell Wei to pick her up."

2

___

IRIS

THE GIRL IS SO PRETTY IN THAT BLUE DRESS. SHE WAVES AT me, like a friendly mermaid, her smile radiant. Her eyes sparkle like jewels, and I smile and wave back. Can we be friends? Maybe she can teach me to swim. And maybe I can teach her to play the piano. A lovely exchange.

Suddenly, murky water surrounds us. She tries to swim away, but can't. The car seems to shrink and close up around her, enclosing her like a cage. I search for something I can use to free her, but there's nothing. The current starts to carry me away, and I shake my head, flailing my limbs, trying my best to resist. *No.* I don't want to leave her behind. But the flow of the water is inexorable.

She yanks at the handle, but the door doesn't open. She bangs on it like an angry animal. It doesn't budge. One beseeching hand reaches for me. But I'm outside, too far away. I want to help her, but I can't move. The light in her eyes goes dark. Fear and horror war inside me.

Save her.

Except I don't know how to swim. I never learned. I was too busy practicing the piano. *Forgive me. I'm sorry. I don't know how to save you.*

We can't keep her like this forever. Not medically advisable.

Can't wake her now.

She's never going to be the same. Look at what happened to her head.

She knows nothing.

A blank canvas.

Mentally incompetent.

Iris, you can't do this. I know what's best for you. Let me take care of you...

Cool hands arrive, impersonal and professional. They drag me out of the water, then out of the fogginess. I'm so tired and weak that I can't resist as they move me around like a doll. Too late, I realize they've put me in a straitjacket. *No!*

"We don't want you to injure yourself. You don't make good choices. You're prone to doing rash things, and end up hurting yourself."

No. No, please don't. The straitjacket holds me tightly, and I struggle in its suffocating embrace...

Only to come face to face with Tony and Elizabeth.

They look at me, identical appalled expressions on their beautiful faces.

Don't let them take me away. Please don't.

But Tony and Elizabeth don't hear me. They look away. Tony's the first to speak. "What a sad, crazy girl."

"A shame," Elizabeth says ruefully. "I didn't realize she was this bad."

He puts a comforting hand on her shoulder.

She grimaces. "Makes you wonder about your judgment, doesn't it?"

"Don't let it bother you," he says. "There will be others."

No! Please! I'm not crazy. I'm not mentally incapable. Please!

The scream builds inside; I want to yell, but can't. There's a huge, bearlike paw over my mouth, trapping the words. I struggle even harder to free myself. Tears stream down my face, but the same strong paw silences my sobs of desperation and panic. *Tony, you said you loved me. Don't let them take me away. Please!*

"Nobody cares what you want," someone that sounds like Sam whispers into my ear. "If you'd only been more obedient, we wouldn't have had to go this far. Now everyone will know."

No, no, no, no, no. I begin to sob. My mind isn't broken. It really isn't. *Don't take me away. Don't lock me away.*

"Let me *go*! I'm not *broken*!" I scream, the paw finally gone from my mouth. "My mind is fine!"

"Iris. Iris!" A tight embrace.

My God. The straitjacket. It's so tight around me that I can't breathe. I thrash, using every ounce of strength in a last-ditch effort to free myself. If I struggle hard enough, maybe it'll vanish, like the paw. "No, no!"

But the embrace doesn't loosen. "Iris, it's okay. I'll keep you safe. I promise. I won't let anything happen to you. I swear it." Soothing kisses rain on the crown of my head, my forehead, cheeks and eyes. "You're safe. I swear you're safe."

The voice is low. Anguished. A warm, large hand runs along my back in comfort. More words come, nonsense words said in a soft voice to calm.

Slowly, the panic ebbs away. As my breathing slows, my surroundings begin to make sense. I realize it's Tony holding me, not a straitjacket. I'm not in a mental institute, about to be locked up. I'm home. In our bed.

Sudden relief crashes into me, and I collapse in his arms like a marionette with its strings cut. I clench my teeth, but the tears flow freely now. I can't stop sobbing as the terror of the nightmare lingers, its macabre fingers still trailing over my mind.

"You're safe, Iris. You're safe," he whispers again. "I swear, I won't let anything happen to you. I will always keep you safe."

I look into his tormented eyes and know he's speaking the truth.

I clutch him tightly and press my face to his strong chest. Smell the mix of his warm male scent and chlorine, which brings back the pool at Sam's mansion and the nightmare I just had. I shiver, then finally register that his clothes are damp. I look up at him.

"You're wet." He's in the same clothes he wore at Sam's... when he pulled me out of the water. My memory's a bit hazy after Sam pushed me into the pool, but I remember Tony leaning over me, saying something I didn't quite understand over the thrumming of my heart.

"I know. I was too late. I didn't get there until Sam pushed you into the pool."

I remember Sam's eyes flaring with grim apprehension before he decided to push me back in, knowing I can't swim. If Tony hadn't been there... I shiver, refusing to let my mind go in that direction. "No. You got there in time. You saved me."

The self-loathing in his gaze says he doesn't accept my version of events. "If you hadn't passed out, I would've killed Sam for what he did. How long did he torture you?"

Does he know about the threat Sam made to declare me incompetent? Or is this something else?

What the Tony from my nightmare did flashes through my mind. I turn away. The expression of disgust and pity—I don't want to see that on his face, ever.

Suddenly, I'm afraid to tell him everything, even as I'm desperate to have someone believe I'm not crazy or incompetent. What if he agrees—even a little bit—with Sam? That maybe I *don't* really know what's good for me?

It was just a dream. Tony didn't really do it. Don't push him away because of your nightmare.

I search his face. Even knowing about my messed-up memory, he's never once judged me or treated me like I was weird or pathetic. He's rescued me twice already—from Jamie Thornton and now Sam. He deserves my complete trust.

I take a breath. "It started the day he tried to ship me off to Tokyo. He said he'd find a judge who'd declare me incompetent. It wouldn't be that hard because I'm not...normal like most people. My memories are...patchy. Then he could do whatever he wanted with me. My opinion wouldn't matter at all."

Cursing under his breath, he cradles my face in his large

hands. "Nobody's going to do anything to you. I won't let anybody take you away. I'm sorry I couldn't protect you today. I had no idea Sam would do that."

"That's right. You didn't know. So don't blame yourself." I don't know what it takes to declare somebody incompetent, but if Tony says he won't let Sam do it to me, I trust he won't. He'll find a way somehow.

"But I should've anticipated. It wouldn't have been like him to give up."

Ah, Tony. His self-castigation is just too painful. It's like he can't give himself credit even after winning the battle. I pull back a bit to look at his beloved face, running a hand over his jaw. "I didn't realize how far he'd go. None of us are bad guys for that. Sam's the villain here." I press a kiss on his cheek. "You mind if I use the bathroom?"

He gestures at the en suite bathroom. "Take your time."

"You should change," I say, suddenly realizing I'm in a new set of clothes, but he isn't. "I don't want you to get sick." He starts to get that mulish look. "Please?"

"All right."

I close the door to the bathroom and go to the sink. The mirror above it shows a pale young woman with a blotchy, tear-streaked face. I splash some cold water on it. I'm grateful Tony showed up when he did. When Sam pushed me into the pool...

I close my eyes, gripping the edge of the sink with trembling hands. You'd think falling in a second time would be less shocking, but it was actually worse. The first time was an accident. The second wasn't. Sam knew exactly what he was doing. And from the hard glint in his eyes as I plunged back in, I could tell he wasn't going to pull me out again. It's scary how water can bury you. No matter how I moved my arms and legs, I couldn't propel myself toward the surface. Actually, the harder I tried to swim, the faster I seemed to sink.

Why did he try to kill me? Was it because he realized he could get rid of me permanently? Given how hard he tried to make me leave, my being in Los Angeles is a problem for him somehow. But enough for murder?

Think Tony's still going to want you if he knows what a crazy needy girl you are? Sam's voice asks.

I shudder, blinking. Tony still loves me. I can tell from his voice, the way he holds me. It's like I'm the most precious thing in the world.

But still... I can't stop the humiliation from lapping at me anyway. Tony's so dynamic, so wonderful that I feel like one day he's going to wake up, take a look at me and wonder what the hell he's doing with such a broken mess.

3

ANTHONY

INSTEAD OF CHANGING, I GO DOWNSTAIRS TO GRAB A STIFF drink, my eyes unfocused and unseeing. Iris's painful nightmare cries are still haunting me, ripping out bits of my heart. How she begged, insisted she wasn't crazy, was capable of making decisions for herself. And she dreamed of water again.

Fucking Sam. Just how many times did he throw her back into that pool, intent on making her give in to his demands?

My hands clench into tight fists. A need for violence nearly overwhelms whatever control civil society has taught me. How could I have been so arrogant as to think my declaration to ruin Sam would be enough to stop him?

"Is she awake?" Dr. Young asks from the counter, lowering her tea. I told her to help herself to whatever was in the kitchen while I kept an eye on Iris. She didn't like it, but eventually gave up when she realized I needed some time alone with Iris, even if it was only to hold her hand.

"Yes."

She stands. "I should go check up on her."

"Give her a minute. She's in the bathroom."

"Ah."

"She didn't sound good."

Dr. Young's dark eyes instantly sharpen. "How so?"

"Emotionally. She was crying." I pour myself a generous helping of whiskey and down it.

"The experience had to be traumatizing, based on what you said. Being dunked in a pool when you can't swim is terrifying." She shivers. "I can't swim that well, either."

"Really?" In her mid-fifties, she wears competence like a superhero wears a cape. Her precision when she works reminds of a scalpel, and—other than break the speed limit—she's never struck me as someone who couldn't do something.

She gestures vaguely toward the living room. "Your assistant let a guest in. I offered her some tea, but she declined."

I glance over, and there sits Elizabeth fucking King. Wei is missing.

"What the hell are you doing here?" I say. "Stalking me now?" In my peripheral vision, I note Dr. Young heading upstairs, but my bigger concern is Elizabeth at the moment.

"I'm here to say I'm sorry, Tony. How is Iris?"

"Why? Got more errands for her to run? Maybe next time you should tell her to put on a bathing suit before she goes."

She closes her eyes briefly. "I honestly had no idea."

"Expect me to believe that?"

"It's true. I swear to you. I wish she'd said something—"

"Just like you told everyone about your embarrassing family dramas?"

She flushes, her mouth tight. "You're right. *I* should've been more on top of things. Is there anything I can do?"

What the hell does she think she can do? "Is that a serious offer?"

"Of course."

"Why do you care after accusing me of playing a game at La Mer?"

"Because something's up. After you left with Iris, Sam told

14

me it was an accident, but I don't believe him. If what he's saying is right, he should've brought her out of the pool, not you."

The reminder reignites my temper. "He dragged her out of the pool, then pushed her right back in, knowing she couldn't swim. He would've kept going if I hadn't shown up."

Elizabeth is bloodless now, her fingers over her mouth. "Oh my God."

I run a shaky hand over my face, hating that I couldn't do more to protect Iris or punish Sam. "He threatened her. Tortured her. He..." I can't continue. Not if I want to maintain control.

"I'm so sorry. I had no idea." She shakes her head slowly. "It's my fault. I should've been more thorough. I should've known something wasn't adding up."

As much as I hate Elizabeth's role in the fuck-up, ultimately, Iris is my responsibility. My sun. My moon. My stars. "You and me both."

"Please, Tony, let me make it up to you and Iris."

I stare at her. She's dead serious, her gray eyes solemn. I realize something else, too. Sam's probably expecting me to strike back at him. But Elizabeth? He would never see that coming. And what she can deliver will be economically and socially painful, if not fatal. I have a lot of pull—my billions have given me that—but I don't have the influence of my family, since I'm an unwanted, disowned son. But she's different. She has the power of the illustrious Pryce family behind her. If that isn't enough, she's related to another powerful family through marriage.

"Then hit him where it hurts the most," I say. "And when he's down, put the boots to him."

4

Iris

When I come out of the bathroom, there is a fifty-something woman in the room, standing by the bed. I stop, my breath stuck in my throat.

If she's an intruder, she doesn't look the part. She's tall, rail thin, her expression professionally warm. Although there's a hint of good taste and wealth in the stylish green blouse and brown slacks and the diamond studs sparkling in her ears, the woman has a utilitarian air—minimal makeup, a no-nonsense bob and horn-rimmed glasses.

"Who are you?" I demand in a hoarse voice, wishing I had a stick or something I could use as a weapon. Just in case.

"I'm Dr. Young," she says, extending a hand. "Hi, Iris."

Panic pumps through me. A *doctor*? Here? Why? She regards me with eyes that are far too sharp. Can she tell what's wrong with me?

"Anthony had me brought here to make sure you're all right," she says, her voice low and soothing. "He's worried about you." She takes a step closer, the hand still extended.

I study her warily. Intellectually, I understand she doesn't mean any harm. Tony wouldn't have asked her to come otherwise. And if she tries anything, all I have to do is scream.

But deep inside, I can't shake off the fear. The nightmare with the straitjacket is still lingering in my mind. I hug myself. "Where's Tony?"

She finally drops the hand. "Talking to a guest. Would it be all right if I just checked you over? I did that earlier while you were unconscious—"

"Did you find anything...off?" I ask, my voice almost too harsh. But I need to know if there's anything that could be used against me if anybody found out.

She blinks. "Uh, no. Nothing concerning. But now that you're awake, I just want to check again to make sure." I start to decline, but she adds, "It'll put Anthony's mind at ease."

Argh. I don't want to do it, but Tony... His anguished expression from earlier flashes comes unbidden. He's blaming himself for what happened, and I don't want to worry him after what he's gone through today. I sit on the edge of the mattress. "Can we just make it quick?"

"Of course." She opens a black bag I didn't notice earlier and pulls out her instruments. I focus on something beyond the wall, my mind going over Chopin's "Torrent" étude, my fingers moving to match the notes in my head. She checks my pulse and temperature, flashes a light in my eyes, listens to my lungs and a few other things. Unlike the doctors I dealt with after waking up from my coma, her touch is professional without being clinical. She talks to me the entire time, her voice calm and quiet, explaining what she's doing and why it's important. It's surprising and nice, like I'm being respected, and it's important to her that I understand the process.

None of the doctors Sam got for me ever did that. They went about their business, only bothering to explain if I asked what a procedure was for. Mainly they seemed to be in hurry and looked at me like I was interrupting some critically important routine with my questions. I'm grateful Tony brought me home and had Dr. Young check me out. I don't think I'd be able to bear it if I were in a room that smelled of disinfectant and had some harried intern rushing through everything

"All done," she says, placing a gentle hand on my shoulder. "You're fine. Everything looks normal, although I advise you to take it easy for a few days. Anthony told me you were crying after you woke up. Sometimes the trauma of almost drowning is worse than a physical injury. I'm a terrible swimmer myself." She smiles ruefully.

The revelation seems genuine, increasing my sense of connection to her. I almost always feel like I'm the only adult who can't swim, especially when everyone else seems so good at it.

As she puts her things back in her bag, I realize I haven't paid her.

"What kind of insurance do you take?" I blurt out. Oh, God. What if she doesn't take the plan I'm on at the foundation?

"I don't."

Crap. "But...um... How much do you charge, then?"

She smiles. "Don't worry. It's taken care of."

"But—"

"Anthony pays me a retainer to see to his needs. It really isn't a big deal."

"A retainer? You can do that?"

She smiles softly. "Yes, you can do that. And I enjoy it, since it allows me to spend time with my patients and give them the kind of care I want to provide. You take care, Iris, and let me know if you don't feel well or have any questions." She hands me a business card and leaves.

The card has only her name and a number. Suddenly, I realize I didn't even shake her hand and squeeze my eyes shut with embarrassment. Talk about rude, although she didn't seem upset. I owe her an apology in person.

I place the card on my bedside table and stay seated on the bed. I stare at nothing in particular, waiting for Tony to come in. After a few moments, I realize he isn't.

So I get up, go downstairs...and freeze at the sight of Tony with Elizabeth. She's seated on a couch near the piano, while he's standing over her, his back to me. She's staring at him like he just told her somebody kicked her puppy, her wide eyes full of shock and anger.

How is she here? A metallic, sour tang coats my tongue as I recall the way she turned away from me in my dream. It wasn't real, but at the same time, I'm pretty sure she wouldn't hesitate to dump me if she thought I wasn't all right in the head. She wouldn't want to be near someone like me when she's so perfect.

Now I wish I'd put on fresh makeup. And done my hair. Elizabeth is stunning in her designer magenta dress, like she's just finished a photo shoot.

Suddenly, she notices me. All the shock and anger evaporate from her face, leaving only cordial warmth. Tony turns around, too, then immediately comes over and puts an arm around my shoulders. "Are you all right?" he asks in a low voice.

"Yes." I force a smile, hoping it makes me look as fine as I claim to be. "Elizabeth, what are you doing here?"

"I came to return your purse." Elizabeth lifts up the bag I left at Sam's.

Was she there to see the ugliness between me and Sam? My knees start to feel a bit wobbly. I drag myself to a couch. Tony sits next to me, his arm still around my shoulders. I fold my hands neatly in my lap. "Thank you."

She comes over and crouches by my feet, looking up at my eyes. "Iris, I'm very sorry. I didn't know Sam was planning to hurt you. Just so you know, Tony's going to stop Sam if he tries anything else. If that isn't enough to put your mind at ease, please trust that I will make it my mission to ensure Sam won't be bothering you like that again."

I jerk back. I understand Tony protecting me, but Elizabeth? "But why...?"

"You're part of the foundation, which means you're one of my people. And I also happen to despise bullies." She gives me a blinding smile, the kind that almost makes it seem like there's a halo around her. "Don't worry about anything and focus on getting better. You can take the next week off to recover."

"But I don't—"

Elizabeth squeezes my knee. "I mean it." Standing, she turns to Tony. "We'll talk again soon." Then she leaves.

"Wow," I whisper, watching her go. Then I realize something I've been overlooking. "How did she know about me and Sam?"

"She and I were having lunch together," Tony says.

A clean-cut, thirtyish Asian man comes out from the den behind the kitchen. The blood red of his tie goes well with his charcoal suit and a snow-white shirt. He's slim but on the tall side, his face sharply chiseled—large, slightly slanted eyes, surprisingly high cheekbones, a perfectly proportioned nose and a mouth that's a bit too full and soft-looking. His hair is slicked back, and he sports a pair of rimless glasses and an open smile.

Normally, a smile like that would put me at ease. But not today.

"Everything's been taken care of, boss," he says to Tony. "TJ's taking Dr. Young home, and the rest is...whatever you want to do."

"Thanks, Wei," Tony says. "Iris, this is Wei Song, my assistant. Wei, Iris Smith, my girlfriend."

Wei's smile widens, and he shakes hands with me. His grip is firm without being overly strong, and he makes direct eye contact. "A pleasure."

"Same here," I murmur, studying Tony's assistant. I've never been to Tony's office or run into an employee other than TJ. It's obvious Wei is very close to Tony, but surprising how much of a polar opposite Wei is to TJ. There's nothing Visigothic or rough-hewn about Wei's elegant appearance.

"No wonder he's hardly ever in the office these days," he says, with sidelong glance at Tony. "If you ever need anything, please don't hesitate to call, twenty-four seven." He hands me his card.

"Thank you." I take it with a small smile. He's impossible to not like. And he reminds me of... I scowl as my mind grasps at a faint glimmer of memory.

"You okay, Iris?" Tony asks. "Should I get Dr. Young to come back?"

"What? No. I'm fine. Just...thinking about something." Wei,

too, is looking at me with concern. "I'm fine now. Really. Dr. Young said I was great."

Wei nods. "Of course. If that's all, I'll see you at the office, boss. Again, a pleasure, Miss Smith." He leaves.

The moment I'm alone with Tony, my whole body collapses like a rag doll. I sag bonelessly into his arms. There's no other word for it: mentally and emotionally, I'm exhausted.

Wordlessly, Tony sits, pulling me onto his lap and holding me. I cling to him, my eyes closed. Then, very slowly, I sigh. "Sorry."

5

ANTHONY

IRIS. MY HANDS ARE ON HER SKIN AND HER WEIGHT IS ON MY lap, reminding me that she's still here. Still alive.

When she came down from our room, she looked so pale that I was afraid she'd faint. Why the hell would Dr. Young tell her she's fine? She should've ordered at least a day's bed rest.

I thought I heard Iris murmur something that sounded suspiciously like "sorry," but I shake myself mentally. Why would she say that? She did nothing wrong. I'm the one who screwed up. Again.

She snuggles closer, her hands wrapped tightly around me, as though she can't bear to be separated. I pull her tighter, because I also need to feel her presence as closely as possible. I keep being too late, arriving after she's hurt, but somehow she thinks I'm a hero and clings to me like I'm an anchor keeping her safe. Gratitude that she doesn't hate me for being a step too late wars with fear—that one day she'll realize I keep failing her and despise me.

Just like Mother despises me for not protecting Katherine.

Just like Father does for not fixing things at home almost a decade ago.

"Your assistant's very nice," Iris murmurs.

I almost smile. Everyone thinks he's nice because he never shows them his other side. The glasses are fake—without prescription. He wears them to make himself appear even more harmless. But I've seen him fight. He's an expert martial artist and doesn't mind breaking a bone or two if necessary. "You should put his number in your phone."

"Why?"

"You heard him. In case you need anything."

"But he's your assistant."

"So? Everything I have is yours." Including my shriveled, damaged heart.

"Are you going to tell me he'll do whatever I need—no matter how insignificant?"

"Yes. But there's more. I trust Wei and TJ with my life. It'll make me feel less worried if I know you'll always have somebody to make sure you're all right." Except it still isn't enough. Not for me. Not anymore. I'm going to have to arrange for something more permanent ASAP.

Iris holds my hand in hers. "I'm never going near Sam again. And he's not going to come anywhere near me or my friends." She suddenly jerks up. "I need to call Julie and warn her. What if he's already trying to do something to her to get to me?"

Of all the things for her to worry about. "I don't think so. Sam's an idiot, but he's got a cockroach's sense of self-preservation. And while Julie may be frivolous and spoiled, her family's very protective of her. Sam is no match for the Pearce family, and he knows it."

"But remember when he lied to Julie to get inside and grab my things? He doesn't seem that scared of her or her family."

Maybe not. Maybe Sam's scared of something else more. He's gone to great lengths to keep Iris hidden...then banish her from the States, using what meager power he has.

She gets up and calls Julie. I hear the one-sided conversation.

"Hi, Julie. No, I'm not... Oh. I don't know." Her gaze slides toward me briefly. "No, look, I just wanted to tell you that if Sam calls or tries to see you, don't agree to it. No. He tried to make me leave again. Huh? No. I have no idea. Just promise to be careful. No. It's..." She sighs. "He and I fought, and he pushed me into his pool." Even I can hear the screech on the other end of the phone. "No, I'm *fine*. Tony saved me. Yeah. Of course. Of course. Okay, love you." She hangs up.

"I see Julie didn't take it well?"

"She thinks we should press charges for attempted murder." Sadness shimmers in her gaze, and she quickly closes her eyes. "I... This hurts. I thought he cared about me in his own way."

The only thing that fucker cares about is himself. But that isn't what she needs to hear right now. I pull her back into my arms, willing the ugliness of the day to pass without leaving too many marks.

"Do you think..." She stops. "We should pack for our trip," she says, her tone oddly flat.

This is a surprise. I actually had Wei cancel everything because I was certain she'd want to stay home. "Do you still want to go?"

"We should."

"That's not what I asked."

She bites her lip. "I don't want what Sam did to have an effect on our plans. Plus, I know you've been looking forward to it."

"It isn't about me or Sam. I was looking forward to seeing you enjoy yourself." I push tendrils of hair away from her forehead and cheeks. "If you can't enjoy it, there's no point." I pull her closer, needing to feel her warm weight to remind myself—again —that she's safe and in my arms. "And Napa isn't going anywhere."

She sighs. "If you're sure. To be honest, I want to stay home with you. Wherever we're going to stay in Napa is probably nice and all, but I want something familiar right now. And...is it weird that leaving the city feels like I'm sort of giving in to his demands? He's been so adamant about making me leave."

"No," I say softly, even as murder roils in my gut. If Sam were here, I'd be gutting him like a bayou catfish for all the horrible things he's done. But Iris doesn't like it when I bruise and bloody my knuckles. "But you shouldn't have to do something you don't want to prove a point. That's giving him too much power." I brush the tip of my nose against hers. "Why don't we get you nice and relaxed for the evening?"

Her gaze flickers to my mouth. "What do you have in mind?"

She's so transparent when she wants me. I want her, too, but right now, sex can wait. "How about a nice..."

"Yes?"

"...long..."

"Mm-hmm?"

"...bubble bath?"

She blinks. "Really?"

"Yup." I stand, still holding her, and carry her up the stairs. I want her relaxed and happy. Just because we aren't going to Napa doesn't mean we can't do something special for the evening, and I need her occupied for a bit, pampering herself, while I set it all up.

6

IRIS

I EMERGE FROM THE BEDROOM, PINK AND WARM AND smelling of lavender from the long, sinfully luxurious bath. *Thank God that horrible chlorine scent is gone.* I'm in my favorite Tweety Bird nightshirt and heart-print shorts.

Tony's in the kitchen. He's showered as well, and is wearing a plain white T-shirt and black shorts. I stop at the bottom of the stairs and admire the sight. He's so beautiful under the lights.

I told him once there's a difference between handsome and hot. There are men who aren't that good-looking but sizzle with sexuality. There are men who are ridiculously pretty, but somehow leave you cold.

Tony has both. He's so beautiful that it feels like I'm looking directly at the sun—perfect, brilliant, maybe even dangerous if you stare too long. Those cut-glass emerald eyes that go tender every time he turns toward me. That sweet, vulnerable smile that always makes my heart ache with yearning. I've never seen him show those sides to anyone else. To others, he's cool and polite, a man difficult to approach and more difficult to get to know.

And even from a distance, he makes my heart beat faster, my skin warm and prickly as my nerve endings come to life.

God, I want him. Not just in bed, but in all the ways a woman can want a man. In my life. In my dreams. Lodged so deep in my heart it's as though our souls are merged, inseparable.

"You're out," Tony says with a warm smile. "I prepared something simple for dinner."

"You didn't have to. We could've done takeout," I say, crossing the living room to join him.

"But I wanted to. Don't worry, I'm not that bad. I promise."

I laugh. I can't imagine him being bad at anything. I snuggle against him, inhaling his warm, male scent underneath expensive, minty soap and loving it.

Wrapping an arm around me, he kisses me. "Mmm. Much better."

"Is it?" I ask breathlessly.

"An appetizer. Very delicious." He kisses me again, not full-on deep, but not precisely chaste, either.

Heat curls in my belly. "We should have the main course," I murmur against his mouth.

"Not yet." He pulls back. "We need to get you fed. You didn't even have lunch."

A minor oversight in a messy day. But I don't want to think about the time at Sam's. "I'm not really that hungry for food."

He shakes his head. "Feeding you regularly is part of my promise to keep you safe."

I'm beginning to realize when Tony says "safe," he doesn't just mean "away from danger." He means in every aspect of my life—from sleep to food to my emotional wellbeing. It's like he worries constantly that something's going to happen, and he's going to lose me. I wonder briefly if he lost someone to illness. Maybe anorexia or depression, but I can't bring myself to ask, lest I poke a sensitive spot.

So instead, I press a kiss to his shoulder. From the way his jaw grows tight, I can sense he still holds himself responsible for what happened at Sam's place. It'll be a while before he can accept that he couldn't have done anything to prevent it. And the only thing I can do is make sure he knows I will never hold him responsible for things out of his control. "How can I help?"

"By enjoying the food and being with me." His defenses are down, and his eyes show naked need. Not for sexual gratification but for the assurance I'm okay and with him and everything's fine in our world.

Damn it, Sam. I hate him for having put that pain in Tony. Just this morning, we were so happy, planning our first trip together and saying "I love you" to each other. If it hadn't been for my uncle, Tony and I would be in Napa by now, drinking wine and enjoying ourselves without any of this darkness overshadowing us.

"I can do that," I say lightly. "So what's for dinner?"

"Let me show you." He leads me out to the deck, where the air is cool and refreshing. The infinity pool's covered—most likely in deference to my earlier trauma—and the sight makes me a little sad, because he's never done that before, and it's a beautiful pool. My inability to swim is affecting me and Tony in ways I never imagined. But for now, I push away the regret because he deserves a happy evening after what we've been through today. Hell, we both do.

Large rose petals are scattered all over the wooden floor, still warm from the earlier sun. Countless candles provide a romantic glow around a huge lounge seat big enough for two and a long table to the side. The table is laden with slices of turkey and roast beef, various cheeses and fruits and thin bread and crackers. There are also four decanters, an ice bucket with a bottle of champagne and multiple wine glasses.

"Wow." A tender sort of joy pulses through me. I always think there's nothing Tony can do to make me fall even more in love with him, but he always proves me wrong. "This is amazing. I can't believe you did all this while I was in the bath."

"So you like it? I was going to do tiger lily petals, but they don't work nearly as well as roses."

"It's perfect." I go on my tiptoes and kiss him. "You're perfect."

He nips my lower lip. "You make me strive to be better, Iris."

"If you get any more perfect, my heart won't hold out," I say, feeling like I'm about to burst with love.

"Oh, I think it will." He pulls me down on the seat, and we cuddle.

We're on the top of the tallest building in the area, and I love how close we are to the starry sky. I rest my head on his chest and hear his heart throbbing.

He takes food from the table, placing a thin slice of beef on a cracker with some cheese. He brings it to my lips. I start to tell him I can feed myself, but then I see the shadows in his eyes.

Tony doesn't operate by half measures. What he did to Jamie Thornton fleets through my mind. That was before we started dating seriously. And if I hadn't passed out and needed immediate care, he would've punished Sam in the same brutal way. Or maybe even worse.

Coddling me, to an excessive degree, is how Tony is coping right now, and I accept the morsel from him. I'm not the only one who suffered when Sam pushed me into that pool. If the situation were reversed, and somebody had hurt Tony, I'd be a mess.

The food is delicious, and the different wines he decanted taste like elixir on my tongue. I'm hungrier than I thought, and Tony smiles every time I take a bite.

"This is so lovely," I say with a sigh after a sip of Cabernet. "Still, I'm sorry our first trip had to be ruined."

"Not ruined. Just delayed." He kisses my temple. "Napa Valley can wait."

"Do you think Elizabeth really meant what she said about taking an entire week off?"

"Yes."

"Oh." I blow out a breath. "I don't know what I'm going to do for a whole week."

"You can practice piano in the morning, like before."

"Yes, but..." I turn to him, unsure how to broach the topic. "There's something I want to do." I clear my throat, unable to meet his eyes. I'm not sure what he's going to say, and I'm afraid he might think it's weird. Or worse, pointless.

"What?" Tony feeds me another piece of well-aged cheese. "Tell me and I'll make it happen."

I stare at him, stunned at the carte blanche offer. On the other hand, he wouldn't have said it if he didn't mean it. Suddenly, it feels less daunting. Almost doable. "I want to find out who the girl in my memory is," I say, hope fluttering in my belly.

He grows serious, his eyes intent. "What memory?"

I lean closer and lower my voice. Silly, of course, since it isn't like there's anybody around to hear, but... This is for his ears only —he's the only one I can trust. "I've been having this nightmare. It's me and another girl in a car, and we're sinking. I had it before while napping after a practice, and again after you brought me home. But I don't think it's an ordinary dream. I think it really happened, because the memory flashed through my mind when I first fell into Sam's pool, and it was different from a dream, you know? I feel like finding out who she is will help me remember the rest faster, even though it won't be easy. The only thing I know is she's a really pretty strawberry blonde."

7

ANTHONY

JESUS. EVERYTHING INSIDE ME GOES RIGID AT IRIS's revelation. A pretty strawberry blonde. Just like Iris... "Do you remember where it happened?" I ask, doing my best to keep my voice calm.

She shakes her head. "It wasn't an ocean for sure. Wasn't salty. And the water was really murky. It was raining hard, because I saw raindrops on the surface."

Holy shit. It *is* the night she supposedly died. I tortured myself a million times reliving it over the years—the wind, the storm, the hit-and-run on the bridge, and the horrible, stagnant waters of the bayou covering her as she sank, alone and terrified, the animals within its depths emerging to tear into her. Even now, with her right next to me and indisputably alive, I taste bitter bile.

I take a quick swallow of red. "But you weren't alone?"

"No. A girl was with me."

The body they found in the Lexus. The one everyone said was Ivy. Holy shit, who would've thought Iris would remember *her*?

My brain starts going at a hundred miles an hour. I've got to find out who the girl was, if the accident was random or not, and —if not—who the real target was back then. Then I can figure out how Sam fits into the puzzle...and whether someone else had a motive to hurt either of the girls. That information will allow me to keep Iris safe. I'd rather die before I lose her again.

"Was she your friend?" I'm doing my best to sound normal, but what the hell is normal in a situation like this?

Iris looks down, biting her lip. "I don't know. What kind of person does it make me if she was?" Her voice is achingly small.

She's suffering. This...whatever happened to her... She's paying the price. I kiss her cool fingers and warm them in my hand. "A person who was hurt and is trying to recover, that's what," I say, even though part of me is urging me to probe harder. *Ask. Find out how much she remembers.* There may be clues to discover not only who's behind it, but their motives as well. A young woman doesn't disappear for nearly a decade without some planning. Just what the hell kind of game is Sam playing...and who else is involved?

If I don't figure this out, she could be in danger again. He's done his best to keep her isolated. To banish her from home, from the entire country. When that didn't work, he tried to kill her.

"I wish I remembered more about her," she says. "Maybe her name... Where we met..."

An opening. The need to know wins, so I ask carefully, "What *do* you remember about her?"

Iris nibbles on the tip of her right index finger for a moment. "She was in a sleeveless blue dress. I think she was friendly."

"What did she say?" I ask, waiting, my heart galloping in my chest.

Iris squirms, dropping her gaze. "Not what she said..."

God, she's suffering, and it makes me want to weep for her. Part of me says to back off for now and let her be, but I can't. Not when Sam's willing to cross the line. I hold her hand. "You can tell me anything."

"She *waved*. I mean, in my dream. And in my memory, I wasn't scared of her. I was afraid for both of us. I wouldn't feel that way if she was a bad person, would I?"

"No, you wouldn't," I say, my voice too thick. As I pull her closer, I feel the sun, moon and stars medallion pressing against my chest, reminding me that the cops recovered it from the car. Whoever trying to kill her left the necklace behind, so everyone would assume the girl who died was Ivy.

"But you know what's really weird? It was Sam who pulled me out of the water that time."

"Sam?" I croak, an icy sensation forming in my chest. I feel like someone's thrown me into a tornado, my thoughts spinning in a million directions. Of all the scenarios I imagined... "Are you sure?"

"Yeah. It was definitely him. But when I mentioned it, he pushed me back into the pool. And that's when you came."

"That's all you said, and he did that?"

"Yeah."

Shit. I had it all wrong. He wasn't torturing her like I assumed. It was...what? A panic reaction? Was she never to remember what he did?

Why the hell not? According to her story, he saved her. He's a fucking hero.

Except that doesn't make any sense, either. He has to be one of the people behind her disappearance. Otherwise, there's no motive for him to hide her or try to ship her off to Tokyo.

"I don't know why he did it," Iris adds. "I didn't accuse him of leaving the girl behind or anything, which I'm certain he did, now that I think about it. There was so much blood around her." She starts shaking. "She's dead, isn't she?"

Yes. But I can't bear to tell her the truth, not when she's already so agitated and upset. It's unfair she has to suffer for the misdeeds of others. "Maybe. We don't know," I say gently.

But what I know for certain is: Sam is not the mastermind. If he were, he wouldn't have panicked like that. He would've reacted better, with more calculation. The person who engineered it thought everything through—a strawberry blonde in the same blue dress as Ivy's, the pendant...everything.

What I don't get is: what's so significant about Ivy? She didn't have any money, and even if she had, she was so young there would be no next of kin. She wasn't set to inherit a penny of my family's fortune, so it wasn't like someone who didn't want to see her inherit would do it.

Or maybe Ivy was a tool, and the real target was the girl in the car. But if that was the case, why hide the girl's identity? That doesn't make sense either.

I need to find out who she was, although that's going to be difficult. It happened so damn long ago. There's no evidence, and whatever witnesses might exist won't be that useful. Most people don't remember things that happened that long ago with any degree of accuracy.

"Do you think there's a way to find out who she is?" Iris asks suddenly.

Shit. "Why?"

"I feel like if I can figure that out, I'll remember faster. Like the dream I had with her in it. I think it triggered me to remember it in more detail when I fell into Sam's pool today."

"But you said you don't recall much about her." Have to be careful here. It's one thing for me to figure this out, something else for Iris. I can take care of myself. I would actually welcome whoever was behind the event in Tempérane to come at me. But Iris is different. Not only can she not take care of herself, she's my sole weakness—because she's one thing I can't bear to lose.

"I know. I wish there were clues about her identity, but…" She looks at me, her eyes bright and determined. "Do you remember what I told you about my mind? How my doctor said it's like a broken bowl badly put together, and that's why I don't remember everything?"

Fear is slicing at me, peeling off just a bit more each time, because I know exactly where she's going with this.

"If I know everything, I won't be broken anymore."

People say words can't hurt, but they're wrong. Hers are killing me, and my heart is weeping for her. Here's the most beautiful, gentle soul I know, and she's whispering, eyes lowered, like she's ashamed of herself. I hold her face in my hands, brushing my thumbs over her cheeks. "You aren't broken," I say, my voice cracking. "You're perfect."

"But Sam threatened to declare me incompetent. He wouldn't have done that if he didn't think he could do it, and the only reason he *could* do it is because I'm messed up in the head."

If Sam were here, I'd rip him to pieces with my bare hands. "Let him try. We'll fight him together, and we'll win."

Honor says that I should tell her everything. She deserves to know the truth about herself. Fear says I should hide it all. If she starts poking around, she could draw attention to herself...attention that could get her killed for real this time.

But there's another fear—a small, insidious voice that says when she remembers everything, she might just leave me. I look at her wrist. I don't know how the tattoo ended up gone, but the absence feels like an omen—like she's going to decide she can do better than a worthless piece of shit like me.

"We don't know when or where it happened. She could be anybody," I say, hating myself for throwing up roadblocks. This is the opposite of what I want to be for her. But I'm too selfish to risk losing her.

"Not even narrowing it down to a young strawberry-blond woman who drowned in rivers or lakes?" she asks in a small voice.

Ah, Iris, do you know how many strawberry blondes are out there? How so many of them drove me mad as I drowned in grief and self-loathing? "There are too many. We wouldn't even be able to narrow our search by people who died. What if she miraculously survived?"

"You're right." Defeat crosses her sad gray eyes, slicing me.

So I do the only thing I can—I kiss her.

I kiss her with all the sorrow and shame in my heart. Then with all the desperate love in my soul.

Her mouth soft, she kisses me back. Her tongue flicks across once, twice. My tongue meets hers, then licks the irresistible mole. I pull the full lower lip into my mouth. She clutches my shoulders, her fingers digging into my shoulders as though she can't bear to let go. And I give a small prayer of thanks that she wants me, even if it's only for now.

She slips her tongue into my mouth, then teases mine into hers. Wine, cherry and caramel flood my senses, setting my blood on fire. But I keep the kiss light, afraid she'll slip from between my fingers like a crumbling pillar of salt if I'm not careful. I came so, so close to losing her.

As though sensing my turmoil, she pulls back slightly and puts a warm palm over my cheek, her beautiful eyes on mine. "Tony, I'm right here with you. Flesh and blood. I'm not going anywhere." Then she moves her palm over to my chest, where my heart beats for her. "Where can I possibly go when you have my heart right here?"

"I don't deserve you," I say thickly, guilt and shame rolling through me.

"We'll have to agree to disagree." She pulls me down for another kiss, demanding my all.

I rain kisses on her lovely face—the delicate cheeks and stubborn jaw—then lick the sensitive line of her neck where her pulse throbs. I'm a fucking liar, and she's going to kick me in the balls when she finds out everything, but for now, I have her. I cling to that, revel in that, because otherwise I'm going to go mad.

"You drive me crazy," I whisper against her ear. "I can never get enough of you. Never be connected closely enough."

She sighs. "You're so perfect, I feel like you're a figment of my imagination—and you're going to slip through my fingers."

"I'm never going anywhere." I kiss her talented hands. "All you have to do is call, and I'll come for you, no matter what. You'll never lose me."

Her eyes grow tender. "Take off your clothes. I want to see you."

So I do. I stand before her, stark naked. A soft sigh leaves her lips as she studies me, her pupils darkening and widening. "You're so hot. You make me hot. Crazy horny for you." She runs an index finger over the glistening spot on my cock and pulls the tip into her mouth. "Mmm."

Jesus. My dick's even harder now. Her siren's mouth curves into a smile—all woman, all powerful. Taking my dick in her hand, she wraps her lips around the head, her tongue swirling over it like a lollipop.

Sharp pleasure pulses through me with each lick, each sweet pull of her hot, wet mouth. Her eyes are on mine, her cheeks hollowed, her lips moving along my thick, throbbing shaft. The vision is so erotically intense, it almost makes me lose control. But I don't want to come like this. I want to feel her climax in my arms first.

I gently pull away, pull her up and kiss her, our mingled tastes making me drunk faster than a twenty-five-year-old whiskey. I tug at her shirt, pull it over her head. She pushes her pants and underwear down her legs and kicks them away.

Her nipples bead in the cool evening air, and she cups the undersides of her breasts in a seductive offering. A low growl vibrating in my throat, I take one into my mouth. She gasps, then drives her fingers into my hair. I pinch the other nipple between a thumb and forefinger.

"Tony, oh God."

"I love your tits," I say before moving to the other nipple. "So pretty. So responsive."

I clamp my mouth around it as I wrap my arm around her waist and bring both of us down on the huge lounge seat. I run my free hand along her belly, dip it below to the hot, wet folds between her legs and slowly thumb her swollen clit.

She arches her back.

"You're so wet. I love it."

My two fingers glide into her easily, and her pussy tightens around them, making me groan with the image of it clamping around my throbbing dick. I add one more finger and thrust in and out of her while continuing to run the pad of my thumb over her clit and pulling her nipple back into my mouth.

Iris's breathing grows rapid, rough. A low moan tears from her, and she arches into my hand. "Tony—wait. Stop."

I go still instantly. "What's wrong?" Did I do something to hurt her? She might have injuries Dr. Young missed...

"Not like this. I want to feel you inside me."

So do I, but... "I have to go grab a condom."

She licks her mouth. "Are you clean?"

"Yes, but—"

"I am, too. I'm not asking you to give me a baby, Tony," she adds when I hesitate. "I just want to feel you."

It's such an act of trust. I feel unworthy, given what I'm keeping from her, but I can't turn away from it either, craving every gift from her with the desperation of a man lost in desert craving water.

"Please...?"

Her soft plea breaks me. My existence has no meaning if I can't make her happy. "You never have to say please to me. Everything you want—need—I'll give it to you."

Except the truth, a small voice in my conscience mocks me.

Muting it, I kiss her, our hands linked. Her legs are parted, and I feel her heat and wetness.

"Now," she demands.

I push into her. *God.* The sensation is so intense, it's like I'm back to being a virgin.

Her lips part, her eyes liquid-silver brilliant. I drive into her, angling my hips just so, trying to shatter her with ecstasy. Bliss twists her face, her eyes unfocused and brimming with sensation. I keep a tight rein to make sure she'll climax, even as I'm losing myself within her darkening eyes.

I know the moment she comes—the small hitch in her breathing and the tight spasming as she cries out my name. It feels so fucking good that I almost lose control. I drive twice more into her, then pull out and climax on her belly, shaking and heaving like I just finished a marathon.

When I can see without lights dancing in my vision, I look down. I like the sight of my cum on her. It's erotic. Primitive.

My woman. *Mine.*

She's studying the irregular white trail on her stomach. "It's supposed to be dirty, but it doesn't feel that way," she says finally in a soft voice. "It's hot. Sweet." She lifts her gaze. "I love it. I love you."

My heart is so full that I can barely breathe. I cradle her face in my hands and kiss her. "I love you too." After wiping her clean with a napkin, I pick her up. "Let's take you to bed. I haven't had my fill of you. We can make love for the next thousand years, and it won't be enough."

She flushes, the smile on her face radiant. "*Ten* thousand."

There are so many things still unresolved. But for tonight, I think about nothing except giving her pleasure and losing myself in her.

8

IRIS

I STRETCH, BLINKING, MY EYES ADJUSTING TO THE BRILLIANT wedge of light coming through the gap between the blackout curtains. I check the clock next to the bed. Eight forty-six a.m. Yawning, I ease myself back on the pillow. It's Saturday, and I want to sleep some more, but...

Tony's already gone. *Where did he go?* I wonder vaguely, sleep still clouding my mind. He wakes up so early. Almost unnaturally so, while I'm tired and pleasantly sore from being kept up most of the night.

I should probably get up. I want to write down what happened in my notebook.

I reach into the drawer next to my side of the bed and pull out my notebook and pen. I put them there last week, planning to write my entries before going to bed because I've been too lax since I started working. Unfortunately, I don't get to write anything, because Tony keeps me completely distracted. Once he starts kissing me in the evening, my brain cuts off, and all I can do is feel.

After scribbling today's date, I lean against piled-up pillows and jot down what happened yesterday, starting with the quiet morning ride with Tony, how we told each other "I love you" for the first time (a truly momentous event). The memory still makes my heart flutter, like I just lived through it all over again. I smile, feeling teenager-giddy with love. I don't ever remember losing my heart to anybody, so it could very well be that Tony's my first.

But as I keep going, my mood starts to darken. Audrey's over-the-top, self-centered visit and going to Sam's to get the check... The arguments. *The pool.*

And the girl. I close my eyes, trying to conjure every possible detail, even though it's unsettling to know so little about her. Finally, I start writing again.

Who is she? Is she alive? I hope so. And I hope there's a way to find out who she is. She could've been a friend. A good one. Tony said it's going to be hard...and seems a little reluctant to look for her. Maybe he doesn't want to do something that's not going to pan out...or maybe he doesn't want to disappoint me. He doesn't say anything, but I can sense he's worried about me. Sometimes I feel like if he could, he'd wind bubble wrap and blankets around me and never let me go anywhere. It's sweet, but also exasperating at times. I'm made of sterner stuff than that, aren't I?

Yeah, sterner stuff that sinks like a rock. And can't do anything to defend itself. My teeth clench as a wave of remembered helplessness surges through me.

Don't think about that right now. Finish the journal entry.

On the other side of the spread, I start drawing the girl as well as I can. The oval-shaped face. Large eyes. And...the hair.

I try for a while, then stop, glaring at the portrait. What the heck is this? A bastardized girlfriend of Frankenstein's? It's worse than something from a kindergarten art class. If my artistic side got even ten percent of my musical talent, I wouldn't be having this problem. I tap the end of my pen on the page, then snap the notebook shut with a huff.

Time to move on, at least for now. I should get up, have break-fast and practice the piano. I haven't been doing that much since starting my job at the foundation. But the notion of practice doesn't fill me with the usual joy and anticipation. Instead, restlessness crawls through me.

I stare at the cover of my notebook, frustration slowly bubbling. I can't draw. I can't swim. Utterly useless in the water, both when I was with the girl and yesterday.

If I'd known how to swim, I might've been able to save the girl in the car. If I'd learned after that, Sam's attempt to terrorize me by pushing me into the pool would've failed.

The less capable I am, the more people can hurt me. A cold sliver of fear slices through me as I remember Sam's threat to declare me incompetent. Again—all because I'm helpless.

Then there's Tony. He's so worried about me. He tries to hide it, but I can tell by the fleeting grimness in his gaze and the way he holds me—like I'm some fragile antique that will break at the slightest shock. I don't want him to worry about me. I want to be his strength the way he's mine. I want to be his equal.

And in order to do that, I need to be more capable. No more of this helpless Iris stuff.

I throw the notebook and pen back into the drawer, then put on a long shirt dress, brush my teeth and go downstairs. Tony's already in the kitchen, placing a fresh omelet on a plate. He's in a gray Princeton T-shirt and shorts, his feet bare. His hair's sticking up, but he looks so approachable and adorable. I walk over and wrap my arms around him.

"Good morning." He kisses me. "Mmm. What a sight. Did you sleep well?"

"Yes. Even though somebody kept me up late."

"Selfish bastard. You should have pushed him away."

"I tried, but he was very good with his hands. And mouth. And everything else."

He laughs. "Coffee?"

"Yes, please." I go to the fridge to grab Greek yogurt and some fresh berries.

I sit at the counter next to Tony, who is munching on his omelet and bacon. My coffee is already waiting. I take a sip. *Ahh.* Hot and strong, just the way I like it.

I glance at his food. The bacon looks exceptionally crispy, and suddenly I'm in the mood for a bite. "Do you mind?" I ask, gesturing.

His eyebrows rise. "Sure."

I take a strip and munch on it slowly. Mmm. Perfectly cooked. I can't remember why I didn't like it that much before.

"Want some more?"

"Nope. Just one is good. It's yummy."

He gives me an exaggerated leer. "That's because it comes from *me*."

I chuckle, happy he's in a light, playful mood this morning. "Yes, you do. And I swear if I didn't know any better, I'd say you were trying to fatten me up to eat me. Like that candy house witch in the fairytale."

"I do enjoy eating you out. And I don't mind if there's more of you to love."

Oh God. It's seriously hot and embarrassing all at the same time. My cheeks burning, I elbow him gently. "How can you say that with such a straight face?"

"Because it's true. I don't care how big you get as long as you're healthy."

I finish the bacon and dig into my yogurt. Tony is always worried about me not eating well enough. I remember how he said I was too thin, not criticizing but out of concern. Sam used to say it was great I was on the too-slim side because it made me look good, which—now that I understand him better—probably meant it made *him* look good by association. It's scary how I didn't see the dark, hidden side of his words because I trusted that he wasn't a bad guy. Or maybe I just wanted to believe he was a good guy because he was the only person who'd been with me and taken care of me since my parents' deaths.

I wonder... Did I eat as little as I could because I wanted Sam's approval? The notion is as unsetting as it is infuriating.

So I finish breakfast and even have a small glass of grapefruit juice after my coffee.

"What are you practicing today?" Tony asks.

"Maybe..." I pause. I was about to say Liszt out of habit, but... "Actually, I don't want to practice right now."

He squints. "You feeling okay?"

"I'm fine. It's just..." I lick my lips, suddenly feeling idiotic and vulnerable. I don't know why that is, because it isn't like Tony doesn't know, but saying it out loud myself seems so much worse.

"What?" He places a gentle hand on my shoulder. "You can tell me."

And I should. Besides, he's the most logical person to ask for help, even if I'm feeling awkward and ridiculous about it. "Can you teach me how to swim?"

He searches my face. "Are you sure?"

Looking into his concerned eyes, I know I'm making the right decision. I need to be his equal, the kind of person he doesn't have to rescue all the time. I can't continue to be a mess he has to make allowances for. "Yes. I promise I won't faint like I did before. That was yesterday, and I'm fine now."

"But..."

"I don't know what Sam was thinking yesterday, but I know the first time into the pool was an accident, and the second time wasn't. And he wouldn't have done it if I could swim, right? So it's like, if I can't take care of myself, I'm always going to be at the mercy of others." I cringe, embarrassed. Even though Tony told me he loves me and will do anything for me, I feel like I'm reminding him—again—how unaccomplished I am compared to him. "Wow. That sounds so...needy. It didn't sound that bad in my head."

Tony pulls me into his arms. "It doesn't sound needy at all. It sounds brave and smart. I'm so proud of you. And of course I'd love to teach you."

I swear I must've done something right at some point, because there's no other explanation for my having a man like Tony in my life. "Thank you."

I put on a bright teal bikini I bought in Spain when Julie insisted we hit the beach. She didn't care that I couldn't swim because, according to her, people go there to check out hot potential Latin lovers and tan as much as to get into the water.

Tony looks great in black trunks, his sculpted body drool-worthy, from the wide shoulders and thick chest to the leanly tapered sides and waist. Dark hair dusts his powerful pecs, and I can see a happy trail vanishing into the bathing suit. I swallow a sigh as my skin prickles. It would be so much more fun to seduce him than learn how to swim. And Tony probably wouldn't object.

Except that's a horrible copout and wouldn't do a thing to fix any of my problems. So we go down to the pool together. I glance at the sun reflecting off the surface. It looks sort of deep. I read somewhere that water is buoyant, but my experience says otherwise. It sucks you down like a giant vacuum.

"No jumping in yet. Gotta stretch first," Tony says.

"Why?"

"So you don't get cramps. Or pull something."

Sam probably wouldn't give me time to limber up first. But I humor him, stretching every major muscle the way he's doing. Besides, it's not too terrible, since I get to see his skin go taut over his body. There's not an ounce of fat on that man. His physique not only looks yummy, but supremely functional and powerful. I'll never forget the way he beat up Jamie Thornton so effortlessly, or saved me at Sam's. Or the way he carries me to the bedroom about as easily as he would a kitten.

He gets into the water first. "We'll start from the shallow side, get you comfortable. And I'm going to teach you how to float."

I look at the steps, then Tony waiting patiently. The water only reaches to his hips. It's probably logical to start from here, but...nobody tries to drown you in the shallow end of the pool.

And this isn't just about me learning to enjoy water. I'm trying to avoid a repeat of what happened yesterday with Sam.

"No," I say.

"What?"

I draw up whatever courage I can muster. "Let's do it from the other end. The deeper side."

Surprise crosses his gorgeous face. "Are you sure? It's—"

"More realistic. Exactly the kind of the scenario I need to prepare for." If I let him talk to me in that gentle tone, I'm going to cave and take all the little baby steps I can't afford to indulge in.

"We can still do it slowly," Tony says. "Like learning how to play the piano. You didn't start with Chopin your first day."

"But I can't." I lick dry lips, moving my leaden legs toward the deep end. "If I take six months to learn a piece...nobody's hurt. But this? This is life or death." Like the girl I couldn't save. Or myself when I was drowning yesterday. I was lucky because Tony showed up in time. But the girl... I hope she made it somehow, but I don't have the faintest idea what happened to her. And not knowing makes it worse. If I'd been able to swim back then, I could've saved both of us.

I stand at the edge of the deep end. My stomach grows jittery and weird, like I'm about to get on a crazy roller coaster with a horrible safety record. Tony moves over, and now the water's to his upward-tilted chin.

I flex my toes, my legs feeling unsteady. Water really scares me, even though, intellectually, I understand that once I learn to swim, it won't be scary at all. I inhale. "Okay. I'm going to jump in."

"Whenever you're ready." Tony opens his arms.

See, there he is, ready to catch me, just in case. *I'm going to be okay. Nothing to fear. I can do this.* Millions of people swim all the time just fine. As soon as I hit the water, kick and move my arms just like I've seen on TV.

Squeezing my eyes shut, I push myself off the ledge. A scream wells in my chest, but I don't get to let it out, since water immediately swallows me. I try holding my breath, feeling bubbles tickling my skin. Oh my God, the water's so *heavy*! I kick like crazy, my arms swiveling like a windmill. Except I don't feel myself going anywhere. My toes brush the bottom of the pool.

My hands hit the solid muscle of Tony's torso. I grab him tightly, and he pulls me up. I gasp as my head breaks the surface, my legs going around him so I don't sink back down.

"I've got you," he says. "You all right?"

I swipe the water off my face, sputtering and breathing hard. "No. It's so annoying. Why can't I kick myself up? People do it all the time on TV."

"You're too tense."

"So?"

"Can't float if you're tense. You have to relax."

"I'd *be* relaxed if I weren't sinking!"

"Iris, I know you're in hurry, but you can't rush this. You have to give it time."

"But it looks so easy! Why can't I just do it like..." I try to snap my fingers, but they're too slippery, and I end up looking silly instead.

"Just because it looks effortless doesn't mean it is. When you play 'Mazeppa,' it looks easy. But is it?"

"Of course not," I say mulishly, because I know exactly where he's going with it, and he's right. "But don't tell me it's going to take me years to learn how to float."

"No. But it'll take longer than a couple of minutes and just jumping into the deep end. Can you trust me to teach you how to do it?"

I sigh. He has a point. I could spend the next several months flailing around, or I could let him lead me in this. "Okay."

Tony spends the rest of the morning helping me become comfortable putting my head into the water—like, *submerging* it— and learning to float. He says the confidence of knowing that I won't sink like a rock will help. And it does, because after about an hour and half of trying, I can float, although I can't quite propel myself forward very well.

"See? There you go!" His eyes sparkle, and he seems prouder of me than I am.

"I have a great coach." This is just the first step, but it's still an accomplishment, and I'm too thrilled to stay still in the water. "I thought it'd take weeks to learn to float." Which is why I tried to force it, like somehow if I jumped into the water over and over again, my body would figure it out. But the patient way was better.

"Told you."

"I don't know why I never learned." More precisely, I can't remember. But I'm certain I never took lessons or anything. If I had, my body would've known exactly what to do, just like it does at the piano.

"You were busy," he says.

"You think?"

"Traveling around. Life. Not everyone can swim anyway."

"Can you teach me to swim freestyle?" Julie and I watched the last Olympics together, and freestyle looked like the most natural stroke.

"How about the breaststroke?" he says, looking down at my chest. "I could teach you that in an afternoon, and we wouldn't even need a pool."

"Har har har. I know it has nothing to do with boobs. And it looked really awkward on TV. Like swimmers were slamming their chest against the water to come up out of it and propel themselves forward."

Tony chokes. "Slamming their chest to come up and propel forward!" He laughs, his head thrown back. "That's too hilarious. Not to mention, you're describing the butterfly, not the breaststroke."

I poke him in the ticklish spot on his side. "Laugh all you want. That's how it looks to me."

"I'll teach you how to do freestyle, but the lesson's over for now."

Wait, what? I hold on to his arm, stopping him from leaving the pool. "But why? I'm doing so awesome!" I make myself float. "See? Totally ready for more."

"We've been at it for ninety minutes, and you're tired."

"No, I'm not," I say, even though now that he mentions it, my muscles *are* starting to feel kind of rubbery.

Holding my hand, he pulls my floating body slowly toward the steps. "We don't want to overdo it. There's tomorrow and the day after and the rest of the week...and month...and year. And it'll be better for you to learn a bit at a time. There's some value in consistent practice rather than doing a lot at once. Wasn't that how it was when you studied the piano?"

I scowl, not liking that he's making another great point to make me exercise patience. Although I don't remember exactly how I learned to play the piano, I do know that you can't make up for a skipped practice by just doubling or tripling the next session. We wade over to the ladder together. "All right. We can chill, I guess."

"I knew you could be reasonable."

"You mean agree with you?"

He grins. "One and the same."

We get out of the water. Tony gestures at the private booth by the pool. "Want to shower?"

"I need some real shampoo and conditioner," I say, running my fingers through my tangled hair. "I'll head upstairs to wash, and join you down here for lunch?"

"Okay." He brings a towel out of the booth and wraps it around me. I walk away, feeling the weight of his gaze on my back. I smile, but then let out a soft breath at how heavy my legs feel when I get to the stairs. *Wow. I guess I did do enough for the day.* It wasn't that bad when I was in the water.

Still, I'm feeling pretty triumphant. Being able to float is a big deal. Next time someone pushes me into the pool, I'm going to come right back up.

9

ANTHONY

I SLUICE THE CHLORINE OFF WITH SOAP AND HOT WATER, DRY myself with one of the towels my housekeeper keeps on the racks in the pool shower and put on a change of clothes from the drawer—a Lakers shirt and denim shorts.

Morning exercise is usually invigorating, but not today. Iris's determination is killing me. I understand her desire not to be helpless anymore. But her resolute stance isn't just from a need to be more self-sufficient and capable. She's too driven, almost like she's possessed. It reminds me of myself seven years ago when I decided I didn't want to be a nobody anymore. I did things I would never consider now—reckless investments with huge risks (but a crazy-high payoff), working day and night until my system just shut down to force me to sleep...

I wonder if Iris is also struggling with the girl in the blue dress —who she was, what she meant, what she represented. Iris might not recall that the girl drowned, but that doesn't mean she's completely free of the emotional trauma of the night. And she doesn't have to bring it up again for me to know she hasn't

entirely given up on the idea of finding the girl. Despite her softness and sweetness, Iris is a fighter underneath, with more steel
than most men.

I go to the kitchen, pick up my phone on the breakfast
counter and text Jill Edelstein, my PI. She hasn't yet sent me a
progress report, but she can look into this, too. I don't trust the
Tempérane cops with the information, and most of them are
already overworked and cynical enough that they wouldn't take
me or Iris seriously. As far as they're concerned, the case was
closed years ago—move along, nothing to see here.

*Additional assignment: Find any missing women between 15
and 40, spring or summer nine years ago, in a 40-mile radius of
Tempérane, Louisiana. Thanks.*

It's a long shot. There might be a lot of women who went
missing. The girl found in the Lexus could've run away ten,
eleven years ago...or might not even be from Louisiana. But it's a
starting point.

Iris's phone is lying on the counter. I don't remember seeing
her charging it. Sure enough, it only has twenty-some percent
battery left. Just as I start to plug it into the charge port, it rings.

Marty Peacher.

What the fuck? What does that son of a bitch want?

I drag my finger along the green button. The last thing she
needs is to deal with this subhuman trash.

Before I can say anything, the bastard starts mouthing off.
"You fucking cunt, what the hell did you do? You owe everything
to Dad! Why you gotta be a bitch about it? He was so traumatized
after your attack yesterday, he's lying in bed! You ungrateful cunt!
He should've let you die!"

If the motherfucker were here in front of me, I'd break his
face with his phone, then stomp him like the cockroach he is. He
keeps on ranting, not pausing to take a breath. If I let him
continue, will he keel over from asphyxiation?

I hate men like Marty, who think it's their right to abuse
weaker people. My contempt goes up another notch when they
can't even get creative with their raving. You can't recycle
"fuck," "cunt" and "bitch" over and over again if you have any

pride in yourself. But most importantly, nobody talks to Iris this way.

"Marty, how delightful to hear from you."

His rant dies. "Who is this?" Something rustles on the line. "Wait. Is this Iris Smith's phone?"

"Why, yes, it is. And this is her boyfriend, Anthony Blackwood, speaking."

"Oh. Uh, hi, Anthony. I didn't know you were with her." His voice is significantly subdued. Actually civil.

Loser. Calling him a cockroach would be insulting all the upstanding roaches of the world. He's a gnat on a cockroach's ass.

"Where would I be except by my girlfriend's side?" I can almost hear him swallow. "If Sam has a problem with how I treated him, he's welcome to call. I'm sure his tongue's still functional, despite the trauma of trying to drown his niece and getting caught."

"He didn't try to do that. He was trying to help her," Marty says hurriedly.

How the hell can Sam lie like this when there are witnesses to call him on it? "I'm sure everything he did was for her own good, not his." My sarcasm vanishes from my tone as I deliver the most important part. "Oh, and if you ever talk to Iris again, I'll make sure you sit in a wheelchair for the rest of your life."

"You can't threaten me like that!"

"But I just did. So go ahead. Try me."

"Asshole," he says, then hangs up.

Pathetic. Does he think he won because he had the last word? I plug the charger into Iris's phone and look in the fridge, thinking about lunch. I didn't buy anything for the weekend, figuring we'd be in Napa Valley. Maybe delivery will do.

The intercom buzzes. "Yes?" I say to the speaker in the kitchen.

"A Miss Julie Pearce is here to see Miss Smith," says the concierge.

Ah. Took her long enough. I would have sworn she'd find a reason to visit Iris before now to check me out, to make sure I'm not a serial killer or something. Harry told me once that's what girls do for their friends. I take his word for that sort of stuff, since I've rarely been in a relationship serious enough for that kind of intrusion. "Send her up. Thanks."

I pull out a stack of menus from a drawer in the kitchen. What would Iris like? Hopefully she's built up an appetite after the pool. Chinese and Thai are always great. She seems to enjoy them. Or pizza...

Wait. *Pizza? Why the hell is this flyer here?* I haven't touched a pizza since Ivy's death, and I don't plan on doing so anytime soon. I start to toss it, then stop. What if Iris wants some?

I stare at the colorful picture of a pepperoni pizza. The same thing we had at Cajun Milan when we had our argument. But I'm the only one who remembers. Iris has no reason to not like it.

I put it back on the stack. There are knocks on the door, and I take a breath, mentally getting ready to deal with whatever interrogation Julie's planning. Normally I don't tolerate uninvited pests, but this is Iris's friend. I have to make an effort.

I open the door. And for the second time in a month, I come face to face with Julie Pearce. Long, sleek brown hair and wide blue eyes tinged with wariness. A hot-pink dress and ballet flats add to her appearance of innocence and harmlessness. She's pretty in a soft way, untouched by anything unpleasant. Her parents spoil her, her brothers dote on her and she basically does whatever she wants. The only reason I don't dislike her is because, despite the privileged upbringing, she seems surprisingly down to earth and genuinely nice. Milton had some stories to tell, saying his baby sister could do no wrong.

"Come in," I say.

"Is Iris here?" she asks, balancing carefully on her feet like a doe ready to bolt.

I cock an eyebrow. If she wanted to make sure her friend's home, she should've called first. "She is."

She walks in. I finally note the large plastic bags she's holding. They smell like food. Very delicious, hot food.

"What's that?"

"Chinese. Iris's favorite. Well, she loves Thai, too, but Chinese was on the way."

"I have a microwave," I say dryly. "Does she like pizza?"

Julie frowns as though I'm criticizing her choice. "She likes Chinese more. She hardly eats pizza."

Good. Now I can toss that pizza menu out. "Come on in. We haven't had lunch yet."

"That's why I came early."

"Would've been smarter to call. We could've been out."

"I called Iris already, and she said I could come by and bring whatever looks good for lunch. Besides, seeing her—and you—in person seemed like the thing to do, especially after what she told me yesterday."

The reminder stirs my anger again, but I push it aside. Julie had nothing to do with it. "Want something to drink?"

"Just water, thanks."

I hand her a glass and make myself a gin and tonic. I sit on a chair at the dining table, my legs stretched out, and enjoy my drink.

She places the bags on the table and eyes me, one hip propped against the edge of the table and her arms crossed. She doesn't touch the water. Her eyes are slit, but not from anger. "You aren't what I thought. Not according to what Byron said."

Obviously not. I'd be worried if Byron said anything truthful about me. Except the part about me being a dick. That's definitely true, depending on who I'm dealing with. "What did Milton have to say?"

"He said you're sharp. Didn't say you're nice, which made me a little worried."

That shit, I think with half amusement, half annoyance. "Maybe you should form your own opinion."

"Maybe I should."

"And...?"

"I want to know everything, but you don't seem like the type to spill."

"Perceptive." Nobody knows much about me because I make it my business not to blab.

"I just want to be sure you're good for Iris. Your reputation sort of...sucks."

It's cute how she's trying to sound polite even though there's really no way. I haven't been a nice man. Didn't even want to be nice. "There's no 'sort of' about it. It sucks. One hundred percent."

She pulls back, blinking. "You aren't going to...uh...explain or anything?"

Where did this overinflated sense of importance come from? The only person who has the right to an explanation is Iris. "What's there to explain? It either is or isn't. I told you it's awful."

"But you can see how it makes me worried. I mean, as her best friend."

"Of course. I'd consider it negligent if you didn't."

She considers. "Do you want me not to like you?"

I think about that for a moment, how much Byron would hate it if his sister *did* like me. But...the effort simply isn't worth it. "I don't care what you think about me, Julie. I only care what Iris thinks. Since she likes you, I want to get along with you."

"So if Iris and I have a falling out..."

I shrug. "You'd basically be dead to me."

"Wow."

Just then Iris comes down the stairs. Her glowing, rosy cheeks and small smile of confidence are enough to make every color in the world more vivid.

"Julie!" She rushes toward her friend, then stops. "Wait. Sam didn't try to do anything to you, did he?"

Julie shakes her head. "Nope." She hugs Iris. "Just wanted to have lunch with you. We haven't spent any time together since that evening when Sam, uh, came over."

I should've beaten the crap out of him. Perhaps then he wouldn't have dared to try to hurt Iris yesterday.

"Yeah, me too." Iris shoots me a quick glance.

I smile, not wanting her to feel bad about wanting to spend time with her friend. "Julie even brought lunch."

"Chinese," Julie says. "All your favorites. Beef and broccoli, shrimp in orange honey sauce. Bok choy and mushrooms and peppers, oh my!"

"Hahaha! Thanks, I'm starving," Iris says, patting her stomach.

"You? Starving?"

"Yeah. Come on, let's eat." Iris takes paper plates out from the bags. The food is lukewarm now, so I nuke it in the microwave, and then we divvy it up.

Meanwhile, Julie gives me a look reserved for aliens from a newly discovered planet. I pour a tall glass of pink lemonade for Iris. I know what Julie's thinking. She can't believe Iris has changed—from eating out of necessity to actually enjoying her food.

I let the two talk while we eat, not really paying attention. It's enough that Iris is happy to spend time with her friend. Byron's a dick, but that doesn't make Julie a problem. Look at Milton, her other brother, who's reasonable and amicable. And I'm so proud of Iris for overcoming the trauma of yesterday and learning to float.

And I'll do anything to ensure that happiness never fades.

10

IRIS

AFTER LUNCH, TONY HELPS CLEAN UP AND GOES TO HIS office, leaving me and Julie alone to chat. We sit on a couch, plumping the soft pillows behind us.

"You look really happy and...content," Julie says, searching my face. "I've never seen you like this."

"I *am* happy. I feel like I finally found a man I can see myself having a future with." I stop and hesitate, a bit scared to voice what I've been wondering about at times. "Is that, like, weird? And too soon?"

"No. I don't believe in love at first sight, but I also don't think being together for a long time makes you fall in love with someone. Sometimes you just know."

I nod, relieved. Not that I'd leave Tony if she disagreed, but it's still good to have someone who isn't broken like me confirm there's nothing strange about the way I feel about Tony.

"And he seems to care about you a lot."

"You sound surprised." In fact, she sounds like she never expected Tony to like anybody.

"No, no, you're totally adorable and lovely. It's just that his reputation is bad, you know? Really bad." Julie scrunches her face. "He didn't even deny it when I brought it up."

I purse my lips, annoyed she's basing her opinion of Tony on gossip and whatever junk that's out there, like Audrey Duff's "attempted suicide" over him. "Don't believe everything you read. He isn't the type to defend himself, especially against groundless rumors."

"I usually don't, but you're my best friend. It's my job to worry."

"I know. But don't," I say, slightly mollified. "I love Tony. He loves me too."

"He does?" Julie leans closer. "Did he say it?"

I nod, biting my lip as a smile breaks out on my face. Every time I think about it, it's like the heavens opening up, rainbows shooting out of clouds and angels singing on the tips of dancing unicorn horns.

"Holy shit! When? Details!"

I tell her how I said it first, almost impulsively, unable to contain the words, and he followed me into the foundation's building to say them back. My heart swells, beating faster, just like it did then, and I feel my cheeks warm, my lips tingling, as though he's just cradled my face in his large hands, told me he loves me, then kissed me like he couldn't bear to let go...

Julie squeals. "Oh my *God*. That's, like, *holy shit* romantic! He is totally into you."

Warm shivers are still going through me. "I know."

"Okay. I officially like your man." Julie taps her chin. "By the way, do you think I can call him Tony now?"

"Um... Did he say one way or the other to you?"

"No. Never. Didn't you notice I never refer to him by name?"

Now that she mentions it... I shrug, a bit chagrined. He *is* particular about his name, always drawing a clear line between those he considers close friends and those he doesn't. I have no idea how he decides. He asked me to call him Tony pretty quickly, but others? I don't think even Wei calls him Tony. "Only one way to find out."

She narrows her eyes dramatically. "Next time I'm doing a 'Yo, Tony!'"

I laugh. "Go for it."

"But you have to be there just in case he gets pissy, so I can hide behind you."

"Chicken," I tease. "Fine. I'll be your shield."

"By the way, did you get your first paycheck yet?"

I blink. "Yeah, why?"

"Because we need to celebrate! In the time-honored tradition!"

"There's a tradition?"

"Of course! Shopping!"

Should've known. Julie loves to shop. "We can do that. I could use some new shoes."

"And clothes!" Julie adds, horrified that I might limit myself.

I raise a finger. "Only if I see something I like." Otherwise she'll make me buy everything in sight. And the foundation doesn't pay *that* well.

She pulls out her phone and shows me all the awesome dresses she's been eyeing, as in she screencapped them to be bought later, and I nod dutifully. She makes me swear we're going to buy something—even if it's just a pair of earrings—and leaves, saying she has to meet her mother for some mom-daughter spa time.

Once the door closes, I unplug my phone from the charger. Tony comes down.

"Done with work?" I ask.

He nods. "All taken care of."

I go to him and wrap an arm around his waist. He pulls me closer and kisses my temple. "Anything you want to do today?"

"Hmm..." I say absent-mindedly as I check for any texts or calls, then scowl. "Something's wrong with my phone. It says Marty called, but it isn't marked as missed. I didn't talk to him today."

"Your phone's fine," Tony says. "I took care of it."

"You took his call?" I ask, surprised and vaguely annoyed. It feels like more evidence that maybe he doesn't think I can handle my own problems. Since I'm trying to be more of an equal partner, it's like a little slap in the face.

"He was calling to yell at you, and in very inappropriate language. I set him straight. If he calls again, let me know."

Oh, Tony. Fighting my battles again. It's impossible to stay upset with him. "I can deal with him."

"I know, but I don't want you to see or hear that sort of ugliness."

My heart grows tender. Although Tony merely described Marty's language as "inappropriate," I can imagine. My cousin is a piece of work.

Tony continues, "You should only see and hear beautiful things."

I run my thumb across his cheek, torn between love and exasperation. "Thanks, but I don't want you to deal with that because of me."

"I'm already tainted. Seen, heard and done things nobody should. You aren't like me, Iris. It's better I shield you myself."

"I'm not like that. I'm not perfect. Eventually, you're going to realize that." Sometimes his attitude scares the hell out of me. How can he see flawlessness when he looks at me? It's like he didn't listen when I told him about my brain injury, coma and partial amnesia. But I know deep in my heart that one day, the scales are going to fall from his eyes. And he's going to wonder what the hell happened to the perfect girl he loved. And then I'm going to lose him.

"When sunflowers stop wanting sunlight. That's when I'll think you're not perfect." He glides his finger along the sun on the medallion around my neck.

My love for him wars with worry. I know he thinks I'm like the sun—perfect, radiant and life-giving. But I'm not. How do I show him that now so he doesn't become disappointed later? Disillusionment is easier to bear when you haven't invested so much time and energy into it.

"Are you practicing the piano?" he asks.

"No. My shoulders are feeling rubbery, and I don't think I'll be able to get a decent session in," I say, wrapping my arms around his neck.

"Hmm. I guess we'll just have to find something else to do..." He scoops me up lightly and starts toward the bedroom, running his lips along my neck as he carries me up the stairs.

11

ANTHONY

After dinner, Iris's eyelids start to droop. She had a pretty tiring day. Swimming was a whole new level of physical activity for her. Then there was the marathon sex.

I lay her on our bed, and she curls up, pulling the sheets over her. She's adorable, and I can't stop myself from teasing her. "It's barely eight, grandma."

She opens one eye to look at the clock by the bed, then rolls so she's snuggled against me, closing her eyes. "You better go back to school, because it's almost nine. And it's your fault. You kept me up late last night."

I hold her until her breathing deepens. By nine, she's sleeping soundly. I kiss her on the forehead, tuck the sheets around her and leave, TJ watching the place as I do. Sam and I are due for a chat.

Sam's mansion's gates are still broken, hanging crooked, leaning against their columns like frat boys after too much partying. I smirk with bitter satisfaction at the sight as I drive my Audi through the unsecured gap where they used to be.

At the main entrance, I knock and wait like a civilized man... although the things I want to do to Sam are fairly barbaric. The butler from Friday opens the door, sees me and stiffens immediately. "Master Sam isn't receiving anybody."

"Ah, so he's home. I'm his beloved long-distance relative. I'm sure he's dying to talk with me about how proper lunch meetings ought to be conducted."

"You can't come in," the butler says coldly, although his Adam's apple is bobbing.

"Or what? You going to shoot me?" It wouldn't take more than one good punch to knock him out.

"Why not? You're an intruder!" His voice becomes slightly shrill toward the end, sweat popping along his hairline.

I laugh. "If you want to do that kind of thing, you should go work for someone in the South. Californians don't like it when you brandish guns and threaten to shoot people." I lean closer until I'm right in his face. "Besides, it's not like you know what it's like to shoot a person. If you want, I could teach you."

He swallows loudly, then takes a nervous step back. "I need to announce you."

"Don't bother. Second floor, right? Left or right? Which door?"

"Left. Third—" The butler inhales sharply, slapping a hand over his mouth. "What the hell," he says, horrified. "It's my job to announce you."

"It's fine. Really. I promise I won't get lost." I walk up the stairs. Where the hell did Sam find this butler? The man is worthless.

Sam's study is as ostentatious as the man himself. Instead of being a place to relax and work or read, it's designed to appear important, the kind of place that says, "The man who works here matters. A lot."

I deliberately ignore Sam and let my gaze wander, giving myself time to calm down enough so I don't jump on him and turn him into a collection of broken bones. Leather-bound books fill tall bookcases; there's a ladder installed to reach the upper shelves. Three Monets hang from the wall—imitations, albeit damn good ones, because the originals were in the National Gallery last time I heard. A huge oak desk occupies a prominent place in the room, along with a leather chair. The desktop has a laptop, currently closed, a stack of documents and a Dictaphone.

A weasel-like smile on his florid face, Sam looks at me from the desk. He's dressed in a maroon evening robe and pajama bottoms. The time I gave myself to calm down hasn't really worked. Right now, the idea of dragging him into the en suite bathroom and shoving his face into the toilet is enormously appealing. It would fit better than your standard beating, too. After all, he used water to hurt Iris.

"Anthony," he says, his voice oily enough to make me feel nauseated. He fiddles with his Dictaphone.

I take an armchair opposite him. "I see you're healthy as a horse, despite what Marty said."

"My son worries about me. He's a good child."

My ass. Nothing less than a beating can fix what's wrong with Marty. "Then perhaps you should tell him to be a good little boy and stop contacting Iris. And I know what you did, Sam. Stay the hell away from Iris unless you want to face charges for attempted murder."

"Attempted murder?" He laughs, slapping the desk. "For what?"

I flex and clench my hands, the knuckles cracking. "I saw you push her into the pool." I bite out each word, fury building like a tsunami. "You know she can't swim."

"She slipped. Twice. I was going to get her, but then..." He raises his palms, shrugging. "You arrived."

The toilet bowl is too good for him. "You want me to believe that shit?"

"It isn't about what you believe. It's about what I can convince a jury to believe. I've been a very good uncle to Iris. Her doctors will be more than happy to testify to that effect. You're the weird, controlling 'boyfriend' who wants to take her away from me for nefarious reasons."

A broken nose and a few teeth in the back of his throat would be nice about now. "Try it, asshole. I can ask Elizabeth to testify on my behalf."

The smirk on his face dims. Then he shrugs again. "It doesn't matter who you drag into court. It won't change the truth, or the fact that you can't handle it. Look at you." He waves a hand in my direction. "Still unable to see clearly. The people closest to you can wield the sharpest knives. And in the dark, so far as you're concerned."

What the hell? Is this just bullshit or a clue? He's too gleeful, and I can't decide.

"I'd be careful if I were you. You can never trust anybody. Like Jamie Thornton. Iris thinks I had no clue, but I knew he wanted her and let him go for it. Figured the trauma would make her leave the country. But you had to step in."

I explode out of my chair, ready to beat the crap out of him. What kind of monster engineers the rape of a young woman?

Sam pulls back, raising his hands. "You can't touch me! My butler knows you're here!"

"You think I give a fuck?" I say, walking toward him. An image of Iris from that night flashes through my mind. The shadows in her downcast eyes. Her holding her broken dress strap up, crossing her arm across her torso like a sad shield. The way she flinched, then clung to my jacket. The cut on her lip from Jamie fucking Thornton's teeth.

I'm going to break this motherfucker. Then make him eat his own balls. That's the least Iris deserves.

"If you pull the crap you did with Jamie, you're going to jail," Sam screams, pushing his chair back when I keep coming. "Then who'll watch over my poor little niece?"

I stop, shaking with the need to break his face. He can probably manage that for a short while. His butler will say whatever necessary to get back at me. Although my lawyers will work their magic and bail me out, I can't afford to be stuck in jail. I can't leave Iris defenseless.

"Stay the hell away from what's none of your business, Anthony. Or people are going to get hurt. You don't want to be responsible for that, do you?"

His smarmy expression turns my stomach. But no matter how much I want to thrash him, I can't. He has the upper hand for now. I have someone I'll die to protect; he doesn't. Still, that doesn't mean I'm letting him get away with it. "I'll pay you back tenfold for what you've done to Iris." My voice is taut with barely suppressed rage.

He smiles with the confidence of a criminal beating a charge on some bullshit technicality. "Good night, Anthony. Now get off my property."

12

ANTHONY

THE SECOND I'M BACK IN MY PLACE, I SHOWER IN A GUEST bathroom so I don't disturb Iris. The whole conversation with Sam made me feel like I'm covered in slime. I would love nothing more than to hurt him the way he wanted to hurt Iris, and I hate it that I'm helpless to do anything.

I rest an elbow against the tiled wall and hit the cool, wet surface with my fist a few times as hot water rinses the soap off me.

Have I been underestimating him the entire time? It's possible Mother's blatant contempt for the man has colored my perception. She's always treated him like he's beneath us. But somehow he got the better of her and is forcing her to invest with him even though she doesn't want to. And he's taunting me with Iris's safety.

I wonder if he's the true mastermind behind the accident. Either it was a hell of a coincidence, or he knew enough to be there when Iris's Lexus fell into the bayou and pull her out of the water. The hit-and-run driver could be Marty. That idiot would do anything his daddy asked him to.

But that doesn't quite make sense either. Marty's too head-strong and stupid to have kept something like that quiet all these years. And Sam's smart enough to know that about his son.

The only thing I know for certain is Sam was there when the accident happened. So I need to trace his movements back then if I want a more complete picture.

I get out of the shower and dry off, then text Jill.

Sam Peacher was in Tempérane, Louisiana, nine years ago. I want to know what he was doing in August. Also, I need a list of all his known associates from then until now.

She responds within seconds. *Anything else?*

No. This is the top priority.

I put the phone down and go to the bedroom. Iris is sleeping soundly under the covers. She looks so innocent, her face soft, her lashes fanning on her cheeks like dark crescent moons. The pendant I gave her glints. She hasn't taken it off since I put it around her neck.

I slip under the sheets, moving carefully so I don't wake her up. Then I wrap my arms around her and inhale the scent of my shampoo in her hair. My bed, my shampoo...my everything. *Mine.* Safe and warm and sweet. Her mere presence is cleansing, sooth-ing. I cling to her like my life depends on it, while I consider how much danger she might be in. Sam was okay with her getting raped in order to manipulate her. Then he tried to kill her because he realized she's starting to remember the night of her accident. What will he do next? Fear burns my gut, and I clench my jaw. I won't let anything happen to her. I'll burn the world down first.

13

IRIS

TONY WAS IN A HORRIBLE MOOD ALL DAY SUNDAY. I sometimes caught him staring at nothing, those green eyes narrow and promising murder. I felt bad for the person who put that expression on his face, but at the same time, maybe whoever it is deserves it. Or maybe it wasn't even a person but a work project? He's running a big company. It must have its share of drama and problems.

But Monday morning, Tony is much more cheerful and relaxed. Maybe it's because he realized I noticed his crabby mood. He's surprisingly sensitive that way.

After a quick shower, I go to the closet, half of which is mine now. Starched dress shirts and crisply ironed slacks hang in his section, while mine's full of dresses, skirts and cute tops. I pick out a formfitting sleeveless red dress I got in Barcelona a couple of years ago.

"Why are you putting that on?" Tony says, watching me. He's already in his work outfit.

"Why not? It's a great power dress. And it's conservative

enough for the office." The round neckline is modest, and it has a mid-shin hemline.

"Don't you remember? Elizabeth told you to take a week off."

Pulling my hair to the side, I turn around so he can zip me up. I can do it myself, but I know he enjoys doing small things like that for me, so it's become my habit to let him. "But I'm feeling fine now. I don't see why I should take advantage." Besides, getting back to work is just what I need to prove to myself I'm not some broken doll that needs to be coddled. I can function like any other normal, well-adjusted twenty-something.

He pulls the zipper up, then hooks the clasp at the top.

"Thank you." Facing him, I smooth his shirt. "You look fantas-tic, and I love our morning commute together. Besides, I think TJ is starting to like me a little bit."

"She's going to send you right back home."

"And I'll tell her I can't go because I don't have a ride."

Tony laughs. "You apparently don't know your boss very well, if you think a minor obstacle like that will deter her."

"We'll see." She won't make me leave if I'm obviously fine and already in the office.

We go to the kitchen together. He starts the coffee. As I reach for the fridge, my phone rings. It's Elizabeth. I answer immedi-ately, almost on autopilot.

"Good morning, Iris. How are you feeling?"

"I'm good," I say with an extra dollop of cheeriness so she can tell just from my voice I'm fabulously well.

"Great. I just wanted to make sure you're taking your week off."

Whaaat? I pull my phone away and stare for a moment, my jaw slack with frustration. Did she not hear my extra-healthy voice? I infuse even more robustness into my tone. "Thanks, but that won't be necessary. I'm feeling great!"

"Please don't argue. It's paid time off. You got hurt while working for the foundation. It's the least I can do." Her voice is honey-sweet and warm, but there's a certain tone underneath.

"But I was working on projects—"

"Which can be taken over by Rhonda for a week. She won't mind."

I cringe, then go for another angle. "She shouldn't have to work overtime because of me. She has a kid." *Come on, Elizabeth. Let me live my life!*

"Don't worry. I can manage it all without asking her to stay late. You just take care and get better. See you *next* Monday." She hangs up.

Tony arches an eyebrow. "Told you."

"But why? Didn't I sound like I was bursting with energy?" I look up at the ceiling. "Did she install a hidden camera? How did she *know*?"

"She isn't spying on us. She just knows what kind of person you are." He grows serious. "If you don't take time off, she'll feel awful, and you'll never hear the end of it. It's better this way."

"She's going to pay me to do nothing."

"So? It makes her happy to take care of people. So let her. She's the kind of boss everyone wants. Why do you think the place has almost no turnover?"

"Then how did she end up hiring me if nobody leaves?" I ask sarcastically, too frustrated to care that I sound like a grounded teenager.

He drains his coffee, his face mostly hidden behind the mug. "Maybe the previous employee had to move?" A careless shrug. "She does hire new people. Just not that often." He gives me my morning java. "Now, enjoy a super-leisurely breakfast, and I'll see you for lunch. And try to remember: it's only a week."

"But there are projects to do. And the funding!" I place my mug on the counter with a small thud as a new thought hits me. "I only went to Sam's so I could get that donation for the children's medical fund. Do you think he wired the money to Elizabeth?" I'm pretty sure the answer is a big fat *no*.

Tony snorts. "Are you kidding? That cheapskate?"

"Ugh. That's horrible. It's the least he should do."

"Even if he offered it now, Elizabeth wouldn't take it. He couldn't have dangled more than fifty K or so." Tony sneers at the amount.

But it's no joke to me. That money represents a chance for someone, someone who could use a little miracle. "Fifty K is a lot. It can save a kid's life! Make a real difference. I've seen the photos and letters, Tony. This mom said the foundation saved her daughter's arm. Just think about that for a moment, how terrible it would be to not have a limb! That's why I went to see Sam. It wasn't just about the check."

He nods and places a hand on my shoulder. "You're right. I should be more considerate. I'll send the foundation a check for five hundred."

I blink at the casual way he speaks of giving away half a million dollars, like it doesn't merit any forethought. "I didn't bring this up to make you donate."

"I know, but it's important to you, so I don't mind."

I stare, trying to process it. When you have the kind of money Tony has, I guess it doesn't matter. But his generosity still leaves me speechless.

"Why do you think I made all this money?" he asks.

"Uh...because you like being rich?"

"No. I did it for you." He's looking at me, his eyes entirely too solemn, and I become breathless as my chest swells with hot, sweet emotion. But something is fuzzy, wiggling in the back of my mind.

Finally, I figure it out. "But you didn't know me back then."

A shadow crosses his gaze. He takes my left hand and runs the pad of his thumb over my fingers, then rests it on the knuckle of my ring finger and looks into my eyes. "I knew I'd meet someone I'd want to protect and spoil."

Tears start to prickle my eyes. This man is killing me with his love. I'll never, ever meet another who loves me more...and there's never going to be someone who I love more than him. If I could write music, I'd dedicate a thousand sonatas to him—my heart, my soul. To the man who is more critical to my existence than air or water. "You've ruined me for other men."

He smiles. "I haven't even started."

We kiss—eagerly, sweetly. Our mouths fuse, and our tongues tangle. He tastes like Tony and a hint of coffee, and I devour him, loving the sound of his roughening breathing. The way we share the heated air around us.

His large hands glide upward, from my waist to my breasts, and I arch into him, wanting more. My nipples are tingling, already pointed, and I'm slick between my legs. I rock against his thick, stiff cock and let out a throaty moan. I want him inside me right now—big and hard and greedy. Giving me everything he has to give. Taking everything he wants to take.

The phone buzzes in Tony's jacket. He ignores it, pulling me closer, fisting his fingers in my unbound hair. The phone buzzes again, this time against my breast, and I gasp.

He curses under his breath, pulling away slightly and taking out the phone. He scowls at it. "Wei."

"Anything wrong?" I ask, remembering Tony's dark mood on Sunday.

"No. Just a meeting I can't miss."

Damn it. I wish he could stay. I'm tempted to ask him to call in sick, but I know better. His company isn't just some entity that generates cash. It's responsible for everyone who works there, too. "Then I won't hold you back," I say, licking my lips for a lingering taste of him.

"I wish I could cancel it."

"But you said you can't." I place a tender kiss on his forehead, then lightly stroke his crotch. "Just think about me all day," I whisper. "While you're in your meetings."

He gives a ragged sigh, his lower lip sticking out a little. The unguarded, honest reaction is so adorable that I can't help but laugh.

"I'll be right here waiting for you to come home. Then we can continue without anything hanging over us."

"Okay." He gives me a small smile. "If you need anything, call."

"I will. And I have TJ and Wei's numbers if you're busy."

"I'm never too busy for you." He kisses me, hard, then leaves with a mug full of coffee.

With Tony gone, the penthouse seems much bigger and emptier. Since I have nothing to do—and I'm not quite confident enough to get back into the pool by myself—I practice the piano. I sigh as my fingers move across the keys. People told me, "You're so good, you can skip a few days and nobody's going to know." But I can always tell. Like right now...I'm about half as fluid as I should be.

I should've done at least half an hour of practice on Liszt's "Mazeppa" étude on Saturday and Sunday, because *God* I've lost ground. If the goal is to play like György Cziffra—with minimal pedal, crisp sound and embellished trills—then I've got to do better.

The intercom buzzes, pulling me out of my drills. Wiping the sweat off my hairline, I look at the time. It's about eleven. *Tony?* No. He'd just walk in.

Sam?

I dismiss the thought as soon as it pops into my head. Tony would've made sure Sam and Marty aren't allowed past the lobby. Maybe it's Julie stopping by again, determined to drag me out shopping or something.

I hit the speaker. "Yes?"

"Miss, there is a Mr. Byron Pearce to see you."

Oh. Given how our last phone call went, I don't really want to talk to him right now. He was so nasty about me being with Tony. On the other hand, he's one of my closest friends. I can't just cut him out of my life because of one conversation without giving him a second chance. He was probably just worried Tony was using me because of all that stupid gossip. I just have to set Byron straight, like I did with Julie.

"Sure. Send him up, please."

Byron arrives a few minutes later. I wasn't just giving Tony a hard time when I told him Byron is handsome. All that soft brown hair, those laser-blue eyes and perfectly chiseled facial bones make women go crazy. He totally could be a model if he wanted. He even has the body for it. But he isn't interested in that sort of thing. Just his family empire.

"Hi," he says when I open the door. He's dressed in a white polo shirt and khakis, sporting a new tan from having been in

Hawaii. In his hands are a bouquet of red roses and some dark chocolate.

"Hi, Byron." He isn't starting with the wrongness of my being with Tony, like he did last time. So that's something.

"Would you mind if I came in?"

"That depends." I cross my arms, mentally getting ready to set some expectations and boundaries. "If you're going to tell me how horrible Tony is, then you can turn right around and go back now."

"Nothing like that. I'm here to apologize for the way I spoke to you."

Well. This is unexpected. Byron hates being wrong, and I thought he'd at least try to defend his earlier behavior. I step aside to let him in.

He walks past, then stops at the sight of the white baby grand and the music resting on top.

"Tony plays," I say awkwardly, remembering our brief argument about him wanting to buy a grand piano for me. He said he was going to for Julie, but that was a flimsy excuse.

Byron raises an eyebrow. "I doubt he's good enough for Liszt."

I look away, trying to hide my chagrin. Of course Byron would know what I'm working on. He used to play the piano when he was younger, and he can read music. Based on his flat tone, he isn't really here to apologize, not the way I was hoping. He isn't going to admit he was wrong about Tony.

He places the flowers and chocolate on the coffee table while I stand with my arms crossed. The anxiety and unhappiness I'm feeling are unfamiliar and weird, like being in a dress that doesn't fit right. But then, I've never felt them toward Byron before. Maybe things are too different now. I can't forget how angry and patronizing he was when he learned I was with Tony. He didn't even ask me if I was all right. Just yelled and rebuked me for dating Tony. I never expected Byron to love Tony, but I didn't expect him to be so negative, either.

"Look, Rizzy, I'm sorry. I was...simply worried. Tony's reputation is nothing to be proud of, and you are..."

"What?" I want him to spell out exactly what he sees in me that makes being with Tony incompatible. "What am I?"

He shrugs. "Too nice. Too sweet."

Normally I'd be touched that he thinks so highly of me. But right now, it sounds like a backhanded compliment, a euphemism for "naïve and helpless"—reasons I'm not good enough for someone like Tony. "I'm a big girl, Byron. I can handle myself."

Byron's eyebrows pinch. "I heard about Sam trying to ship you off. And that he tried to force things again last week."

Guess he spoke with Julie before coming over, but maybe she didn't tell him everything. She always says Byron has a temper, even though he rarely loses it. "So what? I'm still here in L.A.," I say, my voice hard.

"But are you *okay*?"

He's peering at me, not with paternalistic judgment but genuine concern. I suddenly feel petty and foolish. It's Sam who hurt me and made me doubt myself. Aside from one phone call, Byron's been nothing but fabulous. He's the kind of friend who'd literally give me the shirt off his back. "I'm fine. I'm sorry I'm a bit...weird today. His second attempt shook me up a little."

"He better not try again."

"I doubt he will," I say vaguely, not wanting him to probe, in case Julie purposely didn't tell him about Sam trying to drown me. There's no reason to upset Byron, and there's nothing he can do about it now.

"If there's anything I can do to help, just let me know, Rizzy."

Suddenly, the girl in the blue dress pops into my head. Tony said there's virtually no chance to discover her identity, but Byron might know a way. He travels in different circles, and has a different network of people. If I know who she is, maybe I can speak to her. Find out how we know each other. Maybe she and I were great friends before my coma. She might trigger more memories. My heart fluttering with muted anticipation, I tell Byron about the girl I remember.

"So...like a repressed memory?" he asks.

"Yeah, something like that." I fidget, feeling guilty I'm not telling him everything about my partial amnesia. He knows my memory is bad, but he thinks it's because of the head injury scrambling my brain a bit, nothing serious. I've never shared the severity of my condition with him because I don't really feel comfortable enough. Tony is the only one I've told the full truth. "I want to know what happened to her. She feels important."

Byron nods. "Easily done. I can't guarantee anything, mind you, but I can definitely look into it."

Yes! His promise is like a breakthrough. Okay, even without a guarantee, at least I'm not just drawing her face in my notebook—badly—and obsessing about it. A thrill races through me, and I hug Byron. "Thanks! You're the best!"

He hugs me back. "My pleasure, Rizzy, I'll—"

"Get your hands off my girlfriend, Pearce, before I cut them off."

14

ANTHONY

Of all the scenarios I expected to see when I came home, Iris in Byron Fucking Pearce's arms never crossed my mind. The sight of their embrace guts me.

Because I know, deep inside my heart, that Byron is the better choice for her.

There's no blood on his hands. His family loves him. Everyone adores him. He has a great reputation. He's a star—a brilliant, beautiful star. And in a million ways, he deserves Iris more than me. But that doesn't mean I'm going to be the better man and give her up.

Over my dead body.

"Tony," Iris says, pulling away from Byron. "I didn't realize it was already time for lunch." She glances at the clock.

"Blackwood," Byron says curtly.

"Pearce." I look at his hands on Iris's arms meaningfully. If she weren't here, I would be breaking them. But, inexplicably, she's fond of him.

He doesn't drop them. Iris subtly moves away, which is the only reason I haven't turned his face into hamburger.

"I haven't had lunch yet," he says to Iris.

"Then—"

"You aren't invited," I say.

Iris gapes at me, probably thinking what a rude bastard I am. I care about what she thinks of me, but not enough to feed the son of a bitch. If he were on fire, I'd pour oil over him.

"Get out," I say.

"I'll talk to you later, Rizzy," he says. "And I'll definitely look into it for you."

When frogs and monkeys have butt sex with each other, I think at the same time Iris waves and says, "Thanks."

I push him out of my place, not touching him but crowding and herding him until he's on the other side of the door. He sneers. "What the hell is wrong with you?"

"You. Trespassing. My home. My woman."

He tilts his chin arrogantly. "Your home, fine. But your woman? Don't flatter yourself."

I clench a fist, wishing Iris were just a tiny bit less fond of this son of a bitch. It'd be my pleasure to break his jaw. But that isn't the only way to bring him down. "My previous business dealings with Milton were exactly that—just business. But things can become very personal, very fast, and you won't like it if they do."

I slam the door in his face.

∼

IRIS

I ALMOST JUMP WHEN THE DOOR SLAMS. I STARE AS TONY returns to the living room. I didn't catch what he was saying to Byron, but from the murderous gleam in his eyes, I can guess. And there's the hard lines of his shoulders and arms, the clenching of his hands, body language similar to when he attacked Jamie Thornton. I'm glad Tony didn't break Byron's nose...or anything else.

"What's that about?" I ask, purposely making my voice light.

"Him. Being here. With his hands on you."

It should sound petty and ridiculous. But the look on his face is pure torture. He's like a man tormented by some irrepressible demon, egging him to feel angry, to feel like he has to compete with Byron for me.

"He's just a friend," I say quietly.

"Right." He rakes his fingers through his hair, then stops when he notices the roses and chocolate on the coffee table. "Did Byron bring those?"

I nod warily. Is he going to start stomping on them, venting his anger on the gifts?

"No one brings roses to 'just a friend.'" Tony glares at the flowers as though they're to blame for an impending apocalypse.

I cross my arms. He's being completely irrational about this, all because he's under the assumption that Byron wants to sleep with me. My telling him he's wrong hasn't made a bit of difference. "He's done it before."

"How would you feel if Audrey brought me flowers and hugged me and I hugged her back?"

You're overreacting is on the tip of my tongue, but he has a point. Tony and Byron don't get along. Tony has never hidden the fact that he doesn't like Byron or that he thinks Byron's out for my body. From his point of view, the hug I had with Byron is a betrayal.

"I would hate it. But she isn't your friend, and we both know exactly what she wants. The wine she threw in my face made that crystal clear." I place a hand over his heart. "I already told you this. I love you. I've never said that to Byron, ever. You're both important to me, and I want you to at least be polite to each other, if being friendly is impossible. I swear to you, Byron doesn't want me the way Audrey wants you."

"You don't see yourself the way he sees you. The way I see you." Tony cups my neck, his bare palm warm. "You're so beautiful, so special, I'm afraid if I blink, you'll disappear like a dream.

You're all that is good and wonderful and worth living for in the world. My sun, my moon, my stars."

My heart flutters at the stark intensity in his eyes. He means it all—really believes I'm that amazing. But even as I shiver at the aching sweetness of his words, fear pricks me.

I'm not as perfect as the heavens, not worthy of such unconditional devotion. I remember the girl in the blue dress. And a woman named Tatiana, who I still don't have a clue about. And the Asian girl I watched and jeered at porn with. I've only recovered a few tiny pieces of my memory. I'm still so broken.

"Don't think," he says. "You're overthinking."

"I just wish you wouldn't consider me so perfect. There's so much of my past missing."

"It doesn't matter."

"What if I never recover from my amnesia?" *What if I'm broken forever?*

"Then we'll make our own memories to fill the void. Regardless of what your doctor said, you're not some piece of hastily mended pottery."

Hot tears prickle my eyes. This man humbles me with his love. I adore him so much. He calls me his sun, moon and stars, but it's really him who is all those things.

I hold his face and kiss him. Sweetly. Lushly. With all the love and yearning in my heart. My rock. The missing half of my soul. I've been searching all my life for this man, who's kissing me back like I'm more precious than air.

Our lips and tongues devouring each other, we rip into each other's clothes, flinging them everywhere, desperate to feel each other in our most vulnerable and primitive state without artifice or shield. My breathing shallows when I see his cock jutting out, hot and hard for me. His eyes are dark, glazed with lust, his cheeks flushed, his mouth swollen and red.

I lick my lips, then lean forward and kiss his nipple, right over his heart, while reaching down and wrapping my hand around him. I'm already slick between my legs. But it's impossible not to be when he's so open about loving and wanting me.

He cups my breasts roughly, his thumbs skimming the tips of

my beaded nipples, knowing exactly how I want to be touched. "I hear music," he says, "and think, *Is Iris going to like it?* I see a piece of art, and wonder if I should get it for you. I feel the sun on my skin, and I wonder if you're feeling it too." The sweet softness of his words contrasts with the ruthlessness of his hands. I pant, incredibly turned on.

I start to drop to my knees to taste him, but he stops me. He takes me to a couch and kneels between my thighs, lapping me with my legs wantonly spread.

He kisses the sensitive skin near my wet folds, his breath ticklish. "When I get a whiff of perfume, I think it isn't as sexy as the way you smell. When I get a taste of caviar, it doesn't taste as good as you." The flat of his tongue runs along the heated flesh from stern to stem. My back arches. "You're the best thing in my life."

He devours me, his mouth greedy, tongue probing, seeking, thrusting. He palms my breasts, toys with my nipples. He's merciless, bringing me to a fast, brutal climax that makes my whole body arch and twist, my sharp cries piercing the heated air. I barely get a chance to catch my breath before I shatter again. And then again. He's like a man determined to prove something—like he has to know he can make me come forever. And I let all my shields down, wanting to help him get whatever he needs, so he can be free of this inexplicable desperation inside him.

"Tony..." I sob as I hit another orgasm. "Tony..." I reach for him, tunnel my fingers into his hair. "Let me feel you inside me. Now."

He licks me softly as though he can't bear to stop, then comes up and kisses me hard. Our tongues tangle, and I nip at his lips, crazy with wanting him.

He pulls away for a moment. I hear a foil wrapper rip, then he returns, reclaiming my mouth and aligning himself. He drives into me, his movements ferocious. He feels so big, the friction unbearably hot against my pleasure-swollen pussy. I sigh with bliss. I love what he can do with his mouth, but this... It's extra special when we're joined like this. It's amazing how I feel so much—the pulsing of his cock, the racing of his heart, the boundless love he has for me.

I feel another orgasm building, ready to rip through me at any moment. I spread my legs wider. "I love you," I whisper. "I love you, I love you, love you, loveyouloveyou..."

His green gaze is so dark, it's almost black. He wraps his arms around me as I come apart, saying fiercely, "You're mine, Iris. *Mine.*"

Yes. Always. Forever.

His thrusts grow more frenzied until he shudders inside me. We cling to each other as our breathing settles. I feel so boneless and satisfied that I can't be bothered to move except to run my fingers weakly through Tony's dark hair. He looks at peace now. I hope that whatever need drove him to push me so hard is sated. And that he knows deep in his heart that he has me. He'll always have me.

When he finally gets up to go to the bathroom, I admire the view—the superb width of his shoulders, beautifully proportioned torso, narrow hips and tight ass that flexes with each step.

Tony says we can make new memories and not worry about my lost ones. But that's not how I want it. I'm going to find them all. If that means getting Byron's help, so be it, because he's just a friend, nothing more, regardless of what Tony thinks. And I need to fix what's broken inside.

Only then might I not feel like I'm unworthy somehow...that what I have with Tony is a sandcastle waiting for a wave to come wash it away.

15

ANTHONY

THE NEXT MORNING AT AROUND TEN, I SWIVEL IN MY OFFICE chair as my phone beeps with a text. I pick it up from my desk and glance at it. It's just Harry, not Iris. How deflating.

Coming back to L.A.

I tap the edge of the phone. Mother's been increasingly agitated recently, and Edgar asked Harry to visit because there's nobody he can't cheer up. Last time we chatted, Harry said Mother fainted dead away.

The old guilt is difficult to shake off. If it weren't for me, Katherine would've lived. Then Mother wouldn't have become so emotionally brittle. *How's Mother doing?*

Okay now. The doc said it was just stress.

My eyebrows rise. *Over what?* As far as I know, the family's doing fine. As it should. Father is semi-retired, but Edgar's smart and driven. Sensible, too. Unlike some who want to make their mark in the world, Edgar is more about growing Blackwood Energy sustainably and ensuring it can continue to provide jobs for people in and around Tempérane. And, of course, keep the family comfortably wealthy.

No idea. Sam, maybe? I overheard them on the phone. She sounded pissed.

A falling out? Edgar said she keeps lending money to Sam. *So she won't be investing with him anymore?* If she dumps him, I'll have more options for dealing with that smarmy bastard.

Dunno. Didn't hear much. She caught me. Got mad. Which is why she's kicking me out.

Ah. That explains Harry's sudden trip back to Los Angeles. Mother usually enjoys having him around. Everyone adores him because he's like a big-eyed puppy you can't stay upset with.

"Sir, you have a visitor," Wei says over the intercom.

Is it Iris, here to surprise me? Nah. Wei wouldn't have called her a "visitor." Audrey can't get through the lobby; building security has orders to toss her out on sight. And Wei would know better than to bother me with her in any case.

"Who? Bobbi?" I say hopefully. TJ's cousin works as a bodyguard, and I hired her for Iris, figuring the arrangement would be more comfortable than having a man.

"No. A woman from the Hae Min Group."

The Hae Min Group? I have business dealings with them, but the last project we did together was six months ago. A huge club and theater. Highly profitable, without any issues, as far as I know.

Still... Something must've gone wrong, very badly so, for the Korean conglomerate to send a representative over without notice. But...a woman? All my contacts there are men, and except for a select few, the company's still testosterone-heavy from the mid- to top management. "Send her in."

A woman and a man walk in together. Since they're from Hae Min, they're dressed well and conservatively. But while the man is in a black suit, the woman is in a pale peach dress, a black lambskin Gucci bag dangling from her forearm. Pricey jewelry glitters on her ears and throat, but there are no bracelets or rings.

From the cool power in her dark, wide-set eyes to the slightly arrogant tilt of her chin to the confident set of her shoulders, it's obvious she's the one in charge, even though she's got to be a decade younger than the man. Her mouth is full and blood red against the pale skin. Long auburn hair, expertly and expensively cut, frames a small, heart-shaped face.

Nothing about her says corporate. Hae Min workers don't dress like that—or exude wealth and privilege the way she does.

She has to be a member of the Hae family itself. But why is she here? We've never met, privately or otherwise. She's not in the management. When I did the basic vetting for the family before doing business with them, Chairman Hae's only daughter showed no interest in ruling the family empire. Have things changed?

"Mr. Blackwood," she says, with almost no trace of accent. "My apologies for this abrupt visit. I hope I'm not interrupting."

Polite. Cautious. *Interesting.* "Not at all. Please call me Anthony. Have a seat." I gesture.

She takes an empty chair, while the man remains standing. She purses her lips, then speaks briefly to him in Korean, her voice low. I only catch his name and title—Secretary Kim. I've picked up a few Korean words for corporate positions because of how Koreans refer to each other at work—Director Park, Auditor Lim, Vice President Choi and so on.

The man murmurs something, his tone respectful. She waves her hand dismissively, and he bows and leaves, closing the door behind him. What is so important—and secretive—that she needs to be alone with me?

She turns to me. "Again, my apologies. He's...sometimes overly concerned."

"No worries. What can I do for you?" I ask. Something about her is vaguely familiar, but I can't quite put my finger on it.

"My name is Yuna Hae," she says, confirming my initial guess about her identity. "I'm here to talk to you about a video. It has you, someone I presume is your date, Audrey Duff and Ryder Reed at a restaurant here in Los Angeles."

Fucking Ryder. If he hadn't shown up, or at least controlled his costar better, then none of this would be happening. He and

Audrey ruined the special dinner I planned to celebrate Iris's first job. And of course any video with him in it goes viral.

But why does this Korean woman care? She doesn't think she can fly all the way out here and get an introduction to Ryder, does she? A lot of women get stupid about him—his looks and Hollywood fame have that effect. Still, I put on a friendly smile. Offending the youngest child of the head of the Hae Min Group wouldn't be a smart move. She might not be in management, but I've heard rumors that her father overindulges her. "I'm not sure how that's a concern for you."

"It isn't. A concern, I mean. I want to know about the young woman who got wine all over her."

"Ah," I say to buy myself some time, my facial muscles like plastic. For a fraction of a second, I wonder if her visit has anything to do with Sam, but Peacher & Son is beneath the notice of an entity like the Hae Min Group.

Is she somehow related to Iris's accident? But Sam implied that whoever hurt me and Ivy in the past is someone in our inner circle. I don't know this woman at all. I wait for Yuna to continue, unwilling to respond one way or the other until I know exactly what her motive is.

"She looks like someone I used to know. Everyone said she died, but I couldn't believe it. I still don't believe it. My men tracked down someone who is supposedly her uncle, but he was rude and refused to help when I went to talk to him last week. He said I was wrong, but wouldn't tell me how to find her. I simply want to see her for myself. Unfortunately, she doesn't have an address in the city that I could track, and I'm too impatient to wait on a private investigator. It's been almost ten years."

"Just who do you think she is?" I ask, my mouth dry.

"My best friend from Curtis. Ivy Smith."

The impact of those seven words leaves me breathless. This is the girl who exchanged piano videos with Ivy, showing off their progress and egging each other on! "Watch and weep," I whisper.

Yuna's face lights up. "Yes! She's alive, isn't she? She was in the video with you, right? You're that middle cousin she was crazy about. I'm the one who suggested a tattoo as a way to show you she loved you."

How the hell...? I put up a hand to slow her down, my brain working to put the pieces together, trying to figure out what to say and how much to reveal. But in the end, I decide she doesn't mean any harm. She knows things that nobody else would know, which means Iris trusted her. And she cared enough to come all the way here herself instead of waiting for a secondhand report. "You don't think she died?"

"No. Do you believe in soul siblings?"

What? "How can an only child have a sib— I'm not following you."

"Not that kind of sole. Americans only believe in soul mates because they obsess so much about romantic love. But that's not all there is. Ivy is my soul sister. There's no one else who got me like her or cheered me on to be the best I could be. I did the same for her." Her hands curl into white-knuckled fists on the armrests. "I would've known deep in my heart if she really died. It would've left a huge, gaping hole that could never have been filled by anyone else." She looks away, blinking to erase the glint of tears.

Her pain is genuine, and I can sympathize. My life was hell without Iris, but I'm afraid what Yuna's presence is going to do to her memory and safety.

Iris is undoubtedly going to probe, and Yuna is going to tell her everything she can. Then Iris will know I've been lying to her. Her name and her true identity... She might even figure out that I'm responsible for the foundation hiring her. If I'm lucky, she'll be upset. The more likely outcome is her hating me, realizing I'm not worth anything after all.

Then there's Sam. Yuna said she met with him last week, and he refused to help her even though he has to know what she could do for him in return. The Hae Min Group is filthy rich, and it could introduce him to the most elite and exclusive eche-lons in Asia and North America. But instead of capitalizing on that, Sam tried to make Iris leave...and, when that failed, *tried to drown her.* I can't even imagine how far he'll go if he knows Yuna and Iris met, and Iris remembers more than just the girl in the water.

A selfish, desperate part of me says lie to Yuna. Meeting her might make Iris remember...and realize I'm a fucking bastard who deserves nothing. But I've already been committing enough sins by lying to Iris. Do I want to compound it by lying about Yuna too, when Iris has so few friends she can trust?

Iris's wellbeing always comes first.

"There's something you need to know," I say. "She's alive—"

Yuna jumps to her feet. "*I knew it!* Where is she?"

"Calm down. You can't see her yet."

She arches an eyebrow. "I *can't*? Why not?"

Clearly this is a woman who's used to getting her way. "Please sit down. I need to explain a few things."

She reclaims her seat and watches me, her gaze calculating.

I meet her stare squarely. She's probably wondering what she has to do to make me come clean. It's obvious she loves Iris, and she'll do everything in her power to keep her safe, just like me. Those tears earlier were raw and real, and she could be a valuable ally. But for that to work, I have to trust her and get her to agree to my terms. "She doesn't remember me," I begin carefully. "She probably doesn't remember you. She hasn't mentioned you once since she and I got together again."

"Impossible!"

"At that time...everyone thought she died. But she didn't. She had a serious head trauma that put her into a coma for a year. Since then, she's been suffering from partial amnesia."

"Why did you hide the fact that she's alive?"

I don't like her accusation. But if the situation were reversed, I might throw a punch first, then ask the question. "I didn't. I had no clue until not too long ago," I say. "There was a body nine years ago, one that everyone thought was her. The police called it a hit-and-run, but I'm pretty sure it wasn't an accident. Based on what I've learned, somebody went through a great deal of trouble to hide her. She was more or less forced to travel the world after she woke up and recovered enough to leave the hospital and not need therapy anymore."

Yuna pales. "You're saying somebody tried to kill her."

I hate it that she's drawn the same conclusion I did because it means I'm not just being paranoid. "Very likely, yes. I still have no clue who did it, or why. But the man you went to see—Sam Peacher—is part of it somehow. He's worried about the videos and people figuring out who she really is. If he knows that she remembers everything or that she realizes her real identity is Ivy Smith, she could be in even greater danger."

She blinks a few times, trying to get her head around it. "I see. So who does Ivy think she is?"

"A girl named Iris Smith from a place called Almond Valley."

"Iris *Smith*?"

"Distantly related to Sam—the uncle you met. He's a... Well, he's an asshole, no other way to put it. From my mother's side of the family. The Smiths. He's claiming that Ivy is Iris Smith."

"Is Iris Smith even a real person?"

"Yes, but she died a while ago."

"I see." Yuna sighs. "Is it safe for her to meet me?"

I debate telling her no. She'll go away if she thinks it would put Iris in danger again. But somehow I can't. I've already lied enough to Iris, all in the name of keeping her alive. When she turned to me for help, instead of promising to do everything I could, I told her there was no way to find the girl in the blue dress. I don't have the heart to deceive her again, even by omission. "I think so, but you can't tell her who she really is."

Her chin trembles, and she clenches her jaw. "I don't want to lie to her. I've never done that."

I look away. I can't claim I've never lied to Iris. And here I am, trying to co-opt Yuna. "It's only until I can get to the bottom of what happened back then and make whoever's behind it pay for their crimes. I have to make sure nobody's going to target her again."

She sits up straight. "Let me help you."

"Thank you, Yuna. I'll certainly ask if I need your help. Believe me, I want to keep her safe as much as you." *Probably more than you.*

"How much of our past can I share with her?"

I think quickly. Iris would want to know everything Yuna can share. I'd prefer that Yuna lie about everything, but given how reluctant she is about hiding Iris's real name, it's not going to be possible. Besides, I don't think Iris can piece together much from hearing about the three years she spent at the conservatory. "It's probably fine to tell her how you met and your time together at Curtis, without revealing her real name or the fact that she and I used to know each other. She thinks she went to high school until she was eighteen. Sam made her believe it."

"That dog. If this were Korea, he would be finished."

I have no doubt. The Hae Min Group is powerful and ruthless in its home country.

"Now, can I see her?"

She's eager and open, and I'm starting to see why Iris became such great friends with her. But too many things are different now. I don't know how Iris will react to Yuna. "Let me ask her first. Just in case. She doesn't remember you or anything that happened at Curtis as far as I know."

"Do you think she won't want to see me?" Yuna's voice is small.

I look at her helplessly. "I have no idea. I don't know what kind of poison Sam put into her mind about her old friends." If that bastard is devious and nasty enough to lie about Iris's past, he's gross enough to lie about her friends. Didn't she imply Sam made her think a lot of her past friends abandoned her or only wanted to use her? "Look, I'm heading home to have lunch with her. Do you mind if I take a quick picture of you so she can see what you look like? Maybe it'll trigger something."

"Of course." Yuna takes a breath, then smooths her hair and smiles.

I snap a shot. Yuna and I leave the office together, her father's secretary following. I climb into my car, with TJ in the driver's seat, and she gets inside a black Mercedes that follows us.

I look down at the photo. Yuna looks friendly, but there's a hint of nerves in her smile. Sympathy stirs. Here's a young woman who easily gets more or less everything she wants. But not this. Not somebody's heart.

I look out the window. It isn't easy to win somebody's heart, and even harder to keep it. The web of deceit I'm weaving around Iris is growing wider and more complex. I just hope that when the time comes, she'll understand I had to do it and forgive me.

In front of my building, I come out and turn to Yuna, who's trotting toward me in her heels. "Wait in the lobby. I'll call the concierge to bring you up if Iris says yes."

"How long do you think it's going to take to convince her?" she asks.

"I don't know."

She takes my wrist as I turn around. "You have to make her understand how much I want to see her." She licks her lips. "Please." The pride has vanished, and in its place is naked longing.

If she were just a little less likable, it'd be easier to pretend I couldn't help her. But she and I share the same pain, born out of our love for Iris. I pat Yuna's hand gently, then pull it off me. Secretary Kim is staring at her like he's never seen her before.

When I enter the penthouse, Iris gets up from the piano and comes toward me. "Hey! You're a little early. Hungry?" she asks with a wide smile and a coy look in her bright gray eyes.

"I missed you." I pull her tightly into my arms. She's right here. With me. But cold fear slithers up my spine, whispering that she's slipping out of reach.

She wraps her arms around me. "I missed you too, Tony," she says, but I can hear the unspoken question—*what's wrong?*

"There's something I need to tell you," I say.

"Okay."

I swallow, suddenly afraid. Is meeting Yuna going to be enough to make Iris remember our last fight? How I hurt her?

"What is it?" she prompts.

I clear my throat and pull out my phone. "A woman came by my office after seeing the restaurant incident video. She says she knows you and that she's your friend. She wants to meet you." I put Yuna's picture on the screen and tilt the phone toward Iris. "This is her. What do you want to do? You don't have to meet her if you don't wan—"

"Oh my *God!*"

"What?" This is an extreme reaction. Is Yuna not the friend I thought? Did something scary happen between them, and is seeing Yuna's picture triggering it?

Iris has both hands over her mouth. "I *know* her! I remembered her while I was practicing!"

What? So Iris is starting to recall her past, albeit in disjointed pieces. How much more does she remember? What else hasn't she shared?

Maybe she doesn't want to tell you because you shut her down when she asked for help locating the girl in the blue dress.

Fuck. Panic and fear twist around me, making me numb and unable to process.

Iris is gripping my wrists. "Did she leave a number or something? I have to see her! I looked everywhere to figure out who she is!"

Holy shit. My discouraging remark didn't make any difference. She's still actively trying to figure out what the fragments of her memory mean. Does Sam know? Now I almost wish I'd told Yuna Iris doesn't want to see anyone from her past, but it's too late.

"She's waiting downstairs." My voice is calm even though dread is clawing at me. "Let me call the concierge and bring her up."

16

IRIS

I PACE. MY TUMMY'S FEELING WEIRD—SOMETHING BETWEEN fluttering and cramping—from too much anticipation. My palms are damp.

Tony pours himself a drink. He offers me one, but I shake my head.

God. I can't believe that girl is here. How did she find me? Does she live in the city? Someplace close?

Crazy excitement is streaking through me. When Tony showed me her picture, I thought I was hallucinating. How could she just magically appear in his office, of all places? Is it because I've been thinking about her a lot? Other than the girl in the blue dress, she's the only person I've been able to *see* in my old memories.

Without any other clues to discover who she is, of course. I still have no idea why we were watching porn together or what she decided to do after finishing high school. I don't even know if we went to the same high school. She isn't in my yearbook.

I've met people who claimed to be my friends from past. All I felt was curiosity and hope when I met them. I wanted to know about people who used to be my childhood and school friends, but had become strangers in my mind. I also prayed that seeing them would jog my memory, making me remember other things, too. But nothing came up.

There was one girl, a pretty redhead named Debra. Claimed we were best friends, told me stories about how we hung out all the time, ran wild with some of the hot boys from school. But I couldn't muster an ounce of emotion.

"You look like you don't care much about all that," she said.

"It's just so long ago. It's hard to feel much about, you know, juvenile stuff." I didn't want to tell her I didn't recall any of those things. Or that my gut was telling me something was off.

She stuck around, and I let her, hoping maybe one day, my old memories would come back just through sheer force, like a tsunami overwhelming a dam. Besides, unlike some of the others who approached me, she didn't try to get to know Sam or show an interest in his money.

Then I caught her in bed with Marty. She wanted him, and he's young, rich and a better catch than Sam. She didn't care about resuming our friendship. After all, I didn't seem that interesting to her, and she had a goal—marrying a young, moneyed guy.

Another disappointment. Another bitter memory. And Sam told me—again—it's hard to trust people when you're related to somebody rich. Eventually, I quit trying to meet friends from my past. It just wasn't worth it anymore. Traveling around the world seemed preferable.

But unlike the previous "friends," this woman is definitely part of my past. I remember her! The Buddhist monk I ran into in Austria was totally right when he told me my past would find me if I stay in the same place long enough. He said the past is about people—and relationships I have feelings for—not just a string of events that happened.

Tony takes my hands in his. "Just so you know, she understands that you don't remember her. She knows that's why you never looked her up."

"Oh no." I didn't want her to know that. What will she think? It's pretty weird, isn't it, that I still don't remember all of what happened? On the other hand, she's here, so maybe she thinks I'm worth seeing anyway.

"She got in touch with Sam before coming to me. She only realized who you were after seeing the video from the restaurant."

Oh, great. I press my hands over my forehead. Sam wouldn't have told her anything nice. Is she here out of some lurid curiosity, then?

"Do you think she'll like me? What if I'm not the person she remembers? What if I'm too different now?"

"She already likes you. Why else would she come visit?"

"But... What if she's here for some other reason?"

"What other reason? She flew here all the way from Korea to see you, Iris."

From *Korea?* That's a lot of effort just to satisfy a little curiosity. Suddenly, I wonder how badly she wants to use me. "Is she rich?" I demand, needing to know before she shows up. I should've asked this first.

Tony stares at me like I've just spouted wings. "Yes, very. At least, her family is."

"How rich?" Rich enough to not want to use me to get to Sam or Marty?

"Her family probably has more money than I do."

The answer unwinds some of the tension. Maybe she really does just want to see me, nothing more.

The doorbell rings, and I look around quickly. The place is immaculate. But there's a pillow that isn't straight. I rush over to set it nicely on the couch, then run my hands through my hair. Maybe I should've told her to come in an hour so I could make sure I looked perfect.

"This is it," Tony says. "If you don't want to see her, just say so. I'll make her go away." His smile is warm as always, but there's a tightness in his gaze.

"It's okay." I take a deep breath. "I'll be fine."

He nods and opens the door. An immaculately dressed young

Asian woman walks in with a man following closely behind her. "Iris, meet Yuna Hae. Yuna, Iris Smith."

Her hands fly to her mouth, her eyes bright with tears. The man comes closer and whispers something in her ear. She finally drops her hands from her face, making a small choking sound.

I can't help staring. She's *exactly* like my memory, only more mature. Except her hair isn't black anymore, but a pretty auburn. My heart starts thudding.

Yuna Hae.

I roll the three syllables in my head. The clever small talk I was hoping to make vanishes from my mind and a million butterflies are fluttering in my stomach. I'm almost vibrating with nerves—excited and anxious about how she'll react to me, what she'll reveal, what other memories she'll trigger.

"Do you remember me, even a little bit?" she asks, her voice trembling.

A couple of quick, relieved nods, because this is an easy question. "The girl I watched porn with." The second I blurt that out, I cover my face with my hands, wishing I could start over. That *seriously* wasn't the first thing I wanted to say. I hope the guy she came here with isn't her dad or something.

"*Yes!*" Laughing and crying, she runs toward me and wraps me up tightly.

I hug her back out of reflex. Teary, emotional hugs from strangers are super awkward and uncomfortable. I'm not too crazy about people I don't know touching me. But this hug is different, even though Yuna's still a virtual stranger in my mind. My instinct—the same kind that helps me remember music I used to practice—says this is a great hug, full of sisterly love.

"Oh my God, I missed you so much. I *knew* you weren't dead. I just *knew it*," Yuna sobs.

Dead? My parents' obituary specifically said that they were survived by me. "Why did you think I died?"

"That's what I was told. But I knew you hadn't. If you had, I would've felt it." She pulls back to drink me in. "Right in my heart." Tears run down her cheeks in rivulets. The guy who came with her hands her a handkerchief. She takes it and dabs at her face.

"Who told you I died?"

"My mom. She said she got a call." She looks at the stained handkerchief. "My makeup's supposed to be waterproof, but look at this. Can't trust anybody these days," she says, half cringing with embarrassment and half laughing at herself. Mascara and eyeliner are smeared around her eyes, but she looks radiant anyway.

Most importantly, I like her. No reservation or hesitation. "You're gorgeous. Don't let some silly makeup bother you. I couldn't be happier you're here."

But in the back of my brain, I'm processing what she just revealed—somebody told her mom I died, and obviously she and her mom both believed the person despite an obituary saying otherwise.

Sam.

He has to be the culprit. He's the only one Yuna and her mom would believe over an official announcement.

But why would Sam do that? Because I was in a coma for so long? Why not just say I was comatose? The more I think about it, the more I wonder if he took me in to screw with my life for shits and giggles. I just thought he was a good guy because I had no one else after my parents' deaths. I desperately wanted to believe that he was a decent man, despite some things that made me uneasy from time to time.

I bet Yuna isn't the only one he lied to. Why stop with her? No wonder all my friends "moved on." They thought I was dead!

And the horrible users who pretended to be my friends—who were they? People Sam forgot to misinform in time? Or something else?

Now I'm shaking harder—with fury. I don't think I can ever forgive Sam for deceiving me and my friends, making us suffer for nothing.

"I'm sorry my uncle lied to you," I say. "I should've done more to reach out to my friends."

Yuna shakes her head. "I should've done more. You're my soul sister, but I didn't do a thing. I'm so sorry."

I don't ask her to explain "soul sister." Whatever it means, it makes me feel warm inside. Like I've found family, someone I can trust and depend on. "But you came for me, so it's all good. Better late than never, right?"

"Yes. It's nine years too late, but yes."

"I hate to interrupt, but it's time for lunch," Tony says quietly. "Do you want to order something to eat while you chat?"

"My goodness, you're right. We should eat. And celebrate. Do you want to go out?" Yuna suddenly shakes her head. "Oh, wait, maybe not. Not when I'm a mess, and I have a feeling I'm going to burst into tears again any minute. How about gourmet sandwiches? Do you think it's wrong to drink champagne this early?"

"Not at all," I say with a laugh.

Tony shrugs. "Sun's over the yardarm somewhere."

Yuna asks us what we want on our sandwiches and then says something to her man in Korean. He leaves, and we move to the dining table. Excitement is buzzing inside me, making me feel almost drunk at the possibility of learning more about my past— my real past, not Sam's fiction. I pull Yuna so that she's sitting to my left. Tony sits on my right.

"Who's the man who came with you?" I ask.

"Mr. Kim, my dad's chief secretary. He's here because Dad was so worried. He didn't think I could handle the disappointment." She sniffs. "When I thought you'd died, I was inconsolable. I even had to take a year off from school. My parents were so freaked out, they even stopped giving me a hard time about my music."

Yuna's talking like I should know this already. It takes me a moment to catch up and piece things together. Still, I'm glad she isn't treating my memory loss like some big deal she needs to tiptoe around. "They didn't want you to do music?"

Yuna gives me a look. "They didn't. That's why the only school I applied to was Curtis. You can attend there for free."

"Oh." I nibble on my lower lip. "Did I know this? Before?"

"I mentioned it to you once, but it was in passing."

Regardless, it can't feel good to realize your friend doesn't remember things she should. Now I almost wish I hadn't met her until I knew more. She hasn't given any indication she considers me damaged or weird, but how will she feel if she learns how little I can recall? I can't even play along like I remember what happened between us, because the only memory I have of us is watching bad porn. After a moment of hesitation, I ask, "Do you remember where I was accepted? For college, I mean."

She nods. "Curtis. That's where we met."

"Curtis?" I wait for something, anything to surface from my mind, but nothing comes. The name is completely unfamiliar.

"It's the most competitive conservatory in the world. Small. Full scholarships for everyone who's accepted. It's easier to get into an Ivy League school than to Curtis, admissions-rate wise. I gave my brother crap about that because he was insufferable when he got into Yale." A smile ghosts over her lips.

"And I was there?" It's crazy that I was that good. Despite what Sam said, I know I'm pretty decent because of the way people who've heard me have reacted. And the pieces I'm able to play—Liszt, Chopin and Rachmaninoff—are technically demanding. But there's good and there's *good*.

She nods. "You were one of the best. We were awesome."

While my mind sorts through the information, I wait, hoping something will pop into my head. My parents, who must've been proud. The excitement I must've felt when I got accepted and started the school. But nothing comes.

Give it time. Not every word out of Yuna's mouth is going to give you back a memory.

I take a breath. This isn't just about me. This is about Yuna, too.

"So what are you doing now?" I ask. "Professional musician?"

"No. I was hoping to do that, but when I heard you were gone, I just couldn't. I still play, but not at concerts. Instead, I started the Ivy Foundation in Korea with my dad's help. It provides financial help to people pursuing careers in classical music so anyone with enough talent and discipline can study without worrying about the cost."

"That's amazing. I'm so proud of you," I say, even though I didn't miss the part about my untimely "death" derailing her aspirations. *Damn you, Sam.* I hate it that he ruined another life with his lies. But this isn't the time for anger. It's time to reconnect with an old friend. She knows so much about me, and I so little—about myself or her. It's kind of awkward, but I'm not letting my discomfort keep me from reconnecting with someone who obviously cares so much about me.

"You should come and visit the office someday. See what we do. It's named after—" Suddenly Yuna clears her throat, then her gaze darts toward something behind me. "That's yours, isn't it?"

I frown at the abrupt change in topic, wondering what caught her attention. I turn and see the white baby grand. "It's actually Tony's."

She swings her attention to him. "Do you still play?"

He nods. "But the piano is really for Iris."

Some understanding passes in her eyes, and I can't sense what she's thinking at all. Before I can puzzle it out, Tony places a hand gently on my shoulder. "Told you you were brilliant."

"Seriously," Yuna says. "You have talent, drive and discipline. Not everyone has all three."

I stare at her, speechless. She isn't just flattering me. It's so weird to go from being told I was just an average pianist who did okay because of hard practice, to being told I'm freakin' brilliant, with everything I need to be a successful classical musician. It's like living your entire life thinking the sky's green, and somebody yanking yellow glasses off your face and showing you it's really blue.

Then I remember another person—someone we're both aware of, if I'm remembering correctly. "Do you know who Tatiana is?"

"You remember her, too?" She shoots a quick glance in Tony's direction before adding, "Our piano teacher at Curtis. She was such a character." She stands and starts to speak with a horrible accent that's somewhere between Russian and French. "All this education wasted! You haven't lived enough to know true love!"

She starts gesturing, her hands fluttering wildly above her head. "How can you understand the meaning of 'Liebestraum' without having loved and lost? Pounding the right notes on the piano at right pace won't make people *feel* the excruciating, *heart*-breaking pain." She throws a hand over her forehead, her spine bent backward in a dramatic pose.

I laugh, even as frustration tears at me for not being able to recall someone so colorful and memorable. "No way. Really?"

She nods, returning to the chair. "Why do you think we watched all those bad porn flicks? We were trying to learn what it was to love and all that. Pure love. Physical love. Sisterly love. Brotherly love. Obsessive love. At some point, I started dreaming I was in pure sisterly love with Tatiana, who wanted me obsessively. It was creepy, because as much as I love Tatiana, she isn't really my type." Yuna looks slightly horrified, but she's laughing.

I giggle too. It's hilarious we tried to learn about love through porn, but we were teenagers who probably didn't know any better. She's doing her best to give me some details, and I appreciate that, even though part of me is sad I don't remember any of it. If I'd recalled even half the things she's telling me, I would've looked her up for sure.

Something that's been niggling in the back of my mind suddenly pops clear. What she told me feels genuine, but the timeline doesn't add up. The accident that killed my parents and put me in a coma happened before I started college. How could Yuna and I have met? Air catches in my throat, and I go still, wondering if she's another of those "friends" from before. But Tony wouldn't have brought her here if he thought she was bad news.

"Did we live in the same neighborhood or something?" I try to make the question casual.

"We were roommates since our first year. We were fifteen when we moved in together."

"*Fifteen!*"

"Told you we were good."

"But fifteen? Sam told me I graduated from high school when I was eighteen. He even showed me the yearbook."

She slowly shakes her head. "He's lying."

"Obviously," I say bitterly as the depth of Sam's betrayal becomes clearer. Rage swells, growing like a tidal wave about to engulf me. I'm not a violent person, but if Sam were here...

Tony squeezes my hand. "Hey, relax. It's not your fault you believed him."

I look at him, the sympathy in his dark green gaze. He's upset because I am. And he's lending me his strength and understanding. "I know. I just feel gullible and stupid."

Yuna says, "It's his fault for lying, not yours for trusting the wrong person."

"You're right." Sam got away with lies and screwing with my mind because I had nobody I could depend on. He made sure I was isolated—which is why he made me travel so much. And why he was determined to put me on a one-way flight to Tokyo when he found about me and Tony.

I look at both Tony and Yuna. And I know they care too deeply to let Sam or anybody else take advantage of me. Gratitude flows through me, dulling the edge of my rage. "I'm lucky to have you two on my side."

"I should've looked you up sooner." Yuna has transformed, and her voice is hard. "I'm not letting him get away with this." It's jarring to see such a murderous look on her small, delicate face... but if the situation were reversed, I'd feel the same.

How can I remember almost nothing about this woman but still care about her so deeply? Is it because all the memories I can't access are still buried somewhere in my mind? My instinct is to rely on them and let them guide me. If I'd listened to it more, I wouldn't have excused so much of Sam's fishy behavior.

Mr. Kim returns with our sandwiches and a perfectly chilled Dom. Tony and I bring the flutes from the kitchen. At Yuna's and my urging, he does the honor of uncorking and pouring champagne for all four of us.

"To my precious friend," Yuna says, lifting her glass. "May we never be apart again."

"And to *my* awesome friend, who never gave up on me," I say, more determined than ever to trust my instincts and never let myself be isolated again.

"To both of you, and your beautiful friendship," Tony says.

Mr. Kim looks at his flute for a second, then clears his throat. "To your happiness," he says with a small, shy smile.

We clink glasses and drink. The Dom is smooth and delicious, the bubbles full of oak and berry undertones. We eat our sandwiches leisurely while talking. Well. The talk is mainly Yuna and me. Mr. Kim is silent. Tony doesn't say much either, but squeezes my hand from time to time to let me know he's here for me. Yuna reveals all kinds of things about herself, which is great, since I'm dying to learn more about her.

I already knew her family was rich, but Tony didn't tell me they're insanely powerful in Korea. Or have the most absurdly archaic ideas about Yuna's future. Her parents had high hopes for her—to go to a good college and marry a suitably wealthy heir to a huge conglomerate.

"To cement a merger? Really?" I gape at her.

"Blood is thicker than contracts."

Blood? "Were you supposed to make a lot of little merger heirs, too?"

"Of course."

She tells me more. Her love for music wasn't in any of their plans. Whatever she accomplished was through her own sheer will and determination.

She waves a hand. "Oh, please. Stop looking at me like that."

"But you did so much on your own." I'm embarrassed that I've let Sam's disapproval stop me so often, while she didn't let anything—not even her parents—get in the way of what she wanted.

"I lucked out. In Korea, people call me a diamond spoon."

"A diamond spoon?" From her tone, it isn't anything flattering.

"Yeah. A spoon, but made out of diamond. It's like a silver spoon, but a lot more valuable. And I was born with one in my mouth." She shrugs like that kind of talk doesn't bother her, not really. "So tell me what you're going to do now. Are you going to pursue music? You should. You'll be amazing."

Looking at the bright sparks in her eyes, I feel a little sad and pathetic, like I've lost something I shouldn't have. "I can't."

"You haven't been practicing?" she screeches.

I wince. She couldn't sound more upset if I were to confess I had unnatural feelings for a cow. "No, no, I have. I mean, I remember the pieces I must've played before, so I've been keeping up."

"Whew. I thought you'd quit, which would've been a travesty. You should totally go for it. I can just see the critics jumping to their feet, tears streaming down their cheeks... *Smith's debut is an unstoppable force!*" She leans closer. "I'm going to ask Dad to sponsor you. And maybe you can even be broadcast in Korea. Think about the human-interest angle. You'll be fascinating."

She's so animated, waving her arms, her eyes sparkling. She's serious about the debut. But the more jubilant she is, the more deflated I become. "I can't."

"Why not? It was your dream!"

"Maybe, but things are different now." I feel as flaccid as a crepe.

"How?" She jumps to her feet and rushes to the piano. "Look at this!" She points at the music. "You're practicing 'Mazeppa'!" She turns to Tony. "Be honest. Does she suck?"

"She's brilliant. The best."

"Seeeee? He thinks you're amazing."

"But I have panic attacks every time I try to perform in public." The confession makes me feel like a broken doll, and I hate it. I glance down so as not to see the inevitable pity in her eyes.

"What are you talking about?" Yuna asks.

Gazing at my lap, I play with my fingers. "I was in a coma after the accident. After I woke up and recovered enough, I tried to have a small recital because I thought I'd be able to reclaim some part of my life that way. But as I was walking toward the piano, I started to sweat and my heart started to beat so hard, I fainted. They actually sent me to an ER to make sure I wasn't having some kind of heart issue, because I apparently collapsed clutching my chest. But doctors ruled it out. So I tried again, but it happened again. That's when I got diagnosed for panic attacks." My voice is small. I'll never forget the way the ER smelled. Or the endless beeping of the machines. Or the clinical concern from the doctors. To them, I was just a girl who didn't know her limits. And I feel like I'm failing my friend by being much less capable and cool than I used to be.

Yuna raises a hand. "Hold on a minute. That doesn't make any sense. I've never seen anybody as incandescent on stage than you. You fed off an audience's energy."

I look at her, unsure what to believe. If Sam told me I was prone to panic attacks, I'd ignore him, since I know what kind of man he really is now. But I actually experienced them myself. Twice! How can she be so sure? "I don't know. But it felt like my heart was about to explode, and I passed out." I might not recall much of what happened before the accident, but I remember everything since.

"If you think it'll help, I could do a duet with you just to get your feet wet, so to speak. But I'm telling you, whatever reaction you thought you had was not a panic attack!"

I frown, unsure why she thinks that's a good idea. Surely she knows my preferences. "I don't like playing duets with people. Or anything that requires me to play with others." Except Tony. But he's different.

Yuna rolls her eyes. "Obviously not, when you don't have me! You didn't like to play with people who couldn't keep up with you. But we did plenty together, and you got invited to play in quintets a few times. I still have the piano quintet you did." She pulls out her phone and fiddles around until she finds the video she's looking for. "See? That's you."

It's a recording of me and four string players, performing Dvořák's Piano Quintet in A major. "Where was this?"

"At Curtis. About a year before...you know."

The quintet is beautiful, and everyone's playing well. But something about the music bugs me. It isn't the phrasing. It isn't that anybody hit wrong notes. But my skin crawls anyway, like a hundred ants are marching along my spine.

Yuna gestures at Mr. Kim and says something to him in Korean, and he nods and disappears. "I know you're skeptical, so I'm going to prove it to you," she says.

I wait, unsure how she plans to do that. Obviously she isn't going to show me any more videos, since she isn't going through her phone anymore. And she's just drinking more champagne.

I look at Tony. He shrugs. "Whatever she's going to do, I'm looking forward to it," he says.

"You're going to weep," Yuna tells Tony. "We're going to be awesome."

"I thought you Koreans like to be modest," he says teasingly.

"Yes, but we value honesty more." She winks.

Something passes between Yuna and Tony, tinged with a hint of awkwardness and another emotion I can't quite place. If I didn't know better, I'd say they did something sketchy—the usual suspects, like cheating. But I know it isn't like that. I trust Tony one hundred percent. And if they'd done anything wrong, he wouldn't have told me about Yuna. And unlike with other "friends from my past," my gut isn't telling me there's something fishy about Yuna.

She asks me how I spent my years since the accident. I skim over all the therapy—it's boring and dreary—and talk about my travels around the world instead. Yuna interjects with the names of Curtis classmates who now live in various cities, mostly in Europe. Yves Lombard went back to Paris; Diane Steinwitz is now teaching in Prague. When I mention going to a concert in Berlin, she says, "Did you get to see Zack? Zack Thames? He's with the Berlin Philharmonic now. Oboe."

"No."

Yuna wrinkles her nose. "That's too bad. He was *totally* in love with you. And he owes you whatever it cost to get a seatbelt fixed."

"What?"

"Yeah, he dropped a paperclip into the buckle and broke it. I swear, he's the clumsiest guy in the world. His fingers are always fumbling, he stumbles everywhere, but somehow he can play the oboe like a god. When he realized he broke the buckle, he stuttered and apologized, like, twenty times. But I think he was also mortified because he had a huge crush on you, and you were totally oblivious. Despite his genius with oboe, him being only sixteen, he didn't know how to approach you, hahaha. The older woman."

"Me? An older woman?"

"You were eighteen at the time. An impossible chasm. I'm sure he thought he blew his chance forever."

I smile, wistful for what I don't remember. "He sounds like a nice guy. Genuine."

"He is. He's married, the last I heard. Expecting his first child. But how about Barry Lim? He was touring in Europe. He was in London, Paris and Rome last year, performing on *Il Cannone*."

"Wow. I'm sorry I didn't know about that. I would've made sure to get a ticket." *Il Cannone* is Paganini's violin, and not everyone gets to play it. The violin may not be my instrument of choice, but that doesn't mean I don't appreciate it.

Mr. Kim returns, and his expression can only be described as grim disappointment. He leans over and murmurs to Yuna.

"Problem?" Tony asks.

She shakes her head. "No. I was trying to have a digital piano delivered, but it seems they can't do it until the day after tomorrow. I hope that's okay?"

"Sure, I guess. But what do you need a digital piano for?"

"To prove my point about her, me and a duet."

"Oh my goodness, you don't have to," I say.

"Yes, I do. I'm not letting whatever happened over the last few years make you doubt your ability or talent. I'm going to fix it if it's the last thing I do."

"What are we going to play?" I ask faintly.

"Rachmaninoff's 'Taranella.'"

I've only heard it once. It's a fast, passionate piece. And since it's Rachmaninoff, it's also hard. Like, really hard.

"You said you can play pieces you've practiced before. We

spent six months on Rachmaninoff's Suite Number Two," she adds.

"Right..."

"You're going to reclaim your music," Yuna says, her voice thick. "And everything else you've lost. I'll make sure of it."

It's a vow. And as much as I want to do what Yuna is saying, I'm afraid of what it will cost—my panic attacks, whether or not I can handle them and what kind of disappointment I'll be if I fail.

17

ANTHONY

I STAY AND WATCH IRIS AND YUNA. AT FIRST, I TOLD MYSELF I wanted to be there in case Yuna did something to upset Iris. But I soon got sucked into Yuna's stories of Iris's past at Curtis, the things I never knew about her. Vignettes of Iris playing Rachmaninoff or Chopin or Liszt unfurl like movie clips in my mind. And the promise Yuna makes to help Iris reclaim her past and music...

I want that for Iris too. I haven't forgotten what she said about not wanting to be an imitation of some other great pianist, but making her own mark in the world. To be celebrated and admired and listened to because she's awesome. Her eyes were sparkling when she told me. Even though she doesn't remember that now, surely the desire is still rooted deep in her heart.

Shine like the brightest star on the stage—that's what she was born to do. Just like I was born to love her.

But I fear what reclaiming the rest means—for us. I have no idea what she'll do if she remembers everything. I was an immature piece of shit all those years ago. I still kick myself mentally every time I remember the way I rejected her love back then. The entire time I told myself it was for her own good, but in truth, it was me letting fear take the driver's seat because I wasn't smart enough or brave enough to let our hearts guide us. If I were her, I wouldn't forgive me. I'd find someone else better...just like she said at Cajun Milan.

Maybe that's why when we move to the living room, I sit next to Iris and hold her hand tightly, like as long as we have our fingers linked, I won't lose her.

Iris asks Yuna more about the people they used to know at Curtis. Yuna obliges and starts telling stories.

"I still wish I'd never asked you to do that double date. I feel like C.T. was my fault. I always had great feel for guys," Yuna says.

"Who's C.T.?" Iris asks.

"Your first boyfriend at Curtis."

Iris had a boyfriend? I guess it makes sense she would—she's beautiful and talented. Any idiot would want to date her. But she was a virgin until we slept together, so it never crossed my mind that she dated seriously. But not even a hint of jealousy stirs. Hard to be jealous of a "boyfriend" who couldn't close the deal.

Yuna continues, "I told you he was bad news, but you wouldn't listen."

"What did he do?" I ask, curious what could earn the expression of utter contempt that's on Yuna's face.

"What *didn't* he do?" She rolls her eyes. "He flirted and paid attention to any girl who looked his way. Even when Iris was standing right there. What a jerk."

Huh. Well, C.T.'s loss is my gain. And I'm never, ever letting Iris go, whether I deserve to keep her or not. I'd walk a thousand miles on my knees if that would redeem me, make me worthy of her.

"Please tell me I dumped him," Iris says.

"Hell yeah, you did! You also told him to find himself a new accompanist for his cello sonata. I think he cried more over the fact you wouldn't make him sound good than the breakup. He asked me next, and I told him I'd be more likely to strangle him with his cello strings."

Iris and I laugh. The image of the tiny Yuna trying to garrote somebody is hilarious, not to mention impractical. Cello strings are too thick.

As Yuna continues, I wonder if having her back in Iris's life means I can look for a way to permanently eject Byron from it. I've managed not to break his face—barely—only because he's one of two or three friends Iris has. But if she has Yuna, why should I put up with him? I haven't forgiven him for visiting her here, at my place, behind my back. It's disgusting how he craves Iris, even if she doesn't seem to notice it for some bizarre reason. The fucker isn't exactly subtle.

My phone buzzes, and I reach into my pocket and pull it out. It's Jill.

Finally. Anticipation pounds through me. She must've found something to call on a Tuesday. She's been texting me on Friday to give me weekly reports—to let me know she's still working on it.

"Excuse me," I say, slowly letting go of Iris's hand. I can't take the call in front of everyone.

I move out onto the deck and shut the door behind me. "Yes?"

"Am I interrupting anything?"

"No. Go ahead." I walk to a chair by the pool and face the inside, watching Iris and Yuna. Mr. Kim is hovering unobtrusively. A rare talent. Iris laughs at something Yuna says. My mouth curves into a smile as well.

"You wanted to know how Sam became so rich. It's your mother, Margot."

My good mood starts to evaporate. Edgar and Harry told me Mother was involved. But at the same time, it isn't like Jill to waste time with something I already know. "Explain."

"She not only invested in his first development project, she championed it and helped him raise capital about nine—eight? —years ago."

"So it wasn't just money?" What the hell is really going on? Mother hates Sam's guts.

"Her money wouldn't have been enough. Your family's rich,

but she can't access that much of it. You know her side of the family's finances."

Mother's side of the family, including Sam, were comfortable middle-class folks. That's why he kept entreating her; Mother was the only one with access to a significant amount of money. But that access wouldn't have been enough by itself.

Jill continues, "The only people who could have invested enough as single investors were your father and Edgar, because they run Blackwood Energy. But her investment, plus her putting in some good words for Sam's initial project, made all the difference. People knew he hadn't been able to convince her before. So they figured he must've found a winning formula. And apparently they were right, because, along with your mother, he became rich."

Edgar and Harry only said Mother gave him money, nothing about the rest. Neither has any reason to hide it from me, so Mother must've avoided telling the family what she was doing for Sam.

I close my eyes, doing some quick math. Nine years ago was when everything happened—the accident that "killed" Ivy and Mother's financial arrangement with Sam. My gut says they're related, but I can't figure out how.

Mother had nothing to do with the accident. She was home that evening, and I can't imagine her hiring someone to harm Ivy. Despite their arguments and differences, she still considered Ivy her daughter. Mother was so broken up over Ivy's death that she had to be wheelchaired to the funeral. It was August—in Louisiana—and still Father put a lap blanket over her because she couldn't get warm.

The only thing I know for certain is Sam was at the scene of accident, but I don't know how that would help him convince Mother to invest with him. If he tried to blackmail her by keeping Ivy from her, Mother would've ruined him outright and reclaimed Ivy. Given my family's power and connections, it wouldn't have been difficult.

Jill adds, "Margot is still one of his staunchest investors. He's made her a lot of money, too. It's a mutually beneficial arrangement."

Except Mother doesn't need the money.

Suddenly, Sam's taunt fleets through my mind...that the people who can wield the sharpest knives unseen are the people closest to us. Was he referring to Mother? But Mother and I are hardly close. She banished me to Europe eighteen years ago. She made it clear she didn't want me back when I returned after graduating from college. I was officially and publicly disowned seven years ago, and as far as I know, she was pleased with Father's decision to do so.

"He doesn't need her anymore to raise funds for his projects, does he?" I ask.

"No, but he asks, and she invests anyway. It doesn't look good when your first investor dumps you, does it?"

Hmm... "Do me a favor and dig a little deeper. Figure out why my mother still invests with him."

"Money? She's been making at least a ten percent return. That's not bad."

"It's not, but she doesn't need it. And she can't stand him. She used to act like she'd rather burn a hundred-dollar bill than to give it to him, so it's weird she's investing with him."

"Blackmail?"

"Possibly," I say, not wanting to prejudice Jill, even though instinct says it has to be blackmail. But what kind?

If Mother were younger or more risqué, I might suspect she took some pictures she shouldn't have and Sam got a hold of them. But she's not. And I know for a fact there's no affair. Mother adores Father. She'd never betray him that way.

So what the hell is the connection between her and Sam? What am I not seeing?

"I'll look into it. Also, I have a list of the missing women."

I pause for a moment, until I realize who they are. Anticipation fizzes in my veins. Maybe the connection isn't Ivy, but the dead woman in the Lexus. That might be why Sam reacted the way he did at the pool.

"Want me to mail them to you?" Jill asks.

"Got photos, too?" I only need a strawberry blonde. Should be easy to pick a few that match the description Iris gave.

"Of course," Jill says, like I'm asking her if the weather's sunny in L.A. "Just so you know, there are over five hundred women."

Damn it. I start to ask her to sort them by hair color, then stop. Women change colors and styles all the time. "Are they the latest photos of them?"

"Whatever's publicly available, so not always the latest."

"Send them to Wei." He'll know what to do once I explain I'm looking for a woman who had strawberry-blond hair around the time she went missing and was never found. He's great at figuring out creative ways to solve problems.

"Sure."

"Send the invoice for the work done so far as well."

"Will do. I'll call you when I have more to report."

"Thanks." I hang up.

I thought if I knew how Sam got his start, I could find a way to deal with him. Instead, all I have is more questions. I look through the window at Iris gesturing wildly at Yuna, who's clapping and wiping her eyes. Iris's presence in Los Angeles must be costing Sam somehow. Otherwise, he would never try to make her leave...or die.

My head starts pounding. I press the spot between my eyebrows. My phone buzzes with a text.

Come on, stop ignoring me. Just one meeting. Face to face.

Whatever. Ryder is crazy—and stupid—if he thinks texting me every day with the same message is going to get me to see him. His betrayal with Lauren—and the whole fucking scene with Audrey—should be more than enough to satisfy his Hollywood drama quota. If not, he'll have to find someone else to costar in his idiocy. I have more productive things to do with my time, and it's better for his career if we don't meet. I can't guarantee I'll leave that pretty face intact the next time we see each other.

Yuna here is because of him. This time that damned video produced a friend, but there's no guarantee it won't bring enemies as well. And Iris definitely has enemies.

I jump to my feet, suddenly too restless and annoyed to sit, and start pacing along the pool. Everything's going so slowly. I understand that not even money can make things go faster, but it's killing me that nothing's getting resolved as fast as I'd like.

If I could, I'd tie myself to Iris permanently, so I could watch over her twenty-four seven. Instead, I have to settle for Bobbi. Assuming she's done with her work today. Told TJ I'd buy out his cousin's contract, but he said she'd never agree to it. Too damn professional.

Come on. That's exactly the quality you're looking for. She won't ditch you for a better offer, leaving Iris unprotected.

I glance at my watch. It's after lunch and Bobbi should've been in contact by now. Is she trying to get fired before she starts? TJ warned me three times that she really wanted to quit being somebody's bodyguard.

Bobbi can do whatever she wants, but I'm not firing her. And she's going to be tied to Iris until I take care of the danger to my woman—permanently.

18

IRIS

WHEN THE INTERCOM BUZZES, I OPEN THE DOOR, THEN STOP at the sight of an unfamiliar honey blonde with a long ponytail hanging down her back. The concierge only calls us if a guest isn't on the approved visitor list, so I didn't think to check, but now I can't help but wonder if I made the right move by opening the door.

The scowl on her face is more suited to a boxer ready to punch somebody out than a friendly guest. She's at least six feet tall, leanly muscled, with a competent air about her. Her sleeveless black top is stretchy and molds to her small breasts and flat midsection. The black jeans she has on are slightly gray now and frayed. But those are the best kind—comfy and soft. Her boots aren't fashionable, but they look like they can hurt you extra when she kicks.

Eyes the color of burnt caramel focus on me. "Iris Smith?"

"Yes?" I say, wondering how in the world she knows who I am. She has to be one of Tony's friends. Or...one of his exes? Like Audrey? I take a slow step back, so I'm out of arm's reach.

"I'm Bobbi."

She says the name like it should mean something. And she sounds unhappy. Not enough to throw wine in my face, but enough to be nasty. Must be one of Tony's exes.

"Ex*cuse* me!" comes an annoyed voice from behind Bobbi.

"Julie?" I crane my neck to see my friend, who's huffing like a pissed-off bull. "What are you doing there?"

"She won't let me past." Julie jumps up and down, waving her arms.

"Why not?" I look up at Bobbi with a scowl. "Why are you blocking her?" I put my hands on my hips. Although Bobbi's badass attitude is intimidating, I'm not backing down. Not when she's the one being obnoxious.

Yuna stands next to me. Her gaze moves from Bobbi to Julie. "Who are they?" she asks, leaning toward me.

"I'm Iris's best friend," Julie says. "Who are you?"

Yuna's perfect black eyebrows arch. "I'm her soul sister." I can sense Mr. Kim gliding up behind us.

"What?"

I stand there with my hands at my hips, and Yuna copies my pose. But I know I can't hold Bobbi off forever. Crap. *Where's Tony?*

As though my thought conjures him, Tony comes in from the deck. He was tense earlier when he went outside to take the call, but now his face is stark with relief. Suddenly, I feel more confident. We could use some reinforcements.

He shakes hands with Bobbi. "Thank God you're here."

I stare, unable to process the scene. *Thank God?* He's actually happy to see this hostile woman?

"Flight delays. Too bad they didn't ground every plane." Bobbi sounds slightly snarly and annoyed.

I agree: it's too bad they didn't. If they had, she couldn't have made it to Los Angeles from wherever she's from. It would've been nice to spend the time without her to ruin it. Tony just smiles, ignoring her less-than-friendly tone. "Come on in."

Bobbi and Julie both enter. Bobbi studies me, her eyes

narrowed, while Julie's checking Yuna out, who is returning the favor with arms crossed.

"She's the body?" Bobbi says, tilting her pointy chin in my direction.

The body?

"Yes," Tony says.

I swivel my head at his ready agreement. "Hold on a minute. What's this 'body' stuff?"

"The person I'm supposed to protect. Don't you know? I'm your bodyguard," Bobbi says with a smile that says she'd rather be eating rusty nails.

"My *what*?" I feel like somebody just sucker-punched me. I could swear Tony hasn't said a word about it. I would remember. And why does he think I need *her*, of all people? I'm not going to be stupid enough to see Sam alone again. And I don't think Sam is crazy enough to try coming after me.

"Perfect! I'm so glad you're here," Yuna says, clapping like Bobbi is an extra Christmas present from Santa.

Julie, on the other hand, is glaring at Yuna, then Bobbi. Finally, she turns to me. "You have a soul sister *and* a bodyguard now?"

I don't have the mental energy to talk to her about Yuna yet, because I'm still trying to process Bobbi. So I focus on the second part. "I'm just as lost as you." I give Tony a stare, letting him know in no uncertain terms that I don't appreciate this particular surprise. "What exactly is going on?"

Tony looks chagrined. "I was going to tell you today—just you, me and Bobbi, but Yuna showed up, who you wanted to meet." He shoots Julie a baleful look. "And she's completely uninvited."

"I need an invitation from you to visit my friend now?" Julie says.

I raise a hand to stop her, because I know that tone. She's about to launch into a long rant. "Don't you think you should've said something earlier?" I say to Tony.

"It's only logical," Yuna says. "If he hadn't hired somebody, I would have."

I turn to her, vaguely irritated she's not on my side in this. She said she's my friend, not his. "This isn't helping."

She shrugs and gives me a look reserved for someone complaining that water is wet.

Meanwhile, Julie moves closer to me, away from Bobbi. "Pretty high-handed of him, getting you a babysitter without telling you first."

The muscles in Tony's jaw flex. If I weren't here, he'd probably kick Julie out.

I rub my temples. There's no way this is going to get resolved with my two friends watching and throwing contradictory comments.

"Can we talk?" I tilt my head upstairs.

"Yes," Tony says, his expression guarded.

Bobbi starts to follow, and I say, "Not you. You can stay here and wait." If she's around, it'll be harder for me to say what I need to say, because this is strictly between him and me.

"Should've warned the body," she says to Tony, a little too gleefully.

"The body has a name," I point out. "Besides, calling me 'the body' makes it sound like I'm dead."

She shakes her head. "Nah. Then I'd be calling you 'the corpse.'"

My jaw goes slack. She's serious. How in the world am I supposed to deal with someone like this? It's obvious she's only going to answer to Tony, not giving a damn how I feel. And if she's my bodyguard, doesn't she have to follow me everywhere? Is she going to go around telling people I'm "the body" or something similarly embarrassing?

I lead Tony to the guest bedroom. I don't want our bedroom to be a place where we argue.

The moment Tony shuts the door behind him, I whirl around. "Why did you hire someone like that without running it by me first?"

"She's highly qualified—and a woman. I thought you'd be more comfortable with her. Besides, she's TJ's cousin, so I trust her. She also has lots of excellent references. None of her clients has ever come to harm on her watch," Tony explains, ticking off fingers.

Anger wells up like a wave. He's being obtuse on purpose. "I don't mean *her*. I mean a bodyguard in general."

He's staring at me like I'm not making any sense. "Why the hell not? I have TJ; Elizabeth has Tolyan. Her husband has a guy—"

"Yeah, but you're all important and stuff. I'm just a"—I struggle for the right word, so he doesn't misunderstand—"a nobody." And a nobody with a bodyguard is going to look weird as hell. People will whisper. Look at me closely. Wonder what's wrong with me, when what I really want is just to be *normal*, like hundreds of millions of people in the country.

He cradles my face in his hands. "You are not *nobody*. You're everything to me, the most important thing in my life."

"But Ton—"

"TJ already knows if it's between you or me, he needs to choose you."

I search his face. He means every word. The notion that he would die so I could live is... My stomach roils. I refuse to even consider it. "How can you say that?" My voice is shaky. He told me he loved me, but maybe I never truly grasped the depth of his devotion, or maybe I didn't want to understand it because I never felt I really deserved it. Not when I'm not whole.

"Like I said. You're the most important thing in the world."

My lips go bone-dry, my heart racing. The fact that I'm this significant to him is humbling. And scary as hell. "You know I'm..." My voice is raspy, and I try to swallow, but it's no use. "You shouldn't... I'm not..." *Perfect. Not worthy of your life that way.* I'm too cowardly to voice the thought, so instead I say, "I'm messed up in the head. What if I never regain my memory? How will you feel if you have more of my old friends popping up in your office, wanting to see me or something?"

"Then I'll ask if you want to meet them and go from there. As for your memory, it doesn't matter to me. I didn't fall in love with you because of what you remember. I fell in love with you because you see the best in me. You always..." His Adam's apple bobs, his thick, long lashes hiding his eyes briefly before he rests his forehead on mine, his gaze boring into me with stark intensity. "You are the compass of my life. You give me hope that tomorrow's going to be better than today. You believe I'm enough—not my money, not my influence, just *me*. If everything I have goes up in flames, you'll be by my side, your feelings still the same. So how can you not be the most important thing in my life? Losing you would be like getting my heart ripped out."

Every word out of his mouth kills me. Despite trembling legs, I manage to stand, utterly overwhelmed. Tony has no defense as he lays everything out, and it's all I can do not to sob as tears flood my eyes. I've never heard anything this honest or vulnerable before. My objection to Bobbi vanishes because it's petty and inconsequential in face of this heartrending declaration, spoken so quietly. The only thing that betrayed his nerves was a slight rasp that edged into his words from time to time. And I realize he's *willing* me to believe him, while bracing himself for the possibility that I might not.

"Tony... The things you say sometimes... I wish you would value yourself more." I reach out slowly and place my palms on his warm cheeks. "I love you so much, sometimes I think my heart is going to burst. What you just said... I feel the same way about you. So TJ better *not* pick me over you."

The smile he gives me is radiant but tinged with sadness. And I know he isn't going to follow my advice.

"I don't need him doing Bobbi's job," I add sternly. "And I'm sure Bobbi doesn't either."

He dips his head for a kiss.

"Hey, at least wait until I'm gone if you're going to kill each other," comes Julie's extra-loud voice from downstairs. "I don't want to be a witness to a crime, as titillating as that sounds. Murder trials are tedious."

He squeezes his eyes shut. "Why is she here?"

"She texted before you came home with Yuna, and I told her she could come by for coffee or something in the afternoon if she wanted." Until she actually showed up, I'd forgotten all about it. It's crazy how much has happened.

He sighs. "It doesn't matter. Yuna's here too. Let's get rid of our guests."

I know what he wants. Normally I would too, but... "Um. It probably doesn't matter if they stay."

"What do you mean?"

"Uh." I squirm, unsure how to say it. I've never had to tell a man about my cycle. "Well."

Instantly, Tony's holding my shoulders, peering at me worriedly. "What is it? You can tell me anything."

"I'm, ah, onmyperiod, itjuststartedthismorningafteryouleft," I say in a rush. My face heats. "So. You know..." I shrug, totally embarrassed now.

"Oh. Okay." Like it's every day somebody confesses to menstruating.

I steal a quick sidelong glance. "You aren't...grossed out or anything?"

"Why? Women have periods. It's biology. What's gross about it?"

His blasé response lessens my awkwardness. "Well. If you feel that way." I clear my throat, then something else occurs to me. "By the way, Bobbi isn't going to be around all the time, right? She isn't going to be hovering over us in the bedroom."

He gives me a horrified look. "That's definitely not what Bobbi's signed up for. Why on earth would you think—"

"I saw it in a movie once."

He rolls his eyes. "Fucking Hollywood. No. Nothing like that. But she'll follow you everywhere else—your office, shopping, all that."

"Okay." I squeeze his hand as we walk down the stairs together. It's the least I can do to put his mind at ease, even though I'm still uncomfortable with the idea of a bodyguard hovering over me like a mother afraid her child's going to scrape a knee.

~

ANTHONY

THE SIX OF US END UP HAVING DINNER TOGETHER—THAI, since it's easy and quick. Mr. Kim looks vaguely unhappy with the food, and Yuna whispers he doesn't like Thai spices because they upset his stomach. So Iris makes him a turkey sandwich, which he nibbles on while the rest of us eat.

Iris and Yuna chat about the Rachmaninoff Yuna wants them to play together. Julie stares at the food, then suddenly says, "Why would Iris want to play that? She shouldn't have to learn a new piece just to please you, Yuna."

"She already knows how to play it. We performed it together before."

"She doesn't like duets," Julie says.

"No, she loves duets. So long as her partner can keep up." Julie turns a dull red, but Yuna doesn't notice. "And it isn't like it's going to be super difficult, even if she has to learn it from scratch."

"Not difficult? It's Rachmaninoff!"

Yuna looks genuinely puzzled at Julie's shrill outburst. "So?"

"So. The woman says so." Julie shrugs. "Well, it's academic anyway. There's only one piano."

"I'm having another delivered," Yuna says, grabbing more rice and green curry.

Julie shoots me an incredulous look. "Seriously? Two baby grands?"

I shrug. I'm not getting dragged into this weird pissing contest between the two women. Julie's on her own.

"The new one is digital," Iris says soothingly. "It's just a duet."

"We're going to try it the day after tomorrow. You're welcome to come listen if you like," Yuna says.

"I think I will," Julie says. "To see you play this 'easy' Rachmaninoff."

"Okay."

I glance at Iris, and she gives me a small shrug. Yuna isn't being rude, but Julie is obviously spoiling for a fight.

It's too bad she backed down. I'd like nothing more than for her to get herself in trouble with Iris. She's Iris's friend, but I know she isn't too crazy about me. And like Yuna said earlier, blood counts. Julie will always side with Byron over me, and for that alone, she'll always be someone I just tolerate.

19

IRIS

"I DON'T NEED BOBBI TODAY," I TELL TONY AS WE'RE finishing up our breakfast the next day. "I'm going to stay home."

"But what if you decide you need to go out? I don't want you to be stuck all day," he says.

"I won't feel stuck."

"I disagree. The second you can't do something, you want it more." He kisses me, lingering. "Like now."

My cheeks warm. "Look who's talking."

"Obviously. I'm addicted to your body. It makes going to work hard."

I laugh. "Stop with your bad sexy talk and go. See you for lunch?"

"Mm-hmm."

I hand him a travel mug full of coffee, and he walks out. Just as the door's about to close, Bobbi slips through it.

Her attitude hasn't improved one bit. She looks just like yesterday: a flat expression, a sleeveless black top, worn black jeans and the boots. The muscles in her arms flex as she pours herself a coffee, and she takes a seat near the Steinway.

Sigh. I don't know why Tony thinks I should be able to ask her to do anything. She's going to bite my head off if I tell her I want to go out. She has that "don't fuck with me" face.

Trying to pretend it's just like every other normal day, I start practicing. But it's hard to focus because she's like a disapproving storm cloud. I swear I can hear a rumble from the couch where she's sitting and drinking her coffee.

After playing arpeggios and scales in D minor to warm up, I grit my teeth and start on "Mazeppa." But after half an hour, I realize it isn't going to work.

Morning, when I'm practicing, is my calm, happy time. When Tony's home on weekends, he works and occasionally listens to me with a smile on his face.

But Bobbi's shooting daggers in my direction on purpose to ruin not just my practice, but my morning. And even though I haven't hit a wrong note or played off tempo, she's the worst audience ever, sighing every five seconds or so like I'm paining her with my practice. Her reactions are throwing me off. *Enough.*

I walk over to the couch and stand with my hands on my hips. She looks up with a slow smile. It's the smile you give an animal that just fell into a trap.

My heart jumps to my throat, but I hold my ground. This is my home, not hers.

"Why are you glaring at me?" I demand, keeping my voice firm. I'll be damned if I sound scared of her, even though she's physically intimidating.

"Glaring? I was looking at you."

Her reasonable tone stokes my annoyance. "With a scowl!"

"So?"

"But why?"

"Does that matter? I'm here to catch bullets, not listen to Bach or whoever."

I inhale sharply at the matter-of-fact way she speaks. I can't decide if she's just screwing with me or serious about the bullets. Probably just joking. Who the hell's mad enough to shoot at me?

Well, maybe her, since she isn't even trying to hide how much she dislikes me. "You don't have to like me, but you could be a bit more pleasant while doing your job."

"Could. But it's a job I don't want."

Oddly enough, the comment hurts. I didn't want her here either, so I shouldn't be unhappy to hear it. But somehow this feels...personal. And vaguely insulting. Like she thinks I'm beneath her. "Why not?"

She leans back, stretching her arms along the back of the couch. "You really want to know?"

Not really. "Yes."

"Poor little pretty girl has a mean old uncle problem. She blows everything out of proportion to cling to her man. I thought Tony would be immune to such a pathetic, transparent drama, especially after he more or less ignored Audrey Duff's 'suicide,' but I guess I overestimated him." She gives me a lazy, penetrating head-to-toe. "You must be *really* good."

I stare at her. At least she doesn't think I'm weird. Just an opportunistic, parasitical man-clinger. I can't decide if I should be happy or offended. "You think I *faked* the problem with Sam? Just *imagined* that he tried to drown me?"

She shrugs. "You wouldn't be the first chick who manufactured a little drama to get some attention. I'm not judging you." She pauses. "Not much, anyway."

"Hey! You don't get to claim not judging while totally giving me that judgey look. I'm not faking anything. He *did* try to drown me."

"Okay. I believe you," she says carelessly.

I cross my arms. If she's going to be rudely honest, I can return the favor. "Tony didn't tell me he was hiring someone. I never wanted you here."

"Great! Tell him you hate me and have him let me go."

What the hell? She's serious about not wanting this job. She really believes I'm just some drama queen exaggerating the danger. "I can't. I promised him. Besides, what are you going to do if you're out of work? You have somebody else to guard? Some hot actor you've been fangirling over?" Two can play this game.

"Don't want to guard anybody. I want to open my own bakery and be a cake decorator. Get married and have babies. As many buns as my oven can handle."

I look at the clearly visible veins in her biceps. *Cake decorator? Married, with kids?* Bobbi looks like she could subdue a rabid hyena without breaking a sweat. Maybe her idea of cake decorating is smearing the congealed blood and powdered bones of her enemies as frosting and sprinkles.

"I'm a damn good baker," she says. "I can bake better than you play that stupid piano."

"Riiight." I infuse the word with as thick a layer of condescension as I can manage. The only reason I played badly is that she kept glaring at me. "So if you'd rather be stuffing your oven, why are you here?"

"TJ made me."

That's news. I'm surprised TJ would go that far for me, even if the bodyguard he sent has too much attitude. "Is that why you don't like me? You think I forced TJ?"

"Nah, he only listens to Tony. And for what it's worth, I don't dislike you. I just want you not to like me. Then fire me before I have to catch a bullet."

"I don't think you have to worry about anyone shooting at me." I doubt Sam would go that far. He's too fastidious, and guns are messy. And leave too many clues.

"That's what one of my previous clients said." Bobbi leans sideways and lifts her shirt. There's a puckered scar on the left side of her belly.

"Oh my God." One hand over my mouth, I stare, my stomach growing queasy. I know it's her job, but I don't know if I'd be able to handle it if she got hurt protecting me. My annoyance with her attitude evaporates.

Bobbi continues, "I took it for a sniveling little bitch who staged a fake attack to get her rich ex back. She's so stupid she didn't think to use blanks. And I got shot, trying to protect her Instagram bimbo ass."

"That's horrible. People actually *do* that kind of thing?" And here I thought Audrey Duff was extreme.

"You think that's bad? My last client decided he should 'reward' me with sex for saving him from a crazy ex, who was so pissed off over losing custody of their dog that she decided to run him over in front of the courthouse."

"Wow," I say, unable to think of anything else. No wonder she wants to quit. "Does he still have his man-bits?"

Her smile is slightly feral. "Only because I'm a professional."

I breathe out long and hard. That explains her behavior. Maybe she's burned out. Does Tony know? Is that why he's been ignoring her less-than-friendly disposition?

Still, I can't have her consider me her enemy. It's going to drive me crazy to live under that glower. "Okay, look. I'm sorry about what happened, but I didn't do that to you, so don't take it out on me. And I swear I'm not a drama queen. If I do something stupid, you're more than welcome to smack me upside the head. I'll put that in writing if it'll make you feel better. I don't want a bodyguard any more than you want to be one, so let's just get along until Tony's satisfied I'm not in any danger. And if you do that for me, I'll...ask him if he'd be interested in investing in your bakery."

"I have my own money," she says stiffly.

"Yeah, but why use your own when you can use somebody else's?" I don't know how much it costs to open a bakery, but it can't be that much for Tony. If Bobbi has a good plan, I'm sure he wouldn't mind putting some money into the business.

She looks at me like I'm the Serpent of Eden.

"I don't have an ulterior motive here. I just want to have a life that's as normal as possible. Please?" I stick my hand out. "Truce?"

A long, assessing squint, then she grips my hand.

20

ANTHONY

I buy a huge bouquet of tiger lilies and a box of chocolate before heading home. That's the least Iris deserves after everything that happened today.

First, I had to cancel our midday plans because the venture I'm doing in Hong Kong required my personal attention, which meant a conference call over lunch with the local partners. Then my afternoon meetings ran late. Which means I didn't get to leave the office until seven.

Finally—and most important—she's been stuck with Bobbi all day.

TJ warned me his cousin might be difficult. But I didn't expect her to be quite this obnoxious. Hopefully, with some time, she'll mellow out. I'm paying double her usual rate anyway. And Iris is an easy client. If I didn't have to worry about my business, I'd be guarding her myself.

Or more like keep her in bed with me all day long. Bed is very safe. Soft. Warm. Fun...

When I arrive home, the scene is so surreal that I can't help staring. Bobbi and Iris are in the kitchen, pulling something out of the oven. Some kind of white powder is smeared over Bobbi's black top, and the place smells like freshly baked cookies.

What the...? I can see Iris getting domestic. But Bobbi? *Bobbi?*

"Hey, welcome home!" Iris says with a blinding smile, putting the baking sheet on the counter.

I go over and kiss her, placing the flowers and chocolate on the counter, away from the hot sheets.

"Look! My first double chocolate chip cookies. Bobbi helped me," Iris says.

Bobbi helped me. "I didn't know you were interested in baking."

"I wasn't, until today. Bobbi said white and dark chocolate tastes great in cookies, especially if you mix in some macadamia nuts."

Bobbi raises an eyebrow in my direction. "I'm actually a pretty decent baker."

I give her a humoring smile. That's the least I can do, since she's here on a job she doesn't like. "I'm sure. Your own recipe?"

"Uh-huh."

Probably toxic. Iris breaks off a small portion, not waiting for it to cool, and puts it in her mouth before I can stop her.

"*Mmm.* Wow. This is amazing! Better than sex." She flushes, shooting a glance in my direction. "Well...almost."

Bobbi snorts, her lips twitching into a reluctant smile. I glare at the cookies. *Better than sex, my ass.* I take one and have a bite.

Holy shit. It's hot. The gooey chocolate explodes in my mouth, the cookie soft and sweet. It is *not* better than sex. But it's close. Really close. "I had no idea you could bake," I say, after swallowing.

"I can do a lot of things well," Bobbi says dryly.

"Obviously."

"Want me to stick around, or are you good now?" she asks Iris.

"I'm good. Tony's home."

"See you tomorrow," Bobbi says to Iris, and leaves.

When the door shuts, Iris gives me a reproachful look. "I think you hurt her feelings."

"She has feelings?"

Iris pokes my ticklish spot. "Of course she does. She and I worked things out. And she's cool. Wants to open up a bakery after this assignment is over." She picks up another cookie off the rack. "You'll help her start her business, won't you? I'll pay you back in installments, every two weeks. I think I can swing that, although it'll take a while."

She's so cute, pouting and fluttering her eyelashes. And I love it, since she almost never asks me for anything when I've been telling her over and over again everything I have is hers. "Why every two weeks?"

"The foundation pays every other week."

"Ah." I lean closer until the tips of our noses almost touch. "No."

"No?" She blinks. "Why not?"

"Because I don't like the way you think." It's about time she understands that all this—my money, homes, clubs, business— isn't just mine. It's hers, too.

Her teeth sink into her pillowy lip. "Is it the interest? I thought maybe I could do it interest-free?"

"No!" I put a piece of cookie into her mouth before she can say anything else. "This is all yours. If you want to invest in Bobbi's bakery, feel free. Just tell Wei."

"But you and I are just dating."

Her answer slices me like a blade. *Just dating.* Transient bull-shit that could end any time.

And then I realize maybe it *is* just dating to her, and the reason she can't accept that what I have is hers is because she considers our relationship temporary. My stomach suddenly feels like somebody's twisting a knife in it.

I wrap my arms around her hard. She hugs me back with a small squeak.

It isn't just dating, not to me. I know of a more permanent way to bind her to me, and I've been avoiding thinking about it. It seems so wrong to push for it when I'm lying to her.

But the anxiety is dripping into my veins like poison, and I know there's no length I won't go to in order to keep her by my side.

21

IRIS

TONY'S BEEN IN A WEIRD MOOD SINCE YESTERDAY EVENING. Although I'm certain I'm the cause, I don't know why. Is it because I asked him to invest in Bobbi's business? All he had to do was say no. It's not like she was there to hear him.

Instead, he clung to me after we went to bed, holding me tightly. If I weren't on my period, he would've kept me up all night, bringing me to one climax after another. Maybe he's feeling guilty because he doesn't want to do it, but at the same time doesn't want to disappoint me by saying so. But this is poor communication, and we can do better.

And I tell him as much while I stir fresh berries into creamy Greek yogurt in the morning.

"What?" He stares at me.

"I'm just saying it's your money. I'm not going to be mad you don't want to invest in her bakery. I'll find some other way to help her."

He scratches the tip of his nose and scrunches his eyebrows

like he's trying to figure out an unsolvable problem. "You think I'm upset because of that?"

"Not really *upset*. A little moody." I take an extra bite of bacon, partly because I'm hungry, but mostly because seeing me eat perks him up. My appetite—or lack thereof—worries him. As a matter of fact, everything about me worries him. He seems to think I'm so fragile that even the slightest thing will fell me. His overprotectiveness is generally endearing, but I can't have him feeling this way about me all the time. I want to be a source of strength for him, too.

"Look. I'll put in as much as Bobbi needs, and you don't have to pay me back for any of it. I like her. And you should spend your money on you."

His voice is too flat, and the look in his eyes is weird. Not confused. Just a little bit grim and apprehensive. I don't think I said anything to bring that out, so... Did something happen at work? Did Sam send a threat? Or Marty?

I want to probe, but I know he's not going to tell me. And I don't want to argue about it in the morning. That sets the tone for the rest of the day.

So I reach over and squeeze Tony's hand. "Thank you. I promise I'll stay home and safe. Bobbi's going to be here, and the piano's getting delivered today. Speaking of which, Julie and Yuna are coming over. Yuna's set on making me play that duet. Are you going to be joining us?"

"What time?"

"About three."

"I have another lunch meeting today." His dour expression says how he really feels about this more eloquently than his rough tone. "But I can cut the day short."

I hide a mild pang of disappointment that he won't be joining me for lunch. But he's a busy man, running a huge company. It's to be expected. "Okay. See you this afternoon, then." I hand him his travel mug, and he leaves after a kiss.

Bobbi walks in just a second later. She grabs a fresh cup of coffee. "This place has the best coffee."

"Tony has great taste."

"He seems to like nice things." She takes a healthy sip, looking at me over the rim of the mug. "So what's on the docket today?"

"Nothing. Just practicing the piano. And I have friends coming over. Please don't, you know, block them or anything."

"Why would I do that?"

My jaw drops at her innocent, confused expression. "You blocked Julie last time."

"Julie? Oh, the attack Chihuahua?"

I almost spew my coffee. Okay, so Julie was a bit hostile last time, and she is small compared to Bobbi, but...

Bobbi waves a hand. "Don't worry. I won't do it again. It wasn't personal anyway."

"I know that...but she doesn't." Speaking of which, I need to find the time to explain the situation to Julie. I don't know how long Bobbi's going to be hanging around, but I don't need any weird tension between the two of them.

While I practice, Bobbi's on her phone. I get a couple of hours in before the digital piano is delivered. I ask the crew to set it up perpendicular to the Steinway and sign the delivery sheet.

Bobbi is super professional, watching the men and standing by me. She doesn't seem to think they pose any threat, but still gives them a flat stare the entire time.

After they leave, she makes four sandwiches—all roast beef with horseradish gravy sauce and crispy lettuce. She pushes one my way. "Here."

"Thanks. But Tony isn't coming."

"Yeah, I know." Bobbi gives me a small smirk and demolishes her three sandwiches before I'm halfway done with mine. She has the appetite of an NFL player. But she doesn't have an ounce of fat on her. Except for her smallish breasts.

"Where does it all go?" I ask.

She flexes an arm. "Gotta be in shape if I'm going to get between you and a bullet in time."

"There probably won't be a bullet."

She shrugs. "Or a knife. Or a baseball bat."

I try to imagine Sam swinging a bat at me, but can't. It just isn't his style. But Marty? Most definitely. He loves to brag about how athletic and awesome he is. I've never seen him play anything, so I don't know for sure. But since he has zero musical talent and everyone's good at something, maybe he's decent at sports. I hope it doesn't come to that, though. Sam likes to be part of high society, and I don't think its members think highly of assault and battery.

"I'll clean up," I say when we're done with lunch.

"Thanks." Bobbi watches me put things in the dishwasher. "You aren't like a lot of clients."

"In what way?"

"You actually clean up after yourself." She looks around. "No servants."

"Wouldn't it be weird to have people in your home all the time? Lack of privacy?"

"Makes some people feel important."

"I don't care about that kind of thing. I just want to be normal." I'm still trying to figure out how to be that.

"You are."

"Really?" I say, happy she thinks so.

"Yeah. Strangely so."

My joy dims. "How can I be normal and strange at the same time?"

"You don't fit your social setting. The women guys like Anthony date, they look like they're ready to attend a fancy party twenty-four seven, plucked and facialed until they're as smooth and glowing as a light bulb."

I feel torn between being flattered and horrified. I didn't need to try that hard to rise above Bobbi's expectations. On the other hand, she's had some shitty clients, so I shouldn't be too insulted. Besides, let's focus on the positive stuff—she thinks I'm normal!

"So you're going to nap now?" Bobbi asks.

"Maybe half an hour." I start toward the deck. Today's so beautiful and warm. I want to sun and doze off for a bit. But then the intercom buzzes. It's Julie. What's she doing here so early?

I open the door. She's in a fancy lavender Gucci dress she got when we were in Rome together last year. Her hair's pulled back into an elegant French twist, and flawless makeup covers her face. Fresh pink lacquer shines on her fingers.

"Are you going somewhere?" I ask, wondering if she can't stay to watch me and Yuna play.

"Nope. Just here."

She swishes inside. I stare at her back, then down at myself. I feel pretty underdressed in a white shirt and denim shorts. And my bare feet! She's in a pair of silver stilettos.

When I just stand there, wondering if there's a dress code I wasn't aware of, she loops her arm around mine. Bobbi watches her like she's an unusual zoo animal.

"Come on. You gotta take a look at this." Julie drags me to the Steinway and slaps a bright yellow book on it.

"What's that?"

"Rachmaninoff's Suite Number Two. You weren't planning on playing it without any practice, were you?"

"Actually, I was planning to do exactly that." I shrug.

"But why?" Julie leans forward as though she's about to impart a secret of the universe. "That woman's doing it on purpose to humiliate you."

I snort back a laugh at Julie's overactive imagination. "Her name is Yuna, and she isn't."

"She wants to feel superior to us. Couldn't you tell?"

"No, and I don't know why you would think that. If she were, she would've picked something more complicated."

"It's Rachmaninoff!"

"So?" Julie's right about Rachmaninoff being difficult, but I'm not saying more. She doesn't know about my memory loss or that I can play pieces I practiced before the coma. I don't plan to change that anytime soon. Yuna thinks it's some kind of demonstration to show that I'm capable of doing duets. What she doesn't know is that it's my test to see if she's telling the truth. If she's honest about us having played it together, I'll hit the notes without much problem.

"She picked it on purpose because I couldn't find the sheet music anywhere around here. I had to drive all the way to

Anaheim!"

"Oh my gosh, you shouldn't have."

"I'm not letting her embarrass you."

"Julie, It's fine. Really. I don't care if I can't play it. And it isn't like I can memorize the whole piece in the next hour and a half or something."

"You don't have to memorize. I can flip the pages for you."

Hold on. Why did I say memorize? Julie's right. Pianists who play non-solo pieces don't have their music memorized. You always have somebody flipping pages. But it just felt so natural to talk about committing the entire piece to memory, like I've done it before with duet pieces.

"Anyway, let's practice," Julie says, interrupting my train of thought.

"No. I'm going to nap for a bit. I have to if I want to be fresh."

"How can you nap at a time like this?" she demands, her voice shrill.

"Very easily. I'm exhausted from my morning practice."

She looks at the music. "You were working on Chopin études?"

"Mm-hmm."

"Oh my God! Aren't you worried?"

Julie's ear-splitting objections are making my head hurt. I raise a hand. "If you'll let me nap for half an hour, I promise I'll practice the piece."

"No! If you're tired, just have coffee. I'll make some for you right now."

Julie runs off to the kitchen, and I thunk my head on the piano. Maybe I shouldn't have invited her. Her indignation and anxiety are driving me crazy.

"Sure you don't want me to run the Chihuahua off?" comes Bobbi's amused voice.

"No. Don't. Just..." I lift my head and sigh. "I'm going to have that coffee and pretend I'm fine." As annoying as the situation is, Julie means well. It could be I'm just being sensitive. My cramps are making me a little crankier than normal.

I sip the coffee slowly. I appreciate Julie trying to help, but

I'm not interested in spending more of my time practicing when I'm already tired. I didn't work on "Mazeppa" for a reason—it's too taxing.

But Julie isn't deterred. She keeps going on and on about how awful Yuna is for forcing this duet on me when I hate it. "You don't like to play with me either, and I get it. I can't always keep up, right? So it's ridiculous she's insisting on this. Like you have to jump to do her bidding just because she's rich or whatever."

"It's not a big deal," I say, trying to keep my voice calm. But honestly, I'm ready to tear my hair out. Bobbi gives me her patented arched eyebrow. This time it means *Sure you don't want me to toss her out?*

I shake my head, then flip the pages of the music Julie brought, hoping it'll shut her up. It does...for about ten minutes. She's upset I'm not playing the music. So I practice scales instead.

"Gotta warm up," I tell her.

Bobbi sniggers.

Thankfully, Tony comes home with a box of chocolate cupcakes. I could kiss him for that, because I so need some sugar. We go to the kitchen together, leaving Bobbi and Julie in the living room.

He brushes his thumbs under my eyes. "What's wrong?"

"Just a little tired," I say.

"Why didn't you nap?"

I don't want to tell him. Tony isn't too crazy about Byron, and I know that dislike affects how he feels about Julie. "It's a long story."

Before I can steal a bite of one of the cupcakes, Yuna arrives, Mr. Kim following in a conservative suit. She's in a fitted shirt, cropped jeans and casual wedge sandals. *Good.* I don't feel that underdressed anymore.

Tony hands me a small glass of grapefruit juice, which I chug down. "Does anybody want anything to drink?" he asks.

"After we're done with Rachmaninoff," Yuna says.

Julie purses her lips. "I don't think Iris is ready."

"Sure she is," Yuna says airily. "It isn't like she's never played Rachmaninoff before."

"She doesn't like duets!"

"It'll be different now. She has me."

Scowling, Julie stands between the digital piano and the white Steinway. Giving her a funny look, Tony sits next to Bobbi.

Yuna flexes her fingers and warms up on the digital piano for a bit. "Not bad," she remarks after a few scales and arpeggios.

"They did a good job setting it up. Which one do you want?" I gesture between the digital and the baby grand.

She shoots me a cocky grin. "I'm going to be nice and let you take the Steinway. Ready?"

I sit at the piano. Julie sits next to me on the bench and opens the music to the right page. I shoot her a quick smile of thanks. "Whenever you're ready," I say.

"Presto," Yuna says.

I don't know if it's for my benefit or out of habit. If we've played it enough for me to be able to pull it off, she should know I know the proper tempo.

She starts. It's as though the few rumbling notes are waking up some dormant part of my brain. I pick right up and play the next part, and we're off in rapid notes and powerful chords, perfectly synced. My fingers are totally loose, and they fly over the keys easily and comfortably, like I've done this hundreds of times before. Julie's flipping music—about half a measure too slow —but it doesn't matter. I don't need it to play the piece. It's like my hands know exactly what to do.

Exhilaration rushes through me. My heart is buoyant. I feel like I can fly. It's fun playing with Yuna. She's matching me note for note, beat for beat. Not even the digital piano can lessen the vigor and verve of her performance. Even my scalp tingles with excitement. We're complementing each other perfectly.

Six minutes later, we're done. I'm panting softly. I turn to look at Yuna, who's staring at me with a huge smile and tears pooling in her eyes.

"Told you," she says, choked up.

"You did. I just never..." I place a hand over my mouth, unable to continue.

We get up and hug each other like we've just had our first successful Carnegie Hall concert, hopping and squeezing.

It's incontrovertible proof—that she isn't just making crap up but truly was my best friend from Curtis. That we spent months practicing together. That a past I don't remember is still in my head—just ready for me to dig down and discover it all.

22

IRIS

BY THE TIME MONDAY ROLLS AROUND, I FEEL LIKE SINGING the "Hallelujah" chorus. My period is over this morning, and I can finally resume normal life, including returning to the job I love. Humming, I put on a power dress—an ice blue one—and pull my hair back into a ponytail.

"Most people aren't that happy on a Monday," Tony says, mildly amused. He hands me a pair of diamond studs, then puts onyx and silver cufflinks in his sleeves.

"Well, I am," I say, putting the earrings on. "I'm back to my routine. I need it."

"Isn't your routine more like get up, have breakfast, practice the piano, eat lunch and nap?" he says teasingly. "Oh, and swimming half an hour or so before going to bed?"

"Hush. You know what I mean." I slip on my pumps and turn to him. "I love my job. I love it that what I do has meaning, and I'm making a real impact, not just making my employer rich."

"Elizabeth isn't getting rich off the foundation, that's for sure."

"Exactly."

By the time we go downstairs together, Bobbi's already in the kitchen, helping herself to a fresh mug of the coffee she loves so much. Tony gave her a key to our place, just like he did with TJ. Since she knows I'm going to work today, she's in a dress jacket, cream-colored blouse and slacks. But the boots are the same. I decide to call them ass kickers, because they're the kind of footwear that says if you mess with her, you'll regret it. Her hair's twisted into a tight updo, making her lean face appear even sharper.

"Coffee?" she asks.

"Sure. Thanks."

She pours me one, then another for Tony.

I eat quietly. After our heart-to-heart, I should be more comfortable with her, but I'm still adjusting to having someone around all the time. Tony told me she signed a nondisclosure agreement to be discreet and keep things secret. But it's impossible to act like she's not here when she is standing right within my vision, her eyes alert and piercing. And nobody's going to act like she isn't watching over me at work. I have no idea how I'm going to introduce her. "This is my bodyguard" sounds unbelievably pompous.

After we're done with coffee and breakfast, we go to the lobby, where TJ is waiting in front of the Cullinan. She and TJ say nothing to each other.

Is she still mad at him for making her take the assignment? Or is there something else? TJ doesn't look like an asshole, but assholes don't have their assholeness tattooed on their faces.

She gets into a black Escalade parked behind the Cullinan. Tony and I climb into the Rolls-Royce SUV, and we start toward work.

I check my agenda for the day on the ride. The gynecologist Dr. Young referred me to last Friday sends me a text, letting me know she can fit me in at eleven thirty today, but otherwise I'll have to wait for at least four weeks. I text her back and let her know I'll see her today. Her office is close to work, within walking distance.

In front of the foundation, Tony kisses me, then whispers into my ear, "See if you can leave a little early today. Maybe around four. I have a week's worth of things I plan to do to you tonight."

My cheeks go hot. "We'll see," I reply before hopping out of the car.

Bobbi is already waiting. She and I walk together. In front of the door, I turn. Tony's car hasn't moved, and he's watching me through the open window. I blow him a kiss and wave.

A crooked grin on his face, he waves back.

Happiness glows inside me. This is probably the hardest thing in the morning—saying goodbye. I know he won't leave until I'm in the building, so I slip inside with Bobbi. At the sight of the security, I falter. Nobody gets inside without an employee badge to swipe or a visitor's badge.

I reach for the sign-in book, wondering what to put down as the reason for her visit. One of the guards shakes his head. "She can go in."

"I thought the protocol was that every non-employee needs to be signed in."

"HR said she's new. So it's all cool."

"I see. Thanks." So Tony already told Elizabeth. Hopefully that will make introductions less awkward if people ask.

When I step into the foundation's office, I see Tolyan at his desk. He's reviewing a document. His face is granite hard as usual, and he doesn't smile when he sees me or Bobbi. I should be used to his brand of greeting—cold gaze and even colder vibe— but nope. Never.

I steal a glance at Bobbi, who's put on a pleasant face. At least my bodyguard isn't a nail eater in public. I put my purse in the bottom drawer at my desk and boot my laptop. While it's starting up, I say, "Hi, Tolyan. This is Bobbi. Bobbi, Tolyan."

"Nice to meet you," Bobbi says, her voice smooth.

"Here's your employee badge." Tolyan hands her a laminated ID with the foundation's logo underneath.

She takes it and clips it at her waist. "Thanks."

He grunts. "You have hair."

"How very observant."

"In a fight, I'd grab that hair and smash your face against a wall," he says pleasantly.

She smiles. "I'm sure you'd try."

Uncomfortable with their interaction, I grab a legal pad and pen off my desk and jump to my feet. "I'm going to see if Elizabeth needs anything," I announce to remind Tolyan that his boss is right here in the same office.

"As well you should," he says coldly.

Ignoring him, I spin around to face Bobbi. "Why don't you wait for me over there?" I point at the two long couches in the vestibule. "You can read magazines or browse recipe sites or whatever you want to do."

"Sure." She gives Tolyan a last look and then parks herself in the vestibule. It's far enough that Tolyan and she can't speak to each other without raising their voices. Hopefully both are well mannered enough to not talk trash across the distance.

Although the door to Elizabeth's office is open, I knock anyway. She lifts her head from the documents she's been reviewing and smiles. "Welcome back, Iris. How are you?"

"I'm fine," I say with extra exuberance so she doesn't decide I need another week off. "Thank you." I take a seat opposite her.

"Excellent. I heard from Tony about the bodyguard. Hope she's comfortable?"

I cringe inwardly. It's one thing for someone like Elizabeth to have a bodyguard, but something else for a lowly assistant to have one tagging along everywhere. Hopefully my boss doesn't think it's weird or presumptuous. It's impossible to tell how she really feels from her smooth voice and perpetually warm expression. "Yeah. She'll entertain herself until I'm done."

"It's a smart move. I'm glad you have somebody watching over you. After what Sam Peacher pulled, I'd consider it negligent if Tony didn't do more to keep you safe. If we don't take care of the people we love, nobody will." She grows serious. "I had no clue what he was planning to do, and I apologize. I should've suspected something when he specifically insisted on handing the check to you."

"No, no." I shake my head, horrified she harbors such guilt

about what happened. "He was using the work we do for children to trick you. Please don't feel bad. I'm sorry my personal drama messed things up."

"It didn't mess anything up. Tony's been very generous to the cause, far more so than Sam intended. I presume that has something to do with you, so thank you."

I flush, chagrined about Sam and happy that Tony's already kept his promise to make the donation. "I don't think Sam will actually donate the money he promised."

Elizabeth's gray eyes are wintry now. "Even if he offered me every penny of his fortune, I wouldn't take it. What he did was unforgivable."

Wow. When Tony said she wouldn't take Sam's donation, I thought he was just saying it to console me. I understand Elizabeth's rich, but it strikes me again just *how* rich to see her easy dismissal of Sam's millions. Sam always told me he was special— somebody important because of his money. "As long as I'm wealthy, nobody can ever look down on me or turn me away."

For a second, I wonder what he'd do if he knew how much Elizabeth disdains him. A petty, vindictive part of me wishes I'd recorded what she just said so I could send it to him.

"But enough about that," Elizabeth is saying. "There's a new project I want you to be part of. I've been wanting to do art and music programs for underprivileged children. I never got around to it because giving children access to art and music can be incredibly cost-inefficient. You can't mass-deliver self-expression."

I perk up at the mention of music. "I understand."

"But we have a partner who wants to do a pilot program with us. It's going to focus on teaching children music. Given your background, I think you'll be perfect for overseeing it with his people."

"Oh my." I bite my lower lip. She doesn't want me assisting someone, but actually *overseeing* a project. I haven't been with the foundation for long, and this is a huge responsibility. Others who have spearheaded projects, like Rhonda, have been with the foundation for years. I wonder if I can pull it off. I've been mainly supporting other people and doing memos and spreadsheets.

Leading a project feels like being told to sight-read a Liszt piano concerto with the Vienna Philharmonic.

Elizabeth senses my nervousness. "I wouldn't be asking if I didn't think you'd be great at it. If you need any help, you can always reach out to me or Rhonda. She's great at logistics and budgeting. And I'm sure Byron's going to have competent people on his side to help you."

I inhale, trying to calm my nerves. Everyone's gotta start somewhere. Elizabeth doesn't want me to fail, and she wouldn't have asked me to do this if she didn't think I'd be good enough. I'll put in overtime if necessary.

Then it finally registers. "Byron?"

"Byron Pearce is the partner," she says. "I think you know him. He said he decided to try it with us because of you."

"Oh." That was sweet of Byron, although Tony might be annoyed. He doesn't even pretend to hide how much he dislikes Byron. Ideally, I'd like to avoid a situation that will upset Tony... especially in social settings. But the interaction I'm going to have with Byron on this project is strictly professional. And while Tony insists that Byron wants to sleep with me, he's never done anything inappropriate in the two years I've known him. Unlike Audrey, he hasn't thrown anything at Tony in a jealous fit. He's not going to decide all of a sudden that he wants to change the nature of our relationship, no matter what Tony thinks. "Thank you, Elizabeth. I'll do my best."

"Excellent. Why don't you see when you'll be able to have a meeting with his people to hammer out the details?"

"Will do. Anything else?"

"Rhonda has a few things for you to look at. That's it."

I start to leave, then stop, clearing my throat sheepishly. "Oh, by the way, I hate to bring this up because I was out for a week, but I have a doctor's appointment this morning at eleven thirty. Is that okay?"

"No problem. You usually come in early anyway, so don't worry about it."

God, I totally lucked out when I got hired here. I can't imagine a boss this easy to work for, especially if half the things on office dramas are true. I go back to my desk and see a huge basket of tiger lilies. I don't have to see the card to know who sent them.

Have a great day at work. And don't let your slave driver boss push you too hard. ;)

—Tony

I tap a corner of the card against my lower lip, smiling. He's the sweetest. Of course, I have a surprise for him too. But the wait feels too long. So I go online and order a basket of healthy snacks to be delivered to his office before lunch. Tony's big on snacking to keep his energy up. Then, on impulse, I send him a bouquet of tiger lilies too, because they remind him of me. I add a message: *Because I love you.*

That done, I spend the rest of the morning sending emails to Byron's assistant, who's in charge of the program on their side, and go over the work Rhonda did for me. She's only heard that I got a bad case of stomach flu and had to stay home. I send a small prayer of gratitude in Elizabeth's direction. The last thing I want is everyone in the office knowing what a psycho my uncle is. I mean, yes, it's true he isn't a good man, but it would be humiliating for my coworkers to gossip about.

By the time I'm caught up on things, it's time for me to leave for my appointment. Bobbi and I walk the two short blocks.

"Do you think we should act normal, like we know each other?" I ask, unsure how this bodyguard business works.

"Not unless you want to."

"Oh." I clear my throat. "Don't you think it'll look less strange if we act like friends?"

"Not really." A beat. "Do you feel weird?"

"Yeah, a little."

"You'll get used to it."

Ugh. That's not why I started this conversation. "Do you like Tolyan?" I blurt out.

"No." Her answer is swift and decisive. Maybe a little too swift and decisive.

Oh my. Does she like him? I want to probe, but we're already at the clinic.

The doctor's office is pleasant and soothing, with plenty of plants and pale mint walls and elegant beige tile. Nothing like the places I went to after waking up. They were depressingly sterile, with functional linoleum flooring and scuffed industrial-white walls. There's not a hint of bleach in the air here, which I appreciate. Dr. Xia is in her late fifties. She's kind—almost motherly—and answers all my questions and guides me through my options.

Half an hour later, I'm finished. I walk out, a secret smile on my lips. My phone buzzes. Speaking of the devil...

Where are you? I'm at your office, but don't see you or Bobbi.

Oh. I left a little early. I didn't know you were coming.

Did you have lunch yet?

Not yet.

Then let's eat together. My treat. Anything you want.

I giggle, happy at his good mood. *If you put it that way, how can I refuse? How about meet me at the Italian bistro across the street from the office?*

Fine by me.

I glance at Bobbi. *What about Bobbi? Should she come?*

Yes. And she should eat.

Hmm. I scowl. She *should* eat, but I was hoping the lunch would be more intimate—just me and Tony. TV celebrities who travel with huge entourages always look so comfortable, but I don't think I'll ever reach that level of Zen.

I can just think of her like Julie or Yuna—a friend. And it'll be fine, even though the knowledge that she's here to take a bullet for me is sitting in the back of my mind like a cold, ugly fact I'd rather not acknowledge.

23

ANTHONY

A MINUTE OR SO AFTER I GET A TABLE, IRIS AND BOBBI reach the restaurant. It looks like they're getting along—no scowling or uncomfortable tension. Iris is radiant, with a small smile on her lips, and I get the urge to lick the mole under her mouth.

I wasn't planning on having lunch with her today. I had a lunch meeting scheduled, but when her gifts arrived, I had Wei cancel it. My team in Chicago can wait, but Iris can't. The sweet scent of tiger lilies drove me crazy all morning, making me miss her with an intensity that left me badly distracted.

Iris sits in a chair opposite me. Bobbi takes an empty stool at the bar, one that gives her a view of both us and the door, and orders her lunch.

"She isn't sitting with us?" Iris asks.

"She probably figured we'll be more comfortable this way, unless you want her to join us." But I'd rather she didn't. Not because I don't like Bobbi, but because I want to have some private time with my girlfriend.

"No. I mean...is it weird?"

"Let Bobbi do what she wants. She's the pro."

Our waiter gives us a wine list and menus.

"Well. I'd believe that if she didn't bait Tolyan." Iris tells me what happened. "I was scared they'd start smashing each other's faces or something."

I laugh. That man should've known better than to comment on Bobbi's hair. "She's a little sensitive."

"Bobbi? Sensitive? Are we talking about the same person?"

"Because she's a woman, men question her competence. She's good at her job and doesn't appreciate it."

"Tolyan actually looks like a God's gift to badassery, so if he and Bobbi go at each other, it won't end well."

"Probably not."

"Maybe Bobbi should stay home when I'm at work. I don't want to upset Elizabeth."

I think it's funny that Tolyan and Bobbi were trash-talking, but Iris is too anxious about this. "They're both professionals. They aren't going to start breaking furniture and rearranging each other's faces for nothing. And Bobbi is *not* staying home while you work. A man's entitled to worry about his girlfriend."

"You shouldn't. Besides, it's totally safe at the foundation."

Iris doesn't get it. And she never will, because I'm never letting her know the kind of horror and despair I felt nearly a decade ago when I thought she died. I can't go through that again. Not with my sanity intact. "It's still my job to worry. Wouldn't you worry if you had a Lamborghini that it might get a scratch or ding?"

She rolls her eyes. "Yeah, but I'm not a car."

"Exactly. I can always buy a new Lamborghini, but there's only one of you in the world." I already failed once. This is a miracle second chance, and I'm not screwing it up.

"I'll be extra careful to keep myself healthy and unhurt. Not even a paper cut." She raises her hand. "I promise."

"Fine," I say, only because this is the most I'm going to get out of her. She doesn't know I worry about losing her through something out of her control, just like on that stormy night in Tempérane.

"What do you think about splitting a pizza?" she says, closing the menu. "Quick and easy."

Fuck. I should've known she'd want pizza. We're at an Italian restaurant, after all. I should act like it's not a big deal. Everyone likes pizza. But I can't get the memory from Cajun Milan out of my head. It's painful because that was the last time I saw her face to face before the car accident. Shameful because I let my fear for her drive me to cruelty.

Iris peers at me, her eyebrows slightly pulled together. "Unless you want something else?"

I force myself to smile. "Pizza's fine. You can get whatever you want, except veggies. I need some meat."

"Don't worry. I like pepperoni."

Of course she does. Her taste hasn't changed much.

I reach for my water. "That sounds delicious." I order when our waiter comes by. I need a new topic to distract myself, so I can pretend everything's fine. "Anything interesting now that you're back? Hopefully Elizabeth didn't dump a week's worth of work on you, did she?"

"Nope. But she put me in charge of a new project! It uses my music training, so it's perfect."

"I thought you were considering Yuna's suggestion to debut seriously," I say. I've seen her play. She's so happy and energetic, and I don't think this new project can give her that kind of joy. I still hate the idea of her in the spotlight—the attention and danger it can bring—but I'm determined to give her the life she deserves. And if I have to hire a team of hotshot mercenaries to keep her safe, so be it.

"I thought about it, but those panic attacks were real." Her eyes lowered, Iris tugs at her napkin. "It could be that I didn't have them before the accident, but now...something's changed."

Her downcast expression hurts. Yuna's right about Iris being a great performer, but Iris is also right about panic attacks, although I doubt they're caused by public performances per se. The accident might've damaged her memory from before, but I don't think it fundamentally changed who she is. I haven't seen any signs—erratic mood swings, forgetfulness, weird bursts of temper and so on.

If she wants to be a concert pianist, I'm more than happy to find a way to help her cope with the panic attacks. That's the least I owe her for my role in what happened to her that stormy night in Tempérane. I know deep inside if I hadn't left for Los Angeles after our fight at Cajun Milan, she wouldn't have been on that bridge. "Iris—"

The arrival of our food interrupts me. The server makes sure that our pizza is properly sliced by running the cutter one more time along the slices, then puts one on her plate and one on mine before leaving.

"It's a good charity project," Iris says. "And it's fully funded. Byron already paid for it."

"Byron Pearce?" Surely that motherfucker wouldn't dare use the foundation and Elizabeth to get to Iris. But she nods.

My hackles rise. I feel like a man guarding a treasure everyone's trying to steal. "Guess he didn't take me seriously," I mutter. This deserves a strong response.

"What?"

"Nothing. I just don't understand why he's funding this. His family has its own foundation. Throwing money at it would've earned him more Brownie points."

"Brownie points? For what?"

"You know he's in a battle against Milton to see who gets the family business."

"Maybe he's doing it with Elizabeth because he believes in her," she says.

Iris thinks Elizabeth is the gold standard for purity and charitable spirit, and it will probably never cross her mind that Byron is a conniving fucker.

"How come you don't like my friends?" she asks.

"I'm fine with your friends. I just don't like *him* because he wants to sleep with you."

"You know what? I'm going to show you something because you're being ridiculous." Iris pulls out her phone and taps the screen a few times. She flips the phone and shows me the screen.

I lean over and squint.

She scrolls down so I can see hundreds of pictures Google has pulled up. "You see all these women?"

I relax back in my seat. I thought she had something serious to show me. "Yes?"

"You slept with all of them. And I never say anything becau—"

"I never slept with any of them. Gossip rags featured me and some new woman every other month or so. That's it." I start to sit up straight, realizing that she must've had a super-low opinion of me all along. Is this why she won't accept that what I have is hers? "What the hell, Iris? You think I just stick it in anywhere?"

"You're a guy. And you're hot, and rich and... I mean, one of your exes tried to kill herself because you dumped her."

I roll my eyes. *Fucking Audrey and her drama.* "Oh, for God's sake. You're as bad as my brother. Look, didn't you say you're a Bösendorfer Imperial among women? So don't you think I—a man worthy enough to be with you—would be more discriminating? That I would need at least a vintage Steinway upright, so to speak?"

She gives me an absolutely deadpan look.

Damn it. I rub my forehead, since pounding on the table in frustration won't solve anything. "Never mind. That didn't come out right." I think for a moment. I haven't felt compelled to explain or defend myself to anyone in quite a while. People's opinions don't mean much to me. But it's different with Iris. I choose my words with care. "I wasn't as indiscriminate as tabloids said. Some of the women who accompanied me to those parties made it look like we were more, and I never disputed that, since it wasn't worth a denial." I hesitate, debating between laying it all out and holding some back, then shake myself mentally. I've already done enough hiding and lying. Iris deserves to know at least this truth. "I spent the last seven years working until I was exhausted to build my company. If I'd known this day would come, I wouldn't have let those women use me that way. I would've made sure my reputation was absolutely pristine." I stop, holding my breath. It isn't easy to be this vulnerable, even to Iris. I wait for her reaction, feeling as defenseless as a blind, hairless kitten just born into the world.

"So you haven't had a serious girlfriend in, like, seven years?"

"I haven't had *any* girlfriend in seven years."

Iris stares at me. Some rapid processing is taking place behind those beautiful gray eyes, but her disbelief is palpable when she reaches the inevitable conclusion. "Are you seriously telling me you haven't had sex in all that time?"

Her skepticism is a kick in the gut when I'm telling her something I haven't admitted to anybody else. But that, too, is my fault for not managing things correctly. Part of me driven to self-preservation says I should give her a wink and turn it into a joke, but I slap it back into place. Even if it costs, I want her to know what she means to me. "Yes."

"But..." She pulls her lips in for a moment. "You're insatiable. You keep me up most of the night. How do you... I mean, aren't blue balls fatal after seven years?"

I laugh dryly. "You have to get blue balls first. And when women leave you cold..." I shrug. I can't explain to Iris how it really was. No matter how celebrated they were for their beauty and bodies, they couldn't stir me. Their hair color was wrong. They didn't smell of tiger lilies. Their breath held something other than cherry and caramel. Their fingers were too short and clumsy. Their eyes weren't gray. My heart remained dark and cold, no matter how they rubbed against me.

"But Audrey Duff is pretty. Didn't she get naked with you?" Iris asks, her voice brittle with jealousy. "She's one of the hottest actresses in Hollywood."

I snort. Did she ever. And God, how annoying that was. Probably humiliating for her, too, when she realized nothing could entice me. "I've seen mannequins that are sexier than that woman."

Iris leans closer. "So you're saying you felt *nothing*? For seven long years?"

She's not going to drop it. Not until I explain it in way she can understand. As annoyed as I am that she isn't taking what I'm saying at face value, I get it. If I were her, I'd be skeptical too. "I'm only going to say this once, so listen. I've had offers. I've gone so far as to get naked. Then one look and I realized they weren't what I wanted after all." *They weren't you. They could never make me feel what I felt with you. Do you know what it's like to feel that kind of empty despair over and over again?* "And that's where it's always ended."

A wince of sympathy, although I don't think she realizes she's empathizing with those women without meaning to. "And they never said anything about it?" she asks. "Called you gay or impotent?"

I almost smile. That would've been amusing, mainly because I wouldn't have given a fuck, which would have upset them even more. The kind of woman I was linked with needs to feel significant and important. They crave the drama and publicity. "Their pride wouldn't let them. They thought I'd slept with all those other women I was seen with."

Iris's eyes are impossibly wide now. "So until the night we played Schubert together, you never...*you know*...?"

"I'm not saying I never jerked off. I'm saying I hadn't touched anyone, not the way you're thinking, in a very long time." I sigh. It's difficult to explain, because she doesn't remember, and I don't dare tell her everything. But I want her to accept at least one truth. "Iris, you have nothing to be jealous about. My heart, my soul, my body—they're yours. Totally and completely. Always will be."

Intense emotions play through her expressive eyes as she regards me. "You shouldn't do that," she says finally.

"Do what?"

"Say things that make me forget why I was annoyed with you earlier."

Is that what she thinks this is about? I wonder, disappointed and unhappy. My baring my soul has nothing to do with Byron or other women. "I wasn't trying to distract you."

"I know. That's why I can't even get upset with you. You have no ulterior motive. At all."

Guilt pricks at me. If she only knew... "Of course I have an ulterior motive." I link my hand with hers, our fingers tangling. I speak frankly as far as I can. "I want to bind you to me, forever. I want you to love me so much that you're blind to my faults."

"I'm not blind to your faults."

My heart stops for a beat. My fingers tense around hers.

She squeezes back. "I love you anyway."

Just like that, she disarms me, putting me at ease. I loathe breaking our physical connection. So we eat with our hands linked, even though it's awkward using my left hand.

Watching her chew her pizza, I suppose I could be just one percent gracious about her doing the project with Byron. Only because she loves me, and not him. And because I'm going to cut him where it hurts the most. Besides, I don't want her to get the impression that I don't trust her with him. It's the other way around.

As we're leaving, she rises on tiptoes, her body molding against mine. My blood heats from a week of celibacy. She whispers something into my ear, her breath hot. I totally miss what she's saying. "What?"

She tries again. "I got an IUD. The doc said it's effective immediately."

I'm instantly harder than I've ever been. "Seriously?"

She nods with a breathless laugh. "You did say you have days' worth of stuff you want to do to me."

I wrap an arm around her waist and pull her closer. "Can you just call in sick? Tell Elizabeth you can't work this afternoon."

"No. I already took a week off." She nips my earlobe then licks it. It's totally not helping. "Behave. It'll be worth the wait."

A growl vibrates in my chest. Fuck it. I'll just call Elizabeth and tell her Iris fainted and had to go home.

I tighten my arm around her, pressing her body closer to mine, then pull out my phone.

"Bobbi, get me out of here!" Iris says, giggling and wriggling. "Quick, before he gets a hold of Elizabeth."

Bobbi is instantly beside us. "You heard the lady. Let her go."

"Hey! I'm the one paying you," I say.

"To guard her from all threats." She squints at my arm around Iris. "Looks threatening to me."

I shoot her an incredulous look. "Really."

"Yeah." She smiles sweetly. "Or you can just fire me. Then I won't interfere in your foreplay."

Making a sound somewhere between horrified sputter and laugh, Iris wiggles her fingers against my ticklish spot. My hold loosens for a second, and that's all it takes for her to slip away.

Bobbi blocking my way as she follows, Iris trots out of the restaurant quickly. When she's safely out of reach, she looks over her shoulder and sticks out her tongue. I give her a look full of promise of lusty retribution, although a faint smile is tugging at my mouth.

She blows me a kiss. Minx.

I'm so hard that it's painful. Lust thrums in my veins as I watch Iris slip into the office building. She's such a tease, but I adore her for it. I love that she's blossoming, regaining her old confidence and spirit.

TJ brings the car around, and I get in.

Since I can't do anything about the state of my cock, I turn my focus to something I can. I wasn't kidding when I told Byron Pearce things could get personal. He should've taken me seriously. There's nothing I won't do to protect what's mine, and him circling around Iris like a mangy dog after a steak is unacceptable.

What would be the best blow? I could go into another profitable venture with Milton, but that seems a bit blasé—a repeat. Byron is most likely ready for that.

But... A smile curves my lips as an idea pops into my head. He spent weeks in Hawaii to hammer out a deal with a Korean company. And it's a subsidiary of the Hae Min Group.

I text Yuna. *Got something to discuss. Is this good time to talk?*

Within seconds, she calls me. "What's wrong? Is it Ivy?"

"Nothing's wrong." The last thing I need is her panicking. "I'm not sure how closely you keep track of your father's company, but one of the subsidiaries was in Hawaii not too long ago to hammer out a deal with Pearce International."

"I might've heard something about that." Yuna's voice is

suddenly guarded and entirely too smooth. The tone of a woman getting ready to deal with unreasonable demands and favors.

"Byron Pearce is the point of contact. I want that deal sabotaged."

"Why?" she asks coolly, every bit the haughty heiress. "We won't be giving the contract to you, if that's what you're asking."

I almost chuckle at her totally incorrect conclusion. "You said you wanted Iris to reclaim her music. How serious were you?"

"Very. But how does that part of Hae Min's business have anything to do with her?"

This is the key. I need to lay it on a bit thick to move someone like Yuna. "Byron Pearce is trying to keep her at the Pryce Family Foundation. He donated a large amount of money and asked her boss to make her the head of a new initiative."

"Ridiculous. Iris turned it down, right?"

Would I be calling if she had? But Yuna's outrage is a good sign. "No. She said yes. She's very fond of her boss."

"Tell him to pull out."

"I already warned him. But you know how people can be."

"Of course. So you want me to punish him."

Now we're on the same page. "Yes. Your father loves you. All you have to do is ask."

"How do you know I have that kind of leverage? I'm just a worthless daughter." She throws it out there like a challenge.

"He let you attend Curtis even though he'd rather you didn't. He let you start the foundation in honor of Ivy's memory. Now he's letting you go to the States to find this dead friend, and even sent his right-hand man with you. If that isn't love, I don't know what is."

She's quiet for a moment. "Fine. I'll ask my dad. And...can I call you Tony?"

"Huh?" What brought this on?

"I heard from my brother about your weird tic with your name."

Weird tic? What the—

"Apparently you only let your family and closest friends call you Tony, and everyone else is to supposed to use either Anthony or Blackwood. Since you're so close to my soul sister, I feel like you're like...how would you put it in English? My soul brother-in-law, or something? I mean, you're going to marry her."

Her conviction about Iris and me... It's touching. I sit there, stunned, realizing that she's the first and only one to express such a sentiment.

"Why are you so quiet? Don't tell me I've misjudged you. It isn't just a 'sex and it was fun, but you aren't good enough to be my missus' kind of thing, right?" There's an edge to her voice now. She's going to reach through the phone line and cut my balls off if she thinks I'm using Iris.

My affection for Yuna goes up a notch. She's exactly the kind of friend I want for Iris. "Of course I'm going to keep her forever. As for marriage, I'm not telling you when I haven't even bought a ring." Then I add, "Thank you, Yuna, for believing in me and Iris. It means a lot to me."

"Any idiot can tell you make her happy. I've never seen her glow like when she's with you...except possibly when she's killing it at the piano. I'd be a terrible friend to not want the best for you two."

"Thanks. But not everyone wants us to be together."

"Julie?"

Julie? Yuna hasn't been around Julie and me long enough to figure out how we feel about each other...has she? "Excuse me?"

"I noticed you don't like her that much. She doesn't seem too crazy about you, either."

"Something like that." But my annoyance with Julie goes deeper than her telling Iris about my shitty reputation. Any good friend would warn her friend about that sort of thing. But her being weird about Bobbi's presence? That I can't forgive. When Iris woke up after Sam's attack, she was worried sick about Julie's safety, but Julie doesn't seem to prioritize Iris's safety. If she did, she would've done her best to convince Iris to accept Bobbi.

"You're angry she objected to you hiring the bodyguard," Yuna says.

"How do you know?" I ask, surprised.

"Because you looked like you were itching to strangle her."

She laughs lightly. "She's just an ordinary girl. Most normal people don't understand how serious things can get for people like us...when so much money and power is at stake."

I find myself nodding. Yuna understands. But then, she's seen all that stuff her whole life. It's as natural to her as drinking water at a dinner table. "Julie isn't some regular person. She's Byron Pearce's sister. She should know better."

"Really?" Displeasure colors that one word. "I'll do what needs to be done on the Hawaii matter. But I need to offer another firm to do the project. My father doesn't like proposals that cost him money, and he's already invested a lot of time and effort on the negotiations."

I chuckle. "Oh, I don't think you'll need to find another firm. How about just changing the liaison on Pearce International's side?"

"To whom?"

"Milton Pearce. And Yuna?"

"Yeah?"

"You should absolutely call me Tony."

24

IRIS

I WORK LIKE BLAZES ALL AFTERNOON LONG TO WRAP UP everything I need to for the day. I leave the office fifteen minutes early after texting TJ, just in case. Normally Tony comes to get me, but since I have Bobbi with her Escalade...maybe not? I wish we'd talked about the logistics earlier.

Anyway, Bobbi takes me home. She's a careful driver, not a mile over the speed limit, and using her blinkers judiciously. She curses a few times at other drivers. But she brings me home in one piece, safe and sound.

"Are you coming in?" I ask casually as we reach the door.

Bobbi's phone buzzes. She checks the text and smirks. "No. I'll see you tomorrow."

I smile, relieved she's going home now. It would've been awkward telling her to leave so Tony and I could get dirty. "Great. See you tomorrow."

My body fizzes with anticipation as I unlock the door to the penthouse. I want to arrive early so I can freshen up and change into something sexy before Tony gets here. The goal is to drive him insane with lust. The knowledge that we're going to do it without a barrier adds a sharp edge to my need. It's ridiculous, since it isn't spontaneous—I've planned things so there aren't any unintended consequences, but still... It feels extra naughty.

"Finally!" Tony wraps his arm around me the minute I step into the living room.

"Oh! When did you get here?"

"I left the second you texted TJ."

Maybe I shouldn't have bothered if I wanted some freshening-up time. On the other hand, I don't think Tony cares at the moment.

His breath has a hint of whiskey. "I had to text Bobbi to let her know it's not cool to drive like a blind granny."

The start of my giggle is cut short when his lips crash down on mine, his mouth hot and demanding. As he pulls me closer, his thick erection pushes against me, and I shift to fit against him better.

His tongue sweeps into me. I taste the whiskey and Tony, a crazy-sexy combination. He is insatiable, teasing me, stroking his tongue against mine, luring me into his mouth—giving me the permission to do everything I want to do.

I sense him unzipping the back of my dress, then tugging it down until it falls at my feet. He cups my breasts encased in their lacy bra and brushes his thumbs over the peaks. I cry out, the sound muffled against his mouth. He hasn't touched me in, what —six days?—but it feels like it's been forever, my body hypersensitive to him.

Instead of undoing the bra clasp, he pulls my breasts over the cups, creating an indecently deep cleavage, my nipples pushed close together. "Fuck, that's hot," he says.

The harsh rasp of his voice hits me like liquor, filling me with a greedy heat that leaches all the strength from my limbs. My fingers dig into his warm, silky hair as he flicks his tongue over the pointed tips of my breasts, then finally pulls one into his mouth. He toys with my other nipple with one hand, and the other slips between my legs, his knuckles ghosting over my clit through the satin. The barely-there touch makes me greedier. I want firmer strokes. And his cock inside me—filling me until I'm screaming with bliss.

He lavishes attention on my other nipple and pulls roughly at my underwear. I shimmy, helping him get them down my legs.

"I missed the taste of you," he growls, his breathing shallow and fast.

"I missed you too," I whisper.

"You always taste amazing." He kisses my belly, pushing me backward until the back of my knees hit a couch.

I lose my balance, sprawling on the white cushions, my breasts still pushed up over my bra, my legs spread wide, my pussy totally exposed to his heated gaze. Going on his knees, he throws my thighs over his wide shoulders and runs the flat of his tongue over my flesh.

Electric shock streaks through me, and I tilt my pelvis in a blatant offer. His clever mouth moves over me while his long, beautiful fingers fill me. I watch his dark head buried between my pale thighs, white-hot need pumping through me. I never knew until now what a turn-on it was to have a powerful man in his full trappings of wealth and status kneel between my legs and eat me out like this was what he was born to do.

I can't tear my eyes from the view. I'm so turned on that I can feel the wetness trickling down. Tony takes it all, his tongue swirling over my swollen and sensitive clit, setting my nerve endings on fire. His fingers bend slightly, hitting the little bump in my pussy repeatedly, pushing me higher and higher until there's a mountain of pleasure rising inside.

Suddenly, he pulls my clit into his mouth, hard. The coiled tension inside me snaps, and I come, screaming until my throat grows hoarse.

I don't know how much time passes before my breathing settles. But Tony is still between my legs, licking me, this time to soothe rather than stimulate.

"It's gratifying to see you so helplessly out of control," he says.

"Is it?" I say.

I feel him nod against my skin. "I'm horny for you all the

time." He runs the edge of his teeth gently along my inner thigh. "You kept me hard all day long."

"I didn't tease you this morning."

"All I have to do is think about you. And look at the gifts you sent."

My need should've been sated after the awesome orgasm he just gave me. But I'm hot for him again from listening to him talk about wanting me. I want him too. Endlessly. Crazily. His body, heart, soul—everything.

I spread my legs wider. "Put your cock inside me," I say, the intense need for him making me shameless.

His eyes flare with heat. And his reaction adds to my reckless need. "I didn't go see my doc just for a little oral. I did it so I can feel you—just you."

He curses under his breath. His expensive clothes are ripped, buttons flying everywhere, as he strips and kicks everything off.

His cock is so hard and thick, pulsing when I wrap my hand around it. "Now," I demand, letting go.

He pushes into me, long and hard, stretching me and filling me all the way. He feels so good. Perfect.

"Tell me how it feels," I whisper.

"Incredible. So intense, knowing this is where it's going to end, not outside your body." He pulls out and pushes into me again, his glittering eyes on mine. "I love the way you keep me wet. I can sense every small contraction of your pussy."

Holy shit. His frank talk is making me hotter, every cell in my body prickling with sexual tension.

He reclaims my mouth and plunges into me over and over again, each thrust more powerful and pleasurable than the one before. I cling to him, trusting him with my body and heart as he takes me to the height of bliss, where I shatter, sobbing his name and my love for him.

He pushes into me one last time before shuddering. I feel a warm wetness flooding me. It's different from him climaxing in a condom. More intimate and raw. Messier.

It's a while before Tony pulls out. He looks down, his eyes going dark. "I've never done that before—come inside someone without rubber. You're my first and only. And it's hotter than spilling on your belly. Dirtier." He strokes the pad of his thumb across my pussy. "I want to do this over and over and over again, just to fill you like this."

My face heats, half with embarrassment and half with fresh need. Although at times he says the most heartbreakingly sweet things, he can be totally blunt and raw about what he wants, too.

"Are you shy?" he teases.

"No one ever talked to me like this before," I blurt out.

Shadows cross his eyes, then vanish before I can make sense of what's wrong. "Because they're all idiots. There's nothing better than watching the woman you love come and coming inside her."

I'm sprawled on the couch with my legs still spread, dripping and messy and swollen from two orgasms, and Tony's stark naked, his cock still hard and wet from being inside me. But somehow, what he just told me feels more romantic than a love poem recited across an intimate dinner table under a moonlit sky.

I start to reach for him again, brushing my fingers over his hair.

Abruptly, my stomach lets out a loud growl. I flush, then laugh when Tony starts chuckling.

"I guess your belly's not going to wait anymore." He takes a handkerchief from his pants and helps me get clean. "All right. Let's get you fed."

"What are we having?"

"Cheeseburgers and fries. I just have to put the fries in the oven and cook up the patties."

I raise an eyebrow. "That's a lot of calories."

"Gotta keep our strength up." He kisses me. "We have a long night ahead."

And he keeps me up all night long.

25

IRIS

THE NEXT MORNING, WE'RE RUNNING TEN MINUTES LATE. But Tony's acting like we have all the time in the world, pressing his chest against my back and wrapping his arms around my belly. He buries his face against the nape of my neck and breathes in.

"Today's not a holiday," I say, slapping at the hands locked around me. "Come on. You're going to get me fired for being late."

"I'll start a My Girlfriend Is Too Hot Foundation, then. You can be the director."

I bite back a laugh. "What the heck does it do?"

"Whatever you want." He presses his erection against my butt. It's hard and thick again already.

"We did it in the shower. Control yourself or I'm going to ride in with Bobbi without you."

He spins me around so we're face to face. "That's not fair."

I run my thumb over his lower lip, which is slightly sticking out. I love this playful, boyish side of him. He can be too serious and intense. "We have a whole evening and night ahead of us.

Don't act like this is the only time." I yawn loudly on purpose. "Look how tired I am because somebody kept me up late."

"Fine." But he doesn't forget to pinch my butt playfully.

On our ride to the office, I check my agenda. I have a meeting with a rep from Byron to hammer out some of the project details at ten. The person emailed me a PowerPoint file to review late last night. I should get that done ASAP.

Tony looks at it over my shoulder. "The music project, huh?"

"Yes." I slide him a glance. "You aren't going to fly off into a weird, jealous fit, right?"

"Nope." He leans closer and whispers, "I was inside you all night long."

I elbow his side, my face warm. "Behave."

He laughs.

And just like that, I'm happy. He needs to laugh more. He hasn't laughed much since the incident at Sam's mansion.

In the office, I go to my desk and immediately start going over the PowerPoint presentation. Bobbi parks herself in the vestibule, which is good, because I don't want any conflict between her and Tolyan. He shoots a squinty look in her direction, but she ignores him.

Go, Bobbi!

At ten, I head to a small conference room. Bobbi follows. I start to say she doesn't have to tag along, then change my mind. It's better that she come with me than get left where Tolyan can throw out some inappropriate comment. Like "You have breasts."

I open the door and stop abruptly at the sight of Byron alone in the room. Bobbi almost runs into me.

Byron's dressed in a conservative charcoal suit that says he's all business. But his expression is anything but. It's warm and personable.

"Hey, Byron," I say, walking inside, wondering where his people are. "What are you doing here?" I take a seat. Bobbi stands behind me.

"I decided to see to the project personally." His eyes flick to Bobbi. "So that's the so-called bodyguard Blackwood hired."

"She is a bodyguard," I say, not liking the "so-called." He shouldn't be so dismissive and rude.

"She's a spy."

What is Byron saying? It isn't like him to jump to the worst conclusion possible. He's usually laidback and friendly. "I'm sorry?"

"Julie told me. Blackwood got her so she could watch your every move and report to him."

"Is that what Julie said?" I ask, incredulous. I know Julie isn't too crazy about Bobbi, but this is slanderous, and not at all like her. There has to be some kind of miscommunication. If not, I'm calling her to set her straight.

"Not precisely, but it's obvious."

For God's sake. I don't have the patience to put up with Byron's unreasonable assumptions after dealing with Tony's yesterday. "She's a bodyguard. She's here to keep me safe. If you have a problem with that, you need to take it up with Tony."

"I'm trying to protect you."

I cross my arms. Tony's the last person Byron needs to protect me from. He needs to get it through his head that whatever issues exist between us have no bearing on my relationship with Tony. Not to mention Byron doesn't know enough about my circumstances to say stuff like this in the first place. "From what?"

"Blackwood is trying to manipulate and control you."

"Like you're not?" Bobbi says. "Calling me a spy without a reason?"

Really, Bobbi? I grit my teeth with irritation. I don't need her participating in this ridiculous conversation, any more than I need Byron's ludicrous attitude. "Stop. Both of you. This is a meeting to talk about the music program. If we're not going to talk about that, then we're done here."

Bobbi crosses her arms and leans back against the wall, her eyes narrowed. Byron glares at her, then turns his attention to me. His scrutiny is sharp—a blade scraping over my skin.

He shifts his weight. "Before we begin...just so you know, I'm still working on finding the girl you mentioned."

The girl in the car. Tension winds inside me. Why is he

bringing this up now, especially if he thinks Bobbi's Tony's spy? Is he hoping she tells Tony everything, so he'll jump to an erroneous conclusion that we're entirely too close? Or is Byron just dangling it to get me to be more agreeable? Either way, it feels manipulative, and I don't like it. I keep my voice calm. "Are you close?"

"Not yet. There are quite literally hundreds of thousands of missing women who fit your description."

I heave a sigh. I knew it'd be hard, but it's still frustrating. And I'm not sure why he brought it up if he has no update. "Thanks for looking into it," I say anyway. "I appreciate it."

Thoughts are crossing his face. He's not even trying to hide how badly he thinks of Tony, how worried he is about me and how hurt he is at my negative reaction to his concerns. It's uncharacteristic of Byron. He's usually much more circumspect. And nothing really bothers him much. "I know you think I'm just being a dick. But if anything happens...just remember I'm here for you."

"Thanks." Byron and Tony obviously have a problem with each other, and I'm caught in the middle. They're both trying to be somewhat civilized—albeit badly—so I push my irritation with Byron aside and turn our conversation to the project.

26

ANTHONY

THE REST OF THE WORK WEEK PASSES IN BLISS. IRIS IS BUSY at work, but we always make time for each other in the evening (along with at least an hour of piano practice for her). On Wednesday, we invite Yuna over for dinner. She comes, again with Mr. Kim. She doesn't say a word about my favor on Monday, and I don't ask.

Instead, we spend the evening eating and chatting about everything and nothing...culminating with Yuna and Iris doing an in-person version of "watch and weep," each of them playing Liszt, Chopin and Rachmaninoff to impress each other.

I watch them, without judging their performances. I know better. Mr. Kim wisely refrains from commenting as well. It's good to see the fire in Iris's eyes—that competitive spirit rekindled.

When Iris finishes her *Grand Galop Chromatique*, Yuna throws her hands in the air. "You haven't changed one bit! It's so unfair!"

"Haha. I'm going to make you cry when I master 'Mazeppa.'"

"Aren't you done with that étude?"

"Not done enough." Iris's gaze slides toward me. "Tony sent me an MP3 of György Cziffra's performance, and you know what that means."

Yuna shakes her head. "Cziffra probably drank Liszt's blood. It's the only explanation for his talent."

"That's gross. And jealousy is an ugly emotion."

"Not jealousy. Facts." She checks the time. "Oh, it's already nine! I'm going now, so you two can get lovey-dovey and get some sleep before work tomorrow." She hugs Iris and me, then leaves.

"She's just too awesome. I can't believe she gave up her dream to be a concert pianist," Iris says.

"Sometimes people's dreams change." Just like mine did. Owning clubs and becoming rich were never my goals until I learned of her death and experienced the ravaging betrayal of Lauren and Ryder. What I really wanted was something that allowed me a super-flexible schedule and the ability to work remotely. That way, I could go with Iris when she toured the world as a celebrated pianist. I suspect Yuna's dreams changed when her "soul sister" died. She and I have a deep grief in common.

Iris shakes her head. "I wish Sam hadn't lied and told her that I died. I feel like that has something to do with her situation now."

"You shouldn't blame yourself for Yuna's circumstances. You didn't make Sam lie." He lied because there was a benefit for him somehow, even though I still haven't figured out what that is. And I'm going to make him pay for the pain he's caused and the destructive path it put me on. I was a mess after I lost Iris. Ended my friendship with Ryder. Then threatened and fucked with his pregnant fiancée. She could've lost her baby because of me.

Jesus. I'm ashamed to think back on it. I wanted to lash out and punish everyone and everything that hurt me. The entire world was my enemy.

Iris cuddles next to me on the couch. "You know what's weird, though? Since her last visit, Julie hasn't sent me a single text or anything." She opens her mouth as though she wants to continue, then purses her lips with a scowl.

"She's probably just busy," I say, doing my best to hide my satisfaction. I don't really want Julie around Iris. Yuna's firmly on Iris's side, and she wants Iris and me to be together. Julie is on Iris's side, but she doesn't care for me. And when push comes to shove, she will, of course, side with her brother Byron over me. I already have enough obstacles. I don't need Julie in my way as well.

"Maybe. I'll text her tomorrow or something."

Since I don't want her thinking about hanging out with Julie, I distract Iris the best way I know how—amazing sex.

But afterward, when she's sleeping peacefully curled against me, I stare at the ceiling and think back on what Yuna said.

Soul brother-in-law.

All through the week, I think about it. Iris's husband. Yuna's soul brother-in-law.

I'm scum for even contemplating the idea. I haven't come clean to Iris about our past. I don't know how I'm going to do that, or if it's even possible. But I can't give her up now. Death would be preferable.

Part of me says if I marry her, we'll be bound together, and I can make everything up to her by treating her like a queen. Give her the world. Fill her life with joy and happiness. I'm not the helpless young man I used to be. I have wealth—and power.

By Friday, my mind's made up. I visit a jeweler after dropping Iris off at work. If I'm going to propose, I need something extra special.

It takes me less than ten minutes to decide I don't like anything they have. I have a very specific design in mind. Something unique. One of a kind.

I say so to one of the clerks, and she goes back and brings out their senior designer, Masako Hayashi. She's a rail-thin woman with a precise black bob and sharp eyes. Her dress is professional and expensive. Her jewelry is feminine and original.

"What are you in the mood for, Mr. Blackwood?" she asks after a quick introduction.

"Not diamonds, because everyone does diamonds," I say, thinking of Iris that morning as she got ready for work. And the sweet kiss she blew at me before going into her lobby. I felt it like a physical touch, right over my heart, warm and sweet. "Something exceptionally large and radiant. Glowing, almost. Precious. Beautiful. Irreplaceable. Just like the woman."

"She must be someone special."

"Very."

"Any particular preferences? Traditional? Contemporary? Something classic and timeless?"

"Classic and timeless, but unique. It needs to make a statement."

"If you don't like diamonds, but want something classic and timeless, I suggest a large pearl. We recently acquired a sixteen-millimeter—perfectly round. Exceptionally lustrous and virtually flawless. Which is rare. When pearls grow that large, they generally acquire blemishes, you know." Masako gestures at a clerk. She brings out a velvet box, and Masako opens it for me. "What do you think?"

I lean closer. The single pearl is huge. Almost as big as a dime. It has a faint pink tint that's gorgeous.

"This is the top one percent," Masako says. "But a pearl alone can be dull. So I say platinum, small diamonds and maybe sapphires?"

"If you think they'll work well together."

"Great. I'll send you a few sketches by Monday. Once you select the design, we can get started right away."

"I want it done ASAP."

"Of course. But with custom work, it will take some time."

"I don't want to wait long." Why can't people get things done when I want them done, especially when I'm paying top dollar? "Within a week."

"It won't be cheap."

I scoff. She knows people who care about cost don't commission pieces from her. "I don't care."

Brimming with anticipation, I walk out...only to promptly and literally run into Byron Fucking Pearce. He's carrying a Starbucks cup and curses as the hot brew spills over his hand. I manage to step away just in time. His face twists into pure hatred when he sees it's me.

"You fucker."

"Good to run into you too, Pearce," I say, enjoying the brown stain on his shirt. "How's business?"

Byron stares at me for a moment as he puts it together. Then he snarls. "Do you know how long I worked on that Hae Min deal?"

I smile smugly. "Told you it could get personal."

"You petty fuck. That was pure spite."

Pinching my eyebrows together in an exaggerated frown, I stick my lower lip out. "Aw, what are you going to do? Run to Iris and cry? 'Your boyfriend is a meanie.'" I wipe at my eyes.

Violence coils within him. I can sense the tension in his muscles, see the darkness filling his eyes. "You aren't fit to be near Rizzy."

I hate that he dares give her a nickname, as though their relationship is something more. "That isn't her name."

"Really? She answers to it, *Tony*. You're just like Sam."

My teeth clench, and it's all I can do to not break that perfect nose of his. But Iris would disapprove. "Sam and I are different. I love her. He doesn't."

"Oh, of course! That's what guys like you say until you get bored. Then you toss her away like trash."

"Shut the fuck up, you son of a bitch. You know nothing about me or my feelings for Iris. Can you say you're just being her friend when you talk shit about me? Swear you aren't jealous that she's in my bed, but not in yours?" I want him to throw the first punch. Publicly. Totally lose control. It'd humiliate him, and satisfy me no end.

"And can you say everything you're doing is *purely* for her sake? That you aren't trying to make her dependent on you like that slimy uncle of hers?"

His words are like bullets, and they hurt. But I'll be damned if I let him see it. "No," I say coldly.

"Liar." Byron sneers, somehow holding on to his temper

despite the frustration and anger etched in every taut line of his face. Then abruptly, he walks away.

I turn to the waiting Cullinan. TJ opens the door and I get inside, still tense. I wanted Byron to lose his temper. Make a total spectacle of himself, even if he wasn't going to punch me first.

My mood is in the toilet now. The fucker doesn't know shit. He's lashing out blindly, hoping something will penetrate.

The thing is, he struck much closer to the heart of the matter than I'd like. There is a part of me that hopes Iris will remain just a tad dependent, so she'll never leave me. I can't even deny that I hope she won't regain all her memories. The things that happened between us...

I close my eyes, pressing a thumb and forefinger against my eyebrows.

Iris's recollection of Yuna is all positive. She could barely stay still while waiting for her to come up to our place. But with me... She recalls nothing. Not only that, when we first ran into each other at Hammers and Strings, she cried.

That was all that I was to her in the deepest recesses of her memory—the guy who made her sad, not even worth a conscious recollection. When we were together in Tempérane, I thought I could protect her by pushing her away and rejecting her love. I wouldn't let her tell me she loved me. When she got a tattoo to show me she loved me, I rejected it coldly, telling her she was being rash and she'd regret it. All the while, I craved her love like a thirsty man lost in a desert, hallucinating an oasis. By the time I figured it out, it was too late.

So this time I'm not pushing her away. I'm going to tie her to me, even if she ends up hating me. I'd rather die by her hand than go through what I went through nine years ago.

My phone buzzes. A text from Iris.

Hey, are you doing anything tonight? I thought it'd be fun to go clubbing with Yuna and Julie. Want to come?

I thought Julie went incommunicado, I respond.

That's why I want to lure her out. Give her a few drinks, get her talking. And to make it extra special, I want to take them to Z.

I've never been, and I think it'll be fun. And I want to get the Owner's Girlfriend treatment. :)

It's true; she hasn't had a chance to go yet. Suddenly, I want to show her my first club, the place where my fortune was built. Male birds display colorful feathers or a newly built nest to entice a female they want. Why shouldn't I do the same to convince Iris I'm not a total screwup? That if she stays with me, I'll always have the means to take care of her?

Of course. You're the VVVVVIP.

Awesome. Thank you!

Everything I have is yours, I reply. And I'm going to show her what *everything* means.

27

IRIS

ABOUT TWO HOURS AFTER TONY AND I GET HOME, MY friends descend upon us. Julie arrives first, fashionable in a skintight electric-purple dress that she pulls off with a confident strut. Her hair's teased to the nth degree and looks great. Her eyes stand out, mesmerizingly, thanks to extra eyeliner and mascara. We hug. She's apparently been busy, but I'm so glad she accepted my invitation.

Yuna comes with Mr. Kim. I swear the man never leaves her side. She's in a super-adorable sleeveless white top and a merlot-colored skirt with an asymmetrical hem. The heels she has on look lethal—high and sharp. Unlike Julie, she hasn't teased her hair, opting to let it fall naturally around her shoulders and back. A great choice, since she has such amazingly thick, straight hair. She's done smoky makeup and fake lashes that flutter like butterfly wings every time she opens and closes her eyes. She takes one look at me and shakes her head. "Come on, Iris. This isn't a white-collar job interview."

"Don't worry. I'm going to change before we go."

Yuna lights up. "Let me see what you got!" She starts dragging me up the stairs.

I look at Tony over my shoulder, but he merely smiles and waves, mouthing, *Have fun*.

Julie follows us, and soon, both of my friends are in my closet. Well. Tony's and my closet.

"Wow. Your man has great taste," Yuna says, checking out his clothes.

"Don't touch his stuff," I say. "He's peculiar," I add, just so Julie doesn't join in.

"He's not going to know. My hands are extra clean. Mr. Kim gave me hand sanitizer before I came here."

"Hand sanitizer?"

"Just to be safe. He's a little OCD about stuff like that," Yuna says, now finally in my part of the closet and going through my dresses. "I think Dad put him up to it, to make sure I don't get sick in the States. I told him this is a first-world country, but..." She shrugs, then pulls out a bright red dress. "How about this one? It shows off your neck and shoulders and a bit of cleavage. And it's short."

"I love it," Julie says, watching us with her arms crossed.

"Of course you love it! You made me buy it," I say.

"Because I'm awesome like that."

"You have good taste," Yuna says to Julie with a grin. "This is exactly what Iris needs for clubbing. And those." She points to a pair of silvery stiletto sandals. "They're broken in, right?"

"No," I say. "Impulse buy because they looked pretty."

"No biggie. If the straps chafe, just put on some Band-Aids. God gave us Band-Aids for a reason."

"I thought you were a Buddhist," Julie says.

"I am, but it sounds weird to say Buddha gave us Band-Aids, doesn't it?" Yuna says, totally unfazed. "Come on. Strip and change."

I roll my eyes, pretending not to notice the snippy interaction between the two of them. I don't want to intervene and be forced to take sides. I pause when Yuna and Julie don't make any move to leave. "Are you going to give me some privacy?"

"No. Why? Do you think I'm going to pounce on you?" Yuna leans forward. "I thought that was Tony's job."

My cheeks grow hot. "You're terrible."

"Just do it. You don't have anything I don't have...or haven't seen."

She's probably right. According to her, we shared the same apartment near Curtis for three years. You tend to see a lot when you live together. I get out of my blouse and slacks and put on the dress. It hugs me tightly, and the cleavage is a bit more eye-popping than I remember. Have I gained weight?

"You look hot. Put these on." Yuna hands me a pair of long, dangly earrings. "And we're going to work on your makeup."

"What's wrong with it?" I ask, putting on the earrings.

Yuna blinks. "You were going to go like this?"

"I don't know if I need to redo it." My makeup's on the understated side, but that's what I'm usually comfortable with.

"Trust your best friend, then!" Yuna drags me to the vanity and forces me to sit still. "Close your eyes."

"Yes, Mother," I say sourly. Julie isn't moving to help me, which means she must agree with Yuna.

She snickers. "Not even I go clubbing with my mom. You gotta work some magic. You want to look extra sexy and hot. Drive your man insane."

I squirm. If Tony gets any lustier, I'll never sleep. Or get out of bed, for that matter.

"I got us a limo for our night out," Yuna says, moving a brush over my face. "We're gonna club in style. And take lots of selfies."

"You have an Instagram account?" I ask.

"Of course not." She sounds horrified. "The Hae Min Group VP of publicity would kill me. We can only post what's good for the group's image—boring, stoic and hard-working." She dabs something cold along my eyes. "They're to commemorate our time tonight. Sometimes all you have left is pictures and texts."

I crack my eyes open. The line of her mouth is set tight.

I forget sometimes that I'm not the only one affected by what happened nine years ago. Yuna's hurting too—she lost her friend and maybe even gave up on her dream because of it. The fact that

I don't remember her fully is frustrating to me, but it must be painful for her. To her, I'm the best friend who she did all sorts of crazy, fun stuff with. Except now she has to start over to rebuild the lost friendship and trust between us.

"I'm keeping a diary so I don't forget again," I say softly.

Yuna smiles. "I better take up, like, a hundred percent of that space... After your man, I mean."

I laugh lightly, since I don't want to talk about the actual content of my journal. "I don't think the math adds up."

"Well, what can I say? My forte is music." She gestures at the mirror. "So, what do you think?"

I study my reflection, my jaw slack. I look totally different. I always thought I looked nice, and I know how to apply makeup pretty well, but Yuna is magic. My eyes are slightly slanted and much larger, my cheekbones impossibly high and my lips... "I have a pouty mouth," I say, pointing at the mirror.

"I know! There's nothing a little makeup can't do." She turns to Julie. "What do you think?"

Julie looks at my face for a moment. "Nice. Very good."

I frown at her flat tone. It isn't like her to be so subdued and standoffish. She usually gets over whatever's bugging her pretty quickly. It's one of her greatest charms. "Are you feeling okay?"

"I'm fine. Just excited about going to Z. I've never been." She smiles, although not with her usual easy cheeriness.

I want to probe, but don't. If she's not saying anything, it could be because she doesn't want to talk about it in front of Yuna, whom she doesn't know that well. Or maybe Yuna inadvertently did something that upset Julie. I make a mental note to ask later.

We go downstairs. Tony is just finishing his drink. He lowers the glass slowly, his eyes on me. Blatant heat flares in them, making me hot.

Yuna giggles. "Told you," she whispers in my ear.

"Yes, you did." I cover a warm cheek with my hand. I'm pleased with Tony's reaction, and flustered that I'm so turned on by it when my friends are watching.

Tony pulls me to the side and kisses me. "You look...incredible."

"You're welcome," Yuna says. "Now let's go. The limo's waiting."

"Only you would get a limo to go to a club," I tease.

"Might as well do it in style. Selfies, remember? Besides, we have at least six people in our party."

"We do?" Julie asks.

"Uh-huh. You, me, Tony, Iris, then her bodyguard and Mr. Kim."

"Mr. Kim's coming too?" I ask. He doesn't look like the clubbing type. Besides, he's dressed like he's going to a corporate meeting.

"Yes." Yuna turns to Tony. "Unless he's too old for it? Do you care in the States? In Korea, you can't go clubbing when you're his age."

Tony shrugs. "No, it's fine—"

"Why are they coming? We're going to Z, not a war zone," Julie interrupts.

"Mr. Kim can't leave my side," Yuna says. "That's his job. And Bobbi's supposed to be watching over Iris. It's always better to be prepared, because you never know. And I bet Tony would rather relax than hover over us the entire time making sure we're okay."

My gaze darts back and forth. Yuna is totally low-stress and composed, but Julie's another matter. She's like a dog that can't decide between lunging at someone's neck or settling for barking.

Maybe I shouldn't have asked Julie to join us. Except I don't know how she'd feel if I did that. I wanted to make sure to include everyone, but maybe I didn't think it through. "Why don't we get going?"

"Yes," Tony says, putting a hand at the small of my back. "What's that about?" he asks under his breath, as Yuna and Julie file out ahead of us.

"Maybe Julie's upset about something? I wonder if tonight just wasn't that great for her. If it weren't for Yuna, I'd consider canceling, but..."

His hand flexes against my back. "Don't. Whatever problem Julie has can't be dealt with right now, so just relax and enjoy yourself. Please?"

I lean my head against his shoulder. "Okay," I say, even as a tiny knot of worry forms. Our night out might not end up the way I envisioned.

28

ANTHONY

THANKFULLY, THE LIMO RIDE IS MORE RELAXED. YUNA TAKES at least a hundred selfies—alone, with Iris and with everyone else —and makes witty observations. Iris laughs at her jokes, her weight resting against me, which is exactly how I prefer it, so I can feel her warmth and play with her hair.

Julie, on the other hand, is still off. I don't know what her deal is. If she didn't want to come, she should have stayed home instead of ruining the evening.

Wait a minute. Did Byron run to her and cry about how I took the contract away from him? Unless I'm mistaken, she's closer to Byron than Milton. She was even staying at Byron's place earlier. She could've realized Yuna had something to do with Byron's setback.

If that's the problem, she needs to cut it out. Except I can't tell her to do that, not with Iris and Yuna watching. I need to find a way to talk to her privately. If she's got a problem with the way I'm fucking with Byron's life, she can take it out on me, not the women.

Finally, we reach Z. The line's long, wrapping around the block. My hand linked with Iris's, I lead everyone to the VIP lane.

The assistant chief of security lets us in with a polite greeting. He must've heard I was coming to be manning the line himself.

I watch Iris's face carefully as we enter the club. Until now, I've never wanted someone to love my club and feel proud of what I've built. I have no idea how she'll react to Z. She and I never went clubbing in Tempérane, and I've never seen her listen to or play contemporary music. Z is about as far away from classical as you can get.

The loud music throbs at a cellular level. Iris lifts her head, her eyes wide, as she takes it all in—the slick, well-dressed crowd, the multilevel interior with balconies and private nooks and crannies, the bar with all the best liquors. Lots of chrome and glass.

"Wow." A smile breaks over her face. "It's awesome. I can't believe it's all yours."

The coil inside me loosens. "Every bit of it. And there are more." I pull her closer, burying my face in her hair. "All yours, too."

She pokes me in my ticklish spot. "Haha, very funny."

She doesn't understand—all this, I built for her. Seven years ago, when Ryder betrayed me, I swore I'd become so strong that nobody would ever hurt me or take away what was mine again. I learned very quickly that to have that kind of power, I needed to be very, very rich. So I devoted the last seven years of my life to making money—so that if I ever met someone who could be the sun, the moon and the stars of my heart, I'd be ready. But I don't argue the point with Iris. It's enough that she loves it.

"Your DJ has great taste. This is fantastic music," she says.

I pull back to study her face. "Really?"

"What? You don't think I listen to music by people who haven't been dead for at least five decades?"

"Well...yeah."

"Ha! I do, just not that often. Besides, you can't dance to Rachmaninoff."

Laughing with relief and satisfaction, I take everyone to the

VIP section I've reserved on the second level. Yuna doesn't even bother to order a drink. "We gotta get out on the floor!" she says.

"You're just going to skip drinking?" Julie asks, her tone a bit too pointed.

"Later. I don't need alcohol to dance like a rock star," Yuna says. "Come on!" She pulls at Iris's arm.

Mr. Kim says something to her in Korean, and she shakes her head, gesturing at him to stay seated. The poor man looks supremely uncomfortable, although he's doing his best to hide it. He's probably not used to loud music.

"Drinks are on the house," I tell him as Iris drags me out as well.

Julie stays behind. Bobbi follows us, affecting a bored clubber face. But her eyes are watchful.

The second we're on the dance floor, Yuna throws herself into the music. She's a wild dancer—not great but not giving much of a damn as she flings her arms and hair about. A couple of guys join her, and they seem to be having fun. Once I'm satisfied they aren't going to try anything with her, I dance with Iris.

Her movements aren't out of control like Yuna, but she's a fabulous dancer, matching my moves beat for beat. Her body gyrates, her arms raised above her head. She dances in front of me, making sure she's grinding against me.

My blood runs hot, and the dance starts to feel more like foreplay.

After a few loud songs, she puts her arms around my neck and says, "I'm thirsty. Drink?"

I pull her closer and lead her to one of the three bars. This one's in the back, in one of the quieter parts of the club. She gets a cranberry vodka, and I order scotch, neat.

"I had no idea a classical pianist could dance so well," I say.

She giggles. "We aren't that stuffy. Besides, the music's easy to move to. Some music's impossible to dance to." She shimmies closer, rubbing her belly against my cock. "Mmm. You're hard."

"Tease." I brush my mouth against hers, enjoying her light mood.

She gives me a blinding smile. "If I can't tease you, who can I tease?" She knocks back half her drink. "I love it that you're helping people. It's amazing."

"Me? Helping?" I ask, genuinely shocked and confused. What I do is make money. "Are you really working for Elizabeth's foundation? The place that feeds millions of hungry kids and save kittens?"

"Not everyone should go out and save kittens. Some kittens want to have fun. Decompress after a long week at work. Why should everything be about meeting the most basic needs?"

She's looking up at me like I'm some kind of fucking hero, and I feel taller and stronger than a five-hundred-year-old oak. If we weren't at Z, I'd toss her over my shoulder and carry her off to bed. Hell, I might still do that. My office is private.

Somebody slaps me hard on the shoulder. "Hey, bro!"

I turn and see Harry's familiar face on my left.

Iris cranes her neck toward my younger brother. *God damn it.* Harry doesn't know anything about Iris, and the last thing I need is him letting something slip in front of her.

On the other hand, there's no graceful way to avoid this meeting either. *Damn it, damn it, damn it.*

I fist-bump with Harry, doing my best to shield Iris's face from his view. Just my damn luck she's right above the recessed light, which is illuminating her perfectly for Harry.

"I thought I was seeing things. You almost never enjoy your own club." Then Harry finally looks at Iris, pulled tightly against my body. "Oh, I see, you're here to show off."

I know the moment he makes out Iris's face. His eyes bug out, and his jaw goes slack.

"Holy shit, you're..." He looks up at me. "She looks just like—"

Fuck! No! "Harry, you asshole," I say, looping an arm around his neck and putting him in a headlock. *Sorry, kid.* "You think I forgot you owe me money?"

"What? What money?" he rasps.

I choke him, cutting him off. "You thought my jet was free?" I turn to Iris. "This is my little brother. Let me go deal with him. I'll be right back."

"Um...okay," she says, shooting us a curious look.

I drag Harry away. He's strong, but not strong enough to resist me. Besides, I have extra motivation.

I pull him through a corridor in the back until we reach my office. I finally let him go, shutting the door behind us.

"What the fuck, man?" Harry says, straightening and rubbing his neck. "What was that about?"

My heart is still hammering from panic. "Stopping you from making a big mistake."

"But that girl! She's a *dead ringer* for Ivy. Is she the girl in the wine fight video?"

I nod, miserable and annoyed. That damn video! Now I have to figure out a way to make Harry not talk too much. Which means getting another person to lie to maintain the façade I've created. I'm going to hell for this.

He frowns. "And the pianist in that video I showed you after you got me from LAX?"

"Yes," I say, hating that Harry is putting things together so quickly. But he isn't stupid. Just lazy.

"Holy shit. And I told Edgar you were going crazy again." He drags both hands through his hair, pacing. "But...dude. The resemblance is *freaky*. I mean, how the hell can two people look that much alike?"

There's no way to hide this. He knows her too well. He practically grew up with her since she was a little girl. A couple of minutes in her presence, he'll put it together. "Because she is Ivy."

He stares at me.

I go to my liquor cabinet and pull out a bottle of whiskey. I pour both of us a finger. I don't want to drag Harry into my problems, but now that he's seen Iris, he's not going to shut up about it until he gets some answers. "She didn't die."

"What? Who didn't die?" Harry asks, accepting the drink.

I glare at him, annoyed he's suddenly acting like his IQ dropped fifty points. "Who are we talking about? Ivy, of course."

He raises a hand. "Wait a minute. You really, no bullshit, think she's Ivy?"

I nod.

"Tony, I know you're still struggling to accept that she's gone, but this is too much. We cremated her, remember? You were there."

"We cremated a young girl. But it wasn't Ivy."

"Huh?"

I knock back my drink. This is the kind of conversation that requires a case of whiskey, except I can't imbibe like that. "The body in the Lexus wasn't her." And I tell him the gist of what I know.

He stares at me like I'm high. "So Sam's been hiding her all this time?"

I nod, anger stirring again.

"Why didn't she try to escape? Call someone? I mean... What the hell?" His face crumbles. "She knows I wouldn't turn my back on her, doesn't she? And she was in love with you. Why...?" He clenches his hair, pacing, the drink forgotten.

"She would have if she remembered us." Not that she would have called me after that shit I told her at Cajun Milan. But Harry is different.

Harry turns, his hands still fisting his hair. "Huh?"

I don't have the heart to mock his *huhs*, the way I might if circumstances were different. "She had a brain injury serious enough to put her in a coma for a year. She doesn't remember her time in Tempérane. She thinks she's Sam's poor little relative."

"What the fuck?" He lets go of his hair. "She doesn't even know who she is?"

I shake my head. "She remembers some, but not much. She didn't know she went to Curtis."

"She loved that school!"

Looking away, I pour another drink. Guilt tightens its vicious grip on me. If Harry had found her first...things would've gone very differently. He would've told her everything from the beginning.

"Did you tell her about everything? You know, Mom, Dad, me, you...the rest."

I knock my drink back fast. "No."

"Why the hell not?"

"Because she thinks she's Iris Smith now, and it's safer for her that way." And if possible, I don't ever want her to know what I did to break her heart back then.

It wasn't just that I was immature. If it weren't for me being stupid back then, she wouldn't have been in Tempérane that night at all. She would've been in L.A. with me. Then none of the ensuing clusterfuck would've happened.

She wouldn't have been robbed of nine years of her life.

It's the conclusion I've been avoiding all this time, except it's there—an old, festering wound you try to ignore, hoping it'll resolve itself. But I know it'll never go away. The sense of guilt and apprehension hounding me are proof of that.

"How is it safer?" Harry demands.

"Why do you think there was a body? Somebody was supposed to die that night—whether that was Ivy or not...who knows?"

A fast calculation is taking place in his head. "You think... somebody tried to *kill* her?"

"Maybe," I say, even though I'm almost certain. "Sam tried to drown her not too long ago. I'm not willing to risk anything."

"Shit." Harry plops into a chair. "God damn it. Sam has to be the bad guy. He's gotta be dirty."

"Obviously. Even if I discount what he's done to Ivy, he's been manipulating Mother somehow." And Margot Blackwood is not a woman who easily bends to someone else's will.

Harry snaps his head up. "Wait. I forgot to tell you, but she's not the only one."

I lean forward, desperate for any additional clue, no matter how small. "What do you mean?"

"Caleb Wentworth visited soon after her call with Sam. The one I overheard and got kicked out over."

Caleb. The brute I saved Ivy from at a stupid party way back when. I haven't heard that name since I left Tempérane. What I did to Jamie Thornton I should've done to Caleb, but didn't. "What the hell did he want?"

"To see Mom. I don't know about what exactly, but I heard both of them yelling, and Sam's name was in there a few times."

"Who brought it up?"

"Mom, I think. I don't know for sure, though. She sounded almost hysterical. She even threw a vase."

I stare at Harry, speechless. The only time I've ever seen her lash out like that is when Katherine died. "That's...crazy."

"I know, right?" Harry rubs his eyebrows. "Thinking back on it, she was more upset about me seeing Caleb than overhearing her talk with Sam."

I push his drink in his direction. Finally remembering it, he gulps it down with a scowl.

I take some more whiskey. Mother's argument with Caleb makes even less sense. If she needed to speak to somebody from his family, his mother is the most logical choice. And I don't think the Wentworths are investing with Sam. Otherwise Jill would've mentioned it when she gave me her status report. If Caleb is involved with Sam's blackmail...

I shake my head. It doesn't make sense. That punk has nothing on Mother. And even if he did, he's a selfish bastard. He would've helped himself, not Sam.

"Anyway... What do you want me to do with Ivy? We're bound to run into each other again, and I don't want you putting me in another headlock."

"Just call her Iris for now," I say, hating that I'm dragging Harry into my deception. "And you can't let her know you know her from before."

He holds out his glass, and I pour him an extra finger. He takes a quick swallow. "Doesn't it bother you, though? You're calling her by a name that isn't even hers."

Spoken like a kid who's never been given a second shot. "Who cares what name she uses? I have another chance with her. That's all that matters."

29

IRIS

"Who was that cutie, and why is Tony dragging him away?" Yuna shouts in my ear. We're sort of swaying to the music, but we aren't dancing anymore. People around us are, though.

"His brother. Sounds like he owes Tony money or something." I wish Tony would have introduced us before dragging him away. Although Tony knows Sam and Marty—the only two people related to me—I haven't met anyone from his family, extended or otherwise. As a matter of fact, I don't remember him ever even talking about his family. Does he not want me to know about them? Or is what Marty said the truth? That Tony's really been disowned?

"Ooh, he's in trouble. In my family, if you owe and don't pay up..." She runs a finger across her neck.

"I thought your family was in a respectable business." I looked up the Hae Min Group. It's as legitimate as other big Korean conglomerates like Samsung or LG.

"Of course it's all proper. I mean figuratively." Yuna looks down at her feet. "I'm getting tired. Mind if we go sit down for a bit?"

"Sure."

A few guys try to get us to join them as we slice through the crowd. As if. None of them can measure up to Tony. A couple of them reach out to grab at me, but Bobbi cuts them off with her body. The look that she gives them makes them step back.

Wow. I totally need to learn that skill.

"Ladies," Bobbi says, herding us toward our table on the second-level balcony. The noise level is about a hundred decibels lower here.

"I'm going to the little sopranos room. You go ahead," Yuna says.

I glance back and see a long line snaking toward the ladies' room. "Good luck."

I go to our table with Bobbi. I ask the server to give me whatever's Tony's favorite. I'm curious what he likes to drink when he's out. He had something amber-colored at the bar, but I didn't catch the name. Mr. Kim hasn't touched anything except a bottle of water in front of him. Julie signals for another drink, her mouth set in a mulish line.

"You don't like the club?" I ask, sidling closer so we don't have to yell so much.

"It's fine."

"You aren't dancing or having fun. It isn't like you." Julie *adores* clubbing. She did her best to drag me out every time we spent any time together overseas. Besides, if she's upset with Yuna, she's been holding it in for way too long. She's more the type to just talk stuff out, even if it creates a big mess, than pretend everything's fine.

She looks over her shoulder, toward the bathroom, then turns back to me. "It's Yuna. She just...bothers me."

"She does?" I blink, trying to remember what Yuna might've done or said that could've upset Julie. "Why?"

"Just... I don't know. Arrogant and spoiled." She slumps.

"Did she say something to upset you? If she did, it's probably just some cultural miscommunication." It's a flimsy excuse. Yuna speaks English perfectly, and she isn't personally weird. At least, I haven't gotten any odd vibes from her. As far as I know, Tony hasn't either. Yuna doesn't seem to have any problem with Julie, and I want the two of them to get along. I have so few friends, I want to be able to keep and hang out with all of them without making one or another feel bad.

Julie cocks an eyebrow. "Really?"

"She's nice if you get to know her, and doesn't sugarcoat anything or fawn over you. What you see is what you get. Just give her a chance."

My attempts only seem to upset Julie more. She starts to cross her arms, only to be interrupted when the server returns with our drinks. She grabs hers and gulps down half of it.

"I don't know. I'm not a music prodigy, and didn't grow up with such power and influence," Julie says.

"Did Yuna say that?" I ask, stunned Julie feels this way.

"Didn't have to. I can see it in her eyes."

What the hell? Julie may not be a prodigy, but she's a gifted pianist. And it isn't like her family's poor. The Pearces are old money and well connected. I don't understand why she suddenly has this inferiority complex with Yuna. Honestly, I'm the one who doesn't measure up. I'm a poor relation to a man who's a manipulative jerk. Oh, and I forgot my cousin, who thinks I'm too ugly to be raped. Except for my talent with the piano, I have nothing—no money, no fame. The crazy wine fight video doesn't count.

Frustrated with Julie's weird attitude, I knock back the drink. A fireball explodes in my mouth and nose, and I start coughing hard.

I swear I asked for Tony's favorite, not napalm.

A soothing hand pats my back, while I gasp and sputter. "Hey, you okay?"

I look up, and reality seems to warp. But I'm not seeing things. It is...*the* Ryder Reed. One of the hottest and biggest stars in Hollywood.

Patting my back.

Oh. My. God.

My brain quits working. Even the coughing stops. He's even more stunning the second time around, with those dark good looks and arresting blue eyes. Unlike Audrey Duff, he actually looks better in person than on screen. Which is unbelievable.

And he's looking at me expectantly.

"Hi," I squeak.

"Are you okay?"

Oh. My brain finally starts kicking in. "Yes. I'm fine. This new drink..." I gesture at the liquid. "Wow."

"What is it?"

"It, um... Actually, I don't know. Tony's favorite."

Ryder's lips twitch. "Whiskey can be hard the first time." He gestures at the booth. "Do you mind?"

Why is he even asking? Julie and I immediately scoot away to make room for Ryder. Julie is staring like he's a divine blessing.

"Uh, so... I'm Julie," she says, extending a hand.

He shakes it. "Hey. Ryder."

She turns bright red, a stupid smile on her face. "Oh my God. You're, like, *the* hottest."

"Thanks." A megawatt smile, and Julie becomes a puddle. "Great to meet you." He turns to me. "Anthony around?"

"He was here, but he's gone to talk with his brother."

"Okay. Don't know if he relayed the apology, but I'm really sorry about what happened at the restaurant. I ruined what should've been a nice date."

"It's okay. It wasn't your fault." I mean that. That's the night Tony and I took things to the next level and finally slept together. I'm not sure if it would've happened if Audrey hadn't thrown wine at me. Ironic, since she was doing it to get me away from Tony.

"I'm also sorry Audrey harassed you at work."

"How did you know about that?" Then the purpose of her visit pops into my head...along with a possibility. "Did she give you a paper saying I'm cool with her? Like, with my signature on it?"

"Yeah."

"Oh, she did *not!*" If she were here, I might throw what's left of my whiskey in *her* face. "I never signed anything!"

"I know you didn't. Audrey forgot Elizabeth is my sister."

That's right. Sometimes I forget that too. Ryder's got dark looks and muscles, while Elizabeth is a delicate blonde. "Thanks for checking. And not letting her use me or you."

He searches my face as though he can't decide if I'm being truthful. Then, finally, he smiles. Not a smile designed to turn women stupid, but, I suspect, a genuine one reserved for people he's interacting warmly with. "I'm—"

"What the fuck are you doing here?"

Tony is standing over us, his face white with anger. *Oh no.* Why is he so upset? Does he still blame Ryder for what Audrey did? Tony was furious at the restaurant. The last thing I need is a scene ruining our night out.

"Tony, it's okay," I say.

Intense hostility continues to pour off him. I'm certain if Julie and I weren't here, he'd be flipping the table and breaking Ryder's nose.

"Just checking up on your girl while waiting for you to show," Ryder says.

"She doesn't need your concern," Tony says. "Nobody wants you here."

Ryder leans back. "Really? Why don't you ask Iris? Or her friend here?"

Crap. Why does he have to drag me and Julie into this? I shake my head slightly at Julie, but she only has eyes for Ryder.

"Of course he's welcome to join us," she says. "Isn't he, Iris?"

Et tu, Julie? My gaze ping-pongs among the three. I hate to have to choose sides. But what Tony wants means more than some Hollywood actor. If Julie wants to hang out with Ryder, she can do that away from us. "I think it's best if you leave," I say to Ryder. "It's my night out with my friends and Tony." There. That subtle emphasis on "friends" should do it.

"You want *me* to *leave?*" The smile he shoots me this time is dialed into turn-women-stupid territory. Then he gives me a wink and chuckles, like we're in on some joke together. "Preposterous."

I stare in stupefaction. The man's utterly shameless. Or deluded. Or can't imagine why any woman wouldn't want to be his friend.

Okay, fine, under any other circumstances, I'd be ecstatic to have him sitting at my table. But not even the hottest Hollywood actor can measure up to what I feel for Tony.

"Ryder, with me. Now," Tony says between clenched teeth.

Ryder shrugs, an *Oh well, ladies* pity shrug, stands up and follows Tony away. I watch them leave, worrying. Hopefully they have enough sense to talk things out in private without resorting to violence. We don't need another YouTube video.

Once they're gone, the tension in the area suddenly drops. I let out a long breath, a hand over my eyes.

"So I guess I can sit now?"

I drop my palm and look up to see the brother Tony dragged away earlier. "Sure. Do take a seat...unless Tony told you to go away."

He grins. "He didn't." He plops down next to me.

I study him in the dim light. Something about him seems very familiar, although I can't quite pinpoint what. Is it his physical appearance? He's leaner than Tony, but the facial features are very similar—the same thin-bladed nose, the shape of his mouth, the high cheekbones. They also share the same dark hair, although Harry's eyes are blue.

"Do I have something on my face?"

"Huh? No! I'm, uh... It's just that you look a lot like Tony."

"Yeah. He and I took after our mother." He watches me intently. Expectantly.

Except I'm not sure what he wants me to say. So I opt for flattery. "She must be beautiful."

He looks away, deflating slightly. "So people say."

Oh crap. Did I say something I shouldn't have? As far as I know, Tony's mother hasn't passed away. I read a few articles about Tony and his family earlier when Julie and Byron reacted so oddly about him, and there was nothing about his parents being dead. But maybe she's sick or... "I'm sorry if I said something to upset you." I don't know how I could've caused him distress, but I feel bad about it anyway, especially if I touched a sensitive spot.

Propping his elbow in his knee, he looks at me for a moment. "I don't understand how..." He blows out a breath.

Now I'm feeling worse. His mother is definitely a touchy subject. I'm not sure why calling her beautiful was upsetting, but maybe she got into an accident and is horribly scarred or something. How do I fix this?

Yuna shows up, breaking the awkwardness. "Ugh, that line! It's like everyone in the club had to pee at the same time," she says, plopping down between me and Julie, where Ryder was sitting. "So what did I miss?"

"Oh my God, you're going to want to kill yourself when you hear!" Julie becomes extra animated, but I don't like the uncharacteristic edge of gleeful malice to her excitement. "You just missed Ry—"

"Nothing." I'm not letting Julie make Yuna feel bad. And given Tony's mood, Ryder isn't coming back to join us. "You didn't miss anything. Now, let's order some drinks."

30

ANTHONY

Back to my office again. This time with Ryder. I kick the door shut behind us and turn to face him. "All right, you stalker. Let's hear it."

"I wasn't stalking you. I just happened to be here."

"Right." He needs to do better if he wants me to believe him. I get bimonthly lists of all the celebs who visit my clubs from my manager. Ryder's name hasn't on them for a long, long time. "You just happened by. Alone."

"No. Elliot and Lucas came with me."

I snort at the mention of his twin brothers. I don't have to be told to know he probably dragged them here, especially Lucas. I heard he went reclusive after an accident permanently scarred his previously pretty face. And the Elliot I know prefers strip joints to clubs like Z.

"Damn it, I want to fix things with you. Is that too much to ask?" Ryder says.

Yes, because I don't want to, and I don't understand why you should. "Why do you care? It isn't like it's the first time you've made a spectacle of some social catastrophe."

He flushes. "I told you I didn't know. I can't control Audrey. The woman's unhinged enough to stage a 'suicide' over you dumping her."

At least he isn't dumb enough to believe Audrey really meant it. Maybe there's hope for him after all. "If you're really serious, have Elizabeth cut all ties with Byron Pearce."

"Done," he says immediately.

"Just like that?" I cock an eyebrow, surprised and curious as to why he's so confident he can get it done. Elizabeth can be more stubborn than a donkey.

"She's been wanting us to reconcile. If it'll help, she'll do it."

"What about the Pearce money?" The bastard must've offered a handsome sum to entice Elizabeth.

"What about it? She can flutter her eyelashes and Dominic will hand over however much she needs, no questions asked."

True enough. It's no secret her husband is totally devoted to her, and the man is filthy rich.

"I never meant to hurt you with Lauren, Tony." Ryder ends with the nickname I haven't allowed him to use in the last seven years.

It sounds familiar and painful. He was my best friend since I was exiled to Europe when I was twelve. We connected immediately and did all sorts of things together. Double dates. Crazy stunts at ski resorts, memories of which raise the hair on the back of my nape with horror now. A couple of summers I spent with him and his grandfather in Tuscany.

Ryder is the one who helped me see I was fucking things up with Ivy. He's the one who asked me to come to L.A. to regroup after she "died." He... I would've given my life for him until the day I found out he'd been fucking Lauren behind my back.

Except he swore—still swears—he didn't know she was my girl.

I study him. He seems sincere. But he's a great actor. People think he's made his fame solely on looks, but nobody becomes a star this big without real talent and brains.

Let's see what's really going on. "Paige isn't your typical Hollywood beauty. Everyone says she won't last long." His wife isn't a size-zero model. Paige has lots of curves and looks like a regular, everyday American woman. And the Internet trolls loathe her for snagging Ryder Reed.

Ryder's face twists. "Shut the fuck up. My wife's awesome."

The skin around his eyes has gone tight, and he's genuinely pissed off at the slur against his wife. If he weren't feeling so guilty about what happened between us, he might be kicking my ass. Or trying, anyway.

And just like that, I know he means everything he just told me. The tight knot I've been carrying for over half a decade loosens a bit. I start for the liquor cabinet to get the whiskey, then realize I left it on the desk when I was talking with Harry. "She *is* awesome. She can certainly do better than you."

Ryder shoots me a barely mollified look. "Which is why I'm trying to be a better man every day."

I pour a whiskey and hand it to him. He eyes the drink like it's a trick. "This mean what I think it means?"

"Which is what?"

"I'm hoping it means you're going to at least consider forgiving me."

All he's asking is for a chance. He doesn't need to go to this length. He's rich, well connected and powerful in Hollywood. My forgiveness of him, or lack thereof, won't make a particle of difference in his life and continued success.

But perverse side of me whispers that maybe my forgiveness does matter. And if I withhold it, he's going to suffer. Shouldn't he suffer for what he did? Feel like shit for the rest of his life?

I finally understand how Mother must've felt when I crawled back home begging for absolution. No wonder she told me she didn't even want me dead. She said it was because she didn't want me to be with Katherine in the afterlife. But maybe she also didn't want my torment to end so quickly and easily.

"Why are you doing this, really?" I ask. "Is Paige making you?"

He shakes his head. "I've always felt guilty about Lauren. She lied to me and used me, but I should've seen something wasn't right. I was too young and high on success and fame to understand how much you were suffering after you lost Ivy. Which makes me a shitty friend, because I asked you to come out, ostensibly to support you. But until I met Paige, I didn't really understand how bad it was for you. I mean, I sort of understood in my head. But I didn't really *get it*. Then I finally fell in love, and it was like...whoa. If anything ever happened to Paige, I don't know what I'd do. That's when I really got it. How monumentally I had screwed up." He sighs heavily. "I just want a chance to make things right."

It's a humble plea. Sincere. It reminds me of my efforts to seek forgiveness from my mother. She didn't want to give it to me. Nor did she want to tell me what I needed to do to fix things. With the memory comes the crushing despair I felt. It's as though she's just lobbed more hurtful words my way.

Although I understand how Mother felt, I also know exactly how I felt all those years. The weight of the guilt I carried. The struggle and fumbling. It's one of the reasons why I handled things so badly between me and Ivy.

Who am I to deny Ryder a chance to fix things? It would be more than hypocritical.

The real source of my anger with Ryder is from the fact that I believed he stole Lauren from me, knowing how she was just like Ivy. Except I was the only one who thought she was like Ivy. Even Edgar was appalled when he found out what happened, because he couldn't believe how blind and stupid I'd been.

"I believe you."

His mouth parts, and he blinks. If I were in better mood, I'd be pointing and laughing at his dumbass expression.

"What? You want me to take it back?"

He snaps his mouth shut. "No! I just... I thought you'd make me jump through, like, hoops of fire first."

I laugh dryly. If he'd made the same plea just a few months ago, before I met Iris again, I might have. "I miss my old best friend. But don't expect everything to be like before. There's going to be some adjustment."

"Obviously. Thanks anyway. That's all I'm asking."

We clink glasses and drink our whiskey.

"You know I really prefer scotch, right?" he asks after finishing his glass.

I almost roll my eyes. It's just like him to whine about the drink offered. Despite what I said about some adjustment needed, it's like we've never had the last seven years of estrangement. "Shut up and enjoy what I give you. And if you want, you can join us."

"Really?"

"I'm sure it'll make the girls' night."

"More like their decade."

I laugh, this time with genuine humor. But before we go, I tell him about the connection between Ivy and Iris, and swear him to secrecy. "You can't tell Paige, either."

"Dude. I hate keeping secrets from her," Ryder says.

"I get that. But somebody out there tried to kill Iris once already, and Sam tried to drown her. How would you feel if Paige was in danger?"

Ryder pales, then nods grimly. "All right."

We grab Ryder's brothers, Elliot and Lucas, go join everyone and happily subject ourselves to hours of squealing and star-struck faces for the rest of the evening.

31

IRIS

"I WANT TO KNOW WHAT MAGIC YOU PULLED," I SAY AS TONY and I walk into our foyer.

"Magic?"

"*Ryder Reed* just showing up? And joining us?" I poke Tony in the side. "You know that's crazy, right?"

"He just happened to be there. And we worked out some issues between us."

"I'm glad. He seems like a nice person." I was dazzled by his fame and the Hollywood glamour, but once that wore off, it was obvious he's just a guy who happens to be extraordinarily handsome and makes a lot of money off his work. There's such a carefree and easygoing nature to him that I think it'll be good for Tony to hang out with him to have some of that rub off. Tony's too serious at times.

I want to play the "Torrent" étude a few times before going to bed. I know how much ground I lose when I don't keep up. I reach for the digital piano, since it's late and I figure Tony wants some peace and quiet after the loud club, but he shakes his head. "Play on the Steinway."

"Are you sure?"

He nods, sprawling on a couch that faces the piano.

"I'm going to practice 'Torrent,' so it's going to be sort of loud."

"I don't mind. I love listening to you."

"If you say so." I warm up briefly, then let my fingers fly along the rapid notes of the Chopin étude. Something about the way I'm playing the piece is bugging me. At around the later part, I seem to lose steam. Ugh. Ridiculous. The music is barely two minutes long, even though it has more notes to hit than most other compositions that short.

I practice the part over and over until I'm satisfied that it has sufficient power and drive to push the piece to the climactic finale.

"Stunning. Maybe you'll be another Pollini."

A thrill runs through me, and I laugh. "No, I won't. He's totally sublime, and I used to listen to his Chopin recordings all the time, hoping I could play like him. But Pollini is Pollini, and I'm me. I want people to listen to me because I'm awesome in my own way, not because I'm an imitation of Pollini."

The smile I receive for that is full of warmth and pride. I'm bursting with happiness and love.

I stop, blinking. The other person was a man. I'm certain of that, but it wasn't Sam or Marty. They probably think Pollini is some kind of Italian food. His voice is familiar, but sort of muddled...and his face is hazy too. Like most of it is hidden in a blinding light.

Who was it? Maybe another instructor from Curtis?

Impossible. Unless I'm mistaken, I had my head in his lap. I'm sure I didn't do anything like that with one of my teachers. *Did I?*

Or maybe I did. I was in love with whoever it was. I'm sure about that. Maybe if I'd remembered it earlier, I might not have recognized the feeling. But it's the same thing I feel for Tony. Did the man in my past love me back? Was I told I died, just like Yuna? Did he cry? Did he despair?

What about him that made me fall in love back then? Can I find him? Let him know I didn't die and Sam lied?

I shake my head. What's the point of trying to find him? It's been so long. He most likely moved on. Maybe even got married and now has kids, a minivan, dogs and a white picket fence. Living the dream.

People don't dwell on the dead forever. The living go on living, no matter how much it hurts. I did too, after learning my parents died.

Me showing up on his doorstep would only be awkward. Weird. And...

My gaze drifts to Tony. Slowly I stand and kneel in front of the couch where he's sprawled with his eyes closed. He's breathing deeply and quietly. He must've been exhausted to sleep through the "Torrent" étude.

I study his face. The bold slash of the straight, dark eyebrows. The set of his eyes. The straight blade of a nose. The beautiful mouth. I bring to mind the way his brilliant green eyes light up at the sight of me. The way his voice deepens, gains a raspy edge when he's feeling a particularly strong emotion or is going crazy wanting me.

And my heart is aching, full of love for this magnificent man who never puts up a shield between us. I've seen how cool and controlled he is around other people. Being so vulnerable to me can't be easy for him, but he does it anyway to show me how much I mean to him.

I run my fingertips gently across his brows. He stirs, blinks, then smiles at me. "Finished?"

"Yes." I kiss him. "Let's go to bed."

He picks me up and carries me up to our bedroom.

The man in my memory is one chapter of my life I don't need to recall. I have Tony. He's my present...and future. And I don't need anyone else.

32

IRIS

THE NEXT COUPLE OF WEEKS ARE SUPER BUSY AT THE foundation. The first phase of the music program finished a few days ago. Byron pulled out for some reason, although Elizabeth told me he was never planning to go beyond this point. The explanation doesn't make sense. What's the point of sponsoring a program only a quarter of the way? But I can't get any explanation from Byron either. He isn't returning my texts, which isn't like him. I can't decide if he's angry with me for some reason or he's too embarrassed to offer a reason for quitting the project early.

I text Julie to check up on Byron. She won't say anything except her brother's under a lot of pressure and stress. I can't help but feel like maybe I'm to blame for that. Was the project too much for him? Is that why he decided to cut his losses and quit?

Thankfully, Ryder is stepping up to sponsor the rest of it. In a way, I think it may work out for the best. As maybe the world's biggest movie star, he has a huge platform. When he talks, people notice, and it's going to help bring attention to the importance of music in children's lives, and how we're trying to give them another way to express themselves and find solace and comfort that goes beyond just food and shelter.

After lunch, I go through the mail like always. Elizabeth has another huge stack of letters. I sort them by projects and urgency. Then I see a padded white envelope at the bottom. It's not big and must've been hand-delivered by a courier. It merely says "Iris Smith," no address.

I tap the perforated edge and grin. Is this a secret gift from Tony? He surprises me with presents from time to time. The last one was a huge box of German chocolates, which I split with everyone in the office. Except Tolyan, but only because he said he doesn't like chocolate. The more I get to know him, the more I'm convinced he's inhuman.

Anticipation simmering, I rip the bag open. Some blue fabric spills out. I pick it up, shake it out...and drop it like anthrax when I realize what it is.

A sleeveless blue dress. *Exactly like the one the girl in the car in my memory was wearing.*

My hands shake, and I clench them. I never told anybody, not even Tony, exactly what she was wearing. How could this have been sent specifically to me?

I see a note on the floor. I snatch it up and read it.

If you want to talk about the dress, meet me at the Starbucks two blocks from your office at 2 today. Come alone or I'm not telling you shit.

−Sam

Oh my God. I cover my mouth with a hand as a sick, bitter taste hits the back of my throat. Of course he'd know. He pulled me out of the water.

I don't want to see him alone, especially after what he tried to pull last time. But this dress isn't something I can ignore. If he has it, he probably knows who the girl was, too.

What to do?

I press my knuckles against my lips and drum my fingers on the desk, fear burning through me. The Starbucks near the office is usually very busy. He can't do anything there without having witnesses. And I really want to know about the girl and what happened. There's no guarantee he's going to tell me the whole truth, but he might drop enough clues for me to remember who she is.

There are three fire exits on the floor. I can pretend to get some coffee and maybe sneak away. In movies, it looks super easy to lose your bodyguard. But...

Don't be stupid and go alone. Sam is a sneaky man. He lied to Elizabeth to get her to send me his way. He could have some other trap set to get me.

Bobbi's here to protect me, even though she'd rather bake cakes and make babies. Tony's trusting me to cooperate. His stark white face after what happened to me at Sam's house flashes through my mind. If I snuck away and put myself in danger, I'd be betraying his trust.

I look at the note again. Sam probably doesn't know I have Bobbi. It isn't something I've been advertising, and people who know aren't on speaking terms with him.

I go to the vestibule, where Bobbi's reading something on her phone. "Can I talk to you?" I ask.

"Sure." She puts her phone away. "What is it?"

"This way." I take her to an empty meeting room. After closing the door, I tell her about the note from Sam without mentioning the dress.

"My advice? Ignore him," she says.

She's probably right. But my instinct is telling me the risk will be worth it if he tells me who the girl is. Byron said hundreds of thousands of women matching the description I gave him go missing every year. Seeing Sam is the most efficient way to narrow that down. "I can't. I need some answers." Then something else occurs to me. Ugh. I should've asked her this before telling her. "And you can't tell Tony. It's only going to upset him." *An understatement.* He'll literally kill Sam if he knows.

Bobbi cocks an eyebrow, regarding me silently.

My nerves start to fray. I lick dry lips. "You're supposed to be my bodyguard, not his spy. I don't want to be stupid and sneak around and make your job that much harder. But if you don't respect my privacy, I won't have a choice."

"You sound just like that worthless pretty boy. I thought you meant it when you defended me."

Pretty boy? Oh... Byron. I flush over my hypocrisy, but this is important. "I didn't think you were going around telling Tony everything, but there's nothing stopping you from telling him if he asks."

"You mean aside from the NDA?"

"He's the one paying you, not me."

She gives me a flat stare. "And I have my own code. Part of that being, I don't rat on clients I'm guarding. If Tony wants to spy on you, he needs to hire a PI, because that isn't my job."

Oh shit. *She's insulted.* I wish I could go back and pull the foot out of my mouth. "I'm sorry. I didn't mean to question your professional ethics."

She considers, then finally nods. "We have an hour before the appointment. Let me go scout the area. If everything looks okay, I'll text you and pick you up outside the building here. Don't act like you know me. Walk straight to Starbucks. I'm going to follow you, my nose buried in my phone. At the store, you need to let me grab a drink first, then go talk to this Peacher guy. If it looks like he's trying to intimidate you or harass you, all bets are off, and I'm going to beat the shit out of him."

Bobbi going berserk on Sam will create another viral video for sure. Half the people in the place are going to be on their phones. But from the flinty glint in her eye, I know this is the best offer I'm going to get. "Okay."

I go back to my desk and try to work. It's impossible to focus. I make three typos on an executive memo and glare at the monitor. I do not make typos. My fingers are too precise for that. But my mind's not on the task.

Finally, my phone buzzes.

All clear.

At five to two, I leave the office. As soon as I hit the street,

Bobbi's half a step behind, a Bluetooth headset jammed in her ear and speaking Spanish. Her voice is dulcet, as though she's talking to a lover. To anybody who's looking, she and I are strangers.

We step inside Starbucks. I spot Sam immediately. He's all the way in the back of the café, sitting at a booth. The impact of seeing him again is like a rumbling quake, sending chills down my spine. He's dressed in a button-down shirt and slacks, looking like any other well-heeled white-collar professional taking a break. Last time he attacked me, he was calm and almost superior. This time, he's hunched in his seat, his body language radiating tension. What is he planning now? Did I make a mistake by coming here?

Bobbi orders. Her cool, flat voice reminds me I'm not alone or helpless this time. She takes a small table for two by the door, and I grab a fresh cup of Americano and walk past her, my gut knotted tight.

I sit opposite Sam, pull the dress from my purse and throw it on the table. "How come you have this?"

He barely glances at it. His predatory gaze is on me. "Why wouldn't I have it? I was there."

My heart thunders, pumping anxious anticipation in rapid, erratic beats. "Where did it happen? Who is she? Is she alive?"

"First, make Anthony back off. He's fucking with my livelihood." Sam's voice has lost its usual oily smoothness. It's taut now. Ugly. "All my investors pulled out. Make him change their minds."

"That's ridiculous." Tony has influence, but this much? "How could he make *all* of them change their minds?"

"He's the one behind it."

"Oh, come on." I laugh. "You always say you can get whatever you want because you're rich. So how can Tony mess with your investors like that? By threatening them? Beating them? Maybe trying to drown them?"

The last one hits the mark. Sam flinches. "He's a devious man. You don't understand how devious."

"I think I understand enough." I'll never forget Sam's grim

face as he shoved me into the water. There wasn't a hint of human decency. "He's the one who saved me."

"Don't be so sure, Iris. You don't know anything. He has money, and with money comes connections. He's fucking with me. And I will not be a nobody. Never again!" He points a finger like it's all my fault.

"It isn't my problem if your investors don't want to do business with you." And I can't blame them if he's anything like this in his dealings with them. "You have money too. So use your connections to fight this if you want, but don't drag me into it. I'm not lifting a finger for you after what you've done."

"*I saved you, you ungrateful bitch!*"

Of course. It always comes to that. Him saving me. Keeping me alive on the life support. Not giving up on me while I was comatose for a year. "Yeah, and then tried to kill me. Don't expect me to be grateful anymore."

Red floods his pudgy face. His chin trembles.

"You dangled the dress and the girl in front of me, but all you really want to talk about is your money and company. Were you planning to tell me anything?"

"I will if you'll just agree to help! All you have to do is bat your pretty eyes and whisper in his ear that you'd appreciate it if he'd let me be. Men are exceptionally malleable after sex. By now, you should know how to give a decent blow job."

My lips curl with disgust. I hate Sam for even thinking about turning sex between me and Tony into some kind of transaction. I've never shared my body with Tony for anything other than love and mutual pleasure, and I'm never changing that, even if somebody holds a gun to my head. "I'm not going to become a whore for you. And we're done. Don't ever contact me again." I start to get up.

"You little bitch," he hisses. "You think you're so clean? We all have dirt we'd rather not show the world."

Is he implying he did something terrible on the night he pulled me out of the water? Bad enough that he'll murder to cover it up? "Is what why you tried to kill me?"

"No. That was a mistake." His gaze turns inward. "I panicked because you remembered her."

Suddenly, my belly's full of buzzing bees. There's more to his reaction than just my remembering the girl. He must've done something that night. Something bad. And he's not going to talk if he thinks I want to know everything. So I try a different tack. "I just want to know who she is."

He narrows his eyes, a feverish calculation taking place. If he changes the topic again, I might just jump across the table and strangle him. I'm so close to finding out what happened, filling in the blanks of my missing memories.

Finally, he heaves a long, heavy sigh. "She was your close friend."

My hands start shaking, and I wrap them around my coffee cup like it's an anchor. *Was. My God.* Tony warned me she might be dead, but I didn't want to believe him. I'd hoped she somehow survived. "What happened? Why were we in the water?"

The look gives me is full of pity and contempt. "You were driving. Speeding like all idiot teens do when they're feeling invincible. You lost control of the car on a bridge. It fell into the water. You made it. She didn't."

"Liar." I smack the table with my palm. A tiny bit of guilt unfurls in my chest. "How could she not make it when I did?" Sam has to be lying. Another attempt to manipulate me. Since gratitude isn't working anymore, he's going for shame.

"Because your seatbelt was working, but hers was broken. The cops later found out something was jammed in the buckle, and she shouldn't have been riding in the car with you, not when the seatbelt was broken. You felt awful about it. You knew it was broken, but didn't get it fixed right away. Didn't think it was a big deal. Your mother blamed herself for that, too. Said she should've made you take the car in to the dealer."

I start to deny it, then stop. Yuna mentioned I gave a ride to a guy...an oboe player. He broke my seatbelt buckle. Did this happen after? Somewhere near Curtis? Was the girl an aspiring musician?

Hot, bitter bile floods my mouth, and I quickly sip the coffee.

Self-loathing tears at me. My negligence cost a girl her life. Even though I don't remember who she is, she was a friend.

Sam continues, "You remember me pulling you out of the water, right?"

"Yes," I answer, my voice hoarse. My memory is a bit hazy around all the details, but I know he dove for me.

"Do you also remember I pulled you out first?"

I nod. Cold dread slices into my heart like a blade, waiting for Sam to twist...

"You know why? Because you were alive. She wasn't."

Icy pain blooms in my chest. "No."

"There was so much blood, it was obvious she was gone. The coroner said she hit her head and chest hard, and the trauma killed her. If she'd been strapped to her seat, maybe she would've lived."

Denial builds inside, but I can't voice it. I know he's telling the truth. Did I not see blood clouding around her head in my memory? If she weren't hurt, there wouldn't have been so much blood, would there? I feel sick to my stomach. I wish I hadn't had lunch, because it's churning hard.

"You killed your friend because you were too lazy to fix your car."

I stare in horror. I didn't know until now how mere words could cause so much pain, but each syllable out of Sam's mouth is slashing me like a machete. I breathe slowly. "How do I know you aren't lying?" I demand. Just because Yuna said my seatbelt was broken doesn't mean Sam's version is what really happened.

He shrugs. "I know you're beginning to regain your memories. It'd be stupid of me to lie now. So go ahead. Remember it all. Recall the expression on her mother's face when she confronted you about what happened."

The taunt sends a fresh wave of terror through me. I can't sense he's lying. He's too assured. Still... How can he be telling the truth? How could I have killed someone and not remember everything that happened?

Just what the hell kind of person was I back then?

"Why do you have her dress?" I ask, grasping for something, anything to discredit his story.

"Because her mother gave it to you, hoping you would never forget you murdered her daughter."

Oh my God. I bury my face in my hands, unable to face the world. I'm too ashamed, too guilty.

"Like I said, you aren't that clean, Iris. If you don't want your precious Anthony to stay ignorant of what a stupid bitch you are, you'll do as I say!"

I barely register Sam's hateful words through the roaring in my head. I stand unsteadily and rush to the bathroom, then throw up until there's nothing in my belly. Even then, I can't stop heaving.

The girl... I might as well have drowned her with my own hands. She died because of me. And her mother... I don't remember her at all. She must've hated me. I don't know how she could not. And for me to forget it all...and live like I've done nothing wrong...

I was so worried about not being broken anymore that I never thought about what I looked like whole. The idea that I could be so ugly never crossed my mind.

"You okay?" Bobbi says from behind me.

I wave her away. No need to watch me puke.

Did Tony know deep in his heart that my past could be less than pretty? Is that why he was so reluctant to help me find the girl in the car?

Finally, when my body stops trying to hurl up my intestines, I slowly rise to my feet. Bobbi's thankfully gone, and I'm alone in the bathroom. I splash cold water on my face. I look horrible in the mirror—pale and glassy-eyed. My lips are trembling, and I can't stop shaking.

What if Tony learns what kind of person I was? What if he thinks less of me?

I always thought he'd wake up one day and decide I was too broken for him. But now it seems like he might not want me because I'm just not good enough for the kind of devotion he has for me.

I drag myself to the table. Sam's gone. Bobbi's there, watching my things.

"You're pale," she says. "Are you all right?"

No. But I can't tell her. I can't explain to anybody why I'm not okay. "I'm fine."

"Did he threaten you?"

I start to shake my head, but my vision dims for a moment. So I grip the back of the seat instead. "No. Let's get back to the office." I pick up my purse, and we return together.

Not even the California sun can thaw my icy body. My teeth start to chatter, and I clench my jaw so Bobbi doesn't notice.

Once we're back in the office, I pull out my phone. It's an effort, since my hands are so clumsy. I text Byron. Given how he's been ignoring me, I don't know if he's going to ignore this too, but I have to try.

The girl I asked you to look for. Don't do it.

Instead of a text saying okay, I get a call. Maybe it's better to just talk to him. It's taking me too long to type.

"What's going on? Why the hell not? You said it was important," Byron demands angrily.

"It's not, okay? Just...don't argue with me," I plead, doing my best not to cry.

"Is Blackwood forcing you?"

A hysterical laugh bubbles in my raw throat. "No. It's all me. My decision." Because I'm a coward. I'm too scared to know everything now.

"Rizzy, talk to me. I know he's been manipulating you."

"I just did talk to you." Tears flow anyway. My jaw trembles. "I gotta go. Elizabeth needs me," I lie, since I can't tell him anything. I'm being a shitty friend.

At least you haven't killed him. That's an improvement, a voice that sounds just like Sam whispers in my head. I slowly bury my face in my hands.

What Sam said keeps circling in my mind. I try my best to push it aside, but can't. Now I wish I'd never gone to see him. Or tried to remember my past. Or tried to be unbroken.

"Iris, are you all right?"

I lift my head and look at Elizabeth.

She gasps, her hands resting on my shoulders. "Oh my goodness, what happened? You look awful." She places her palm on my forehead, then turns toward Tolyan. "Can you get Bobbi and ask her to take Iris home? She's burning up."

"No, I'm fine." If I act like nothing's wrong, nothing will be wrong. I'm going to pretend I never met Sam. Never heard what he said.

"Don't be absurd. Go home and rest. If you don't feel good, don't come in."

"But—"

"That's not a request, Iris. Go home. Have Tony nurse you back to health."

33

ANTHONY

Masako presents the ring on a tray covered in black velvet. It wasn't finished as quickly as I wanted, but I had trouble deciding between sapphires, rubies and yellow diamonds. I told her maybe we should create one of each—there are anniversaries to come. However, she informed me dryly that the pearls of such size and quality are very rare, and she doesn't have three if I want all of them to be exactly of the same size, luster and flawlessness.

So at the end, I chose rubies. The platinum band is gorgeous, with tiny diamonds embedded all around, set to look like twinkling stars. In the center sits the huge white pearl with a slightly pink tone. It glows as though emitting its own light. Tiny rubies surround the perfectly round stone like flames of the sun. Every gem is of exceptional quality, and as a whole, the ring is superbly elegant and beautiful.

Exactly what Iris deserves.

"What do you think?" Masako asks.

"Perfect." I hand her my plastic.

"Your fiancée will be the happiest woman in the world when you give her this ring. It's some of my best work."

I grin. I can just see Iris. She'll place her hands on her face in shocked delight, her eyes glinting with joy. Then she'll say yes to my proposal. I'll put the ring on her slim, delicate finger so everyone knows she's mine. All mine.

As one of Masako's clerks puts the ring in an elegant black box and wraps everything up, my heart is swelling with possibilities and exuberant happiness.

"A pleasure doing business with you, Mr. Blackwood," Masako says.

"You can call me Anthony," I say, taking the ring.

My phone rings. I check the number. Byron Fucking Pearce. What the hell does he want? Did he lose the succession war because of me? I almost snort. Hope he's not expecting sympathy.

"Blackwood," I say coldly.

TJ opens the car door, and I hop in. He starts driving back toward the office.

"You manipulative shit. What the fuck did you do?"

"That's a pretty broad question." If this were several days earlier, I might think he was mad about Ryder taking over the music initiative, but he should've gotten over that by now. "Be specific. I've been very productive since last time we saw each other."

"You don't deserve Rizzy. I don't give a shit what garbage you're filling her head with."

Ah. He's upset because he's finally realizing he has no chance as long as I'm around. I concede—only to myself—that I probably don't deserve Iris, but that doesn't mean I'm ever giving her up. Or putting up with abusive calls. "Too bad she's with me, not you. And never will be with you." Petty feelings of jealousy and hatred entwine in my heart, and I add, "You've been friend-zoned, buddy. You're done." I end the call.

The ring sits perfectly on my palm. I turn the box, studying the elegant container. Engagement. Marriage. The next logical steps in our relationship. Even three months ago, I didn't think I'd ever marry. But here I am. All because I found her again.

I want her to have everything I can give her—my money, my influence, my name. The next time Sam threatens to declare her mentally incompetent, he's going to have to go through me. Husbands have a lot more say than boyfriends. And I'll destroy the motherfucker for daring to come near my wife.

My phone buzzes with a text. Jesus. Will that loser ever give up?

I'm tempted to ignore it, but glance at the screen.

It's Elizabeth.

Iris isn't feeling well, so she went home. Thought you should know.

"Turn the car around. We're going home," I say to TJ, my throat suddenly dry.

Every time Iris isn't well, I'm scared shitless. Logically I know she is going to get sick from time to time, but emotionally I can't shake off the dread of something happening to her and me being too late. It's happened so many times already. I was too late to stop two fucking rapist wannabes from touching her. And Sam at his home. Again too late to stop him from pushing her into the water...

"Step on it," I add, my heart no longer racing with joy but with apprehension.

I start to call Bobbi, then stop. If she's driving, she shouldn't be on the phone, not even on speaker, and get distracted. I call Iris, but she doesn't answer. I hang up and text her. *Call me.*

She doesn't.

~

IRIS

BOBBI DRIVES ME HOME. SHE IGNORES ALL MY protestations that I'm fine.

"If I'd known you'd react like this, I wouldn't have let you meet that man," she says, her jaw flexing.

I wouldn't have gone to see him if I'd known. Thoughts jumble and circle in my head. If I hadn't driven so recklessly, I wouldn't have lost control of the car. If I'd gotten the seatbelt fixed, the other girl could've lived. If I'd learned to swim back then, maybe Sam could've pulled her out instead. Maybe the first responders could've saved her. Then her mom wouldn't have been so torn with grief and anger. She must hate me.

The weight of guilt suffocates me. I should at least remember the mother's face. Her pain. Instead, I'm living a happy life with a man who loves me. I've felt no remorse anywhere along the way. Nothing for the friend I killed. But the girl...she should be the one living a happy life. What a self-centered hypocrite am I to think I'm making a difference just because I work at the foundation? It isn't enough to erase my debt.

And I didn't even get her name. Just what kind of horrible person am I that I forgot to ask?

Bobbi escorts me all the way to the living room. It's freezing, the air conditioner blowing quietly.

"You can go now. You don't have to stay," I tell her, and go out onto the sunny deck.

My legs are shaky, but they hold. I take off my shoes, but my feet are too icy to feel the warmth of the sun. The infinity pool sparkles like a rectangular diamond. My bare feet curled over the edge, I look at the water. A gentle breeze ruffles the surface, making beams of sunlight dance on the bottom of the pool. The fluid motion beckons me...

Jump in and remember.

❧

ANTHONY

I'M PROBABLY OVERREACTING. IVY'S PROBABLY JUST A LITTLE under the weather, I tell myself. She was fine in the morning. Upbeat. She had a good appetite. She's been eating well enough that she's filling out, regaining the weight she lost since the accident in Tempérane.

Bobbi calls me as TJ's a block away from home.

"What's wrong? Why is she home?" I demand before she can get a word out.

"She's not feeling well. She dismissed me for the day, but I'm not sure about leaving her alone."

Smart woman. "See if Dr. Young can come by."

I jump out of the Cullinan before it comes to a complete stop and rush into the building. The elevator goes up and up and up. *Jesus. Why is it so slow?* Sweat beads and trickles down my back as anxiety drums in my veins.

When the damn car finally stops on my floor, I burst into our home, ripping my jacket off. It's too damn hot in the place. Bobbi's in the kitchen, on the phone, probably with Dr. Young's receptionist. I swivel my head around, looking for Iris.

"Where is she?" I say.

Bobbi points to the deck, and then her face goes white.

~

IRIS

I FIRST REALIZED THAT THE GIRL IN THE CAR WAS SOMEONE from my past when I fell into the pool at Sam's. If I jump in again now, knowing her mother gave me the dress, will I recall more? Will that lessen the guilt? I *should* remember. That's the only thing the girl's mother wanted me to do.

The time I remembered her... I fell into the water alone. Sam jumped in afterward to pull me out. I've never gone into the pool at Tony's without him around because I'm still less than confident about my swimming ability.

If I plunge into the water now...alone...maybe I'll know more.

I step off the edge.

34

ANTHONY

I SPIN AROUND AND SEE IRIS IN HER DAY CLOTHES VANISHING into the pool, like a slow-mo segment from a horror flick. The water plashes, but I hear nothing. The place is soundproof.

I start to run before Bobbi can. Iris can swim, I tell myself. I taught her how. So she should be okay. I know she should. But she isn't coming up.

I jump into the water, phone, shoes, watch be damned.

Iris has her eyes squeezed shut, her palms pressed against the sides of her head. She's bent forward, staying under the water. What the hell? Is she panicking and forgetting to how to float?

I wrap an arm around her and start to pull her up. She struggles. Her fists hit me, but I hardly feel them. The only thing that matters is getting her out of the pool. *Now.*

Finally, I manage to push her onto the edge, and Bobbi pulls her out. I drag myself up.

Iris is curled on her side. I inhale a lungful of air, ready to scream at her for being so foolish. Reckless enough to *jump into the pool.* If this is a prank, it isn't funny.

But the glassy look in her eyes stops me before I can start my tirade. "What's wrong?" I demand, my voice taut with the unspoken anger and terror.

"I can't remember, Tony," she says. Lost. Broken.

All my senses go on full alert. I've never seen her like this, not even when she told me about what happened to her before—what Sam did to her. And I know whatever made her feel sick and come home isn't just mere illness. But what triggered it? "What can't you remember?"

"The people I should. I don't remember the people I should. I even tried to stay under the water and think about them. But nothing came. Absolutely nothing." Her chin trembles.

My heart breaks for her. And I realize that even if I tell her everything I know, it won't be enough. She still won't have her memories. There may be more Yunas in her past, but none of them will matter because she doesn't know them. She doesn't have anything in common with them. She has to re-create old connections, while feeling like she's working extra hard to catch up because of her lack of context.

I pull her into my arms. "Let's change you into dry clothes, then we can talk. How about that?"

She just sits limply.

"I'm not changing until you do. We'll both catch cold."

She looks up at me slowly. "I don't want you to get sick because of me, Tony."

"Then let's go."

I get up. She stands, but her legs are too unsteady. A shudder racks through her, almost making her lose her balance. I pick her up.

Bobbi's watching us, her face drawn. "Do you need anything?"

"Get Dr. Young here ASAP."

She nods.

I carry Iris to the bedroom, wishing I could lend her my strength...or take some of her pain. I'd gladly give up an arm if she'd never suffer like this again. Quickly, I peel the wet clothes off her, towel her down and put her in her favorite Tweety nightshirt. I strip mine off and put on a white T-shirt and denim shorts, then finish drying her hair, using the dryer she likes so much in the morning.

She closes her eyes.

"Can you tell me what happened to make you want to remember?" I ask softly.

She's quiet for so long that I start to wonder if she heard me over the sound of the dryer. But finally, she shakes her head. "Please don't ask."

She's too brittle. If I ask, she might just crumble.

Give it time. When she's calm, you can ask again and fix what's bothering her.

By the time her hair's all dry, Bobbi comes up. "Dr. Young's here," she calls from outside the door.

I pick up Iris's hand. It's like ice. I envelop both her hands in mine, trying to warm them. "Let's get you checked out and make sure you aren't sick or hurt."

Iris looks like she's about to argue, then finally sighs. "Okay."

~

IRIS

THE FIRST THING DR. YOUNG DOES WHEN SHE WALKS INTO our bedroom is shoo Tony out. "I can't let you stay here. Privacy laws, you know? So out. If she wants you to know, she'll tell you later."

Tony glares at her like he wants to put up a fight, but leaves without a word.

Dr. Young turns to me. She's in a bright purple dress today, her hair sleek and perfect. Compared to her, I'm underdressed in my nightshirt. At least my hair's dry, thanks to Tony.

I know why he called her in, but I don't know how she's supposed to help me. It isn't like she can wave a magic wand and fix what's broken in me. It's just going to be a tiring episode of me trying to hide what's really wrong, so I can reassure everyone I'm fine.

She takes me to the edge of the bed and has me sit down. The she pulls a chair from the makeup vanity, sets it opposite me and takes a seat. Her sharp eyes probe, but not unkindly. "I heard the general gist from Bobbi. How are you feeling?"

"Tony shouldn't have asked you to come," I say, not wanting to even think about Sam or his visit.

"Why not? I heard you jumped into the pool downstairs."

"I just slipped." I hate to lie to her, but I can't tell her why either.

Her expression remains the same. Not even her eyebrows twitch. "He's worried about you."

She's being too kind. And I can't stand the reminder that I'm making him worry. "He shouldn't be. I'm not worth it." My voice cracks.

Finally, a frown furrows her forehead. "Sure you are. He adores you."

"He only loves an image. He doesn't know the real me." He doesn't know I killed someone.

"Then show him the real you."

"I can't." I wouldn't be able to bear it if he turned away from me in disgust. Or worse, in disillusionment and disappointment.

"Is there something that's upsetting you? You can tell me. I'm bound by law to not discuss it with *anybody*."

I stare at her. I want to tell her—get some advice. I'm too confused to sort things out on my own. And I have no one to talk to. As much as I like Yuna, I can't just call her and demand that she tell me about such an ugly and shocking event from my past. And Tony... He's the last person I want to discuss it with.

But to talk about it... It's like baring my shame to somebody. Inhaling deeply, I try to gather some courage. "I did something no decent person should ever do. And the worst thing is, I don't really remember exactly what happened."

"I see." She regards me with empathy. And it chips at me like a chisel. I don't want to share the story with anybody, but she's looking at me too kindly, and I'm so desperate for guidance...and reassurance that I'm not a monster or that I'm going to be okay...

My shield cracks and falls apart. I tell her about the accident, my words pouring out in a torrent. She listens, without uttering a single sound.

"I feel like I *should* know, but I don't. I only remember a little bit. What does that say about me?" I ask.

"Nothing. Sometimes when we experience a great trauma, we don't always remember every detail. Haven't you heard that eyewitnesses are notoriously biased and inaccurate?"

I shake my head. She has a remarkable gift of compassion and kindness, and I'm grateful there isn't even a hint of judgment on her face.

"Ask two people about the same event, and you'll get two very different answers. There have been studies. And let me give you a piece of advice, as someone who's had more life experience—not as a doctor." She leans forward. "Everyone's done something they're ashamed of. We may never talk about it, but we react to it in some way. When something reminds us of it, we tend to withdraw or lash out more harshly than we would otherwise."

The shame she's talking about has to be something along the lines of pocketing an extra dollar or two when somebody gave you too much change. What I did is way, way past that. "I might have killed someone."

"Or not. Maybe it's the car maker's fault the seatbelt buckle didn't work because of a paperclip. Or really, it's the fault of the boy who dropped it into the buckle. For all we know, the girl could've died even if everything worked perfectly in your car. Are you the only person who could've prevented the accident? Be honest."

"I was speeding," I point out, in case she forgot about that.

"So? Millions of people speed every day. Right at this moment, hundreds of thousands of people are speeding and breaking other rules. Are they all guilty?"

I shake my head, frustrated she doesn't understand. It isn't just that I sped, but that I killed somebody. Not only that, I don't remember the incident. So I've been living guilt-free, while the girl's mom has lived every day in pain. But what was I expecting? Dr. Young isn't a shrink.

"Be kind to yourself, Iris," she adds. "You're an exceptional young woman."

I look away. Her words make me feel worse. It amazes me that a woman as smart as her can't see I'm a fraud.

A soft sigh. "Let me check you over." Her tone is brisk now. "Make sure you aren't coming down with anything."

35

ANTHONY

IT'S TEMPTING TO SIT OUTSIDE THE BEDROOM DOOR, MY EAR pressed against it to hear the conversation between Dr. Young and Iris. I'm desperate enough to stoop that low to find out what made Iris behave this way. But I'm also rational enough to know if I do that, she'll never trust me or agree to be treated by the doctor at home again.

So I go downstairs. Bobbi's in the kitchen, helping herself to another cup of coffee.

"What the hell happened?" I ask.

She shakes her head. "Can't tell you."

"*Why the fuck not?*"

"Iris doesn't want me to."

I press my lips tight to contain the ugly words I want to spew at her. The fear and frustration that have been accumulating and bubbling are ready to erupt like a volcano and destroy everything nearby. Instead, I press my fists against the cold counter and give her a level stare. "You work for me."

"You're paying me. There's a difference." Her voice is flat.

"I'm not a spy. The second Iris thinks I am, she won't trust me or listen to a thing I say. Then I won't be able to do my job, and you'll have to find someone else to watch over her." She takes a small sip of coffee. "That what you want?"

Damn it. Bobbi's right. And that is not what I want. I need to find out some other way. But first...

I call Wei. He answers instantly. "Boss?"

"I need the pool at my place ripped out." I glare at the long, rectangular expanse of water outside. The image of Iris's blood-less face and tormented eyes digs into my heart. No more. Iris is never going to try to torture herself like that again.

"I'm sorry, what?"

If this were any other time, I'd laugh. I've never heard Wei sound so blindsided.

To make sure he understands, I speak slowly. "I. Want. My. Pool. Ripped. Out."

Bobbi gestures at me.

"Hold on, Wei." I turn to her, pulling the phone away from my mouth. "What?"

"Don't do that," she says.

"You're not a spy, fine. You're also not a home improvement consultant."

She sighs. "If Iris wants to jump into water, she'll find a way. Wouldn't you rather have her do it here than somewhere else next time?"

I begin to snarl that there won't be a next time, but catch myself. That's what I thought after I rescued Iris from Sam's, too, but look what happened.

"The better idea would be to install a sensor that alerts you every time somebody's on the deck. And a camera system to monitor it."

She has a point. Unless I plan to rip out every pool and drain every lake and pond, what I'm thinking about doing to my home is a Band-Aid solution.

I return to my phone and tell Wei the new instructions.

He sounds relieved. "Getting rid of the pool would be bad."

"Why?"

"Pools add value."

For fuck's sake. I'm this close to telling him nothing is more valuable than Iris's health and safety, but I stop. He doesn't know what happened. And as my assistant, it is his job to look out for me. "Thanks, Wei. Just get the sensor and camera stuff done ASAP."

I go to the foyer to retrieve the jacket I tossed on the floor. I take the ring out of it and put it in the pocket of my shorts. As I drape the jacket on the back of a couch, Dr. Young finally comes downstairs. She's frowning slightly.

"What's wrong?" I ask. "What's making her like that?" I point my finger upward.

"I can't tell you."

"You don't know?" I ask. What the hell am I paying her for?

Not even an eyelash flickers. It's as though she's been expecting me to react like this. "I said I can't tell you. Privacy laws."

"Bullshit!" I slam my fist on the wall. I'm sick of people saying they can't tell me. This isn't some trivial issue—this is Iris. I didn't make all this damned money or gain this much influence and power so I could just sit on the sidelines and watch her suffer. "How the hell am I going to help her if you don't tell me what's wrong?"

Dr. Young continues calmly, as though I hadn't just fractured my plaster. "Feed her something easy to digest. Don't probe about what's wrong or try to fix it. Men always do that, and this isn't something you can fix."

"What do you mean it's something I can't fix?" I manage to spit out through the thick lump of fear in my throat.

"Exactly that. The only thing you can do is be kind to her. And fill this prescription."

I eye the paper. "What is it?"

"A sedative. She said she didn't want any, but if she becomes too agitated, you might want to offer it to her. If anything else happens, call me, regardless of the time."

She leaves, and Bobbi takes the prescription. "I'll get this filled. Why don't you go to Iris? She needs you," she says quietly, and leaves.

Finally alone in the living room, I think about what the doctor said. That I can't fix it—I can only be kind to Iris. Like that's even a question.

I go up to our bedroom, then stop at the door, suddenly nervous. What if this is the kind of wedge that I can't do anything about? I've never seen her like this before. She's always been so brave—such a fighter—that I didn't realize she could break.

It doesn't matter, I tell myself, doing my best to push my nerves aside. She's here. She's alive. I can work with that. Everything else can be fixed.

I knock quietly, open the door and walk inside. Iris is perched on the edge of the mattress, her shoulders rounded and hunched, her head low. Her elbows rest on her knees, her hands loosely linked together.

She looks defeated and wan, all the vitality gone. I sit next to her and pull her toward me. As I wrap my arm around her, I feel her against my side, the slight weight. I hold her hands in mine. They're usually so warm and limber. But now, they're cool and stiff.

Her body tenses, and she clenches her hands around mine until her nails whiten. I can sense the muscles in her jaw working. Her chest starts heaving...slightly at first, then more. Sobs tear from her throat, and she presses a fist against her breastbone.

What could be causing such torment? The sight of her hurting is unbearable. I thought—in my utter arrogance—that all that I had...money, power, influence...would protect her. But there's nothing any of it can do to lessen her anguish. The same dark helplessness that I felt watching Katherine die threatens to overwhelm me. But somehow I hang on to my sanity and composure. I can't break, not when Iris needs me to be strong. "It's okay to cry," I tell her softly, kissing her cold fingers. "Let it out."

"I hate making noise. I don't want people to know I'm crying."

Maybe she doesn't realize what she just said, but I do, and cold fear and rejection slice through me. I hate that she's guarding herself so fiercely with me, when just this morning, she was so open and sparkling. Doesn't she know I'm always on her side? "It's just me here, Iris." My voice is rough, and it cracks as I add, "It's okay."

She shudders against me. I don't know how long she sobs quietly. The seconds grow into minutes...and longer. I wish I could do something for her. I wish I could figure out what exactly happened to trigger this so I could prevent it in the future.

Finally, her tears subside. She wipes her face with the backs of her hands. "What's the limit?" she asks, her voice thick and wet.

"What limit?" I keep my tone soft and safe, just like Dr. Young said.

"When do you decide you don't love me anymore?"

My hold on her tightens. I hate the doubt, the anxiety. It shocks me to realize we share a fear of losing the other's love. I deserve to lose her love. I've never been lovable...a screwup. Everything I've done has been an attempt to make up for the fact that deep inside, at my core, I'm not really worthy of her. But Iris... She's warmth, light—all that is beautiful and wonderful and special. "Never. I'll never stop loving you."

She turns, pulling away a little, so she can face me fully. Tears glisten in her eyes, her cheeks. Her nose is red, her mouth white. "What if there are things in my past that are ugly and wrong? What if I'm a bad person?"

I cradle her head in my hand with infinite care, wishing with all my heart I could communicate how precious she is. I'm the one with the ugly, fucked-up past, not her. "You could never be a bad person. Every time I look at you, I wonder how I ended up with such a gentle soul, and I want to be the kind of man who deserves you."

Her eyes are still haunted. I'm not reaching her.

Desperation makes me talk faster. "You're the best thing that's ever happened in my life. If someone asked me to choose between you and everything else I had, I'd choose you."

"You shouldn't." Her voice breaks.

She's withdrawing emotionally and mentally. I feel the loss as keenly as a rasp along my skin. If I don't pull her back, she's going to drift away, lost forever. The notion is terrifying, a bleak, lonely future unfurling in my mind like a tattered tapestry. I have to anchor her to me, make sure she never leaves...never doubts my heart.

I slide down the bed and crouch in front of her. I squeeze her hands, willing her to really listen to me. "I love you, Iris." I look into her eyes, now dim and dull as unpolished silver. "I love you so much that I want to spend the rest of my life with you." I pull the box from my pocket and flip the lid open.

The pearl glows like stardust. The diamonds and rubies sparkle, reflecting the soft light in the room.

Iris stares at the ring mutely. Then tears start to flow.

"What if I'm not the person you think I am?"

It breaks my heart. I know better than she knows about herself. And I'm not the man she thinks I am. "I know exactly who you are—the only woman I'll ever love."

Say yes. Her eyes are sad, but as long as she says yes, I can fix the rest. I know I can make her happy. Just this morning, she was smiling sleepily, her hair spread on our bed, her cheeks flushed from lovemaking. I'm still the same man from those hours.

Pain is etched in every line of her lovely visage. She squeezes her eyes shut and puts her hands over her face.

She isn't saying yes. She won't. I have to change her mind somehow, but I don't know how.

She doesn't want your love. She doesn't want your money.

She thinks she's a bad person because she can't remember something that happened long time ago. And I've painted myself into a corner where I can't tell her everything without losing her. In all my dealings, professional and otherwise, I could get what I wanted by bluffing or cajoling or being well informed. But Iris isn't going to be won that way.

"Don't let the past define your future. *Our* future." My voice is taut and hoarse. "Only your choices now have the power to do that."

Her shoulders shake. I know I've failed to penetrate that fortress of pain to reach her. All that I have to offer isn't enough, and the weight of futility and helplessness presses upon me until

I can't stand. Maybe her heart knows, even without the memories, that I'm flawed. A sister killer. A disowned son. A cold, callous bastard.

I'm tempted to take a page from Audrey's book and stage a fake suicide. Iris would then...

I stop myself. What the hell is wrong with me to even consider that? What would that prove, except how undeserving I am? It'd only earn Iris's contempt, and rightly so.

My heart slowly shrivels until I'm frozen inside. I stay at her feet until the sun disappears under the horizon.

36

ANTHONY

THE WEEKEND IS AWFUL. THE AIR IS CHARGED WITH tension, anxiety and fear. Or maybe I'm the only one who feels it.

The Steinway remains silent. Iris doesn't even glance at it. It's as though her love of music—the one constant in her life—is gone. And I worry that her love for me is gone as well from the way she avoids eye contact.

She sits on a couch, hugging her legs until the knees touch her chest. An afghan is wrapped around her. She's so pale, her eyes puffy from crying so much. Even now, tears trickle down her cheeks from time to time. It's as though she isn't even alive, not where it counts.

She doesn't touch her food. I can't eat either, not when my stomach is knotted so tight. She only drinks water if Bobbi brings it over and hands it to her. Bobbi says nothing as she watches over Iris.

Barely three words are spoken the entire weekend by anybody. I don't touch Iris. Not that I don't want to, but I'm too afraid. She looks ready to shatter, and I don't know if I can put the pieces back together.

I text Elizabeth. *Did anything unusual happen at the founda-tion? Did the project go bad or something?*

Not that I know of. Why? Is Iris okay?

What the hell kind of question is that? Would I have contacted her if Iris were? I rein in my frustration. This isn't Elizabeth's fault. *No. She hasn't been well since Friday. I think it's got something to do with what happened at work.* It has to be.

Let me see what I can find out. I'll be in touch. Also, I'll assume Iris is too sick to come to work on Monday. Let her rest a bit. Maybe I made her work too hard. The project she's on has gone through some upheaval over funding.

That's Elizabeth. Always gracious, even though she and I both know I'm the reason the project had the "upheaval over funding."

She doesn't text me back. I know it takes time to figure stuff out, but my patience still wears thin. Every second that ticks by, Iris is drifting further away from me. It's as horrible as watching little drips of acid eat away at you.

Monday morning, things aren't any better. My eyes are gritty from a lack of sleep. A day's worth of beard covers my jaw. My stomach burns from hunger.

Iris is curled up in bed. Her eyes are closed, but I know she isn't sleeping. Her body's too tense, her breathing too shallow and rapid. For the last two nights, she's flinched and cried out in her dreams, her words too soft and fast for me to catch. *What night-mares are driving you?* She didn't let bad dreams get to her after Sam tried to drown her. Whatever's haunting her now has to be worse than her own possible death.

I pick up my phone and call Wei. "Cancel all my meetings. I'm not coming in today."

"Of course, boss." A beat. "Are you all right? You don't sound good."

"I'm—"

"You should go to work."

I see Iris sitting up like an old woman with creaky bones. "But..."

"I'm going to work, too." Her voice is rusty. She hasn't spoken since Friday. "Go shave and get dressed."

I take in her wan, pale face. Dark half-circles look like bruises under her eyes, and the sight hurts. "Elizabeth said you don't have to go in if you don't feel well."

"I can't stay here all day. We have things to do, Tony. And you don't have to babysit me."

I want to argue, tell her she's wrong, that I'm going to stay with her and help her sort everything in her head until she realizes she's worthy of every amazing thing life has to offer. That I'm the one who doesn't deserve her, but is too selfish to let her go.

If she were showing even the slightest vulnerability, I'd push. But her lips are set in a firm, straight line.

"Boss?" Wei's voice from the phone jerks me back to my assistant.

"Never mind. I'll be in." I end the call.

Iris drags herself out of bed and showers first. I don't join her like I normally would. I go in after she's out, then drag a razor carelessly over my face, cutting myself in three spots. I press them for a minute, trying to get the bleeding to stop. For some reason, when I pull my hand away, the sight of blood on my fingertips reminds me of the day Katherine died.

Some fucking poetic reminder of why my life went wrong. Just like a shirt that's been buttoned wrong from the very beginning. Impossible to fix, unless I could go back in time and resurrect my sister.

Then I wouldn't have been banished. Or spent so much time wallowing in guilt. I would've been able to fall in love with Ivy without Mother's hatred hanging over us. I wouldn't have turned my back on Ivy when she got the tattoo to express her love for me.

Perhaps this rejection is nothing more than what I deserve. Tit for tat. Why should Iris want to accept my proposal when I wasn't brave enough to accept her tattoo? She erased it after, scrubbing her body clean of any declaration of love, just like she scrubbed her mind clean of my presence.

When I finally emerge from the bathroom, Iris is already dressed in a blue tunic top and black pencil skirt. She's put on some makeup, but it can't hide the dark circles under her eyes or the way the ends of her mouth curve downward.

Wordlessly, she leaves the closet and walks out of the room. It feels too much like a final goodbye—the way Mother turned her back on me at the terminal when she was sure I had the boarding pass for my one-way flight to Zurich. I start to follow, then stop and put on my work outfit in record speed before bounding downstairs.

Bobbi's handing Iris a cup of coffee. Iris holds it for a moment, then takes a small sip before setting it back on the counter.

"Iris," I begin.

"I need to get going. I'm going to be late." She looks at me with infinitely sad eyes and walks away.

Bobbi mouths, *I'll keep her safe*, and follows Iris out.

Iris slips out of our home like sand sifting through my fingers. Panic pulses, growing louder until it drowns out everything except one thought—whether she learns the truth or not, I'm going to lose her.

37

IRIS

"HERE." BOBBI PUSHES A TRAVEL MUG IN MY DIRECTION AS she drives her Escalade to the office. "It's tea. Hot. You need fluids."

I take it, but don't drink any. There are burning holes in my belly, and I can't tolerate any food or drink right now.

"You're really not going to tell Tony anything?" she asks.

I don't know what I'm going to do. I've been thinking all weekend, but haven't come up with anything coherent.

"He's worried about you."

I close my eyes, wishing she'd stop. I saw the pain in his eyes and face firsthand, and don't need her to tell me. But it's impossible to say yes to the proposal when I don't know what I am.

He asked me not to let my past define me. It's easy for him to say because he knows exactly the kind of person he is—honorable, brave, protective and sweet. I thought I couldn't be so bad. I mean, I feel sympathy for people who aren't as fortunate as me. I try to be fair as much as I can.

But what if what I've done is an attempt to compensate for

things I've done wrong? Even when I can't access the specific memory, it must be in my head somewhere, influencing my decisions and behavior.

That uncertainty makes it impossible to say yes, even though he looked at me with love in his gaze and proposed with the most beautiful ring I've ever seen in my life.

I rub my index finger across the astrological medallion he gave me. I've never taken it off. The rough surface scratches my flesh, and I wish I could have half the belief in myself that he does. But since Friday, every time I sleep, I dream of the accident. My mind supplies more details—probably helped by Sam's description of the event. The bridge. Water. The broken seatbelt. The girl.

Last night her mother came to me in a nightmare. I couldn't make out her features. They're always hazy. She threw the blue dress in my face. Called me a murderer and a monster, incapable of shedding a single tear of remorse at the funeral. Her words *I'll never forgive you* rang in my ears when I started awake. I clutched the pillow and breathed, hoping they would fade. But they remained, circling like vultures, ready to rip me apart. I don't know how I could've cried for two days straight, but not cried at the funeral. Too deep in shock to react? Too guilty to cry?

No answers come, and I want to scream with frustration. Break something. But that won't solve anything. Part of me says I could've imagined the mother's raging over not crying, but then why did it feel so real?

When I finally arrive in the office, Tolyan cocks an eyebrow, but doesn't comment on how awful I look. Elizabeth says hello, walking by, and does a double-take. She asks me to come to her office.

"Close the door and sit down," she says, taking a seat at the couch and patting the empty spot next to her.

It feels like an electric chair, but there's no graceful way to demur. I sit down and look at her, waiting for her to start.

"Didn't Tony tell you you could stay home? I told him if you didn't feel well, you should," she says.

"He did. But I really don't like taking time off." Plus, staying at home and doing nothing except thinking about the girl and her mom would drive me insane. I need some normal in my life right now. "I'm fine."

Elizabeth looks skeptical. She opens her mouth, closes it, then tries again. "If you need someone to talk to, I'm here for you."

She's such a sweet woman. I wish I could tell her, but I can't. She's so perfect, so angelic, she not only wouldn't understand, but would be horrified someone like me is working for her. "Thank you," I say. "I think it's best if I just focus on the project. I don't want to fall behind. Is there anything else you want to discuss?"

"No...that's all."

I go back to my desk and do my best to focus for the rest of the morning, ignoring the huge waves of numbness that threaten to overpower me. I can at least do this much to make the world a little bit better place.

I have the tea Bobbi gave me earlier for lunch. It's lukewarm, but the travel mug kept it from going totally cold.

The afternoon is more of the same. Around four, I get a text from Yuna. *Any plans for this evening?*

No.

Let's have dinner together. Bring Tony. Or would you rather do something dirty and couple-y together?

Tears prickle my eyes. Oh shit. I don't want to cry at work. I already made a spectacle of myself on Friday. *I can't.* Then, without any conscious thought, I write, *He asked me to marry him,* and hit send before I can catch myself.

Crap. I didn't mean to share that with anybody. I don't know what made me text it.

Yuna calls immediately. Bracing myself, I drag my finger on the green button.

"*Oh my God!*" she screeches into my ear. "When? Where? Tell me everything! And when's the engagement party? I need to go shopping. *We* need to go shopping!"

A sob spills from between my clenched teeth. I cover my mouth to contain the sound, but it's no use. Keeping my head down, I rush to the bathroom and lock myself in a stall.

"What's wrong?" Yuna asks. "Are you crying?"

"I couldn't accept."

"What? You told him no?"

I start to shake my head, then realize she can't see me. "Not exactly. I sort of left it in limbo." It was awful to see the aching hope in his eyes, knowing I shouldn't—*couldn't*—say yes. I took the coward's way out and covered my face and cried because I knew if I didn't, I would say yes like a greedy child. But at the end, my silence hurt him as much as an outright rejection. It was in his pained gaze all weekend long. Him watching me, tragic and tormented.

"Why not? Talk to me. Stop crying like the world just ended. Did he screw up?"

"No." I sob harder. "It was the most perfect proposal. I was in my Tweety shirt and looked awful, but it didn't matter. He proposed anyway, in our bedroom."

"Um." She sounds hesitant. "When did this happen?"

"On Friday. He...he says he loves me."

"Of course he loves you. I've never seen a man who loves a woman more. Look, I'm coming over to pick you up right now. I should be there by five. You and I are going to have a talk and a lot of good drinks to sort this out, okay?"

I want to tell her it'll never be okay. Or that she doesn't have to bother. But at the same time, I need somebody, and Yuna feels like the safest person for that. "Okay."

38

IRIS

YUNA PICKS ME UP FROM THE FOUNDATION A LITTLE BEFORE five. Her eyes go wide, but she wisely keeps quiet about how I look. Bobbi follows in her car.

Yuna has Mr. Kim drive us to her hotel. I don't say anything, since I'm feeling awkward with him around, and she doesn't try to make me talk.

She has a suite on the top floor, with a two-hundred-and-seventy-degree view of the city through walls of glass. There are numerous vases full of red roses, and a black Yamaha baby grand sits on a platform.

She gestures at me to take a seat. Mr. Kim and Bobbi go to the coffee bar to help themselves to what is undoubtedly gourmet java. I curl up on one of the couches, making myself as small as possible. I wonder if Yuna knows about the girl. And if so, how *much* does she know?

Or maybe she doesn't know. That's why she treats me like a sister. A soul sister, she called me. I don't feel I deserve a title like that. But Yuna mentioned the broken seatbelt. So it doesn't make sense she wouldn't know about the girl who died. Does it not bother Yuna that I killed someone?

Yuna takes the armchair, kicks off her shoes and rests her feet on an ottoman. A gift basket full of mini-bottles of liquor and wine is set on a glass-top table between us. She takes one and hands it to me.

"Merlot. It should be tasty. Want a glass?"

I shake my head. I open the screw-top and take a sip. It's pretty full-bodied. I take another swallow and feel the alcohol warm my body.

"I feel like it's my fault you're in this emotional mess," Yuna says, helping herself to a Chardonnay. She doesn't bother with a glass either.

That surprises me. It isn't like she knows why I'm upset... Or does she? "Why?"

"Because I wasn't around." She looks at her hand for a moment. "I should've looked for you harder."

"You found me now." Since I'm not ready to talk about me and Tony yet, I say, "By the way, is your dad okay with you staying here for this long?"

She purses her lips like she doesn't like the topic, then shrugs. "He isn't happy I'm not rushing back home, but I told him if he had a long-lost soul brother, he'd understand."

I wonder how understanding her dad would be if he knew I was a killer.

"Even if he weren't okay, there's nothing he can do. My grandfather left me a sizable trust four years ago when he passed away, so I don't need Dad's approval. But I try not to cross him if I can help it."

We plunge into an uncomfortable silence. What I really want to know about is the broken seatbelt buckle. How much of what Sam said is true? Did Yuna know the girl I killed—her name and her mom? Yuna told me some guy broke the buckle, but not the consequences. Maybe she doesn't know about the accident. Or she doesn't want to upset me by talking about it.

"Want something to eat?" Yuna says finally.

"Not really." Just the idea of solid food is revolting.

"If we're going to drink, you should have some dinner." She gestures at Mr. Kim, who comes over instantly. She speaks to him in Korean, and he nods and disappears.

"What did you tell him?"

"I asked him to get you some mild abalone porridge. It should help settle your stomach. I eat it every time I need something easy to digest." She crosses her ankles and smooths her skirt. "So tell me what happened. He proposed, and you didn't say yes or no?"

I take another sip of the wine as the gut-wrenching memory of Tony at my feet runs through my mind. I'm exhausted, but I feel like I can make sense with Yuna. She might even help me find a way to make it not hurt for Tony. "I wish I could've said yes. I wanted to, but I just...couldn't."

Yuan blinks. "Why in the world not? I thought you said he told you he loves you?"

"He did, but he deserves..." I pause to think of the right word to describe what I'm feeling. "He deserves better."

"Better than *you*? Are you kidding?" She shifts around until her legs are tucked under her. "That's for him to decide, not you."

Except he doesn't know much about me because of my partial amnesia. There's no way he can make a real decision without knowing all the facts. "You know I don't remember my past. What if I did something bad?"

"Like what?" She frowns. "Smoking pot?" She leans forward and whispers, "Did you? I won't judge if you did."

God. I wish my biggest problem were having smoked pot. I shake my head helplessly, frustration over my broken memory bubbling over. "I don't know because I don't remember! That's the problem!"

"How's it a problem? He already knows you don't remember your past, but loves you anyway. He probably already thought everything through before proposing."

"He might not have imagined the kind of things I could've done."

"Meh. Everyone's done something stupid they regret later. Tony isn't perfect as you think. Neither am I." She comes over to the couch and sits next to me. "Look, Iris, do you remember how I said my parents are planning to marry me off in a merger?"

I nod.

"Even though I hate the whole plan, a small part of me knows it's probably better that way."

I stare at her, utterly flabbergasted. Just what century is she living in? "You do? Why?" Yuna is so beautiful and smart. She should settle for nothing less than love.

"Because I'll never know if a man wants me for me—Yuna Hae—or as the only daughter of Chairman Hae. But you... You know exactly what Tony wants. He'll never care what's in your past."

Not even killing a girl? The words shoot up all the way to my tongue, but I click my teeth shut. I drink more from the bottle. "Do you think love never changes?"

"No," she says. "But the kind of love between you and Tony? That won't ever change."

How can she be so sure? I'm feeling a little dizzy. The room's not spinning, exactly, but my body doesn't feel super steady either. "How do you know?"

"He looks at you like you're the only thing worth getting up for in the morning. Love like that doesn't change. If I hadn't seen that on his face, I would've never agreed to— I would've never let him come near you."

It's too much effort to stay upright. I lower my head until it hits the couch cushion. "Yuna?"

"Mmm?"

"Can you tell me stories from those years ago? When you knew me at Curtis? Good, bad, ugly, whatever. Everything."

"Of course."

Yuna starts, her voice soft and gentle. I close my eyes, willing my brain to soak everything in.

39

ANTHONY

THE PENTHOUSE FEELS EMPTY. COLD. BUT NOTHING HAS changed, except Iris isn't here.

Bobbi already texted me that Iris is going to be spending the evening with Yuna. I want to go bring her back, but Bobbi added, *I think she needs time.*

If she needs time, she needs time. I know hurrying her or trying to force things won't solve the problem.

Without bothering to turn on the lights, I sit on the couch that faces the Steinway and stare at it. In my mind's eyes, I can see her at the piano, dazzling me with a brilliant Chopin or Liszt. "Bravo," I whisper.

I need to get off the couch and eat something. At some point, my body's going to give out. But I can't seem to muster the energy.

My cold, barren home feels like an omen. Should I have pushed Iris to share what's bothering her? Should I have forced Bobbi to tell me anyway? There are other bodyguards available if Iris gets mad at Bobbi for caving in to my demands.

Don't be an idiot. Iris will never trust anybody on your payroll.

Right. She'll hate me.

My phone buzzes. A text from Yuna.

Iris fell asleep. Probably best if she spends the night here.

It's not even nine, but she hasn't been sleeping well. She must've been exhausted. It's logical to let her get what rest she can instead of waking her up and bringing her back home.

But dread inside me grows like cancer. During the weekend, even though we weren't talking or touching, at least we were sharing the same bed. Now...

I hurl my phone. It dents the wall and drops to the floor.

Panic digs its talons into my heart. Is this the end? Is she going to leave me? I don't even know how I screwed up. Was it something subtle, something I didn't even realize would be a problem? If I ask, will Iris tell me?

Suddenly, my bitter confrontation with Mother floods my mind. I begged her to tell me how I could earn her forgiveness. She wouldn't. Said if I had to be told, it wouldn't count. I needed to figure out what I needed to do on my own to be truly forgiven. Then she delivered the final blow—and made it clear how much she despised me.

If Iris ever looks at me the way Mother looked at me then...my heart will literally cease beating.

Give her time. Maybe she just needs to think about the proposal. It was spur of the moment and badly done. Who the hell just yanks out a ring? I should've reserved an entire restaurant and filled it with tiger lilies. Then hired a quartet to play something lovely while I told her how much I adored her.

Besides, I trust Yuna to keep Iris safe. Maybe talking to a friend will be a good thing. Yuna is sensible, wants us to be together and knows what's really going on with Iris.

I make my way upstairs. Iris is going to need to toiletries, makeup and clothes for tomorrow. Yuna could buy some for her, but Iris wouldn't be comfortable with that. I run shaky hands over Iris's things, praying with all the desperation in my heart that she realizes we can overcome anything so long as we're together.

I pack her a bag and debate going to Yuna's hotel myself, then change my mind. If I'm there, I'm not going to leave without Iris.

Even now, every wild instinct in me is screaming to drag her back here, whether she likes it or not—she belongs with me, and no one else.

I go to the living room and pick up my phone. It's cracked, but still working. I call TJ. "I need you to come get a bag for Iris."

He comes up to the penthouse a few minutes later. I tell him to take the bag to Yuna's hotel, and he grunts and leaves.

I stay unmoving on the cold floor of the living room long after.

40

IRIS

When I open my eyes, I'm in an unfamiliar bed. I jackknife up, my heart drumming a thousand beats a minute. What the heck happened?

I look down and realize I'm in my underwear. Who undressed me? Where am I?

Slowly, my brain starts working. I realize I'm in a hotel room. Yuna's suite.

Oh crap. Did I take her bed? I slip out, dragging a sheet with me, and go to the bathroom. A fresh robe hangs from a hook on the door, and I put it on and gingerly step out.

"No need to tiptoe. I'm already up," comes Yuna's voice from the coffee bar. She's in a pair of pink pajamas, her hair messy. She must've gotten up not too long ago, because her right cheek still has pillow marks. "Sleep well?"

I start to say yes out of reflex, then I realize I actually do feel rested. "Yeah...I did. Did I take your bed?"

"Nah. This suite has three bedrooms."

"Oh. Mr. Kim's in the other one?" I look around, wondering

when he's going to pop out, fully dressed in his black suit and ready to go.

Yuna laughs. "If my dad heard that, he'd go into shock. Actually, I think Mr. Kim would be more mortified. He's in a different room. Two floors down."

"Oh." It seems kind of wasteful to get a three-bedroom suite and only use one.

"Why don't you shower, and we can have breakfast before you go to work."

I shift, feeling like a person who left home without an umbrella despite the storm warning on TV. "I don't have anything to wear."

"Not true. Tony sent a bag last night. I put it in your room."

"He did? How did he know?" I didn't text him because somehow talking to him, even via texts, feels awkward, and I didn't expect to stay for more than an hour. He must've been frantic. Another black mark against me.

"I let him know. Didn't want him to call the police and file a missing persons report. Going to jail for kidnapping would suck." She winks.

I let out a small laugh, then stop. I haven't laughed in...days. Since Sam sent me the dress.

It feels good. Almost normal. But guilt immediately pricks me for daring to feel good while knowing what my negligence did all those years ago.

"Let me get ready," I say, the moment gone.

The overnight bag is on the bench at the foot of the bed. I unzip it and look inside. Tony thought of everything. All my toiletries and makeup are here. He packed two fresh sets of underwear and clothes and nude pumps.

After a quick shower, I put on a chartreuse dress and shoes. They look good on me. Tony always knows what I need.

As I tuck in my old clothes in the bag, I see a white piece of paper on the bottom of the bag.

I love you.

—Tony

An excruciating pang rips through me. I pick it up reverently, then press it to my heart. *I love you too, Tony. I wish I were a better person—somebody who deserved you.*

I put the note in my purse and go out to the living room. Mr. Kim is arranging three chairs around a wheeled dining table that has appeared. Room service obviously delivered breakfast while I was in the bathroom. There are poached eggs, toast with butter and various jams on the side and a pot of fresh coffee.

"Ta-da!" Yuna says, taking a seat. "Looks great, huh?"

"Yes." I smile wanly. "I'm not that hungry, though."

"Oh no. You aren't pulling that crap. You're going to sit and eat."

"But—"

Yuna lifts a finger. "No *buts*! Unlike Tony, I have no problem having Mr. Kim hold you down while I shovel food into your mouth."

I snort at the ridiculous threat. "He wouldn't do that."

"Mr. Kim was on the Korean national team for taekwondo and is still a total badass," Yuna says.

That clean-cut, straight-laced corporate man? He beams at me.

"Okay, fine." I force myself to have one poached egg and half a piece of dry toast.

Yuna nods approvingly.

I should be irritated at her high-handedness, but she means well. And if our positions were reversed, I might do the same. She hands me a cup of coffee and waves goodbye when Bobbi shows up to take me to the foundation.

Although guilt over the death of the girl is still nipping at me, I can manage to push it aside so long as I'm busy in the office. I even offer to help Rhonda with her executive memos when I have half an hour of downtime.

Yuna comes to see me for lunch, again with Mr. Kim, who will again be happy to hold me down, never mind that we're out in public. Bobbi smirks, but doesn't try to stop Yuna or Mr. Kim. I guess it's not her job to defend her client from nutrition. So I choke something down. It tastes like sawdust, even though the restaurant is ostensibly a four-star establishment.

If I were only dealing with the guilt and an overbearing friend, I might be okay. But at the most random moments, without any rhyme or reason, Tony pops into my head.

Our first meeting when I cried. That night he rescued me from Jamie Thornton and took me home. The date—us playing Schubert together...then finally spending the night together. Him taking care of me after Sam's attempted homicide. Tony asking me to marry him.

Every exquisite memory tears a small strip from my heart. Sometimes the pain is so agonizing that not even tears come.

Even as I pray the hurt will stop, I know it won't. Because I'll never stop loving Tony.

41

ANTHONY

MY OFFICE IS DARK. I CAN'T STAND BRIGHT LIGHT NOW. My eyes are too gritty and sensitive.

It's already Thursday. But Iris hasn't texted me or left a message. Wei already knows he's to interrupt me, no matter what, if she calls.

My new phone vibrates on the desk. I pick it up. Yuna's text pops on the screen.

She had Greek yogurt and fruit. Also grapefruit juice and coffee. She said she slept okay, but I heard her cry out in her sleep. Sounded like "I'm sorry."

I hover my fingers over the report. I didn't ask her, but she started sending me short updates from Tuesday. I'm glad Iris is eating and taking care of herself. She was a wreck over the weekend.

The fact that Iris seems to be doing better with Yuna is the only thing stopping me from bringing her back home. I miss her so much that I'd rather have every bone in my body broken than spend another second without her.

I probably screwed up when I asked her to marry me. She was upset, and instead of focusing on her problem, I was trying to bind her to me.

A new email arrives on my phone from Jill with the subject line FRIDAY. I open it immediately.

Iris left the office five till two to get coffee at Starbucks nearby. There she spoke with someone. Per one of the baristas, the man was Caucasian, well dressed. But the details are vague. The location's always busy. Its customers are mainly white-collar professionals.

This man... He has to be the reason Iris is slipping away from me. I flip through a mental catalogue of people with this kind of influence over her. My first instinct is Sam, but that can't be right. He used to have power over her, but not anymore, not after he tried to drown her. Iris wouldn't believe anything out of his mouth.

Which leaves only one other option: Byron Fucking Pearce.

Has to be. He hates my guts, and he'd love to poison Iris against me. He's furious that I pissed all over the deal he had with Hae Min Group, so he's trying to hit back, below the belt.

Murderous rage beats in my veins. I jump to my feet. I'm going to kill the son of a bitch. I'm going to find him and teach him what getting hit below the belt really feels like. And once he's down, I'm going to kick him until he can never get back up.

I throw the door open to my office and stalk out. Wei leaps to his feet. "Boss?"

TJ rises too. "What's going on?"

"I'm going to hunt down Byron Pearce," I say between clenched teeth.

One look at my face and TJ grows stony. "No. You need to calm down."

"Don't tell me to calm down! I have every right!" How dare he get in my way? I'll fucking kill him, too, if I have to.

A few heads pop up over the cubicle partitions. TJ grabs me and pushes me toward my office, abusing his size and brute strength. He kicks the door shut behind us.

"I'm not paying you for this!" I scream, an inch from his nose. "Let me go or you're fired!"

"Don't be stupid!" TJ's voice is cold. "What do you think Pearce did?"

"He spoke with Iris on Friday! That's why she's not here where she needs to be. She's out there"—I gesture at the city —"without me."

"Is that what Jill said?"

"Yes."

TJ narrows his eyes. "She said Byron Pearce is responsible? She named him specifically?"

Why the hell is he so hung up on technicalities? "She doesn't have to name names. It's obvious. No other man in the city could have this kind of power over her! She thinks he's her fucking friend!"

TJ grabs my shoulders. "Just stop and think. You don't really know who she spoke to. Do you honestly believe if you charge over to Pearce International and beat him up, Iris is going to come back to you?"

I glare at him. I hate him for asking a question I can't answer. I want to break every bone in Byron's body—which is nothing less than what he deserves. But my mind is whispering that Iris will think I'm a sociopath if I do.

"If you attack him without being sure, it'll only drive her away," TJ says, as though he knows exactly what my traitorous mind is telling me.

"Drive her away? She's already gone!" Wrenching away from him, I swipe my hand across my desk. Everything crashes to the floor. More than a few items shatter. But the fury inside me is still raging.

I clutch the edge of my desk, shoulders tense and head hung low. My ragged breathing drowns out even the sound of my racing heart.

This singular taste of defeat is so bitter that I nearly gag. It's almost as bad as her death. She never once said she didn't love me. In fact, I know she *does* love me, and she knows I love her. But somehow, it isn't enough to fix this.

"This isn't good for you." TJ's voice is soft. Almost kind. "If she doesn't come back, you need to let her go."

My knuckles whiten around the desk. "I can't." My words crack. "I'd rather die."

"Yeah? Well, if you don't start taking care of yourself, you'll get your wish."

～

IRIS

IT'S ALMOST ELEVEN BY THE TIME THE WEEKLY THURSDAY status meeting ends. I've never had to attend one before, but now that I'm in charge of an initiative, I'm required to report on progress. I was nervous the first time, but I'm more relaxed about it now. The purpose of the meeting is mainly to see if anybody's lagging behind and provide help. So many of our projects are time-sensitive. And everything's on target so far.

Clutching my notes, I leave the conference room with everyone else. As I reach my desk, I spot TJ saying something furiously to Bobbi and stop.

My heart skips a beat as apprehension drips into my veins. Did something happen to Tony?

Almost immediately, I shake myself. If it had, somebody would've called. And Bobbi wouldn't be staring at the messenger with crossed arms and a sour face.

So what's going on? Did Tony send TJ to bring me home?

It's been days. Maybe Tony ran out of patience. But I'm not ready to face him yet. I haven't worked through my guilt or the fear of all the bad things I could've done. It's one thing to be broken. Another to be vile. I honestly have no idea what I'm going to do, stuck in this weird limbo of not knowing and unable to make decisions. I have no clue if it's even possible to come to grips with this kind of paralysis...or if I can be with Tony when I have all these messed-up things hanging over me. I start to turn away.

"Hey! Stop!" TJ yells.

I look over my shoulder, and TJ's thick index finger is pointed at me. This has to be the first time he's said so many words to me at once. He's definitely here at Tony's request.

He starts toward me. Bobbi yanks him back. Tolyan slowly stands, eyes hollow and cold, and moves around the desk.

Suddenly, the air is crackling with aggression. If I leave now, Bobbi, TJ and Tolyan are going to go at it.

The foundation is what's keeping me sane. I can't afford to lose my job here over a brawl. I turn to Tolyan. "You can go back to your desk."

He arches an eyebrow, like he's mortally offended I'm in his way. Annoyance pushes into me like a needle. I inhale, then pull myself together. He can't make a scene in the office.

I look at Bobbi. "It's fine."

Her gaze slides in TJ's direction, her lips pursing. She looks like she wants to punch her cousin out, but she finally backs down.

"And you." I point at TJ. "This way."

I start walking toward one of the smaller meeting rooms. He follows, quietly for such a large man. My coworkers crane their necks at the sight of the Visigoth. Embarrassment unfurls in my belly, and I stomp on it. Nobody knows who TJ is or why he's here.

We enter a windowless room. A round table and three chairs fit in there, but that's it. He shuts the door behind me. My mouth dries at how much space he takes up, the hostility coming off him. His eyes are narrow. His whole mien is like a bull about to charge.

And I'm the red cape he wants to trample. I should've at least gotten a room with a frosted glass wall.

TJ points at me, his head thrust forward and beard bristling. "Do you enjoy tormenting Tony?"

"What?" I say blankly. He can actually have a conversation. And he's talking rather than thrashing me the way his gaze says he wants to.

"What did he do to you?"

I look away. "Nothing. It's not him. It's me."

"Horseshit! That's what women always say when they're mad but too bitchy to say why."

Is this what Tony thought? But I've never said I was upset with him. Why is he assuming he did something wrong? "I'm not angry with him."

"Then why are you torturing him? The only crime he committed is loving you too much. And the sad fucking fact is, you don't deserve it because you don't value it. Audrey Duff deserves him more. At least that bitch wants him badly enough to fight."

Excruciating pain explodes in my heart. TJ might as well have trampled me.

"He isn't eating. He doesn't sleep," TJ continues relentlessly. "The only reason he goes to work is all the employees and their families depend on him to put food on the table. Otherwise, he'd hole up in his room and never come out."

Aching regret pours through me. I never wanted that for Tony. He shouldn't suffer because of me. He doesn't deserve this. I don't deserve him.

"He was an SOB before he met you, but that's better than what he is now. If you aren't strong and brave enough to accept his love and love him back, then let—him—go." TJ leans closer until our noses almost touch. "Or I'll do it for you."

His eyes are feral. This is a promise. He leaves quietly, not bothering to slam the door.

I should be scared, but I'm not. Only the most crippling pain and self-loathing are slicing through me. My mind conjures an image of Tony, hurting—not eating or sleeping. He's so full of vitality and vigor that it's impossible to imagine him that way, but TJ was telling the truth.

Audrey Duff deserves him more.

That crazy, self-centered bitch does *not* deserve Tony! She'd make him miserable.

But I'm doing the same thing to him, aren't I? At least if she left him, he wouldn't care that much. With me...

I look down at my hands. My fingers shake. Tony loves them, even though they're weirdly long and sort of ugly. He loves every-thing about me, doesn't care about my partial amnesia or my horrible uncle or cousin. Nothing matters to him as long as I'm with him.

"You okay?"

I raise my head and see Bobbi at the doorway. Her eyes are flinty. If I tell her no, she's going to go find her cousin and try to beat the crap out of him. "I'm okay."

"TJ didn't do anything? Hurt you, or...?"

"He didn't touch me. Just wanted to talk." I give her a reassuring smile. But I don't tell her I would've preferred that he punch me instead.

42

IRIS

THE REST OF THE DAY IS A BLUR. MY MIND KEEPS BRINGING up what TJ said. Then it argues with me about how stupid I'm being, its voice gravelly and low-pitched like TJ's.

Just take what Tony's offering. Run with it. Forget what happened before. He doesn't care. He doesn't have to know.

By the time I make it to Yuna's hotel, my head is pounding. She's curled up in her seat in front of the TV, watching BBC News. She frowns and turns it off. "You look awful."

"Just a headache. Do you have any aspirin?"

Mr. Kim immediately appears and hands me a couple of white pills with a glass of water.

"Thank you." I smile weakly. After taking the medicine, I kick off my shoes and sit down next to Yuna.

"Tough day at work?"

"You could say that." I sigh, closing my eyes. *Audrey Duff deserves him more.*

A fresh wave of outrage rips through me. She doesn't deserve

Tony at all. Her idea of fighting for him is faking suicide. That's all kinds of messed up.

But are you worthy of him, you little chickenshit?

That's what I'm trying to figure out, so shut up.

"Hey, do you think I'm a coward?" I ask.

"You? A coward?" Yuna shifts her weight. "Says who?"

I'm not getting into TJ's visit. She wouldn't take it well. I don't want to see Mr. Kim try to hold TJ down so Yuna can lecture him about being nicer. "I'm just asking."

"No. You're one of the bravest and most resilient people I know."

Her answer leaves me touched and embarrassed. My friend. Always seeing the best in me. Doesn't she know I killed someone? Or does she not care?

"What brought that on?" she asks.

"I was thinking..." I hesitate. I don't want to discuss TJ's accusations in detail. But I can maybe tell her some of the arguments my mind's been throwing at me. "How do you make a decision when you don't know something?"

She considers. "Do you actually have to make the decision?"

"Yes." I can't let Tony suffer in limbo. TJ's right about that part.

"My dad once told me there's no certainty in life. You have to make so many decisions, and you never know all the facts. For example, you make a decision to go outside. But you don't know if it's safe or not. A drunk driver might hit you when you try to cross the street. Or there could be some psycho terrorist about to strike where you're going."

Maybe I should've been a little more specific. Fear of drunk drivers or terrorism isn't going to help me figure out what to do. But Yuna's looking at me like I should get it now, so I say, "So you just...do it?"

"Well..." She props her chin in her hand. "You're probably talking about decisions that are a bit more complex than just going outside, right? So in that case, you can only look at what you know for sure and then decide. I usually write things out. Two columns. One for the things I know for a fact and another for the things I don't know. Then I weigh my options."

That sounds so logical and straightforward. But there's got to be a landmine somewhere. Nothing can be that simple, especially when it involves a matter of the heart. "Have you ever regretted a decision you made using the two-column way?"

She taps her lower lip a few times. "You know what? I can't think of any. But I remember regretting not taking chances. Basically, everything is a risk. The times I let some small risk stop me, when I was afraid...I've regretted some of those."

"You? Afraid?" Yuna's one of the most fearless people I've ever met. Not to mention she has rich parents to bail her out.

She nods. "Sometimes I feed it, giving it more power than I should. You know, like when you're a kid. For example, I refused to swim in the ocean."

It's hard to imagine. She seems so capable all the time. "Why?"

"My brother told me stories about water spirits that wrap around your legs and drag you down into the depths." She shudders. "I believed it, and kept thinking about it, and then...just couldn't go into the ocean, even though I could swim better than him. Water spirits could be hiding in the waves." She wrinkles her nose. "Silly, huh?"

"No." The little Yuna standing at the edge of the ocean, too scared to go in, is so vulnerable and real. I wish I could hug the girl she was. Since I can't, I hug her now. "Thank you."

"For what?"

"For being such a clear voice of reason." I let go. "I need to think."

"What about dinner?"

"I'm not hungry." I can't eat, not when my nerves are prickling with anticipation and apprehension. I jump to my feet and head to my room.

"But you have to eat somethi—"

"This is more important!" I shut the door behind me.

I pull out my notebook from the drawer next to the bed. Then I arrange the pillows and lean back with a hotel pen. After flipping to a blank page, I draw a long vertical line down the middle. On top of each column, I write, *certainty* and *uncertainty*.

Certainty is easy.

I love Tony.

Tony loves me.

I don't remember my past. (*It's possible I'll never remember it.*)

Uncertainty is harder.

I could've done something bad in my past. (*Sam said I did, and I think he's telling the truth, sort of.*)

Tony could find out whatever bad things I've done and not love me anymore.

I could be a weakness for Tony. He isn't taking care of himself because of me.

I

My pen stops working, and I make rapid circles, trying to draw out more ink. But it just makes circular grooves in the paper. I throw the pen in the wastebasket near the bed and glare at the page. That third uncertainty really bugs me. I never want to be the reason he isn't doing well. I always thought if I regained my past, I wouldn't be broken anymore and would be somebody he could depend on and draw strength from.

My gaze shifts to the last item on the certainty column. *I don't remember my past. I might never remember it.*

If I never remember my past, am I always going to be a weakness? Somebody who burdens him?

Frustrated and confused, I tilt my head and look at the ceiling. My mind swirls with a billion thoughts. I try to calm myself, needing to think things through logically, one thing at a time.

Did Tony act like I was a burden to him? He worried about me, sure. He was furious when Sam hurt me. When I just moved food around on my plate, he'd offer something he thought I might like better. He could've at any time told me he was tired. Or if he didn't want to say it out loud, he could've just dumped me like he did so many other women before me.

But he didn't.

I think about my feelings for him. Wouldn't I have reacted

with worry if Tony didn't have a healthy appetite? Wouldn't I be furious if somebody tried to hurt him?

Of course. Of course I would, because I love him and want the best for him.

And right now, he's suffering because of me. Is that what I want? Is that what's best for him?

Every time I give him a smile... Every time I'm happy... Every time I make myself a little bit more vulnerable to him... He reacts like it's everything he's ever dreamed of.

If you aren't strong and brave enough...

I always reacted like I was somehow less because I didn't have my memories. Sam certainly told me it was a problem. Threatened to use that to declare me incompetent. But I don't feel incompetent. My head is clear. I remember what's happened to me since I woke up from the coma. I have journal entries to prove that I recall them correctly. I'm certainly competent enough to learn how to swim and create complex Excel spreadsheets for the foundation. I can still master new skills and improve.

I let myself believe I couldn't be more if I didn't regain all my lost memories. The doctor's explanation that my mind is like a broken bowl that's been put together with some missing pieces has been playing in the back of my head, stoking self-doubt and worry.

But everyone has problems, visible or not. Those who are happiest are the ones who don't let their problems define them. I've been letting my memory loss define who I am. And, in the process, hurting myself and the person who loves me the most.

Sam's vile words come rushing back. But this time, instead of reacting with gut emotion, I make myself pull back just a little bit. He's always given me just enough breadcrumbs of information to manipulate me. He lied to me about my high school. Always highlighted how much he's done for me. When nothing else worked, he tried to put me on a one-way flight to Tokyo...then drown me outright.

And with the facts laid out plainly, a sudden grimness grips me. He's pissed off that his investors pulled out, and he's blaming Tony for it. I can't think of any weakness Tony has that Sam could attack, so he's striking at Tony through me. Maybe I was negligent back then when I was driving the car. Maybe I wasn't. I'll never know for certain. But I can't live my entire life torturing myself over it because it won't bring the girl back. If she was my friend, like Sam claimed, that's not what she would've wanted for me. And I don't want to give up on Tony and our love because of it.

TJ is right. I have to be strong and brave if I want to be worthy of that love.

I roll over and reach for my phone, ready to call Tony...then stop. *Three thirty-six a.m.?* How did the time pass so fast?

Impatience mounting, I punch the pillows a few times. Ugh. I couldn't have thought faster, could I?

I can't call him now. Maybe he's finally tired enough to fall asleep. *Tomorrow. I'm definitely going to make it right tomorrow.*

Two hours later, I roll out of bed, too buzzed to get any sleep and anxiety still riding me hard. I want to apologize to Tony for being stupid and tell him I love him, now and forever. I shower, get dressed and come out to see Yuna sipping coffee.

"I'm going to see Tony right now!" I say.

She gives me a small smile. "For what?"

"To tell him yes."

"Yes!" She pumps a fist, almost spilling her coffee.

I turn around and smooth my blue dress. "So how do I look?"

Yuna studies me critically, then finally nods. "You look fine, but you can't do it right now."

"What? Why not?"

"You can't just go over there and say yes. There has to be a proper set-up for this sort of thing."

"But—"

Yuna raises a finger. "Shut up and listen. The man has waited for days. He can wait a few more hours. Then you can accept his proposal in the most memorable way possible. You're only going to do it once, right? So you should make it something neither of you will ever forget."

"But—"

Yuna wags the finger. "No. You give me your key to the penthouse and go to work. And I'll take care of the rest. Trust me."

Trust her? "You've done this before?"

"No, but I imagined how mine should go. Come on. You know I'd never steer you wrong. And after you tell him yes, you're going to text me afterward with a picture of the ring, because I'm going to throw you an engagement party."

43

IRIS

YUNA TAKES MY KEY TO TONY'S PENTHOUSE FOR THE PREP, which is taking all day long, according to her texts. When I ask her what she'll do if Tony's working from home, she says she already checked by calling his office. My Friday is shot because I'm too distracted. I have no idea what she's planning, and I don't know how Tony will react. I wonder if I should've just asked him out to a romantic restaurant, but it's too late now. That would be snubbing Yuna.

Around lunch time, Yuna texts me, insisting I leave work three hours early because I need to do something about my appearance.

You said I looked fine! I text back.

That was then. This is now.

I roll my eyes. She's too invested in this being a huge production, when all I want is to go to Tony and fall into his arms.

Still, she's been the most awesome friend, so I humor her. "It's going to be super boring," I say to Bobbi as she drives me to the address Yuna sent.

"You aren't my first client to spend hours at a spa or whatever. Don't worry."

The moment we arrive, Yuna drags me inside the salon to get my makeup and hair done professionally. "Ethereal and radiant," she orders before I can get a word in.

The stylist beams. "Perfect."

"Are you going to have her wax me, too?" I ask Yuna, my tone extra dry.

"You didn't shave this morning?"

She's serious. "Never mind."

"No, we can probably add that. They can do a full-body wax while she does your face."

A vivid mental picture pops into my head. Me lying down, my thighs spread indecently, with wax all over my legs, armpits and crotch, while a makeup artist is wielding a brush over my face. Shudders run through me. "No! I was being sarcastic."

"But waxing does look better. And it feels nicer when..."

"No! Absolutely not."

"If you're sure..."

"Very," I say. If she doesn't back off, I'm going to get Bobbi to gag her. Yuna isn't the only one with hired muscle around here.

The makeup and hair go smoothly. The stylist knows exactly how to enhance my eyes and cheeks. She puts a lovely shade on my lips that she dubs "bridal pink."

"I'm not getting married," I say.

"Close enough." Yuna gestures to Mr. Kim, who's been sitting in the waiting area.

He brings over a garment bag and a box.

"Ta-da! The perfect dress for you!" Yuna says, unzipping it.

The maxi dress is white with a lovely hint of pink. The mesh bodice is held up by two thin straps. The neckline is a little too plunging for me, but the rhinestones, sequins, iridescent beads and tiny pearls look amazing on the top half the dress. The skirt is unadorned and plain, but it makes the dress even more elegant and sweet.

"It's gorgeous, but I don't know... Don't you think the neckline is a bit too low?"

"We could always do a nun's habit, but come on. You want this to be memorable. This dress will make a statement. And I promise, it will not make you look slutty. Put it on with these shoes." She hands me a pair of silver stilettos.

The stylist takes me to the changing room. I put on the dress. It fits perfectly. Ditto for the shoes. Yuna must've put a lot of thought and effort into finding them. I can't wear anything underneath, though, because of the plunging bodice and the skirt showing the panty lines. Thankfully, Yuna tosses a glossy black bag over the door to stuff my bra and panties.

Although I'm feeling a bit bare underneath, the dress is an ethereal promise of a lovely future. Exactly what I need when I see Tony today.

I come out of the changing room. "What do you think?"

"You look amazing." Yuna circles me. "If I were Tony, I'd do you first, then ask you what you wanted to say."

I almost choke with laughter. Mr. Kim looks at me with a small smile, while Bobbi smirks.

"Diamond studs. And you need a diamond drop necklace," Yuna says.

My hand wraps around the sun, moon and star medallion from Tony. "I'm not taking this off."

"But it's not going to look right."

"I don't care." It's custom-designed, one of a kind. He gave it to me after we slept together for the first time. It's too sentimental and special for me to replace with some generic diamonds.

She gives me a look, then finally throws her hands in the air. "Fine. At least put on the studs. They're mine, but you need them more than me."

"Thank you."

"Don't forget to text me how it goes! I want to be the first to know."

"I will. And Yuna...I don't know how to repay you for everything you've done."

She waves it away. "Please. That's what friends are for. And the dress wasn't even that expensive. But for the wedding, I expect nothing less than a Vera Wang original." She rubs her hands together. "I'm already halfway finished with your engagement party and bachelorette party plans."

Her eyes are full of anticipation and happiness. When she told me she was my soul sister, I thought she was being overdramatic. But everything she's done for me proves she's my biggest ally and supporter other than Tony.

I hug her. "You're the best."

"I know." She pats my back. "Now go get your man!"

44

ANTHONY

MY OFFICE IS DARK. THE BLINDS ARE DOWN, AND THE LIGHTS are off, except for the small lamp on my desk.

It's Friday, and Iris is still gone, not a word from her one way or the other. I only have a single text from Yuna.

Iris didn't sleep well last night. Actually, I'm not sure if she slept at all. Her appetite was meh, and she didn't eat much breakfast.

I read it over and over again, hoping I can penetrate the surface to something deeper underneath. Yuna said Iris was sleeping and eating better earlier this week. Why is she back-sliding now? Is she remembering what happened last Friday? Still sorting through it?

My desk phone beeps. It's Wei. "Would you like me to make a room reservation for tonight?"

TJ must have told Wei about my not going home yesterday. I couldn't bear to be in the place without Iris. It didn't used to be so big and cold, but now, it's about as inviting as an industrial meat locker. So when I saw a hotel on the way, I asked TJ to stop and spent the night there.

When I don't answer, Wei clears his throat. "Boss, there's something else, too. You have an invitation from Ryder Reed. A private dinner at his Hollywood mansion with him and his wife."

That one's easy. "Not going." Even though I've forgiven him, the sight of him and his wife is going to be too much. According to the latest trashy gossip, he's upset the baby isn't pretty enough to be his, and he's going to divorce her for it. But I know the truth. He worships the ground she walks on, and she adores him. The public's upset with the tabloids for dragging a baby into it. "Get me a room at the Ritz," I add.

"Got it." Wei hesitates. "Just so you know, his people met with Iris yesterday at the foundation. So he could've heard something."

"Well, then for fuck's sake, obviously I should go!" What the hell happened to Wei that he keeps the most important thing for last?

"Okay. I'll let him know."

"Wait!"

"Boss?"

"Sorry, Wei. I shouldn't have snapped at you."

"It's okay." He doesn't say more, but there is a pregnant silence. *I'm worried about your mental state. You haven't been yourself.*

I text TJ to bring the car around. There are a couple of glossy bags, one blue and one pink, in the Cullinan. "What are those?"

"Gifts for Ryder and Paige. Wei got them," TJ says.

I glance inside. A bottle of a pricey red, some flowers and a frilly stuffed animal toy. Those should do.

"You sure this is a good idea?" TJ asks.

"It is the best damn idea I have for the evening." Maybe Ryder will say something about Iris. He's close to Elizabeth, so he could've gone to the foundation himself yesterday. Iris might've told him something. His pretty face has the power to make women reveal way more than they should. Maybe I should use *him* as my spy, since Bobbi won't do it.

Ryder's place is more like a fortress than the typical fancy mansion you see on TV. Unlike Sam's frilly so-called security, it has sturdy, functional gates designed to keep intruders out. The thick gray concrete walls are tall, with barbed wire and security cameras on top. He installed those after some psychopath stalker fans tried to sneak into his bed and other ridiculous escapades. The only thing he needs to complete the "keep out, assholes" vibe is a machine gun nest.

When TJ identifies himself and me, the gates open, revealing a perfect slice of SoCal paradise. Colorful flowers bloom in the lush garden. Green shrubs have been recently shaped and trimmed. A huge swimming pool sparkles like a man-made lake off to one side. Normally, there wouldn't be anything around it except lounging chairs and umbrellas, but now, it sports a four-foot-tall fence to keep the baby out. The mansion at the end of the driveway is gigantic, with columns and double doors. Even though Ryder's mother comes from old money, the place looks like nothing but new money. It makes sense; he didn't take a penny from his parents. The money he's made is all from his looks and some shrewd investments.

I step out of my car and walk up the steps. Before I can ring the bell, the double doors open, and Ryder comes out, dressed casually in a polo shirt and shorts, his feet bare. "Hey, ma—" He stops abruptly, his gaze raking me from top to bottom. "Holy shit. Did you catch the flu or something?"

I'd laugh if I didn't felt so terrible inside. "Do I look that bad?"

He nods.

"I'm not contagious, if that's what you're asking," I say, trying to put his mind at ease, especially with the baby at home.

"I wasn't," he says, recovering. "You just look like shit. Well, come on in. And invite your driver in, too."

I hold out the bags Wei prepared. "For you, Paige, and the baby."

"Thanks." He leads me to the huge sitting area that overlooks a rose garden. "Something to drink?"

"Anything's fine."

He pours two glasses of his favorite scotch and hands me one. We clink silently.

"Is Iris coming after work?" he asks after a sip. "She could've told Elizabeth she wanted to leave early."

"She isn't coming."

"Why not?" A shadow crosses Ryder's blue eyes. "You still think... You still don't trust me?"

I shake my head. "You're so far off the mark, you aren't even on the board. If I didn't trust you, I wouldn't be here at all." I try to brace myself for the pain, but it's pointless, like trying to shore up a dam after a flood destroyed everything. "She's gone."

"Gone?" He looks at me like I'm speaking Martian. "But she's still at the foundation."

"Something happened to her. I proposed, and she just..." I can't continue. Saying it out loud makes it feel too real. Something set in stone.

"She said no?" His voice is soft with sympathy.

Somehow, the sympathy makes me feel even worse. Is my situation that obvious? She didn't exactly say no. It's so much worse—I can't fix it. I've failed somewhere along the way to protect her and make sure she's all right. "She left."

"She *what*?"

"She's staying with Yuna now."

"But dude, she loves you. No woman could look at you the way she did at the club and not be totally in love with you."

"I thought that too." And that's why the rejection wasn't just unexpected but unrecoverable from—a KO that left me so punch-drunk that I can never get back up.

"Did you screw up? Forget the ring?"

I laugh hollowly. "I got a custom Masako Hayashi."

"Okay, fine. It wasn't the ring." Ryder runs a palm down his face. "You think she's starting to remember the past?"

I already considered that possibility. "No. If she were, she wouldn't have looked so sad." She would've slapped my face. After cutting my balls off.

"Don't you think you should tell her, though? I mean, before someone else does?"

I swallow a mouthful of scotch. I know I should. I've been avoiding that because I don't know how to do it without making her hate me. And there's the matter of timing. How am I going to just blurt out that I knew who she really was all along but didn't tell her? How am I going to deal with the nuclear fallout? "I've come too far to do that."

"Hey, it's never too late."

Spoken like a man who has everything. "It is this time. I built a castle on a poor foundation. To fix it, I'd have to wreck it and start over...except I don't think I can."

"Nothing stays secret forever."

I drink more scotch, trying to soothe the acid burn in my belly with the liquor. Ryder's right, but I don't want to think about it. Besides, unless Iris regains her memory, nobody's going to tell her. Yuna and Harry won't. Harry will already have told Edgar—Harry tells Edgar everything—so my brothers won't be talking. My parents disowned me, so nothing's going to come from that quarter. Sam and Marty are too dirty to talk. As a matter of fact, they'll do their very best to hide who Iris really is because they gave her the false identity.

"It's going to be worse if she doesn't hear it first from you," Ryder adds.

I know that, but... "If I tell her, she'll hate me for sure."

"How can you be so certain?"

"Because she's the way she is because of me." Since I can't dwell on it without losing my mind, I add, "It's complicated."

I tilt my empty glass, and Ryder pours me more scotch. He's right about everything. Keeping up the lies is a shitty thing to do, except I have no idea how to get out of the situation. Maybe the time to be honest was at Hammers and Strings.

I don't know how many more scotches I have. Paige joins us after a while, curvier than ever from post-pregnancy weight. Her honey-golden hair is in a messy bun, and her face is scrubbed clean of makeup. Although she's no stunner, she's naturally beautiful and wholesome. I tried to use her to get back at Ryder, but ultimately couldn't. Those liquid brown eyes made me feel like scum every time I contemplated doing something nasty.

NADIA LEE

"Hi, Tony. I'm so glad you could join us. Where's—"

Ryder shakes his head. *Thanks, buddy.* Now I don't have to do an explanation encore.

"Oh. Well." She smiles. "Do you want to have an early dinner? I think it's ready. I hope you like Mexican. I've been craving it." She laughs. "You'd think the random cravings would be gone by now, but..."

"That's fine." I'm not here for the food. I only want to know how Iris's doing.

We move to the dining room, where Ryder's cook has everything prepared. Tacos and fajita fillings and soft tortillas are spread out, undoubtedly delicious, but I reach for more scotch. I have no stomach for anything solid. Paige pushes a few platters toward me, but eventually she quits, for which I'm grateful. It's already bad enough to see the obvious love and affection she and Ryder have for each other in the small touches, the faint smiles...

Time to get to the real reason I'm here before I start to feel any lonelier and more pathetic. "I heard you had a meeting at the foundation yesterday." *Come on. Give me some clues as to what's up with her, so I can fix it.*

"My new assistant did," Ryder says. "Iris is managing her first project well. Everything's on track."

Pride stirs. That's my woman.

Is she still? the annoying voice whispers in my head.

She is until she tells me it's over.

Nothing says "the end" like walking out.

Fuck. I finish the drink, wanting to drown out the infuriating points my mind is making.

When my glass is empty, Ryder pours me more.

"Shouldn't you eat something?" Paige says.

"I'm not really hungry." It's the truth. I haven't been hungry in days.

From the disapproval in her gaze, she disagrees. "You'll scare all the girls away looking like that."

I laugh hollowly. I only want one girl. As I consume more of Ryder's best scotch, my mind starts to relax a bit. I should talk to Iris tomorrow. It's been a week, and she'll have gained some perspective on whatever's bothering her by now. If not, I'll just kill Byron Fucking Pearce, because it's gotta be his fault. I don't need TJ to drive me. I can find that bastard on my own.

Well past nine, I stand unsteadily.

Ryder puts a hand on my shoulder. "You can spend the night if you want."

"Nah. I got a reservation." Even if I didn't, I'm not staying here. Not with those two lovebirds. They're restraining themselves on my behalf, but I can still see and hear how they're finishing each other's sentences. Sometimes all it takes is a single glance to communicate. It only makes me miss Iris more.

"You aren't going home?" Paige says.

"No. Wei made me a reservation." I beam at her. "I'll be fine. It's a suite!" Or at least I think it is. But it doesn't matter. A roach motel would do.

"Maybe you should go home," she says. "What if she wants to talk to you? How is she going to find you if you aren't where you're supposed to be?"

Ah, my best friend's wife is ever so hopeful. I'm not. Life has taught me that hope doesn't usually pan out. "She hasn't texted me in a week. She doesn't want to talk."

"Don't do what Ryder did to me. I had to fly halfway around the world to talk to him."

I squint at Ryder. "Did you do that?"

"Something like that." He laughs. "You know how it is."

"Well, it's just a hotel, not halfway around the world."

Ryder and Paige walk me to the door.

"Thanks for dinner," I say.

"You didn't eat a bite," Paige says.

I grin shamelessly, refusing to let her make me feel bad about having Ryder's scotch. I haven't had this many calories in days. "Hey, liquid dinner counts."

I stumble out, and TJ helps me into the Cullinan. I close my eyes. The car is quiet except for the sound of my breathing and the purr of the engine as we drive away. Did Wei get a room at the same hotel Yuna's staying at? Maybe I could accidentally run into Iris. Or maybe...maybe...

My head is swimming. I reach for a bottle of aspirin I keep in the car and take four with some water.

Drinking close to an entire bottle of scotch was dumb. Ryder's the one with the titanium liver and immunity to alcohol, not me. But it felt so good. Nice to have a burn in my gut that isn't caused by acid.

The Cullinan finally stops. The doorman rushes over and opens the door. I stare bleary-eyed at the hotel. It isn't Yuna's. And...

How is she going to find you if you aren't where you're supposed to be?

That's a damn good point. What if Iris wants to talk to me? Not that I think that's going to happen. But you never know. Miracles do occur.

One already did when she came back from the dead. You screwed up. Again.

Just one more time. That's all I ask.

"Shut the door," I say to the doorman. To TJ, I say, "Take me home."

45

IRIS

I PACE. IT'S ALREADY AFTER NINE, AND TONY'S NOT home yet.

Where is he?

I even managed to send Bobbi home, after swearing I wasn't going to jump into the pool or do anything crazy. It's impossible to be romantic and intimate with an audience.

I stop and take in the romantic scene. Yuna did an amazing job. Countless candles emit soft light from the floor, on the table, along the stairs. If they were real tea lights, they would've burned out by now, but they're electric. Instead of a bare bulb sticking out on top, each one blows a gentle breeze through a hole in the center, which makes a flame-shaped piece attached to the top dance. It makes the light look real and natural.

The dining table has platters of cold cuts of meat, cheese and chilled champagne. Well, it isn't that chilled now because the ice cubes have melted. Eight vases of tiger lilies emit a soft fragrance, but they only remind me I'm alone here without Tony.

I pull one long stem from the vase on the table. Suddenly,

exhaustion crushes me. I slump on a couch, the tiger lily resting on my belly. I was so sure he'd be home. Maybe I should've considered Tony might have plans on a Friday. He's a busy man. Maybe Audrey came back. Maybe...

I stop. *He wouldn't go back to Audrey. That's crazy.* I'm just tired. I haven't slept much, and disappointment is leeching away what little reserve of energy I have.

Tony could've gotten tired of waiting for you to make up your mind. A week is a long time.

Maybe. But I'm not leaving until I talk with him. I didn't go through all this just to give up...

A prickling of awareness runs through me. I open my eyes, then blink to focus.

Tony's crouched in front of me, his gaze intent on my face. Air sticks in my throat. His cheeks are hollow from weight loss. His green eyes are bloodshot, and several days' growth of beard covers his face.

He's completely still, not even blinking. I can barely feel his breath, although I can smell alcohol on him.

I sit up slowly, sorrow blooming in my heart. No wonder TJ was angry with me. I didn't realize Tony was suffering this badly. I should've rushed here at four a.m. yesterday instead of waiting until now.

"Tony," I whisper.

His gaze is roaming over me. "Are you real or am I dreaming?"

"I'm very real." I lay a hand over his cheek so he can feel me.

He places a tender kiss in the center of my palm, his eyes still on mine. He hasn't blinked even once, as though he's afraid if he lets me out of sight even for a millisecond, I'll vanish. "I didn't mean to wake you."

"It's okay. I didn't mean to fall asleep." I flush with embarrassment. "Listen, Tony. There's something I have to say."

"Are you leaving me?"

"Uh, what?" I look around. The faux-candles are still glowing romantically. And the tiger lilies are the same. What gave him that impression?

His whole body's wound tight. "Thought maybe you were. This looks like a last supper or something."

Guilt and remorse bloom in my heart. His reaction isn't even rational, and all I told him is I needed to talk to him. Didn't the candles give him any idea that this isn't a goodbye? "I'm not leaving you."

The wariness doesn't ease.

"And you ought to eat. I can't believe you, after nagging me for weeks to take better care of myself." I stop, then shake myself mentally. I'm not here to talk about that. "About what I'm here to say..." I inhale deeply to gather courage. I've never been this emotionally vulnerable to someone before. Even though Tony's never been anything but supportive, it's still scary. "Last Friday, I learned something upsetting and scary about myself. I've been so obsessed about it that I didn't realize how I was hurting you. I want to be strong for you—and brave enough for you. If you'll still have me..." I lick my lips, then reach out and hold his face between my palms. "I love you, Anthony Blackwood. You're the only man I've ever loved, and I know you're the only one for me. There are times I'm really, really scared because you're so perfect that I don't think I deserve you. But I can never give you up. Will you marry me?"

He finally blinks. I can see all the thoughts and emotions drain out of him as my words sink in. My heart racing, I stare into his eyes. Sanity returns first, then joy...the most blinding and brilliant love fills his gaze.

"Yes. God, *yes*. A billion times yes."

His mouth crashes down on mine. Relief and joy overflows my heart. I return the kiss, desperate for him. It's been so long since we touched. Loved. Took pleasure in each other's bodies.

I glide my tongue against his and shiver with delight. He tastes like hard liquor and frenzied lust.

Our hands are clumsy. I fumble with his shirt buttons, dying to feel him. His heart beats hard and fast. I pull away just long enough to say, "Take off your clothes."

The buttons explode, flying everywhere. The shoes and socks

are next. He pulls down his pants and underwear and kicks them off.

His mouth rushes back to mine, devouring me. I sob with relief that he still wants me like this, because I want him just as much.

He runs a large, hot palm along my leg, making the bare skin tingle. When he reaches the flesh between my legs, he groans. "You aren't wearing anything underneath."

"Panty lines. You know."

He glides the pad of his thumb along the slick folds, bumping against my clit. I cry out, my fingers digging into the bunched muscles in his wide shoulders.

"God, it's been so long," he whispers, his breath hot against my neck.

"I know. Don't make me wait another second." I nip his earlobe and spread my legs shamelessly. I need him *now*. Inside me.

I shift so his hard shaft is positioned at my pussy. My whole body vibrates with anticipation. "Now, now."

Tony pulls my nipple—the mesh bodice and all—into his mouth and drives into me in one powerful thrust.

Arching my back, I cry out. He feels so good—so large and pulsing. I missed this—the connection, pleasure...and stark vulnerability so private and exclusive that I'm the only one he shows it to. I love him so much more for it, and all of my shields come down, leaving me totally exposed to him in return.

His name is a prayer on my lips as he moves, the fast, desperate friction of our bodies creating blinding bliss. He knows exactly how to push me higher and higher. I clutch him to me hard and look into his eyes.

"Come with me," I whisper.

White heat flares in his gaze, his muscles tight and trembling. He drives into me one last time, grinding against my clit. Pleasure explodes inside me. I sob out his name before his mouth reclaims mine, his hands crushing my hair.

He pulls me tightly toward him, and we cuddle, our hearts racing. When my breathing settles, I note the cool hardness underneath my feet. I realize we're half on the rug in front of the couch.

I'm still in my dress, the skirt bunched around the waist. Tony's completely naked. Without changing our position, he fumbles for his pants and drags them over.

"Now. This goes where it belongs." He takes the ring box from the pocket and puts the ring on my finger. A possessive gleam glints in his brilliant green eyes.

My breath catches at the rightness of having the symbol of our commitment on my hand. The pearl is huge, flawless, almost a celestial object in its beauty. The rubies are stunning, and diamonds sparkle like unshed tears of a happy bride at her wedding. "It's perfect." I kiss him. "You're perfect." Then I pull back with a frown. "But you've lost too much weight." I trace my hands over his ribs, more prominent now. TJ said Tony stopped taking care of himself, but I didn't realize how bad it was. "I'm sorry. This is all my fault."

He holds my hand and kisses each fingertip. "No. It's enough you're back. Nothing else matters."

I look at his soft expression. He's totally justified in being upset for what I put him through. He could totally demand to know why I stayed away. But none of that's important to him.

I'm the only one he cares about.

His love touches me to the core. I have no idea what I've done to deserve this complex, powerful man who's only vulnerable to me. "I've been selfish," I whisper. "I hurt you, and I shouldn't have. I should've been stronger." I should've never let Sam or a past I can't remember get to me like that. The guilt I felt should've been mine to deal with without causing Tony any suffering.

"Everyone deserves to be a little weak." He kisses me. "I love you so much. If you hadn't come tonight, I was going to go to Yuna's and drag you home."

I gasp, finally remembering my best friend, who put all this romantic scene together for us. "Oh my God. I totally forgot. I was supposed to text her."

"About what?"

"That we're together! She's throwing an engagement party for us."

He frowns. "She is?"

"Yes. She insisted, and I said sure, why not." I rub the frown lines as though I could erase them. He needs to stop acting like this could vanish in an instant. "We need to celebrate our happy moments."

Tony picks me up and stands. "Then I'll never get anything done, because I'll be too busy celebrating." He kisses me sweetly.

And I vow I'll never hurt Tony again because of Sam or my past. I'm going to be strong enough for our love.

46

ANTHONY

IF IT WERE UP TO ME, IRIS AND I WOULD NEVER LEAVE THE place or let anybody visit. But late Sunday afternoon, she stretches lazily in bed and says, "Yuna's coming over for dinner."

"She is?" I wrinkle my nose, pulling Iris closer, not wanting to get out of bed yet. It's not even five. We ate a few times to keep our strength up, but otherwise, we've spent the last two days entwined with each other in bed.

"Uh-huh." She rubs her eyes. "She wanted to visit yesterday morning, but I held her off as long as I could."

I try not to make a face because Iris adores Yuna and I owe her one. But damn. I even forced Bobbi to take the weekend off.

She pokes my ticklish spot. "Can you be a little less enthusiastic? She says she's going to bring food and drinks."

Whatever. It isn't like I can't afford to feed us. But Iris looks too happy, and I guess it was bound to happen. After all, don't all women want to admire engagement rings? Iris's finger sports the pearl, and it's a stone to be proud of.

She holds up her left hand in front of her face. "I seriously love this."

"Really? In what ways?" I ask, not fishing. Okay, very much fishing. But I deserve that after a week of hell.

"You're very traditional."

"Me?" I've been disowned by my family and made my money with clubs, where people drink and gyrate away until dawn.

"Yup. Protective. Insist on paying for everything when you don't have to. Indulge me even when you don't want to. I think you let me get away with a lot of things because I'm a woman."

I grin, but don't correct her. How I treat her has nothing to do with her gender. She gets to get away with murder because I love her. "I see."

"So I knew you'd go that route, but the pearl was unexpected. And I like it better than I would a diamond."

"Do you?" I ask, happy I got it just right and pleased she's so thrilled with it.

She shifts and turns so she's facing me. "Yes. Everyone has a diamond. This ring is so us—different, but somehow we work really well."

"We do." I link our fingers and kiss her knuckles. "So let's not have guests over."

She laughs. "Don't be bad. If I cancel, Yuna's going to show up here anyway...and probably sooner than tonight."

I let out a theatrical sigh. Iris probably tried her best to hold her friend off as long as she could.

"And we both need to get out of bed and get ready. I do not plan to greet Yuna naked," Iris says, hopping off the mattress and starting toward the shower.

I stay in bed, enjoying the view, then finally get up when she shuts the door. I should be gracious. Yuna hasn't just been supportive of Iris; she probably helped me stay on this side of sanity with her text updates. It's just unfortunate Yuna doesn't have the patience to wait a month before barging in on us.

She shows up at five till six, dressed fashionably as usual in a soft orange fitted tunic, white cropped pants and chunky sandals. Mr. Kim's in a suit, of course. I don't think he has anything else in his wardrobe. I almost blink when I spot Julie, too. I could swear Iris didn't mention Julie. Or was I just so distracted I missed it?

"Welcome," I say, remembering my manners. "Come in."

"Congratulations! Oh my God, you're going to be like my brother-in-law!" Yuna hugs me.

Mr. Kim gives me a bland smile that says in no way am I going to be anything like a brother-in-law to Yuna.

"I'm so happy for you," Julie says when Yuna's finished with her enthusiastic embrace.

I look at her, gauging her emotion. She doesn't like me that much, and isn't she on Team Byron?

"Oh, come on! You don't have to look suspicious," she says. "If Iris agreed to marry you, then she must really love you. I'm big enough to say I'm fine with you as long as you make her happy."

"It's my life goal to make her happy."

"Then we're good." Her tone is decisive and clear.

Suddenly, I'm glad Julie's here too. Although she can be a bit impulsive, she means well. Iris doesn't have a lot of friends, and it matters that she's surrounded by people who want the best for her.

"Where's the star of the evening?" Yuna demands.

"You mean it isn't me?" I say with a grin.

She pulls up short, then puts a hand on her chest. "You just made a joke."

"I'm not *that* bad." At least, I don't think so.

And then Iris comes hopping down the stairs. A bright red top and skinny jeans look fantastic on her. But most of all, I'm drawn to the gentle radiance of her expression, the beauty of her soul. No matter how long I live or how many people I meet, I'll never find a more splendid woman.

"You're *here!*" She hugs Yuna and Julie in one big embrace.

"Show us the ring!" Yuna says.

"Yes, the ring!" Julie reaches for Iris's left hand.

Iris lifts it up, tilting it this way and that. Much squealing ensues.

"Oh my God!" Julie's eyes widen. "It's *huge!*"

"Aww. It's gorgeous," Yuna says. "Custom-made, right?"

Iris glances in my direction. I put an arm around her waist and say, "Yup."

"Who?" Yuna asks.

"Masako Hayashi."

"A great choice."

I grin. "I know."

"Who's that?" Iris asks.

"One of the best jewelry designers in the world. I think she makes bridal pieces," Yuna says. "You have to have her do them for your wedding." She gives me a look. "You're going to, right?"

"It's going to be ridiculously expensive," Iris says.

It's adorable how she's worried about things like that. How many times do I have to tell her everything I have is at her disposal? But at the same time, I understand where Iris is coming from. I've seen her passion and dedication at the foundation. She sees the poverty and misery of the world, and it's difficult for her to imagine spending that kind of money on herself. "We can totally do that," I say. "Then, if you'd like, we can auction the pieces to raise money for charity afterward."

She looks up at me, her gray eyes shining. "You think so?"

I nod, ignoring the stunned expressions on Yuna and Julie's faces.

Iris's shoulders droop slightly. "But who's going to buy them? I'm not famous or anything."

"We'll find a PR angle. My team can come up with something." They better if they want to keep their jobs. Making my fiancée happy is their new responsibility.

A call from the concierge interrupts us. "Uh...sir? Mr. Black-wood. Uh. There's...Mr. Ryder Reed here to see you. You know, the actor."

"I can't believe I'm not on your approved guest list!" comes his voice in the background.

I roll my eyes. It's just like him to show his big-ass ego everywhere he goes. He's probably here to check up on me to make sure I didn't do something crazy after the dismal and depressing dinner on Friday. Speaking of which, Paige is the one who advised me to go home. I owe her for that. A lot. "Let him up. And his guests, if he has any." I hang up.

"Who was that?" Iris asks.

Yuna and Julie also wait for my answer.

"Just a friend dropping by," I say, not wanting to tell them now and get them overexcited. It's going to be bad fast enough. At least there are only three women.

A few minutes later, Ryder walks into the place like he owns it. All three women yelp with surprise. Julie's in particular is piercing. I wince. Maybe Byron Fucking Pearce is trying to turn me deaf using his sister.

Even Mr. Kim's normally stoic demeanor cracks slightly. "I don't know why they're reacting like that. It isn't like you cured cancer," I say.

"Don't hate the player." Grinning shamelessly, Ryder gives me a man-hug, slapping my back. "I see Iris is here, so we all good?" he says into my ear.

Before I can answer, Yuna says, "They're engaged!"

"What? Did I say that loud enough for everyone?" Ryder asks.

"Yes," I say.

I herd everyone into the living room so we can all sit down. Iris and I share a loveseat, and Ryder's wedged between Yuna and Julie on a long couch. Mr. Kim almost vanishes into the background. It's a talent.

Ryder gives me the smile he reserves for billboard advertising. "So, engaged! I knew it! You lucky dog. I'm happy for you, man."

"Thanks. Where's Paige?"

"Stayed home. Benni's been fussy all day, and she didn't want to leave her with the nanny." Ryder leans back in his seat with a satisfied grin. "So I'm your best man, right?"

Again, before I can answer, Yuna and Julie gasp like they just won the jackpot, hands over their mouths and chins.

"Why are you so excited?" Julie asks Yuna.

"Why are *you*?"

"Because I'm going to be Iris's maid of honor."

Yuna rests her hands on her hips. "I don't think that's been decided yet."

"Ladies, ladies! I'm a married man." Ryder spreads his arms innocently.

I don't buy the act. He might be married. He might be devoted to his wife. But he's still a showman. He thrives under the attention. "I haven't decided who's going to be my best man," I say.

Ryder snorts. The meaning is clear—who could possibly be better suited for best-manning than him? "You have other candidates?"

"I don't know. Maybe one of my brothers?"

"Oh come on! You know Harry'll lose the ring."

"That's slander. Besides, I have two brothers."

"*Edgar?*" He laughs. "Are you trying to have a wedding or a funeral?"

I have to laugh as well. "Edgar's a rule follower, but he isn't that bad."

"Dude. I haven't met a single rule follower who was any fun."

Iris loops her arm around mine. "You have two brothers?"

I nod. Soon, she's going to get to know them all, and I need to prep Edgar. "You already met Harry. Edgar is older and lives in Louisiana."

"Why do I feel like there's so much more to know about you?" she asks.

Because I haven't told you everything, especially about my family. It's one topic I almost never discuss. "Because I'm mysterious, with lots and lots of layers. You need to stick around if you want to peel them all," I whisper into her ear.

Before Iris can respond, Yuna raises her hand. "Since I'm in charge of the engagement party, I feel like I should definitely be the chosen one."

"That's not fair. I never got a chance to volunteer for the position!" Julie says.

"Nobody volunteers." Ryder waves a hand. "You just do it. Tell me more about this party you're planning. I love parties, and I know exactly what makes them memorable." Then he pauses. "And somebody order dinner. I'm getting hungry."

47

ANTHONY

AFTER DINNER, I LEAVE RYDER TO ENTERTAIN THE WOMEN and go out on the deck for some peace and quiet. My eyes started glazing over when Yuna brought up engagement party favors, and Julie decided they should be fun and eclectic and unique. They want the event to be one for the ages. I shudder. That's the last thing I need when there's a killer out there I know nothing about.

All I want to do is marry Iris. That's it. But at the rate things are going, I'm going to have to participate in all sorts of parties and other junk. I'm only indulging Yuna and Julie because Iris looks so happy, and Yuna repeatedly made the point that Iris is getting married *only once*, so I owe it to her to ensure it's something *she never, ever forgets*. And it's true. Iris does deserve to have some joyful new memories to make up for all the ones she's lost. I'm going to make sure that this time, she won't lose any of them.

The door opens and closes, and I sense Ryder's presence. "Got tired of listening to the menu?"

"Yeah. I said fun, not food. They're acting like they've never eaten shrimp before."

Just like him to complain about that. But when he has parties, he has a team to manage the details. He just shows up.

"You okay?"

I shrug, then blow out a breath. Here I thought I was doing a good job of hiding how I'm really feeling about the engagement party. "Do I look that bad?"

"Nah, you're doing all right. But you're no actor, and I've known you for a long time."

"I don't like the party idea," I say. "If it were up to me, I'd cancel, but..." I have no idea how I got myself in this jam. This is not how I envisioned my proposal to engagement to...post-engagement stuff.

"Then cancel. You're the other half of the couple."

"I owe Yuna one." Actually more than one, for not only taking care of Iris but keeping the secret. "And look at Iris. She's thrilled."

"The shit we put up with for our women." Ryder clasps my shoulder. "You'll survive. It really isn't that bad. All you have to do is smile and look happy, which shouldn't be too hard. Besides, the girls might not even find a suitable venue."

"It's not the venue. It's the security." Anxiety keeps pushing all my buttons. "Parties like this get picked up by bored 'journalists' all the time. Headlines pop, and people notice." Sam flipped out over the videos that went viral. The last thing I need is him losing it and making a scene, humiliating Iris. Or for the real villain from nine years ago to realize she survived the crash and come back.

"Eh, what can you do? Comes with the territory." Ryder looks out over the city contemplatively. "Money. Connections. Fame."

"The killer from Tempérane is still out there. Somewhere." I hate that I still don't know who it is and where he or she might be. Jill is working too damn slow for my taste. "What if they come back to finish the job when they realize Iris is alive?"

Ryder's eyes are alert now. "You really think she was the target?"

"I don't know. But even if she wasn't, she's a witness. If I were the killer, I would want her permanently silenced."

He rubs his jaw. "Shit."

Frustration and stress stick into me like a hot poker. A hotel is going to be way too open. I can't not invite Ryder, and that means party crashers. It'll be hard for Bobbi to guard Iris.

"I got a solution. A big scandal right before the party. Nobody'll care about your event." Then he adds quickly, "In a good way. You know."

I almost roll my eyes. In Hollywood, nobody giving a shit is probably worse than some faceless assassin trying to kill you. I'm tempted to take him up on his offer, but I know better. "I can't let you do that. You gotta think about your wife." I don't want her to suffer on my account.

"What about it?" Ryder's face clears. "Oh, you think I'm offering to star in this one?" He guffaws. "Please. I don't do low-budget scandals. It's Hollywood. Scandals are dime a dozen and cheap to produce. Just leave it to me. I'll give you a scandal so bad, it'll overshadow everything short of an alien landing. And if you're worried about hotel security, I'll host it at my place. Nobody can crash it."

It's true. Ryder's place is like a reverse prison. You can't go in. Not without an invitation. "That would be great. Thanks."

"What are friends for?"

I give him a faint smile. But I can't shake off the unease in my gut.

48

ANTHONY

WHAT I WAS REALLY HOPING WAS THAT YUNA WOULD LOSE interest in the party nonsense. But once Ryder volunteered his mansion, she became even more determined to make it a huge success.

Normally I'd be touched—on Iris's behalf, since I don't care about the engagement party. But this isn't a normal situation. And it's crazy how Yuna has maintained her enthusiasm for three whole weeks.

At least Ryder came through. A sex scandal broke last night. It features a barely legal porn star and the former mayor of some little town in New York. Normally nobody would care. But the porn star is about to be in a non-porn film, and the politician has a big platform among young voters. He was a shoo-in for senator, and some thought he might even get the nod for the presidential election in the next few years.

Sucks to be him. He shouldn't have been cheating on his wife, who was going through liver transplant surgery when the sex tape was made.

It's just a party. It's going to be over in less than six hours. We can do a lavish but intimate ceremony, not too many guests.

It's clouding over outside. While Iris is in the shower after her swim, I check my phone. A text from Jill arrived a couple of minutes ago.

Got what I need. Can we meet and talk this evening? I'm at SFO. On my way to LAX.

Finally! I've been needing this information for weeks. *What are you doing in SFO?*

Peacher's business got its start in the Bay Area. He moved it to L.A. after his first project. There are a lot of people here who want to talk if you know how to ask.

Jill does know how to flirt, flatter and stroke male egos. She's also great at conveying sympathy and care, which makes women loosen up. *What time can you get to my place?*

Nine?

No good. Have to attend a party.

Tomorrow morning, then.

No. I'm not waiting a second more than I have to. *Come to the party. It's at Ryder Reed's mansion.*

Holy shit! For real?

Yes. I'll add you to the guest list.

Will be there. Black tie?

No. But dress nice. You can tell people you're my friend if anybody asks. I don't want my fiancée knowing why you're really there.

Got it.

I run my free hand through my hair. This must be big. Jill wouldn't have contacted me if it weren't.

And sensitive, my mind whispers. Otherwise she would've texted or emailed it.

The unease that's been plaguing me in the last three weeks might be nothing. But my instincts almost never steer me wrong. I usually screw up when I ignore them.

I go upstairs and step into *our bedroom.* I can never get used to how much I love the sound of that. Soon, Iris is going to be my wife. Longing and love swell in my heart until I feel like I'm about to float away like a balloon. The joy she gives me is so intense that it seems like I'm living in a dream rather than an actual life.

Her hands resting on her hips, Iris is standing in the closet, her back to me. She's totally nude, except for the chain around her neck and the ring on her finger. I watch for a moment, and she bends over to check something.

Lust sears through me. I spent hours this morning bringing her to climax over and over again. And now, I want to do it again. Watching her shatter in pleasure is an addiction. I crave it worse than an alcoholic craving another drop of vodka. "Are you trying to decide what to wear to the party?"

"Yes," she says, straightening up and looking at me over her shoulder.

"Yuna didn't pick something out for you?"

"Hahaha. She didn't have time."

I glide forward until I'm standing less than a foot from her. "You look the best in nothing but that necklace and ring."

She laughs breathlessly, her cheeks flushing. "I can't show up at the party like this."

"Obviously not." I look at her nipples. They bead under my gaze. My mouth waters. "This is just for me." I graze my thumbs over them.

A harsh, quick inhale. Her gray eyes darken until they're nearly black. "Tony," she whispers, her voice shaky with desire.

I push her gently against the wall, but my mouth is not gentle. I devour her ruthlessly, greedily, reveling in the cries of pleasure in the back of her throat and loving the taste of her on my tongue.

Iris doesn't get ready for another hour.

49

IRIS

BUTTERFLIES ARE FLUTTERING IN MY BELLY. I KEEP RUBBING my hands, which feel clammy now. Maybe it's the rain.

My dress is a lavender Versace. It's cute and classy, with an off-the-shoulder bodice and a flirty skirt made of thin material that swirls every time I turn. The dress and nude sandals seemed like a great idea back home, but now that we're sitting in Ryder's mansion and about to face the guests, I'm rethinking my choices.

"Do I look okay?" I ask Tony for the fifth time.

"You look perfect." He holds my hand, then kisses it. "Your fingers are cold. Why are you so nervous?"

"Because it's our first public event as a couple." I breathe slowly to make sure I don't hyperventilate. So many people are here, many of them Tony's friends and acquaintances. "What if they don't like me?" What if they think Tony could've done better? That he's, like, settling? What if I do or say something weird?

"They'll love you." Tony smiles. He looks amazing in a white button-down shirt and black slacks and jacket. No tie. Tony didn't want one, and Yuna agreed, saying it's a party, not a "who has the nicest tux" competition.

"I don't know..."

Thunder cracks outside, making me jump and move closer to Tony. What started out as a light drizzle on our way here, making TJ complain that SoCal people drive like crap in the rain, became a full-blown storm after we arrived. I hate it, but not for the same reason. Storms always spike my anxiety, especially when the sky's raging at night. It always feels like I'm being dragged into a horrible pit, which, once in, I'm never escaping from. *Maybe I should just tell Tony I'm not feeling well and cancel...*

I stop, then shake myself mentally. I promised myself I'd be strong and brave. Am I being strong and brave?

No.

Didn't I know it wouldn't be easy to love a man as extraordinary as Tony? I've seen how he is around most people. He won't even let them call him Tony, pointedly reminding them his name is Anthony. He always maintains a certain distance and aloofness, but not with me. From the very beginning, he let his guard down, pulled me closer until I've become the center of his universe—just like the sun, moon and stars on the pendant he gave me.

I can do this. For him. For myself.

"It's time," Yuna says, sticking her head into the room where Tony and I have been waiting.

Our fingers linked tightly, we step out into the huge hall together. Ryder's mansion is gorgeous, contemporary and classy, with beautiful artworks. He's letting us use the ground level for the party.

I blink at the number of people who are gathered, clapping as we enter the hall, Bobbi following discreetly. Yuna said the party was going to be "small." We have to be violating the fire code or something.

I recognize a few guests from celebrity gossip sites. But most are totally new to me. There are so many, all of them wanting to stop and congratulate us, that it's hard to make our way. Tony seems to know all of them and responds politely, but not always with warmth. He also makes introductions, but nothing sticks in my head for more than a second. Trying to keep track of all the faces and names is harder than memorizing Rachmaninoff's entire second piano concerto in one afternoon. And if this many are here for the engagement, how many will come to the wedding?

I whisper the question in Tony's ear.

"It was supposed to be small. People got ten days' notice, so I figured most wouldn't bother," he says, his voice low. "And I thought even if they said they'd come, they wouldn't because the weather's crappy."

"So how come they're all here?"

"Probably because I've never been linked to a woman this long...or fallen in love. You're the only one, and people are curious." A small frown.

I remember how Julie told me about the horrible womanizing reputation Tony has. Maybe it's been bugging him more than it should. I pat his hand with a grin. "They shouldn't care so much about your reputation. You're one of the nicest people I know."

"Is that so?" he whispers into my ear, his hot breath fanning my skin.

I tilt my head, so he can see the truth in my eyes. "Yes. If the rep were real, I would've never fallen in love with you."

Instead of making him smile, what I said seems to bring shadows to his gaze. I don't get it. Is there something else to what people say about him that I missed?

I want to ask him what's wrong, but don't get the opportunity. People are starting to make toasts, and I have to pick up a flute of champagne from a waiter and raise it.

But I make a mental note to ask Tony about it later. I want to fix whatever's making him feel sorrow or regret...just like he's been doing for me.

50

ANTHONY

I SHOULD'VE SMILED AND WINKED WHEN IRIS SAID SHE didn't believe my rep was true. The moment concern dimmed the smile on her face, I knew I'd screwed up.

It's just that my reputation is very well deserved. Manipulative. Cold. Ruthless.

And hiding the truth about her past—our shared past—fits those three adjectives pretty well. Ryder said it'll be worse if she finds out from a third party, and he's right. But even if I want to tell her, I can't figure out how. I couldn't handle her contempt or hatred...or worse, disappointment.

It's the weirdest thing, but I'd rather have her slap me or call me names than be disappointed or lose faith in me. Those seem like the greatest failings I could have, something beyond forgiveness. And I'm going to do everything in my power—no matter how manipulative, cold or ruthless—to ensure it never happens.

Once the toasts are finished, people come over to say a few private words. God. I had no idea there would be this many. If I had, I would've found some other place to meet with Jill. How the hell am I going to find her in this mob?

Yuna and Julie, however, are excited at their success. "Look at the crowd! It's awesome!" Julie says.

"They're all here for you," Yuna says to Iris.

I spot Byron heading toward Julie. Or maybe us. I don't know or give a shit. I didn't want him here, but he's Julie's brother, and ostensibly Iris's friend. It's too bad he didn't crash his Maserati on the rain-slickened roads. My arm around Iris tightens.

"Rizzy," Byron says with a warm smile. Then his gaze shifts toward me, and it turns noticeably cool.

Fine by me, since, if I could, I'd run him over with my Cullinan.

"Byron, I'm glad you could make it." Iris's smile is slightly uncertain.

Oh? Is he on her shit list?

"When I heard from Julie, I had to." He clears his throat. "I hope this is what you want."

"It is."

"Then I apologize for being a jerk earlier."

No! Don't apologize. Stay on the course of jerkhood!

Iris beams, then hugs him. "All is forgiven."

I should definitely run him over for that close contact. And they're hugging for too long. A tenth of a second should be more than enough.

"Thank you," he says.

Yeah, yeah. Petty bastard. He still isn't congratulating her.

"And congratulations."

Damn it. All five syllables without choking. I pull Iris closer with a warning in my eyes. She's mine. She's wearing my ring on her finger. Soon she's going to take my name. And nothing Byron does is going to change that.

The sooner he accepts it, the better off he'll be.

Thankfully, he moves on quickly. Mainly because I'm acting like he isn't there, and there are other people who want to say hello.

Finally, Harry and Edgar reach us. Harry hugs Iris in his

usual exuberant manner, clasping hard, leaving Edgar to gawk. Although he heard from Harry and I spoke with him over the phone earlier to prepare him, he can't hide his shock.

"This is so unfair," Harry whines dramatically, tightening his hold on her and turning her slightly so she can't really see Edgar's face. "Tony takes all the good women."

"All?" Iris says, pulling back slightly.

I raise an eyebrow at Harry. *Explain, you little loose-tongued fool.* But I'm faking my outrage. We're both overacting to distract Iris from noticing Edgar's expression and giving him time to adjust.

"Every time I think I found somebody I want to date, Tony's already dating them." Harry throws his hand over his forehead. "And now, he's taking it a step further and *marrying* you!"

I bite my lip. Iris actually giggles. "Well, Tony can't marry all of them, so why don't you go propose to one of his exes?"

Harry shoots her a look of utter horror.

"But not Audrey Duff. I'm afraid I'm not too crazy about having another wine fight with her."

Edgar's face has finally returned to its normal state.

"Edgar, stop Harry before he embarrasses all of us," I say. "My fiancée is going to think my brothers are idiots."

He turns to Iris. "The sad truth is, Harry sucks at flirting. I'm Edgar, the oldest brother. Welcome ba— Welcome to the family." He hugs her, unshed tears glinting in his eyes. "I'm really happy for you and Tony."

She hugs him back with a smile, but my heart is thumping erratically. *Damn it, Edgar.* I'm going to kill him if he slips up and spills the beans.

After he lets go, she looks at him quizzically. "Are you all right?"

"Yeah, I'm fine. Just a little emotional." He lets out a soft breath. "It's so good to finally see Tony happy. I'm grateful."

The irritation that's been swelling inside me pops like a balloon. How can I stay angry with him after that? Besides, he was a rock when I was at my worst—after Katherine's and Ivy's deaths.

Flushing, Iris beams. "Tony makes *me* happy. I'm the one who's grateful." She squeezes my hand. "You know I don't have any siblings, so I'm thrilled to get two handsome brothers like you through Tony. I feel like this is so one-sided."

"Oh no," Edgar says. "Trust me, you are everything we could want in a sister-in-law."

Harry says something I don't catch, and Iris laughs.

As happy as I am to see my brothers and Iris getting along, I can't help but feel conflicted about my parents. As I'm disowned, they'll never attend my wedding...and probably never care. Normally that wouldn't bother me, but I wonder if it bothers Iris, even though she has to be aware of my circumstances. It's not exactly a secret. We haven't discussed it, mainly because I didn't know how to bring it up, but Iris didn't either. It's as though she's decided until I'm ready to talk about it, she won't push.

For once, I wish she would. Just a little. But part of me is relieved. How do you tell your hard-won fiancée you got disowned because you shot your sister and let her bleed to death? Officially, I got cut off seven years ago. But in reality, I wasn't ever part of the family after Katherine died.

Elizabeth and her husband Dominic King come over to congratulate us. I know of Dominic, although he and I aren't close. He has a face pretty enough to suit a woman of taste like Elizabeth, with near-black hair and intense blue eyes that seem to miss nothing. He's a newly minted billionaire, but unlike me, he didn't come from old money. He made the news a little while back when he took a bullet for his wife.

Elizabeth hugs Iris, then me. He shakes hands with me, but hugs Iris lightly.

"I'm so happy for you two!" Elizabeth holds Iris's hands. "And I owe you one for making Tony and Ryder reconcile."

Ah, here we go, I think with affection. She's still thrilled about that. It's getting embarrassing.

"I didn't do anything," Iris says.

"Ha! I know it's you. Tony wanted to run Ryder over with his Cullinan until you came into his life."

I smirk at her exaggeration. She doesn't know my target's

shifted to Byron. "I wouldn't have done that. The car's worth more than his sorry ass."

"Hear that?" Elizabeth winks with a small smile. "Let's get something to drink. This isn't the kind of event you can do dry." She loops an arm around Iris and takes her away.

I don't want to share her, but I don't object. Everyone seeing her being so friendly with Elizabeth is going to be good for Iris. People love Elizabeth and respect the endless charity work she's done, and not that many are really close to her.

"Liza loves her," Dominic says, watching his wife walk away. "And is very protective. She says Iris reminds her of her younger self."

"Does she?" I can't imagine why Elizabeth would think that. From background to personality, she's nothing like Iris. But does it matter, so long as Iris is put under another layer of protection?

"Something about her being innocent. And youthful."

I snort. "You'd think Elizabeth was in her sixties. Iris isn't that much younger."

Dominic shrugs. "I never contradict my wife unless there's a very good reason."

Ryder comes up and slaps my shoulder. "Tony, my man!"

Instantly, I'm surrounded by Ryder's sycophants, who all decide I must be congratulated, whether they know me or not, regardless of how they really feel about my engagement. I look at them and manage a smile. Ryder always had his share of groupies, but it's gotten worse since he's become a global star.

Over one of the men's shoulders, I spot Jill. *Finally!*

She's sipping a martini in a corner. She's pretty, tall and lithe, with cropped hair the color of a brand-new penny. She's in a tight blue satin dress, which fits her slim frame perfectly.

I gaze at her hard, hoping she notices the stare. She finally looks in my direction and mouths, *I can wait.*

Maybe she can, but I can't. I've been patient for too damn long.

I make my way toward her at the speed of an anesthetized snail. Every couple of steps, somebody grabs my sleeve to congratulate me. I come to a lurching stop and am forced to smile and respond in kind, when I'd rather ignore them all and cut my way straight to Jill.

When I'm a few feet away from her, sudden gasps rise ahead of me. The crowd parts like a startled school of fish.

I see someone on the floor. A redhead.

Shit. Jill!

The martini glass she was drinking from lies shattered on the floor. She's clutching her chest, her other hand a white-knuckled fist. She convulses, beads of sweat popping over her oddly pale face.

"Jill!" I say, rushing to her and kneeling by her side. "*Jill!*"

Her glassy eyes turn to me. She blinks a couple of times. "Tony..." A soft breath slips between her trembling lips.

"I'm right here." I put a palm on her cheek. It's cool and clammy. Something is very wrong.

From the look in her gaze, she knows that too. "Have to tell you..."

I lean closer until my ear is almost at her mouth.

"Careful... Your mother..." She gasps, and her whole body tightens. Her teeth clench. The pain and fear of death rip across her face like they did with Katherine all those years ago.

My gut makes the same old knots it did eighteen years ago. "Jesus. *Somebody call 911!*" I scream.

Jill isn't breathing anymore. She's too still. I start compressing her chest. *She can't die like this. No, no way. She's going to live. She has to.*

The muscles in my shoulders ache and my arms feel rubbery, but I keep going. I will her to live the way I willed Katherine. I am *not* having her die on me. I'm going to save her, and she's going to be fine. *She is not going to die. Not going to. Not!*

The paramedics come. People pull me away. The EMTs do their thing and check Jill out. Try to revive her over and over again.

I watch, my heart in my throat.

But eventually, they shake their heads.

And I know I failed.

51

ANTHONY

RYDER SENDS EVERYONE HOME QUICKLY. HIS PEOPLE USHER Iris, Bobbi, Elizabeth, her husband and Paige to another room. Harry and Edgar leave with Yuna and Julie.

I try to get the paramedics to tell me what happened to Jill. I want them to tell me they can revive her if they take her to a big hospital with real doctors and lots of equipment. But they don't. They just take the body away.

The body.

She's not even a person now.

Ryder takes me to the room where everyone is, and I sit on a couch, hollow and shaky. Iris quietly puts an arm around my back. Ryder's pacing, speaking furiously on his phone. Elizabeth, too, is on a call. Dominic rubs a soothing hand along her back.

I look down and see my hands. Trembling. A little damp in the palms. But when I turn them over, there isn't any blood.

Might as well be.

I clench them. I learned how to do CPR and other basic first aid. It was supposed to help me not repeat the tragedy of the past.

I should've been able to save Jill. If I had been better, maybe. If I'd been thinking more clearly...

She had to have been poisoned. Healthy people in their prime don't just keel over and die. And certainly not when she was just about to tell me what she'd found.

It's all my fault. I should've told her the people she was digging into were dangerous. If I had, she might've been more careful. Might still be alive.

I think back on what happened since I spotted her in the crowd. She looked fine, drinking her martini. Who could've poisoned her? When? Ryder's place has tight security. The catering company came highly recommended.

A large hand thrusts a glass full of clear liquid in my face. I look up and see Tolyan, of all people. *When did he come here?*

"Drink. You look like shit," he says.

I take it and finish the whole thing. It's vodka.

"Jill was a good woman. It's nasty business, people dying at your engagement party."

No shit, Sherlock. It's nasty business to have people die on you, period. Then I wonder if he knows something. Elizabeth's "assistant" has a certain reputation. I stand and tell Iris, "I'm going to get another drink. Do you want anything?"

She shakes her head.

I head toward the wet bar, gesturing at Tolyan to follow. He helps himself to Ryder's best vodka when we get there.

"Whatever Jill was after...she got too close," he says.

I nod, gratified Tolyan agrees with my unspoken theory. "It was no accident."

"She was here to see you. Ryder doesn't use her. She wouldn't have gotten in without an invitation."

There's no point in feigning ignorance. "Yeah, I hired her."

His eyes grow remote. "Stop unless you plan to go all the way. And unless you don't care who you have to hurt to get justice. It could be a hollow victory."

What does he know? "I'm not stopping until I find out who did this to her."

He grows even more emotionless. "That's for the police. I

mean the thing you wanted her to look into. Obviously some-body's willing to kill to keep it buried."

Willing to kill...

Suddenly, it clicks. The answer comes like a lightning bolt. Sam. He was there in Tempérane. He did some things he shouldn't have. He tried to hide Iris. Then forced her to leave the country. When that failed, he tried to drown her. Whatever Jill discovered must've been damaging, and he had to do something about it.

Jesus. Blinding panic tears through me. "Where's Iris?"

Tolyan tilts his chin. "Same place you left her."

Right. Of course. She's still on the couch, still safe. Surrounded by people I trust. I set the empty glass on the bar counter and return to her.

"A little less shaky now?" Iris says.

I nod, lying. I'm anything but.

"Was she your friend?"

"She's—was—somebody who worked for me and my company."

She reaches out and holds my hand. "She must've been close to you to be invited. I'm sorry."

I squeeze her hand back, maintaining our physical connection because it's the only thing that's making me not lose my mind right now.

This should've been one of the most amazing, unforgettable nights of Iris's life. Well, it's unforgettable, but for all the wrong reasons. I hate it that I couldn't keep the ugliness from slipping through and touch her.

"Let's go home," she whispers, brushing her fingertips tenderly along my cheeks and jaw. "Let's get you away from here."

We say goodbye to everyone and exit. The cops have my contact info, in case they need to get in touch.

TJ brings the car out. After dismissing Bobbi, I hold an umbrella over Iris.

Our ride home is quiet, except for the sound of raindrops knocking on the Cullinan. The thunder and lightning seem to be over, but the road is full of creeping drivers unable to figure out what to do on roads that aren't bone-dry.

Iris holds my hand in hers, a silent gesture of comfort. I'm grateful for her understanding, although I know I don't deserve it. If she knew the whole truth—what I'm hiding from her, who Jill is and what she's been doing for me—she'd hate me. If she could, she'd flip the Steinway over on me.

When we step into our place together, I make sure to lock the door and pull away from her gently. I don't want her to think I'm upset with her, but Jill's death...Sam... The ugliness of the night keeps circling in my head, and the guilt and self-loathing are twisting around me, leaving a slimy, toxic fog over my mind. I don't want Iris to touch me and become tainted. She should be clean and safe. She should never know what it's like to see some-one's life snuffed out like that.

"Don't pull away." She reaches for me, wrapping her hand around my wrist with surprising strength. "You don't get to do that. Ever."

"Iris—"

"I know you're bothered by Jill's death. But it wasn't your fault. Nobody could've predicted it."

Her understanding and kindness shred me. She always sees the best in me. She can't imagine what a shitty deal she got by agreeing to marry Tony Blackwood. She thinks I'm giving her a family—my brothers—and my fortune, while she isn't bringing enough to our relationship. She alone is worth more than all my money and other material junk combined. She is the heart—without her, there's no life.

When I remain stiff and unyielding, she tilts her head, regarding me quietly. She places her palm on the center of my chest and slowly pushes me backward until my spine bumps against the edge of the kitchen counter.

"Do you love me, Tony?" Her voice is quiet and steady.

"Yes. Always," I answer in the same tone, wondering why she's asking me this. Can she sense I'm holding something back? Is she trying to reassure herself I'm one hundred percent truthful?

"Then promise me you won't move or stop me until I'm finished."

Her eyes are as luminescent as the moon. I should reject the comfort and love she's about to offer. But I'm selfish and craven enough to want everything she has to give.

She takes my silence as a yes, and kisses me. Just a feathery brushing of our lips, our breath mingling. The touch is so sweet that my heart aches for her. Her mouth moves over mine leisurely. This is her time—she sets the pace. I let her lead. I ruined the party, but I can do this for her.

Her hands tug at my shirt, untucking it. Without breaking the kiss, she pulls each button out of its hole until the garment opens, exposing my torso. She strokes me, every touch light and gentling, as though calming the beast writhing with self-recrimination and anger. Her lips follow her fingertips. My breathing shallows, grows rougher. She's killing me slowly. But I can't move. This is what she wants, even though I'm not worthy of it—not really.

Her warm breaths fan over my skin. She unbuckles my belt, unbuttons my pants, then tugs the zipper down, its whisper loud in the quiet apartment. She pulls down my slacks and underwear in one smooth motion.

My dick springs out, already hard. Iris's face is so close that I can feel the heat from her parted lips.

"I love how honest you are with me—your body never hides anything."

Her words slam into me like a roundhouse kick. But my dick grows harder, defenseless against her nearness.

She places little kisses along my shaft, which throbs unbearably. Between the achingly tender caresses, she whispers to me, "You take on the world, Tony... You believe you should be able to control everything... When you can't be a god, you torment yourself. But you're a man... A brilliant...sexy...hot man. The only man I've ever loved... The only man I'll ever love."

Oh God. Just words. But they're hotter than any pornographic sex trick, making my heart overflow with tenderness and love for her.

Iris wraps her lips around me. I grip the edge of the counter and tilt my face forward so I can watch.

She's beautiful, kneeling before me in her classy Versace. She pulls me in as much as she can, her tongue, lips and cheeks working. But more than her actual technique, what gets me is the pure bliss crossing her exquisite face.

My brilliant North Star. She's guiding me out of the dark pit where my mind has gone—to the bright, warm land of the living. The slimy, toxic fog dissipates.

The pull of her mouth is irresistible. I'm drowning in sensation so pleasurable it's on the edge of pain. She's chipping away at all my defenses, leaving me vulnerable. But I feel safe and strong with her.

"I'm going to come," I warn her.

Her hand tightens, her eyes open and welcoming.

At her silent permission, my control breaks. I come violently, everything in my body tensing. Her lips tighten around my cock, and I feel her mouth and throat moving as she swallows.

La petite mort.

The first person to come up with the phrase must've been like me. Every time we're together like this, a little bit of darkness inside me dies, and her love fills the void left behind.

Dropping to my knees, I kiss her deeply.

"Tony..." She flushes. "I, uh...just..."

"What? If I can't kiss my fiancée, who can I kiss?" I say, tossing back what she said in the club about teasing me. I place a long, lingering kiss on her mouth, licking her lips. Then, remembering she's been on her knees for a while, I shrug off the rest of my clothing and carry her to our bedroom.

"No bad feelings tonight," she says, looping her arms around my neck.

"No bad feelings," I promise.

52

ANTHONY

My EYES OPEN, MY MIND IN THAT HAZY STATE BETWEEN sleep and alertness. The bedside clock says it's only six thirty. Iris and I spent most of last night wrapped around each other, but I'm still too wired from what happened at the party to sleep.

Iris, on the other hand, looks so peaceful. I watch her chest rising and falling slowly and take comfort. I don't want to see a still torso ever again.

I start to reach for my phone, then realize it's in my jacket... which is downstairs. I look back at her, not wanting to leave and content to watch her sleep. But there are things I need to do. Quietly, I pull on some shorts and go to the living room.

Time to make Sam pay.

I text TJ. *Find out where Sam was last night during the party.*

The fucker wasn't invited. I made an executive decision to snub him. Iris hasn't commented either, despite my concern she might want to invite him, if only for appearances' sake.

But just because he wasn't invited didn't mean he didn't try to crash it. Although Ryder's security is top-notch, no system is infallible. Sam could've snuck in, using his relationship to Iris. The guys checking the list might've thought we made a mistake. Or they let him in anyway because he's Iris's uncle, and why wouldn't a relative want to stop by and congratulate his beloved niece?

After a while, I begin to lose patience. I start to write a follow-up text for TJ when he responds.

He's dead.

I stare at the two words, then shake my head and read them again.

Still the same.

Dead? Absolutely no way. Maybe TJ got mixed up. I had a small business dealing with a man named Sam Lincoln a few years ago. *I meant Sam Peacher,* I reply.

TJ calls me. "I know you meant Peacher. He's dead."

Holy fuck. Shock tears through me like a tornado. Fortunately, I'm standing beside a couch, so I sit.

Dead. How? When?

"When did it happen? Was it after the party?" Maybe the motherfucker got what was coming to him after he fled the scene.

TJ's next word smashes my theory into smithereens. "During."

"How?" I demand, as the realization dawns on me that he and Jill died at the same time.

"Someone ran him off a highway. No witnesses. Died of internal bleeding. If the other driver had called 911, he could've lived." TJ considers for a second. "Or maybe not. People here can't drive for shit in the rain. The cops think the weather was a factor."

They're wrong. Sam used to live in Louisiana. Torrential rain is nothing, thunder and lightning par for the course. "Anything else?"

"Funeral's in a week."

Jesus. "That fast?"

"Guess his son wants to wrap it up. He's getting Daddy's money."

Damn it. This is not what I wanted to deal with, so soon after the darkness of Jill's death. Iris is going to have to be involved, since Sam's her uncle. Is Marty going to expect her to show for the funeral? Does she want to? "Update me if you hear anything else."

He grunts, and I hang up.

I place elbows on my knees and run my hands over my unshaven jaw. Two seconds later, I jump off the couch and start pacing.

I was convinced Sam was behind Jill's death, but... If he didn't do it, who did? A co-conspirator from nine years ago? Somebody else who doesn't like it that I'm digging into the past? Or was it just some unrelated personal vendetta?

The last option is unlikely. Getting to her at Ryder's mansion is too difficult for most people. And she only decided to show in the first place because I asked her to come to tell me about the findings.

It has to be either Sam's co-conspirator—if he had any—or somebody else who wants to hide the truth. If they knew Jill was after them, they could've had her followed.

Storm. Another hit-and-run, pushing the target's car off the road...

The whole thing sounds too much like what happened to Iris in Tempérane.

But wait. Sam and Jill died at approximately the same time. That means there are at least two killers. *Fuck.*

Is the hit-and-run driver the same one from before? If so, why kill Sam? Why now? And who killed Jill? For what reason? And are the killers working together? Now I'm beginning to wonder if she died for reasons that have nothing to do with my assignments.

I stop when I remember something Yuna said.

She told me she found Iris because of the wine fight video. But because she wasn't able to track Iris's address, she went to Sam first because her investigators found out he was Iris's uncle.

Sam's killer could've done the same thing.

Frigid terror grips me. I swivel my head toward the huge windows looking out at the city. The killer is in the city right now. Unlike before, Iris is no longer anonymous. Any idiot can Google and find out that Iris and I are engaged. My address isn't exactly a secret. And it's only logical that if they killed Sam...the next target is Iris.

No. *No.*

I pick up my phone and call Bobbi. She answers on the first ring. "Yes?"

"Bobbi, come to my place ASAP. Armed."

"What's wrong?" Her tone is sharp.

"It's her uncle. Sam Peacher." I glance over my shoulder at the stairs to the second level. I walk out to the deck and close the door, looking at the rooftops of the tall buildings around me glowing in the early morning light. "He's dead."

"Sam Peacher, that shit? How?"

I pause at the sneer in her voice. I don't think I ever mentioned him to her...and as far as I know, she's never had any contact with him. "Hit-and-run. Did you know him?"

"A long story. Can't tell you the details. Anyway, what about it?"

"Whoever killed him is most likely coming after Iris." *Will* come after Iris.

"Why?"

"Another long story. But you have to watch her even more closely, twenty-four seven. As a matter of fact, why don't you move in? Until we catch the killer?"

"That's...pretty open-ended. What if you never catch this guy?"

"I will." I have to. I can't have a threat to Iris out there. I'll hire a team of international mercs if necessary. I'm not going to fuck it up this time and lose her again.

"All right. But only because I like your fiancée, not because I really like being somebody's bodyguard."

"Thanks." I mean it. Other than TJ and Wei, Bobbi's the only person I can trust with Iris's safety around the clock.

"You owe me one."

"I'll build you a bakery anywhere in the world, no questions asked."

She snorts. "I'll be there ASAP." She hangs up.

I blow out a breath. It's going to be okay. I'm doing everything I can to keep Iris safe. If I have to, I'll tie myself to her with a rope.

When I go back inside, Iris is already in the kitchen. She's put on my shirt and is making coffee.

Suddenly, coffee sounds like a great idea. I haven't had any since I got up. I pull Iris into my arms, needing to feel the solidity of her delicate form. To reassure myself that she's still warm, breathing and alive. My brilliant light. And I hate it that I have to add to the ugliness from last night with the news from TJ.

"Are you okay? You don't look so good," she says, searching my face.

Am I that transparent? I school my features, settling them into impassivity.

"Don't do that. Tell me what's bugging you instead of shutting me out."

"You might want to sit down first." Although she ended up not liking Sam much, the news of his death is going to be a blow. She's known him for so long, and he did take care of her earlier, when she was just out of her coma and vulnerable.

She perches on a stool, her eyes not leaving my face. "What is it, Tony?"

I place my hands on her shoulders. There's no gentle way to put it. "Sam's dead."

Her eyelashes flutter, and she opens and closes her mouth. Finally, she shakes her head. "What? That... There must be a mistake. Some kind of mix-up."

"I'm sorry, Iris. He died in a car accident last night."

She presses trembling fingers over her mouth. "Oh my God. Why didn't anybody call..." She stops. "I have him and Marty blocked. Oh no."

"Listen to me," I say, tightening my hands on her. She needs to focus. This is too fucking important. "It was a hit-and-run. The cops are looking for who did it. And Bobbi's moving in with us."

"But why?"

"To be on the safe side." I can't quite meet her gaze, so I go grab two mugs of coffee. "She's going to keep an eye on you." I thrust a coffee at her.

She doesn't take it. "What are you not telling me?"

Even if I want to, I can't tell her about the killers and the crazy kind of danger she's in. She would worry endlessly, and I don't want to see that anxiety and fear in her eyes. "The funeral's next week."

"Tony. I'm going to ask again. What are you not telling me? Why does Bobbi need to move in with us?"

I'll tell her the only truth I can. "Just trust me, Iris—"

"I'm your fiancée, not your kid! You can't make decisions without any explanation and expect me to be okay."

Beyond the angry façade, I glimpse a hint of fear. Sometimes not knowing is worse. It twists and morphs into a monster that makes you scream in your sleep and look over your shoulder during your waking moments.

"Sam had enemies," I say, choosing my words with care. "I think whoever killed him last night could've been one of them. I don't want them to come after you because of your relationship to him. That's why."

"Why didn't you just tell me?"

"I didn't want to make you afraid." *I can't let you know the full truth.* Not yet. I'm not ready. I'm probably never going to be ready.

She finally takes the coffee from my hand. "I'll be careful. And I promise I'll be a model client for Bobbi."

That should reassure me. But somehow it doesn't. Nothing will put my mind at ease until whoever's responsible is put away forever.

53

IRIS

EVEN THOUGH I MANAGE A SMILE FOR TONY DURING breakfast, my thoughts are in turmoil. *Sam. Dead!* I can't believe it. It hasn't even been a month since he tricked me into meeting him at Starbucks. He was so alive, his eyes blazing with temper.

I was furious with him for the way he manipulated me, but I never wanted this. He saved me from the water when I had the accident, and kept me safe while I was in my coma. I only wished he'd stay away if he couldn't be happy for me.

And stop trying to use me to get to Tony.

That poor woman at the party, and now this. Maybe the storm last night really was an omen. When I return to the bedroom, I sit on the bed, pull out my notebook from the drawer and jot down the events in short, succinct sentences. Then I add: *Why does this feel like a warning? Or am I being melodramatic? Even though I didn't know Jill, and Sam and I had problems, their deaths leave such a shadow—an emptiness I can't quite describe. But what bothers me is that I'm not that sad for Sam. I wasn't struck by grief over Jill's death because I didn't know her. But*

Sam? Even if I ended up angry with him, shouldn't I feel more than just a passing melancholy? I feel sorrier for Marty that he lost his dad. What does that say about me?

Tony walks in. "What are you doing?"

"Just making an entry." I close the journal and put it back in the drawer. He knows I write more or less daily, but I've never shown anything to him. He's never asked, either, probably out of respect for my privacy. "I...I feel awful." Then I quickly add, "Especially for Sam."

"You knew him for a long time. It's only natural." Tony sits next to me and lends me a shoulder to rest my head.

"I just wish we hadn't had such an ugly falling out." *I wish he weren't such an awful person, so that I could experience the grief I'm supposed to, rather than regret over not feeling sad enough.* I close my eyes as guilt winds around me like a vine. I shouldn't think so badly of the dead, even though part of me is wagging a finger, saying it's all true: he was manipulative and terrible.

"It wasn't your fault," Tony says quietly.

I snuggle closer, finding comfort in his words and grateful he's not judging me for not shedding any tears for Sam. We stay quiet like that for a while. I enjoy the emotional connection, but then doubts start to slither over my head like snakes.

The storm. Two deaths. How they feel like fateful warnings.

"Do you think it's an omen?" I ask.

"What is?" he asks.

"Last night. Jill and Sam. They both died when we were having our engagement party. The storm, too. I really hate those."

"It's not," Tony says decisively. "Even if it were, I'm not changing anything."

How can he be so resolute? "But Tony..."

"Do you believe in destiny?"

"Yes, but—"

He places a finger over my lips. "I know exactly what you mean. Now here's what *I* mean. If we aren't fated, then I'll fight fate for another moment with you."

Just like that, the darkness that's been clinging to me since I heard about Sam's death dissipates. Tony says I'm the sun, moon and stars of his existence, but he's the light of mine. The one who illuminates the underlying, basic truths of life. It wasn't until I came to L.A. and met him that I started to remember more of my past, become stronger and more resilient.

We spend the rest of the day together, just the two of us... Well, Bobbi too, but she's very good at making herself unobtrusive. After lunch, I call Yuna and Julie and Tony's brothers, making sure they're all right.

Finally, I stare at Marty's number. He's an ass and a horrible misogynist. Regardless, I should call and offer my condolences. He never had a mom growing up, and now he doesn't have a dad either. I know how painful it is to lose parents.

Inhaling deeply, I hit his number. It rings and rings and forwards me to his voicemail, which is full. Part of me is relieved and grateful. I start to text, then stop. That's too impersonal and rude. I'll just have to try again later.

On Monday, when I show up at work with Bobbi like any other day, Elizabeth gives me a concerned look. "Are you all right?"

"I'm okay," I say, forcing a small smile. Besides, it's really better if I keep working.

I try calling Marty during lunch, but still no luck. He's probably just overwhelmed. With his father gone, Peacher & Son is his responsibility now.

On Wednesday, a small but sturdy cardboard box arrives at the office. It's from an attorney, but I'm not familiar with the name. It's specifically addressed to me with CONFIDENTIAL: TO BE OPENED BY ADDRESSEE ONLY in bright red.

I hesitate. We normally get letters and documents for the causes the foundation's working on. This feels personal. Like the blue dress Sam sent. Besides, wouldn't a lawyer send a letter or manila envelope?

Just to be safe, I Google the man's name. He's a real attorney, specializing in estate and family law in Los Angeles. His firm is large and prestigious, with high-net-worth clients.

Ugh, I'm just being paranoid. Sam's gone. He can't send me

anything. The lawyer is legit, and he probably isn't sending me anything creepy.

I run a box cutter along the clear tape. Inside is a small item covered in layers of bubble wrap. I open it slowly.

A music box falls into my lap. It's small, no more than two inches square, and old, the enamel on its plain white cover slightly discolored and chipped in a corner. As I turn it in my hand, something rattles a bit, like a small part has come loose inside. The bottom has two initials—WS, which means nothing to me. After winding it, I open it, and it plays Debussy's "Clair de lune," the sound tinny and small. I close it, and the melody stops.

What's this about?

I look at the bottom of the box and see a white envelope. I take out the letter inside and start reading.

Dear Ms. Smith,

My name is Joseph Lawrence, and I am a lawyer representing your late uncle, Mr. Sam Peacher. Please accept my sincerest condolences for your loss.

The enclosed is a music box Mr. Peacher wanted you to have upon his passing. It used to belong to his mother, Wilhelmina Smith. As you are a fan of Mozart sonatas, he thought you would appreciate it and keep it with you safely.

The rest is the typical closing, and I drop the letter back in the box. Resting my elbow on the desk, I prop my forehead in my hand. It's so like Sam to misidentify the composer and the piece. Tears prickle in my eyes. Why did he have to die and leave me his mother's music box? It's such a worthless item, but also weirdly sentimental. Didn't he hate me for staying in L.A.? Or refusing to manipulate Tony into helping Peacher & Son?

I should hate him for making me cry after doing his best to make my life as difficult as possible when I decided to quit traveling. But my mind keeps bringing up all the ways he tried to keep me safe—pulling me out of the submerged car, warning me about my emotional condition when I told him I wanted to try performing in public, encouraging and paying for my trips...

The tears that fall are bittersweet. Keeping my head down, I pluck a Kleenex and dab at my face. Sam's dead. I can let go of our differences and just grieve, because a person I depended on for so long is gone in something as senseless as a hit-and-run accident.

54

IRIS

SAM'S FUNERAL IS AN ODD MIXTURE OF SOMBER AND SHAM.
Everything's proper—from the white roses to the chokingly
delivered eulogies. Marty looks almost dashing in a conservative
black suit and slicked-back dark hair, although his hooded blue
eyes, which normally hold vague dissatisfaction, are bloodshot.
But except for him, nobody seems to be grieving for real. There's
some sniffling, and some of the women even dab at their eyes. But
there are no tears or any air of sadness over the attendants, just
the avid alertness of wild animals scenting fresh blood.

Tony, seated next to me, isn't bothering with a display of grief.
His face is hard and watchful. He's only here because of me.

"Thank you for coming," I whisper into his ear. I know Tony
thinks very badly of Sam, and he's been busy at work. Bobbi could
sit with me here, while Tony got caught up on his projects. But
instead, both are here, one on each side of me.

He squeezes my hand. "It's for my peace of mind."

I don't bother to argue. Ever since the engagement party, he's
been impossibly protective. Something about Jill's and Sam's

deaths really shook him up, and somehow he's connecting them to my safety—or lack thereof. I don't get his logic, because Jill had a heart attack, and Sam was a combination of bad luck plus some horrible hit-and-run human being who didn't think to stop and call 911. But it's hard to listen to logic when strong emotions are overwhelming you. I just wish I could reassure Tony that I'm not going to keel over. Our lives are just beginning, and there are so many things I want to do together.

The back of my neck prickles, and I glance over my shoulder. My gaze collides with a fifty-something blond woman. She's sitting a few pews back. The black veil from her hat covers half her face, so I can't really make out her features, but what I can see is fine and delicate. A simple, chic dress covers her slim, almost frail-looking shoulders. I don't think I've ever seen her before, although something about her feels just a tad familiar. Maybe Sam's lover?

No. Her mouth is off. It isn't set in a flat, pressed line of barely contained grief. It's... It strikes me that she's smiling, ever so faintly. *Good riddance,* it seems to be saying.

The fine hair on my neck bristles, and I feel cold fingers of apprehension gliding up my back.

Do you think he'll shed a single tear when you die? Do you think you're special enough to make him cry?

A woman's voice I've never heard before rages in my head. I inhale sharply, my insides twisting at the palpable fury in each word. Is it the blue-dress girl's mom? Am I finally remembering her now?

But that can't be right. She wouldn't be talking about this "he" or the weird thing about "crying."

"Are you okay?" Tony whispers.

"What? Oh, yeah. I was just thinking." After a few moments, I surreptitiously look back again, but the woman's gone.

I blink a few times, then turn my attention back to the funeral. I must've imagined it. What kind of person comes to a funeral with a "good riddance" smirk? The snippet of memory that popped up must've distracted me and made me see things.

How weird. I've never remembered just words without any visual to go with them.

As soon as the service is over, we stand. Tony glances around and takes my elbow. "We should leave before it gets too crazy outside."

"I need to have a word with Marty."

"For what?"

"I haven't been able to get in touch with him all week." I feel like I should express my condolences. Even a jerk deserves a few kind words when he must be reeling from the abrupt death of his dad. Besides, this is a good opportunity for a clean break. I don't plan to see him or speak to him again. "It won't take long."

Tony's eyebrows pinch together. "That little shit's been snubbing you. Like he matters anymore. Without his daddy, he's nothing."

It's like him to think the worst of Marty. Not that it isn't deserved. "Sam was my uncle, and he kept me on life support for a year."

Tony sighs. "Okay. Let's go find him."

"Thanks." I squeeze his hand.

The line of people wanting to talk to Marty isn't that long. Sam was the face and brains of Peacher & Son, but it's obvious from the mildly amused way people regard Marty that nobody considers him a serious successor.

When the three people in front of us murmur a few things and disappear, Tony and I step up. "Marty," I say. "I'm sorry for your loss."

He gives me a sharp look, his eyes bloodshot and slightly glassy. He shoots a sneer in Tony's direction. "Here with your fiancé?"

Oh crap. I hope Marty doesn't make a scene. He helped Sam manage Peacher & Son, so he must also believe Tony's the one behind making all the investors pull out. And unlike Sam, Marty has very little filter between his mouth and brain. "Yes. He decided to join me to pay final respects."

"Did he now? How generous. And how nice of you to finally

remember what my father did for you." Suddenly, his face crumbles, and he envelops me in a tight hug before Tony can stop him.

Tony bristles, but I push him back with a hand. Marty just lost his father. When I lost my parents, it was the worst. I'm willing to comfort him for a bit.

He buries his nose in my unbound hair, his breath gross against my skin. "I know about the blue dress and the real reason Dad kept shit from you," he whispers. "If you want to know more, meet me in the women's bathroom in the hall in five minutes."

He tightens the hug, then pulls away. I stare at him, wondering if I misheard. But no. His eyes are too shrewd...too scrutinizing.

I want to ignore what he said and leave with Tony. Marty can't possibly know anything about the blue dress...or can he? Or why Sam lied to me all these years and told everyone I died?

But...

Marty is leaving the reception line after announcing a bit loudly that he needs a private moment to regroup. He makes a left turn at the main entrance to the parlor.

Sudden urgency thrums in my veins. Other than Sam, he's the only one who might possibly know something about my past. And he has no real reason to lie about it, does he? If he starts spewing garbage to drive a wedge between me and Tony, it's not going to work. Sam already used that tactic. I'm not falling for it again.

My mind made up, I turn to Tony. "Do you mind asking TJ to bring the car out? I need to use the ladies' room, but I'm ready to go."

"Sure."

"I won't be long." I go out into the hall, Bobbi following. I spot the bathroom. "You don't have to come in," I tell her. "But if I'm not out in three, come get me."

She squints at me. "What's going on?"

"Just a quick talk with Marty."

"He's a weasel. I'm coming with you."

"If you're with me, he may not talk. If he tries anything, I'll scream loud enough that you can hear it."

Bobbi nods, then leans next to the door, checking her watch.

I go inside, my palms slightly sweaty. Marty's already there, standing by the sink.

"Couldn't resist, could you?"

The sneer on his face makes me wonder if I'm wasting my time. "You have three minutes. Get to the point."

"Your real name is Ivy Smith."

I snort. *Seriously?* "Then why don't I remember ever answering to Ivy?"

"Because your head is fucked up."

"You're lying." I'm starting to get disgusted with myself for ever thinking he knew about me or my past. "I can't believe I thought you might have some genuine information."

Suddenly, he grows serious and his eyes narrow. "Iris was a distant cousin on my grandma's side of the family. You fit her well. Do you remember your name, or did you assume Iris has to be your name because everyone called you that when you woke up?"

"Of course I remember my name!" I say. Of course I remember...

When I first opened my eyes...I saw Sam, whom I didn't recognize back then.

"Iris, you're awake," he said. "Finally! Doctor! We have to call your doctor..."

Tremors run through me like the start of an earthquake, small but growing more powerful. "I'm from Almond Valley," I say, more for myself than Marty.

He shoots me a superior smirk. "You're from Tempérane, Louisiana. Just like Anthony. Oh, right. Your fiancé didn't tell you, did he? You guys used to date...snuck around a bit. He's known all along, including the story behind the blue dress Dad showed you. You dumb whore. You were supposed to make Anthony back off, not break off with him and then run back." Marty's practically spitting at me.

Tony and I knew each other before? Preposterous! Blood roars in my head, drowning out whatever else comes out of

Marty's mouth. Shaking my head, I back away from him, so he can't taint me with any more of his lies.

If Tony and I knew each other, why didn't he say so? And his brothers, too! If I'm from Tempérane like Tony, Edgar and Harry would've known me too, but they acted like they'd never met me before. Did Tony ask them to do that? *No, no,* I tell myself as soon as the question surfaces. What is this, some huge conspiracy? I'm not important enough for that.

And Yuna! Wouldn't she have called me Ivy if that really were my name? It isn't like Tony hired her to fake a friendship. She's genuine...and plays the meanest Rachmaninoff, Liszt and Chopin!

And the girl in the blue dress? Tony doesn't know her. I told him how important it was to find her, and he said he couldn't help.

Because he didn't know. If he could, he would've done everything in his power to find out who she was. He loves me. He adores me. I look at the ring on my finger. The symbol of everything he feels for me.

Marty's doing this as a final blow against me and Tony. Marty knows I don't like him. He blames Tony for investors abandoning Peacher & Son. He's just angry he doesn't know how to attract investors like his dad did.

"You're pathetic. Don't ever come near me again," I say, turning away.

"You stupid cunt, shut up and listen!" He starts toward me.

The door opens, and Bobbi pokes her head in.

Marty comes to an abrupt stop. "Use the other one on the second floor," he says.

Her gaze flicks to him for a fraction of a second, then returns to me. "The car's here."

The car. It jolts me, and I start moving. I have to go. If I leave this horrible space with two stalls and two tiny sinks and Marty sneering at me, I'll be okay.

My legs tremble as I walk out. When I'm past her, she lets go of the door, and it closes behind me. Suddenly, my knees buckle. I slap my palms against the wall for balance, Bobbi's arms supporting me.

"What did he do to you?" she asks.

I shake my head. I can't tell her.

"I'm going to kill that weasel."

"Don't. I just need a minute. Feeling a little dizzy." And clammy.

Bobbi reaches into her jacket pocket and gives me a handful of M&M's. "Here. Eat these."

I take them and dump every single one into my mouth. The sugar tastes good. So does the chocolate. The area stops spinning, and my muscles no longer feel like old rubber.

But now that I can stand upright without the hall spinning, my mind whirs faster, processing Marty's lies.

Because they are lies. There's no way my real identity is Ivy Smith or that Tony knew me from all those years ago—

The Ivy Foundation.

Everything inside me freezes. Yuna said she started it to provide financial help to Korean kids who study classical music. I didn't think anything of the name, but...

When I was having my first nightmare about the girl in the blue dress, I was with Tony. And when he woke me up, *he called me Ivy.*

Suddenly I can't move. If I leave, I have to face Tony. And I'm going to want to know for sure. I can't *not* confirm.

Come on. Marty's lying. The name of Yuna's foundation is a coincidence. You don't think she should've named it after you, do you? And Tony said he misspoke in panic. Are you going to believe Marty over Tony?

But...

I press the heel of my palm against my forehead. Marty is a jerk, but he isn't stupid. He wouldn't lie about something that could be disproven in seconds. But who can confirm for sure?

Not Tony or his brothers. Not Yuna. No one from the high school I supposedly went to, since that's a lie Sam made up. So who else is left...?

My brain churns through everyone I can think of, throwing

up one objection or another as to why I shouldn't contact them. Ugh. There's nobody who can tell me for sure? Did I go to a middle school then? How about somebody from Almond Val—

Curtis!

I attended the school, so they must have a record of me. If I call and ask, will they tell me? Or are there privacy laws preventing them from doing so? I can't get a lawyer for this. I want to get it resolved quickly and quietly.

But wait—I don't have to call the administrative office. I can simply call one of the teachers I had. And there's one I remember —Tatiana, who taught piano to me and Yuna. All I want is for her to tell me that I—Iris Smith—studied with her. And if she wants, she can share some stories that might trigger more memories.

I pull out my phone and start typing, then stop. I don't remember her last name. I Google for her first name plus "piano faculty at Curtis," but it only returns her bio, without an office number or email address I can use to reach her. It does have her last name, but I can't find her home number under Tatiana Seger. Smart of her to keep the information off the Internet, but it's frustrating that I can't just grab her contact info off Google.

"Bobbi," I say, my voice rusty. I clear my throat. "Can you do me a favor?"

"What is it?"

"Do you know how to find someone's cell phone number? If it isn't listed?" *Say yes.*

"Yeah. It isn't that hard."

I let out a small sigh of relief. I wouldn't know where to start looking for a reliable PI. There's no way I can ask Byron or Julie for help with this. "Do you mind finding this woman's number, then?" I copy and paste Tatiana's info and text it to Bobbi.

She looks at her phone. "Shouldn't be a problem."

"Great. Thanks. Let me know how much it is, and I'll take care of it."

"What do you mean?"

"I don't want Tony to know." I can't let him know. He'll think I'm doubting him. And to be honest, part of me is ashamed I'm not taking him and Yuna at face value. But I can't let go of my misgivings without checking them out first. Otherwise, they're going to come back over and over again.

"Then I won't tell him, but you don't have to pay me. Consider it an engagement present."

"Thank you. Regardless, I owe you one."

Bobbi shrugs, looking slightly uncomfortable. "Now, are you well enough to get going?"

Not really. I don't want to go anywhere until I can talk with Tatiana and get my answers, but... "Yeah. I think I've kept TJ and Tony waiting long enough."

"They're men. They're used to it."

55

ANTHONY

"It's taking too long," I say, sitting in the Cullinan.

"They're women," TJ says.

He's right. But I hate that Iris is in the same building as Marty. She didn't look well after that parasite hugged her. Of course, I wouldn't look so good either if I got body-locked by a slimy leech.

"If they aren't back in the next five seconds, I'm going in," I say.

"They're in *the women's bathroom.*"

"And?"

"What do you think is happening? Sam's boy is attacking her?" He snorts. "Bobbi picks her teeth with guys like that."

I start opening the door. I'm only going to check up on her, in case she isn't feeling well. I should've insisted she skip this travesty of a funeral. It isn't like either of us is really sorry Sam's gone.

Just as I'm about to step out, I spot Iris and Bobbi coming toward the car. Iris's complexion is completely bloodless. It reminds me of the way Katherine looked in her casket.

I jump out of the car. "Are you all right?" I hold her hands. They're icy.

"Just not feeling well." She gives me a wan smile.

I give Bobbi a quick look past Iris and mouth, *Marty?* Bobbi shakes her head. The tightness inside me eases a bit. The bastard didn't touch Iris again. I lead her toward the Cullinan and help her get in. Bobbi rides shotgun.

"What's wrong?" I ask Iris as TJ pulls out of the driveway. "Should I have Dr. Young meet us at home?"

"No. It's just the breakfast. Isn't sitting well."

She didn't eat that much in the morning, and I chalked it up to nerves. After all, seeing a little shit like Marty couldn't be good for one's digestion. Even I don't feel so great. But it upsets me that her stomach issue is bad enough to make her this unwell.

"TJ, pull over when you see a store," I say.

He grunts. A few miles later, he pulls into a strip mall, and I run inside the grocery store to grab a bottle of ginger ale. I remember how it used to settle Mother's stomach when she had indigestion.

I return to the car, twist the cap and hand it to Iris. "Here."

She stares at the drink for a moment, her eyes oddly remote. Something I can't quite name slides cold talons along my shoulders.

"Iris? You don't want the ginger ale?"

She blinks once, then looks at me. The smile she shoots me is half-hearted. "Sorry. Got distracted. Thank you." She takes the bottle and takes a small sip, closing her eyes the entire time.

Somehow it feels like she's shutting me out. I'm being ridiculous, of course. She's just tired. But I can't shake the ugly apprehension.

"Tony?" she says suddenly, her eyes open now.

"Yes?"

She lowers her voice until it's barely a whisper. "You know it bothers me I don't remember everything, right?"

"Of course." Do I ever. She jumped into the pool and tried to drown herself to find some missing pieces of her past. The pain she carries still breaks my heart, every time I think about it. I wish there were a way to fix it all for her, but I know there isn't, short of some medical miracle or magic.

"If you knew something...anything about me that I didn't know, you'd tell me, right?"

I go still, surprised and uneasy over why she's asking me this all of a sudden. The question is a no-win—a choice between a minefield and sinkhole. The only right answer is yes, but that isn't the truth of what I've been doing. If I tell her now...

She waits for an answer, her body tense.

Nothing stays secret forever.

Ryder told me that. I've been ignoring it, hoping if I do, maybe it won't come true.

Every little lie spins another, until the skein is as complex and inescapable as a spider web. The only way to start over is to destroy it, clear every strand, but if I do that, I'm going to lose Iris.

"Of course." I reach over and hold her hand in mine. "I'm going to do everything in my power to keep you safe."

The tension in her eases. I force a smile despite my apprehension, and count my blessings that she didn't notice my evasion.

56

IRIS

ONCE TONY AND I ARE HOME, I KICK OFF MY SHOES, CHANGE into a comfy T-shirt and shorts, and practice Liszt for hours. I need to channel my restlessness into something, and nothing focuses me like Liszt's études. The technical demands shouldn't leave any room for unhelpful thoughts.

Tony offers me soup, but I decline. It's impossible to eat, especially after what Marty said. Even though my fingers are moving over the keys, my mind keeps bringing up what he said...and Bobbi agreeing to get me Tatiana's number.

I should've asked her how long it's going to take. What if Tatiana is out of the country and is impossible to reach? Don't musicians travel around the world? Maybe she's on a music tour. Or on a safari—an adventure to experience life to the fullest.

Around five, my phone vibrates on the Steinway. I pick it up, my heart pounding. *Want anything for dinner? I'll pick it up on the way.*

I stare, confused, until I realize it's a text from Yuna. We're planning to have dinner together. *Anything's fine with me. You might want to ask Tony.*

OK.

My fingers hover over the keys. Questions swirl in my mind. *What's my real name? Why did you decide to call the foundation The Ivy Foundation? Why did Marty say those things to me?*

In the end, I don't write any of them. I start to put the phone back on the piano, but it buzzes again. A text from Bobbi.

Cell, it says. Ten digits follow.

Tatiana's number. My hands shake. That was quicker than I thought.

Sweat slickens my palms. This is it. The answer I'm looking for. I go to the kitchen and drink a glass of water. It's not quite nine o'clock in Philadelphia. If I call her now, I can put the uncertainty to the rest once and for all.

Tony's working on his laptop. He's in a gray Lakers T-shirt and loose shorts, his bare feet propped on an ottoman, ankles crossed. He looks so serious when he goes over his company's numbers and reports. I remember what TJ said—that even when he was hurting while I was floundering over Sam's revelation about the girl in the blue dress, he kept working because his employees depended on him doing his job. I'm with a man who's just that responsible and caring.

Tatiana's going to say she had a student named Iris Smith. A smart girl. Needed more life experience. I'm going to feel super sheepish and ridiculous for having ever doubted Tony.

Then why are your legs so unsteady?

Probably because I'm about to speak to another person from my past. Somebody who meant a lot to me. It has nothing to do with Tony or what Marty said.

I walk up to our bedroom and close the door. I don't want Tony overhearing me and realizing I've been doubting him. I'll make it up to him somehow later. I just need to talk to Tatiana in private...and say everything I need to say to her.

I sit on the edge of the bed and call the number. My stomach churns like I'm waiting for the results of a brain scan. I've had to do that a few times, none of them pleasant, all of them disappointing.

"Hello?" comes a dulcet, youthful voice. The same one I heard in my memory.

My heart thumps hard. "Hi. I'm trying to reach Tatiana Seger."

"This is she."

I close my eyes. "I don't know if you remember, but I heard you used to teach a student about ten years ago. Iris Smith."

"Um... What did you say her name was?"

Stupid phone. Are we having a bad connection? "Iris Smith."

"I'm sorry. You must have me confused with some other teacher. I've never had anybody with that name."

No, no, no. My stomach feels like somebody put broken glass in it. This has to be a mistake. I must be breaking up badly. I'm getting a new phone with a different carrier as soon as I'm done here. "No, I mean *Iris Smith*," I say, enunciating carefully. "Aren't you at Curtis?"

"Yes."

"Then you have to be the right one," I say, needing her to remember me—Iris Smith. "You taught Yuna Hae at the same time. You remember her? She's from Korea, and—"

"Oh, Yuna! Yes, of course. Such a lovely girl. She dropped out after her friend died, but are you sure you didn't get the names mixed up? Her best friend was *Ivy* Smith, not Iris."

My vision dims for a moment, and I blink furiously to refocus. "I'm sorry, what?"

"Ivy Smith. Not Iris."

"That can't be right. It's gotta be Iris Smith. Yuna's best friend is Iris Smith." *Because I'm Iris Smith!* The hysterical words stay trapped in my throat, making it hard to draw in air.

She sighs. "I'm sorry, but I remember all my students, and Ivy in particular was an amazing pianist. So full of potential. She died in a car crash years ago."

"But that can't be right. I know..." What the hell *do* I know? I don't even have the right name. "She died," I say, my mind numb.

"She died in..." Tempérane or Almond Valley? I don't know what I'm supposed to say.

"Her home town in Louisiana. So tragic."

Oh my God. Tempérane. It has to be. Bile rises, flooding my mouth with a bitter tang.

"Look, you have your names mixed up. But regardless, if you're attempting to pull some kind of scam with Yuna Hae, I wouldn't bother. She's too smart to fall for it, and she'll destroy you. If you need money, get a job. Karma's a bitch." She hangs up.

I clench my phone. My entire body shakes uncontrollably.

Ivy Smith. That's my name. And Tony lied. A bomb seems to go off inside my head at the realization. So did Yuna. A smaller bomb this time, but it still puts spots in my vision. I shove my fingers into my hair and clench, pulling at it tightly until it hurts. Why? Why did they fool me like that? And Edgar and Harry... They lied to me too, probably at Tony's request.

I realize than I'm hyperventilating. I try putting my head between my legs like I saw on TV once, but I lose my balance and fall forward instead.

Has anything Tony said been real? According to Marty, Tony and I dated before in Tempérane. Is this some kind of sick revenge because I did something he didn't like back then? Or did I snub him at some point? I can't think of any other reason for him to tell me nothing but lies when he knows how much I need the truth about my past.

Or maybe this is some weird competition with Byron. Tony made it clear how much he despises Byron.

But he's been so sweet to you, a small voice in my head whispers.

Only because he needed to in order to make me believe him, I think bitterly. I wouldn't have trusted him so fully if he were a dick like Marty. The pearl on my finger glows. I thought it was the most beautiful ring ever. Now it seems tawdry and vile—a mockery of everything I ever felt for him.

Sam called me a blank canvas. Maybe Tony came to the same conclusion. A blank is more malleable...full of possibilities. For all I know, he sought to mold and bend me into the woman he wants

—a stupid, gullible idiot who would believe every piece of crap out of his duplicitous mouth.

And he lied to me again today. In the car when I asked him... because I needed to know...

What did he say? *Of course.*

My chin shakes, and tears prickle my eyes. I clench my jaw, my teeth digging into my lip. The coppery tang of blood fills my mouth. Instead of easing the tension, I bite down harder. The physical pain is anchoring, so the emotional blow doesn't blast me into oblivion.

I stand and look around the room. The bed where Tony and I shared our bodies. The closet where we helped each other get ready in the morning. The shower where we washed each other and then got hot and heavy.

There are too many memories tearing at me. And when I face him again, he's going to expect me to smile and wrap my arms around him and kiss him and let him fuck me into a moaning ecstasy. The notion is revolting. I press my hands over my mouth, so I don't throw up. I don't have time to waste with that sort of thing.

I have to get out of here—away from him—*now.*

I pull out my suitcase from the closet and throw it on the mattress. Then, quickly, I grab my dresses and work clothes and shoes and start dumping them into it without bothering to sort them...until I notice the lavender Versace I wore to our engagement party. The gorgeous outfit mocks me, reminding me of the party where all those people looked at me with smiles on their faces. Were they in on the fucking farce, too?

A rage of humiliation sweeps over me. Even this morning, our engagement was the culmination of our love and commitment to each other. Now it's a joke. A third-rate show for some sick entertainment.

I pick up the dress and try to tear it apart, but, infuriatingly, the material holds. *It looks so easy on TV.* I hurl it to the floor and kick it, wishing it were Tony instead.

There might be scissors in the bathroom I can use. I go there, then see my lotions and toiletries. I spent my own money on them, and I'm not leaving anything of mine here. Breathing roughly, I grab them all and add them to the pile in the bag. I spot a bottle of perfume Tony bought for me a while back, but ignore it. He's not going to claim I took anything of his.

I want nothing from him.

The door opens, and Tony walks in. Snarling inwardly, I zip up the bag. Guess I won't be cutting up the damned dress after all.

He takes one look at me, and rushes forward. "Iris!"

How dare he! I slap his hand away, hard. He stares at me like he doesn't recognize the person he's looking at.

Of course he doesn't recognize me. I'm not Iris Smith. Not anymore.

Fury builds inside me, slowly at first, then with more momentum and speed, like an avalanche. "You bastard."

"Iris...what's wrong?"

I despise the concern on his face. It looks so damn genuine, and it hurts. I hate it that he still has the power to make me feel this way. "What's *wrong*? You're asking *me*?" Wrath racks me. I've never felt this out of control. My fingers are twitching, and I can't command my body parts to do what I want. It's as though the anger has given them independent wills of their own.

"Iris—"

If I could stop myself from shaking so much, I'd slap him. "How about you stop with the 'Iris'? You know that's not my name."

57

ANTHONY

I FEEL THE BLOOD BRAINING FROM MY HEAD, LEAVING ME dizzy and reeling. Every muscle in my body tenses to keep me upright. I can't go down, not when Iris—Ivy—is ready to walk out on me. The suitcase makes it abundantly clear. I need to say something—*anything*—but nothing comes.

She glares at me, her eyes like chipped ice. Fresh blood beads on a cut on her lower lip. Just what kind of frenzy was she in to injure herself like that?

"We came from Tempérane, Louisiana. We knew each other before. We dated, didn't we?" she says, her voice like a naked blade.

We did, but how does she know all this? Did her memory return since we came back from the funeral? *How do I fix this?*

"What's the matter? Nothing to say? That's fine. I'd rather you stay quiet than throw more lies at me." She shakes her head. "Why would you lie to me? Why would you call me by another woman's name *when you know it isn't mine?*"

That I can answer, even when the room's spinning around.

"Because your name doesn't matter. The only thing that matters is you're alive and here with me." Each word comes out taut and raw. I will her to believe me that much, even though I know I have no right.

Her eyes soften for a second before she firms her mouth. The sight is like a shiv into my heart. "So you thought I died, too?" she says in an ugly, mocking tone I've never heard her use before.

I'm going to lose her if I don't fix this now. My head finally kicks in, my tongue no longer thick and stupid. "Yes! I thought I'd lost you after the accident. When I saw you again, I thought I was going insane—seeing things—because I missed you so much."

"So when you realized who I was, why didn't you tell me?"

"I was afraid." My answer is honest, no bullshit.

Ivy looks at me like she doesn't understand what I mean. No —worse, she looks at me like she doesn't believe me, period.

Lay it all out. Like you should've a long, long time ago. Her suitcase is packed and lying on our bed. *Do it now, before she walks away.*

But I can't. If I tell her everything... I pick up on the one thing I can tell her—the least damaging reason I was scared shitless for her safety. "Listen to me, Ivy. Everyone thought you died—me, my brothers, the police, *everyone*—because we found a body in your car in a bayou. In it was the body of a young woman who was damaged enough that her face was a mess. But she had strawberry-blond hair like you, and she was in a blue dress—the same type you wore that day. We also found your pendant—the one I originally gave you back in Louisiana, the one you're wearing right now—and your purse, so the cops decided the body was you. Everyone thought you were gone."

I see her eyes flicker as she puts the facts together. I almost wish she were just a little bit slow. But I know better. My Ivy is brilliant. She'll get it quickly enough. Trepidation winds through me.

Finally, she inhales sharply. "That's the girl in the blue dress I told you about, isn't it? The girl you said you couldn't help me find."

I close my eyes briefly, wishing with all my heart that I could give her an answer that won't make her hate me more. But I can't. "Yes."

She looks away as though she can't bear the sight of me. It's the same reaction Mother had when I went back in Tempérane to seek her forgiveness. She treated me like I wasn't there, then, when I confronted her, she told me that not even my death could make up for what I'd done.

The despair I felt back then resurfaces, gripping me so hard that I can't breathe. Urgency loosens my tongue, and words pour out of me like a monster flood breaking through a dam. "Ivy, *I couldn't tell you.* Someone out there killed that girl. Even though the cops back then didn't think so, it was a deliberate murder—the car was hit twice. And Sam's accident looks exactly like that one—the storm, the nighttime hit-and-run... everything! I couldn't let the killers know you were alive. They could come back to finish you for real this time—either because you were the real target or to get rid of a witness to the crime. And Jill's death wasn't an accident either. She was looking into it for me."

She stares at me long and hard. I can't tell what's in her mind. *Please. Let it be something forgiving. Let her remember how much she loves me.*

Certain sins can destroy that love. You killed your mother's love. Surely, Ivy's love isn't any stronger than your own mother's.

I grit my teeth. I don't need this right now.

"You know when I came home and jumped into the pool, to try to trigger more memories?" she asks, her voice awful. "You proposed to me that day."

"Yes," I whisper, goosebumps breaking out down my arms at the memory. I'll never forget the horror of that as long as I live.

"I did that because earlier than afternoon I had seen Sam. He told me I was driving the car when it went over the bridge, and I was the reason the girl died. He said the girl's mom blamed me and wanted me to remember what I did forever—that I was a killer."

Oh no, Ivy. Painful regret surges inside me. I know what it's like to carry the burden of somebody's death on my conscience.

I've lived with it for most of my life, and even now it's weighing on me. Ivy should never have experienced that.

She continues, "If you'd told me the truth, I would've known better than to believe him. And I certainly wouldn't have suffered for nothing. And to think I felt guilty for hurting you by not being able to accept your proposal..." She shakes her head, her lips curling into an ugly line. "I couldn't say yes back then because I didn't feel worthy. What if I was a killer? But the real reason should've been because you're a manipulative asshole. *Just like Sam.*"

"Ivy..." My voice cracks. I can't think of a single thing to defend myself, because I deserve every bit of her hate and anger. But what scares me the most is the way the animated light in her eyes has dimmed, her wan face and the air sawing in and out of her with such labored effort...as though she's slowly dying.

Like when the life leached out of Katherine under my bloody hands.

I did this to Ivy with my lies. Because I was—still am—too ashamed to tell her everything. That I was a pathetic jerk, who wasn't brave or mature enough to accept her love back then. And that that's the real reason why the car went over the bridge and she lost everything—her memory, her future, her friends...*everything.*

I look down at my shaking hands. They feel sticky and dirty, like there's another layer of blood on them—Ivy's.

"What I can't forgive is you made me fall in love with an illusion. We're done."

The finality of her tone jolts me. I jerk my head up.

She's pulling off the ring, her movement jerky and rough. She looks awful, like she's dying, but she isn't dead. Surely I can fix this. Surely the third time will be the charm. I just need one more chance. That's all. "No, don't. We aren't done. If you want me to tell you about your past—I'll tell you everything," I say, walking toward her to block her from leaving.

But the ring's already off her finger. She places it on the vanity. The rubies around the pearl glitter like fresh blood.

Ivy takes a step back, as though my presence alone is enough to soil her. "Do you think I'll believe anything you say now, Anthony?"

I stop. Why is she calling me that? Not even Mother at her most furious called me Anthony. "Ivy...I'm always your Tony."

Her eyes are infinitely sad. And so, so dark. It's as though all the light has been snuffed out.

My fault. I'm destroying my sun, moon and stars...

"No, you aren't," she says, her voice thin and pained. "Tony is the name your family and friends call you. I'm neither. I can't stay here anymore, not without going insane. Do you understand?"

"I love you," I tell her, because that's the only truth that will never, ever change.

She flinches as though I slapped her. Her reaction is like a bomb going off in my belly. "Then you should've told me the truth from the beginning," she says. "Since you never loved me enough to do that, you don't get to keep me."

She pulls the suitcase off the bed. I should stop her, but I can't move. She's so fragile that I'm afraid she's going to shatter if I touch her, and I'll never, ever be able to put the pieces back together.

Just like I couldn't piece together my shattered family.

58

IRIS IVY

WHEN I DRAG MY SUITCASE INTO THE LIVING ROOM, BOBBI
appears, looking concerned. "What's going on?"

"I'm leaving."

I pick up my purse and roll the suitcase to the door. When I
open it, Yuna's on the other side, Mr. Kim carrying a huge takeout
bag that smells like Thai.

"Iris," she says with a smile, which immediately dims as she
notices my lip. "Oh my God, look at your mouth."

She sounds so concerned, but I'm unmoved. Actually, I wish
she'd stop. Were we ever even really friends? Why would a friend
lie like that?

She glances down. "Where are you going? Did you and Tony
have a fight?" She sighs and rolls her eyes. "Just give him time to
apologize. Men always act stupidly."

Of course. But she didn't have to be part of that stupid act. Or
take his side. "Lying bitch," I say dispassionately.

Yuna pulls back, her spine stiffening. Mr. Kim stares, his
jaw slack.

"I know everything," I tell her.

"Iris—"

I'm sick of people *Iris*ing me. It's a reminder of how stupid and gullible I am. "You know that isn't my name."

Her face slowly collapses, tears gathering in her eyes.

I look away, anger and frustration filling my heart to overflowing. Why do liars always act indignant or behave like victims when they get caught? I don't have the patience or energy for either act. I walk into the waiting elevator, Bobbi following.

"Ivy," Yuna says. "I'm sorry."

"Don't ever come near me again," I say.

The elevator closes.

~

ANTHONY

THE DOOR IS AJAR. IVY DIDN'T BOTHER TO SHUT IT.

She's gone. The pressure in the bedroom drops. But that doesn't ease the pain in my heart.

I'll never forget her terrible face—the corpse-white skin, the blood on her lip, the glassy gray eyes. She knows I failed her... No, worse. I *betrayed* her. If she walks out of the building, she's going to be out of my reach. She's going to vanish.

I can't let that happen.

Sudden urgency energizes me. I jump to my feet and rush out.

"Ivy!" *Don't let me be late.* "Wait!"

I take four steps at a time on the penthouse stairs, not caring if I trip and break something. I'd gladly break every bone in my body if I could have her back.

"Tony."

I stop at the teary voice. Yuna. Her face is tear-stained and blotchy. This is nothing like the pampered daughter of a wealthy Korean chaebol family.

Then I spot Mr. Kim standing beside her, holding a takeout bag. I swivel my head.

"Where's Ivy?"

"Gone. She just went into the elevator." Yuna wipes her face with her hands. Mr. Kim silently offers a handkerchief, but she doesn't seem to notice. "What did you do?"

I stare at her, unsure where to begin. What didn't I do?

"She called me a lying bitch. She knows everything, doesn't she?" More tears stream down Yuna's face.

I did this to her, too. She never wanted to lie in the first place. More guilt and shame entwine around me. "Yes."

"How could you have been so careless?"

I wince inwardly, but accept her anger and blame. I deserve them. "It's my fault. I'm sorry. But I have to go get her before she's gone. I have to bring her back." I start to leave.

"Then what, Tony?" The question stops me.

I can't believe I have to spell out everything. "Then she stays with me!"

Yuna lunges in front of me like a shield. "She'll hate you for the rest of her life! And she's going to be miserable."

"I can make her happy." *I'll find a way. I know I will. I love her too much not to.*

"How? Tell me how!"

My mind goes blank because it can't think of a single good plan. Is there a way to come back from this? I killed the light in Ivy's soul. I saw it die in front of me in the bedroom. But I can't give up. I can never give up. "Because I love her! I love her and I'm going to do everything in my power to make her happy."

"So what? She won't believe you. As far as she's concerned, you're the guy who lied to her."

"Shut up. I—"

What I can't forgive is you made me fall in love with an illusion.

Ivy's words come back like a slap in the face. Suddenly, I can't push Yuna out of the way. What Ivy's seen of me is an illusion that I've carefully crafted. I never showed her the ugliest part of me. I only showed her the bits that weren't too objectionable. If I bring her back, she'll want nothing but full disclosure—festering wounds, the blood on my hands and all.

"Do you want to be with a woman who doesn't love you?" Yuna asks sadly.

"Yes." It'll drive me mad. Every day is going to be a slice fileted off my heart. But I'll embrace the pain and her hate if it means being near Ivy.

Yuna shakes her head. "Let me rephrase that. Do you want to be with a woman, knowing she'll always be miserable with you?"

Dammit, Yuna. The selfish, desperate part of me says yes, I would, because life without Ivy isn't worth living. But what little decency remains inside me is repulsed. If I can never make her happy...then she should go out there and find her own happiness.

That's the last—and only—thing I can do for her.

59

IVY

IT'S HARD TO LEAVE WITH MY PRIDE INTACT. HARD NOT TO lose it like a psycho, like I really wanted to. My hands still shake with a violent need to lash out at everyone who was in on this farce.

But figuring out where to go is much harder. And humbling.

I stand in the lobby, hand on the suitcase handle, unsure what my next step should be. I have nowhere to go. I have a job, but not a place of my own. It's obvious now how one-sided my relationship with Anthony was, because now I'm homeless. I shouldn't have depended on him like I did on Sam. Anthony's a liar and a user, just like my so-called uncle.

Even as anger thrums in my veins, grief courses through me, making my eyes prickle. I've been a fool. A naïve, broken idiot who deluded herself into believing her life was perfect.

When Anthony came into our bedroom, I was torn between anger and a crazy need for him to explain. I wanted to know it wasn't just some malicious prank. There had to be some logical excuse for what he did—something that might even redeem him just a little bit. I wanted to believe I hadn't been so off in my judgment.

But I was. He had so many opportunities to come clean. But even when I was at my most vulnerable and susceptible, he didn't.

And I bought everything he said. How he must've laughed. I remember how surprised and touched I was when he told me he hadn't been with a woman in seven years before me. Now I can feel humiliation burning my cheeks. Of course he slept with all of them! Then he told them pretty things, made them think they were special and wonderful. Why else would Audrey Duff go that far? If I hadn't found out about his deception, and he dumped me coldly the way he did his previous women, I might've done more than just throw wine in his date's face.

"Iris—"

"That isn't my name, Bobbi," I say lifelessly. "It's apparently Ivy."

She pauses for a second. "Okay, Ivy. Where are you heading? If you want, I can take you to a hotel or..." She shrugs.

I shake my head. I don't want a hotel. Too transient, and it's going to make me feel like I'm back on the road again, rootless and aimless. I can't have that if I want to remain in control of my life. But where am I going to find an apartment this late on weekend?

Julie!

Unlike Anthony and Yuna and their friends and family, Julie has been a real friend, one who never lied or tried to manipulate me. She has a place in the city. She was staying with Byron, and even if she's still mooching off him, I can ask her if I can couch-surf for a few days until I rent a place of my own.

I call her, praying she picks up. She does.

"Iris, what's up?" she says cheerily.

I inhale deeply, trying to make myself sound normal. "I... Are you still staying at Byron's?"

"No." I can hear a scowl in her voice. "He kicked me out after he came back from Hawaii. Why?"

Oh, thank God. Too many things happened between me and Byron for me to be comfortable crashing at his place. I swallow, embarrassed that I have to ask and angry that my misguided trust in Anthony put me in this position. "I know it's short notice, but would you mind if I stayed with you for a little while? I'll move out as soon as I find something. I promise."

A moment of stunned silence. "I... Well, sure. Yeah, of course. That's fine."

"Thanks, Julie. Can you send me your address?" Weirdly, I've never been to her place in the city. We were usually in some other country when we hung out, and here in L.A. I was staying with Byron until I moved in with Anthony.

"Of course."

I hang up. Bobbi cocks an eyebrow. "So you're heading to Julie's?"

"Yes."

"I'll drive you."

I shake my head, grateful but uncomfortable with her offer. She ultimately works for *him*. "You don't have to. It's over. You're free to go bake and have babies." I force a smile. "Thanks for everything." Anthony is a shithead, but Bobbi's been good to me. At least I know she kept her word about not telling him about Sam's visit...and I'm pretty certain she isn't part of the "let's make a fool out of Ivy" show. Unlike Yuna, Anthony and his brothers, Bobbi and I never had any reason to know each other, and she probably believed whatever Tony told her about me and my situation.

"The day isn't over yet," she says. "And I'm paid up through the month."

I don't argue. She looks too resolute. And I don't have the energy to fight anyway. All I want is to get out of here before Anthony or Yuna comes down to cause a scene, trying to excuse their dishonesty.

We walk to Bobbi's Escalade, and I give her Julie's address. It's a little under half an hour away, and Bobbi drives, obeying the speed limit.

"This have something to do with what Marty Peacher said?" she asks after a few minutes.

"Yes." Unlike Anthony, Marty told me the truth. Only when it suited him, of course, but he did.

"And the number I got for you?"

"A woman who used to teach me at Curtis. She confirmed what Marty told me."

Bobbi sighs. "At least you double-checked instead of believing shit out of that weasel."

"I'm a fast learner." Just not fast enough to catch Anthony's lies before I let him into my heart.

"In case you think I'm doing this for Tony, I'm not. You're my client, not him." Bobbi scowls, her hand flexing and unflexing on the steering wheel. "I've known him for a while, and he never struck me as unfair or dishonest. If he were, I would've never agreed to take this job, even as a favor."

Crossing my arms, I look away. Guess he has Bobbi fooled too. That doesn't make me feel any better, though. It only adds to the list of reasons he's a monster.

The streets of Los Angeles always bustle with cars and noise. Since today's as dry as can be, people are speeding, yelling and being generally over-cocky. But not even the zany cacophony of the city can bring me out of my funk.

Bobbi clears her throat. "I heard you fight."

Great. Just perfect. How loud were we?

"Maybe he didn't have a choice."

"How?" She better not be trying to paint him as the good guy, or I'm going to jump out of the car.

"I don't know." She shrugs. "Blackmail?"

I laugh. "Yeah, right. He'd never let himself be blackmailed."

"For you, he would."

Sure. He'd just find some way to lie his way around it. "I know you mean well, but it's not something I can just accept." I start to bite my lower lip, then wince when my teeth touch the cut. "I'm really tired. Let me know when we're at Julie's." I close my eyes, faking sleep. I don't want to talk or think. I need to make my head as empty as possible so I can pull myself together. I'm not letting Anthony make me fall apart. No man's ever going to have that much power over me.

Bobbi doesn't say anything else.

When we reach Julie's place, Bobbi helps me with my suitcase. She takes me all the way to Julie's unit on the tenth floor. When Julie opens the door, I turn to Bobbi. "You can go home now." When she opens her mouth, I add, "Please."

Her jaw works, but then she turns and walks away.

I slip inside Julie's apartment. It's spacious, but cluttered and messy. Still, not as bad as Byron made it sound. Not a pigsty.

Julie's in a pink shirt that says, "I left my heart in Paris," and yoga pants, her hair pulled up in a messy topknot. "What happened?" she asks. "Did you and Tony fight?"

I press the back of my hand over my mouth, blinking away the tears that come. I wish it were as simple as a fight. A fight would mean we could bicker for a bit, then settle our differences and work things out.

But what happened... It's more than any fight or kept secret. It's a betrayal.

"Iris—"

I hold her hand to stop her. "Why don't you pour me some wine, and I'll tell you everything."

60

Ivy

Julie doesn't probe or ask questions as I go through it. She's uncharacteristically quiet, as though she can sense I'm barely clinging to control. Throughout my talk, she's sympathetic, nodding when appropriate, rubbing my back when I need physical contact and comfort. She plucks a few Kleenex and hands them to me when I start sobbing.

"I'm so sorry," she murmurs. "What a bastard. You should've kicked his ass."

"I know," I say, grateful for her empathy with the despair in my heart. "I can't believe I didn't get to slap him, not even once."

"Next time I see him, I'll do it for you. And you know what? Ivy is a gorgeous name. It suits you."

"Thank you. It's weird. I feel like I'm in some kind of messed-up movie."

She shrugs. "It doesn't matter what your name is. You're still my friend."

"You're the best." I hiccup, then bury my face in my hands when a fresh wave of tears come. *Thank God for Julie.* I need somebody honest on my side. I don't think I could bear it otherwise.

When I'm all cried out, she takes me to a guest bedroom and has me change and lie down. "Why don't you get some rest?" she says quietly.

"Thanks, Julie."

"What are friends for? Holler if you need anything." She squeezes my hand and leaves me alone in the room.

At first, I lie there, thinking there's no way I can sleep when my mind's churning. But I must've been more exhausted than I thought, because before I know it, it's Monday.

I wake up early and get ready for work. I have to stay on a routine or I'm going to drive myself crazy. Routine kept me sane when I recovered enough to leave the hospital after waking up, and this isn't going to be any different. I'm not going to let Ton— no, *Anthony's*—mind games turn me into some kind of helpless puddle of goo.

As I put on my work dress, I notice the pearl ring missing on my finger. The sight sends a sharp pang in my heart, but I clench my teeth. It isn't a symbol of love like I thought. It's a symbol of "Ivy is an idiot." I'm better off without it. Without Anthony.

But, like an idiot, for some reason I can't bear to take off the damned medallion. I stick it under my clothes so nobody can see it. It'll just be my secret shame until I can make myself yank it off and toss it in his face.

Julie's already in the kitchen by the time I come out. Fresh coffee drips from the coffeemaker, and she's munching on dry cereal from a bowl, just the way she likes it. "Want some?" she says.

"Yes, please." I grab a bowl and pour out a handful of cornflakes. I don't bother with milk. That would be too much for my stomach. It already feels like there's an acidic hole in the middle.

"You want anything special for dinner? Otherwise, I'm making spaghetti and meatballs," Julie says. That's her specialty. She claims she got the recipe from an old woman in Sicily.

"It's okay. I'm going to be late anyway."

Julies scowls. "The foundation making you work overtime?"

"No, I'm going to look for a realtor after work." It's about time I become self-sufficient, so I don't have a repeat of standing in the lobby and wondering where to go. And that means getting a place of my own.

"I don't mind if you stay here a while." She clears her throat, shifting her weight. "Actually, it'd be great if you'd stay. My place has four bedrooms, and is really too big for one person. If you don't mind, you know...the clutter and mess."

I give her a faint smile. She doesn't think I noticed, but I saw the furtive concerned looks she threw at me while I told her everything upon my arrival. "Thanks, but it's about time I stand alone on my own. I've been too dependent on other people."

"No woman is an island, and all that. It's okay to lean on people." She gulps down her coffee. "It's in our wiring, or else we'd live alone, like male bears. Not even single mom bears want them around, because they suck." She stops, then makes a "what the hell am I saying" face.

I know the point she's trying to make. But she's so wrong, she can't come up with a good example to support it. "Exactly. Men suck. And even female bears know they need to stand alone." I wash down the last bite of my cereal. "At least I'm not pregnant like those mom bears." That was a real, bright possibility before— Anthony and me getting married...having children eventually. Aren't I lucky I found out what a lying SOB he was before we had babies and ruined their lives, too?

If I repeat it to myself enough times, the hollowness in my heart will go away. I'll go back to feeling like myself again.

There are knocks on the door. Julie scowls.

"Is that Byron?" I can't think of anybody else who would be visiting this early. I doubt Anthony sent somebody to get me. He knows his game is over. What's the fun of toying with a pawn who knows too much?

Julie shakes her head. "He's out of town until next week." She goes over and opens the door. "What the hell are you doing here?" she demands as Bobbi steps around her and walk inside.

"My job. I'm here for Ivy."

I thought I made it clear earlier that she doesn't need to bother. "It's okay. I don't need you around. Not anymore."

"Gotta finish out my contract," she says lightly.

"You don't have to give the money back. I won't tell Ton—Anthony." The correction hurts every time. But it's necessary. He isn't a friend. He's nothing to me. And calling him Anthony is a reminder of what he truly is.

She shakes her head. "Sorry. Professional ethics."

Anthony doesn't deserve her. "You're being a stubborn mule."

"And? Mules are cool." Her voice is bland. "Maybe I'll make that my bakery logo."

Sharp annoyance breaks through the general blueness of my mood. Bobbi's not going to budge. I might as well humor her until I figure out what to do about the situation. "See you tonight," I say to Julie.

As Bobbi drives us toward the foundation, I say, "I appreciate you giving me a ride. But I don't want you around, and it isn't anything personal. Besides, wouldn't you rather be making cakes and cookies?"

"You can do better than that. It totally is personal. You never wanted me around," she says neutrally.

I fidget, hating it that she made the point with such bland accuracy. "I like *you*, Bobbi. I just didn't like having a bodyguard. And right now, you know...you remind me of him." *There. I admitted it.* I sigh, waiting for judgment or some kind of sympathy that's going to make me feel even worse right before work.

"What would you say if I told you Byron's paying me to keep an eye on you?"

What? You're a double agent? I swivel in my seat. "Is he?"

A corner of her mouth twitches up. "Course not. Just hypothetically."

Oh. Right. I feel absurdly gullible, which is annoying. "I'd still ask you to do your own thing, instead of wasting your time with me. You want to live your dream, right? So you should do that. This supposed danger I'm in—whatever Anthony told you—is all fake."

It has to be. He lied about everything. I don't see why he

wouldn't have lied about the "danger," even though he sounded so sincere when he told me about the killers. Besides, if there really were killers, why didn't he go to the police?

Because they're fake. And it's crime to file a false report.

Bobbi pulls into the foundation garage. I climb out, then wonder if Elizabeth was in on the deception all along. She's close to Anthony, and she must've run a background check on me. Which, now that I think about it, is probably another reason Sam never wanted me to get a job, because who knew what a check would show?

What about others at the company? HR? They surely know...

My skin crawls. It seems like everyone knows the truth about me except me.

"What's wrong?" Bobbi asks.

"Nothing." Whether people know or not, that's on them, not me, for being lying jerks. I need to go to work with my head held high.

When Bobbi and I step inside the foundation, Tolyan is at his desk. When he notices me, he lifts his head and nods once. "Iris," he says. That's about as friendly as he's going to get.

"Good morning." Watching him closely, I add, "The name is Ivy, by the way."

There isn't even a mote of surprise in those winter-cold eyes. So he knew about my real identity, too. For how long? Does Elizabeth know? Sudden anger pulses through me at the possibility that she's been in the "Let's Fool Ivy" conspiracy.

I almost roll my eyes at myself over the stupid question. Of course she knows. Tolyan doesn't keep secrets from her.

"Is Elizabeth in?" I ask.

He nods once, watching me with the stillness of a predator debating if he's hungry enough to pounce.

Ignoring the unsettling scrutiny, I step into her office and close the door behind me.

Elizabeth is beautifully put together as usual, her loose hair tumbling around her shoulders, a pale green dress draping over her as though she was the model the designer was dreaming about when he created the outfit. She looks at me, her eyes guarded. My anger turns to bitter disappointment. So. She knows about the fallout between me and Anthony. She must've heard from Ryder or something.

"Iris..." Her gaze drops to my empty left hand, and she presses her lips together. "I'm so sorry."

The sympathy is becoming exhausting —from Tony, Yuna, now Elizabeth. It would've been easier if they hadn't done anything to be sorry about in the first place. "You know Iris isn't my name," I say, taking a seat opposite her.

"Yes." She exhales softly. "The background check we ran on you revealed Iris Smith from Almond Valley died nine years ago with her parents in a car wreck."

So that part about Iris Smith is real. It's just that I'm not her. Wonder why Sam bothered to give me her persona when it's obvious my background isn't like hers at all. My car wreck killed the girl, not me or my parents. Is it because our names are so similar?

"Why didn't you say something?" I ask. "Wouldn't that have been enough to fire me?" I can't think of a single organization where it would be okay for an employee to give wrong information—intentionally or otherwise—about who she is. And that's especially true of a place that handles the kind of money the foundation does.

"Immediately afterward, Sam pushed you into the pool, and it sort of slipped my mind."

"You mean Anthony asked you to lie."

"It was my choice."

She could've thrown him under the bus, but is taking the blame in the situation. I can respect that. But I would've respected her a lot more if she'd been honest with me from the beginning, regardless of what Anthony wanted.

Elizabeth hesitates for a moment. "Is there a name you want me to use instead of Iris?"

Finally we're getting to that, weeks too late. "Ivy. Ivy Smith is my real name."

"I see. I'll do that."

"Thank you," I say hollowly.

"Are you going to quit?"

If she'd asked me last week, I would've been horrified. But now I only feel a mild numbness. "Do you want me to?"

"No!" She sounds stunned. "You know I care about you and value your contribution."

She does...just not enough to be honest. It's so hard to take people seriously when they lie but at the same time claim to care about me. "Then I won't, but only because I believe in what the foundation is doing. But if there's a better opportunity, I'll be leaving."

"That's fair. Thank you, Ivy." She looks at me almost mournfully.

I'm not sure if she's thanking me for the warning or for staying. Regardless, nothing changes. I return to my desk and throw myself into work, because that's all I have left.

61

ANTHONY

"Yeah...um...same as yesterday," Harry says on the phone, throwing a surreptitious glance my way.

I don't have to hear more to know it's Edgar. My older brother's been calling every day since Iris—Ivy—left. Eleven days and ten hours or so, now. Since I stopped answering my phone, he started calling Harry, who moved in with me last Monday. It's funny how my brothers think they're the ones keeping me from going over the edge, when it's actually Bobbi.

The blinds are closed, and the living room's in semi-darkness. I can feel Harry's gaze. He probably wants me to get up. *Not going to.* I don't care. The only reason I don't spend all my time in bed is that I'm afraid if I do, it won't smell like Ivy anymore.

If there's something that requires my attention at work, Wei brings it to me. He's done that twice so far and canceled all my meetings.

I stare at the Steinway. It glows like the pearl I gave Ivy. But without her, it stays eerily silent, its existence pointless.

Just like my life, which has become meaningless again since she left.

Despair seeps through me. I can't decide which is worse—believing she was dead or losing her now. Both times, I was given a taste of heaven, only to have it yanked from my grasp.

And I deserve it.

I vaguely sense Ryder walk in. He sits next to me, placing a bag of food on the table. "Eat."

"No."

"Come on. I got this from Éternité."

Éternité has a three-star Michelin rating, and doesn't do take-out. But since one of his cousins owns it, I guess they made an exception for Ryder. I've never been, but heard great things about it—there's a story about how the owner dedicated the restaurant to the woman he wanted to make his wife. Remembering that makes my whole body tight with pain. Even the name Éternité hurts. Because I'm never going to get my everlasting happy ending with Ivy.

I don't make a move to touch the food. My stomach's too tight for anything. Even water makes me nauseated. "You were right," I say.

"I'm right about everything." When I don't make a snarky comeback, he gives me a wary look. "About what?"

"Secrets."

He exhales roughly. He knows why Ivy left.

"It's my fault." Her eyes were so barren and desolate...like the best in her died. And I killed it. I look down at my hands, seeing the clean, slightly tanned skin, the neatly trimmed nails. I don't understand how they aren't dripping with blood. There should be another layer of old, crusted blood under the nails, too. I've destroyed so much good in the world. Katherine. My family's happiness. Now Ivy. Everything I touch gets fucked up.

"Nothing's unfixable, especially relationships," Ryder says. "You love her; she loves you. You're hurting now, but you can overcome that. You can fix it."

"It's one thing to fight fate to have her, another to fight her." The shattered, contemptuous look in her eyes—I can't face it, knowing I'm the cause. "I'm the reason she felt the soul-shredding guilt of being a killer. She believed Sam because I didn't tell her the truth. I had people she trusted deceive her for me. Why isn't this a fitting punishment? I tried to keep her with lies, and I lost her because of them." I shake my head. "It's like a Greek tragedy or something."

Ryder gives me a look torn between disgust and empathy. "Shut the fuck up, man. I'm telling you, you can fix this. She's had over a week to digest things. She's calmer now. Just talk to her. Make her understand. Or are you going to lose her like this? Just let her go? Have some other asshole snatch her up?"

Bile rises at the idea of another man touching her. Loving her. Being the center of her universe, given the gift of her smile...her love. The emotions that tear through me are dark and murderous, but then guilt pours through like a tsunami, drowning out everything else. "She knows I don't deserve her. I have nothing to offer except money." She can do so much better than a soulless, tainted bastard like me. I didn't tell her—because she didn't ask and because I didn't want to remind her how little I truly have—that my parents wouldn't even have been at our wedding. Or that they despise me.

Ryder's gaze grows somber and sad. "Damn, man. I wish you could see you're worth more than whatever's in your bank account. You're loyal, responsible and so unselfish, it's actually painful to see you like this."

"Then stop coming over," I tell him tonelessly. "Nothing's going to change. It's finished."

"You thought it was over when she 'died.' And I agreed because we all thought she was gone. But it's not over now, Tony. Nothing's finished until one of you is dead, and if you don't fight for her, a girl like that? Some other guy *will*. And when she opens her heart to that somebody else...then it won't just be over. It'll be pure hell—for as long as you live. And you'll always wonder if you could've done something to fix it. Don't live with that kind of regret."

62

ANTHONY

DON'T LIVE WITH THAT KIND OF REGRET.

Damn it. Ryder knows how to get my ass off the couch and make me move.

I shower. Shave. Clean up. Put in some eyedrops to hide the fact that my eyes are gritty and bleary from not having slept well in a week and a half. I select my best clothes—a bespoke shirt and slacks, then slip my feet into the shiniest of shoes.

I have TJ look up Julie's address, and then I drive the blue Audi over. According to Bobbi, Ivy is still there because she hasn't been able to find a place that fits her needs yet. I spot a florist on the way. I'm tempted to stop, but don't. If I'm not enough to convince her to let me fix what's broken between us, no bouquet is going to change her mind.

In front of Julie's apartment, I wait. Bobbi's Escalade pulls up. I honk. It stops, Bobbi sticking her head out for a second, then vanishing. I get out of the car and go to the passenger side of the SUV.

Ivy's there, her face pale and thin. Fresh guilt threads through my heart. She shouldn't have lost weight because of me. Her eyes are dark gray now, without the usual vivaciousness.

"Ivy, I just want a moment of your time," I yell through the window.

She looks away.

Shit. Don't do that. I have to talk to her. *Just five minutes. No, three. Even a minute. I'll take anything.*

I knock on the window. She turns toward me, then slowly opens the door and climbs out. Her hair's pushed back into a low ponytail, and there are dark circles under her eyes.

Ivy. My sun. My light. What have I done?

"What do you want?" she asks flatly.

A million things I want to say, a billion things I want to do, and the only one I want is her. *One step at a time.* "I'm sorry."

Her gaze slides from mine. "You should take Bobbi back," she says finally.

I wish she'd slap me. Or call me names. Anything but this cool, civilized tone. It reminds me too much of how Mother was when I came home after my nine years of exile. She never forgave me, refused to give me another chance. If Ivy didn't look so delicate, I might shake her, but I'm too scared to touch her. "I can't. I have to be sure you're safe."

"You can see that I am. Guarding me isn't what she wants to do."

"I don't care." Nothing trumps Ivy's safety, and I'm not here to talk about Bobbi.

A faint, mocking smile tugs at her mouth, turning it painfully ugly. "You've always been so selfish."

"When it comes to you? Yes."

"Why do you still care?" She looks at me quizzically. "I already know your game. I don't believe that my life is in danger. And I won't be Iris or whatever she represented."

"Iris or Ivy, none of that matters. What matters is *you*. You represent a second chance. A miracle. I thought you weren't you because I screwed up before with someone else, projecting onto her what I wanted, rather than seeing what was really there. If

you were ever curious who I was with two years after you supposedly died, that's your answer. When I realized you didn't
remember me or have the tattoo on your wrist anymore..." I stop.
Her expression is too still. It isn't like Ivy at all to be so emotionless. It sends terror marching through me, as terrifying as the
sound of an enemy army approaching to destroy whatever's left of
me. And suddenly, I can't continue.

I can see her processing slowly. Surprise flickers in her eyes.
She turns her left arm and looks at her scarred wrist. "Why does
the tattoo matter?"

If I tell her, she'll know my past failings. Part of me would
rather die out of shame than to let her know. But I don't want to
lie anymore. I was a fool to think I could keep her with a façade of
words. All I've done is build our future on a foundation so shaky
that the slightest tremor could bring it down. Look how it's
collapsed on me. On her. "You got it to show me you loved me
when we were younger. It was beautiful, too. A tiger lily and our
initials entwined within. Instead of being flattered and happy, I
told you that you didn't know what you were doing."

"So I was pathetic then, too," she says mockingly.

"No. You were incandescent. It was me. I was a coward.
Scared. I didn't think I could protect you, and then, sure enough,
you died. It seemed fitting—you erasing the tattoo along with
whatever memory you had of me."

"But the girl everyone thought was me... Did she have the
same tattoo on her?"

"Probably not. But we'll never know for sure."

"Why not?"

I hesitate, not wanting to burden her with the gruesome
detail, but her eyes are telling me she won't tolerate any holding
back. And this is my fault too. If I'd been honest from the beginning, she wouldn't be insisting on knowing everything. "There's a
lot of small wildlife in a bayou. Crabs, shrimp, all kinds of water
bugs...they tear skin and eat it. The weather was warm, too."

Ivy sways slightly. I start to step forward, ready to catch her.

She raises a hand. "Don't. I'm perfectly capable of standing
on my own."

I freeze. The rejection cuts, leaving a deep gash in my heart. She used to let me support her, lend her my strength and more. And I loathe myself for being the cause of this. How the fuck do you screw up so many damn times?

Ultimately, I have two questions. I'm going to get them out before I leave. "I'm sorry, Ivy," I say again, because I can't say that enough. "Do you hate me?"

A tense beat. "I don't know," she says.

A clear yes or no would've been preferable. This is worse, especially when she speaks so woodenly. It's as though she's so dead inside that she can't even bring herself to hate me. I should give up now, but I can't. I have to ask the other thing, get it all out. "Can you forgive me? Give me another chance?" It's shameless, but I want another miracle. Just one more. For that, I'll sell my soul.

Ivy looks at me long and hard. Suddenly she sighs, her shoulders drooping. "Even if I could forgive you, giving you another chance wouldn't be easy."

My mind holds on to three words—*forgive* and *another chance*. She didn't say it was impossible. Just not easy. Hope unfurls in my heart. I can convince her. I just have to try harder. "I'll make it up to you."

"How? I can never have faith in you now." Unshed tears glint in her eyes. She cranes her neck and blinks fast, before lowering her chin to face me. "You lied to me all along. You were my constant, the one person I trusted from the beginning. Otherwise I would've never let myself fall in love with you so quickly and absolutely."

Her words contain staggering pain. I expected this be difficult —humbling, even—but it's far worse than the time I begged for forgiveness from Mother. She told me not even my death could earn her absolution, and I never got a second chance to fix what I broke in my family. But this situation with Ivy is even more agonizing. Fate, for whatever reason, decided to give me another opportunity. And I repeated the exact same mistake—I let my fear drive me. *Again.*

Ivy saying she no longer has faith in me puts a nail into my heart. I know the kind of person she is. If she's lost faith in me, she'll never love me again, never leave herself vulnerable to me again, and she'll always be on guard around me. Staying with me would cause nothing but misery for her.

I've lost her.

63

IVY

I SLIP INTO JULIE'S APARTMENT, THE HOLLOW EXPRESSION ON Tony's face haunting me. I've given up on trying to call him Anthony. It didn't work to put any emotional distance between us. It only made me think about how he told me to call him Tony from the very beginning, when so many people aren't allowed to.

I wish he hadn't asked me if I hated him. I wanted to tell him I did...that I wanted him to pay. But I couldn't. In reality, I miss him. I miss waking up in his arms, seeing his sweet, boyish smile in the morning, sharing breakfast, talking about our plans, leaning my head on his shoulder on our way to work in his car, and just knowing I'm unconditionally loved by an extraordinary man who knows how broken I am but doesn't care. Learning that he lied to me tore a gaping hole out of my heart. And time hasn't worked its fabled healing powers. I can barely pretend to care about anything anymore.

I thought Tony would try to argue or make excuses when I told him I don't have faith in him anymore. I braced myself for it. But I never expected him to look like I shot him in the heart—

stunned, pained and defeated. He looked ready to crawl into a coffin.

He didn't say a single word. Just got in his car and drove away. The sight should've given me some satisfaction—that I made him hurt the way I'm hurting. Instead, I feel terrible, like I just kicked a baby bird that's fallen out of his nest. And the hole in my heart grows ever bigger.

Part of me wonders if I should forgive him and give him a chance. If not for him, then for myself. What's the point of this breakup if it's stripping pieces of my heart every day?

But I'm not certain that's possible. I'll probably always wonder if he's being honest for the rest of my life. I'd be trading excruciating pain for maddening suspicions. We would never be happy again, even if he swore on his life he'd never dupe me. I'd always remember he made everyone around him lie for him. If he was willing to go that far to deceive me, he could do it again if it suited him.

Julie isn't in, having planned to spend the night at her parents'. I go to the piano and start on Hanon's *Virtuoso Pianist*, hoping the mindless finger exercises will sooth my turmoil. Chopin, Liszt and Rachmaninoff—my usual choices—are out of question right now. Have been since I left Tony.

Chopin's impossible because I realized that the man in my memory—the one who kissed my fingers, and the one who listened as I told him my ambition to be awesomely unique, rather than a Pollini wannabe—is Tony. Liszt... I keep thinking about "Mazeppa" and the recording from Tony. *Grand Galop Chromatique*—I played that in Hammers and Strings, where he and I first ran into each other in Los Angeles. And Rachmaninoff... Yuna and I played the duet at Tony's. He was there to listen to our performance.

So that leaves Hanon. Since it isn't challenging enough for me, I'm playing the whole thing in the fastest tempo—prestissimo. When I'm finished, I see I have another string of texts and missed calls from Yuna. What the hell does she want? I made myself abundantly clear when I called her a lying bitch. She doesn't get to claim to be my best friend—much less a soul sister

—then lie for Tony. That's the kind of betrayal nothing can redeem.

Regardless, she's been contacting me at least ten times a day. By now, she should accept that the game is over, rather than trying to annoy the crap out of me. I've blocked her six times, but she keeps getting new numbers. This has to be harassment. I'm this close to filing a restraining order. And I want to tell her I'm going to sue her ass if she doesn't stop, but I don't. I'm not giving her the satisfaction of a response. She isn't worth it.

I don't care that excising her from my life feels like cutting off a finger. I'll get used to it.

Better to be alone than surrounded by people I can't trust.

64

IVY

WHEN I OPEN MY EYES THE NEXT DAY, IT'S TOO BRIGHT OUT, and I shriek with panic. I know I overslept without having to check the time.

This is all Yuna's fault! She called twenty times last night, and I had to turn off my phone, so I could drink my wine in peace after Hanon. Then I fell asleep on the couch. Unfortunately, my phone also serves as my alarm. And it stayed off the entire night.

I rush out of the apartment, Bobbi in tow. I compressed my morning routine as much as possible, but I'm still running fifteen minutes late.

"Do you think you can drive a little bit faster today?" I ask as we hurry down the steps.

"Speed limit's the speed limit."

"But I'm late, and nobody drives that slow! TJ certainly doesn't. Where's the car?" *Crap, crap, crap!*

"There. I had to park down the street a little. You know how many tickets he's had?"

"If you get pulled over, just flash your most charming smile."

In response, she bares her teeth in a grin Jack the Ripper must've worn when he was stalking his victims.

She's not going to do it. Great. Grumbling under my breath, I open the passenger door, about to hop in.

"Wait! Stop right there!"

The hair on the back of my neck bristles. I don't need to turn my head to know it's Yuna heading our way, but I can't help but look.

In a pink designer dress, she's running straight for me, her feet in sneakers, rather than her usual high heels. She's holding a wide-brimmed hat down with one hand so it doesn't fly away. Mr. Kim is right behind her, easily keeping up in his suit and loafers.

No way, especially not today, not when I'm running late. "There's no time for this. Let's go," I tell Bobbi.

Nodding, she opens the driver's-side door.

"*Stop her!*" Yuna points a finger at Bobbi.

Mr. Kim accelerates like a bullet. I stare at the man, my jaw slack. Although Yuna threatened to use him to hold me down so she could shovel food down my throat, I've never expected her to actually unleash him. On Bobbi of all people.

He grabs for Bobbi, so she can't get behind the wheel. She does something with her hands and he misses his grip; she turns and pushes him away. But he doesn't go down. Instead, he goes after her again, warier now but determined to keep her out of the car.

Yuna finally stops when she's three steps away from me, gasping for air. "Finally!"

"Using Mr. Kim to beat up a woman is rude," I say, my gaze gliding toward Bobbi briefly—to make sure she's defending herself from Mr. Kim—then back to Yuna.

She glances at the two of them. "Bobbi looks like she can handle herself."

"Make him stop."

"No."

This is ridiculous. "Call off your man, and I'll ask Bobbi to let him live."

Yuna looks at me for a second, then says something to Mr. Kim in Korean. He immediately backs off, and so does Bobbi.

Yuna turns to me. "I have to talk to you."

I cross my arms across my chest. "I'm late for work."

"I'll donate a hundred thousand dollars to the foundation if you give me ten minutes."

Wow. This is a new tactic. "Is that the going rate for bullshit these days? Guess if you're poor, you can't afford to lie, huh? But luckily, you have that diamond spoon."

Her cheeks flush, even darker than before under her makeup. "Stop it! Just ten minutes! You owe me that much after what you put me through by dying!"

Oh no. She's not putting that on me. I'm not the liar here, and I never wanted to "die." "I didn't tell you I died."

"I don't give a damn who told me." Her voice cracks, slightly shrill now. "I thought you died, and I grieved for you. Why do you think my dad's letting me stay here with no one but Mr. Kim to watch over me? I was a *wreck!*"

Amazing how convincing she is. And I'm so pathetic that I want to believe her. "If you care about me that much, *why did you lie?*"

Yuna deflates. "That was my fault. You can hate me if you want. If you never want to see me again, then...okay. I deserve that. But not Tony."

Oh, for God's sake. She's here to defend *him*? I glare at her, anger mounting. Is she really *my* soul sister? She sounds more like his. "Why not him? He made you lie, didn't he?"

"Nobody makes me do anything. It was my decision. He told me about the danger you were facing, and I decided to play along to help keep you safe. I couldn't lose you again."

I look away. I don't want to bend. She betrayed me. Made me feel like a fool...

But she also made you feel loved. She was kind and supportive of you when you were floundering after Sam told you all that crap about how you killed the girl. She did that out of friendship, without knowing what was really going on with you. She made sure you were fed, listened when you needed to talk and was thrilled when you got engaged. She cried with joy after playing "Tarantella" together and promised to help you reclaim your music. Who else cares about you like that?

"Patch things up with Tony," Yuna says. "He'll make it up to you. I know he will. He can make you happy if you'll just give him a chance."

I hug myself, suddenly vulnerable and unsure. It's uncanny that she's saying what the shriveled part of my heart suggested last night in a moment of weakness. "How can you be so sure?"

"Because I saw how it was between the two of you all those years ago. You were so in love with him, I could tell you were glowing even over the phone. I'd never seen you like that, ever. And I told you to get the tattoo to show him how much you love him."

The one Tony told me about. The one I no longer have. I glance down at my left wrist.

"How long did it take you to fall in love with him this time, not even remembering him? A week? Two?"

I think back. I can't remember exactly when or how. It just happened so quickly and decisively. Maybe I fell for him again the second I ran into him at the entrance of Hammers and Strings. My reaction to him has always been extreme.

"I don't know if you remember, but I believe in reincarnation. Always did. When you die, your soul goes to the underworld, and before you're reborn, you have to drink a tonic that makes you forget everything about your past life. So then you'd think the person is totally starting over when she's reborn, right? She's going to find a new man to fall in love with, start a fresh new family and everything. But that isn't true." Yuna's eyes are infinitely sad. "Even if you remember nothing of your soul mate, when you're reborn, you seek out and love the same soul through a thousand lives and beyond. That's you and Tony. I've never seen a man love a woman more or suffer more for her. He hates himself for hurting you. You'll never find another guy like him, and you'll never feel alive and whole without him. He's the missing half of your soul."

What she's saying stirs an aching emotion in my heart. It's

small, but it pulses with such raw intensity that my vision blurs with tears. "Do you think all this is going to make me forgive you?" I say, hating her for having the power to pierce through the armor of indifference I've tried so hard to erect between us.

"No. But I want you to be happy and safe." She gives me a long look, then steps back. "Okay. I'm done. It's up to you to decide."

65

ANTHONY

"WHAT THE HELL?" HARRY SAYS FROM ABOVE...PROBABLY the top of the stairs.

I can hear him coming down. What time is it? Morning? Why is he still here? I told him to go home last night.

"Are you trying to suffocate yourself?" He yanks on the pillow from over my face, ripping it from my hands.

I jump off the couch and grab it back, then shove him away, hugging the pillow to my chest.

"Tony?" Harry looks at me like I just escaped from a mental hospital.

"*Don't touch it.*" I hug the pillow more tightly.

"Your pillow? You don't want me to touch your pillow?"

"It's Ivy's. Still smells like her. I don't want you contaminating it."

Harry closes his eyes. "Oh, for fuck's sake."

"Shut up and go back to your place."

"And leave you in this pathetic, unstable mental state? Do you even hear yourself?"

I do, and don't care. "I have so few things of hers left. I have to be careful."

"Is that why you're sleeping on the couch?" He speaks slowly, as though I'm three.

Condescending bastard. "The bedsheets still smell like her, but the more I sleep there, the more they're going to end up smelling like me."

Harry sighs. "You have guest bedrooms."

"She used to sit here." I park myself on the couch. I know I'm being unreasonable, but I can't help myself.

"Why don't you just go get her?"

"Get her?" I already tried that and failed.

"Yeah, get her. Make her come back to you. Isn't that why you made all this money and crap? So you can have her?"

I look around my home. The expensive furnishing. The wide expanses of marble and granite. The creamy-white Steinway. The only thing missing is Ivy. "Money—all of it—is so I can make her happy and give her the world." If I can't do that, it's nothing but numbers on my bank statement.

"So go give it to her and you can win her over again." Harry spreads his arms. "You can do anything!"

"Can I?" I stare at my younger brother. Doesn't he know my history? "I couldn't protect Katherine. I couldn't protect Ivy nine years ago. I still can't do a thing to fix everything I've broken. You're right. If all I want is to *have* her, I can manipulate her into coming to me." In my lowest, most craven moments, I've considered it, despite Yuna's warning. "But then what?" Maybe Harry has an answer. After all, he's spent ten years of his life in college, studying.

He spreads his arms. "Then she'll be yours!"

Ah, Harry. Always the optimist and the charmer. *Maybe you could pull it off, but not me. Never me.* "No, she won't. She doesn't believe in me anymore. If I force her, she'll hate me. She'll grow hollow, bitter and cold. Just like Mother."

The energy seeps out of Harry. His hands slowly fall to his sides.

"I can't do that to her. She's meant to shine." Like the sun, moon and stars.

A beat. "Maybe she'll change her mind."

I prayed for that, too, when I went to see her. But I know better. "Miracles don't happen more than once, Harry. Not to someone undeserving like me."

66

IVY

I'M OVER HALF AN HOUR LATE FOR WORK. NOBODY mentions it, since I'm generally early. One of the things I learned about the foundation is that even though we're supposed to work at least thirty-five hours a week, Elizabeth doesn't care when or how we do our job so long as everything gets done on time.

Fridays can be either super hectic—to get everything done before the weekend—or easy because everyone's a little bit distracted. Thankfully, today's the latter. I get straight to my tasks, doing my best not to think about what Yuna said. She only showed up to demonstrate whose side she's really on. And it's not mine.

Around eleven, I get a text from Byron. He's back in town.

Heard about what happened from Julie. I'm sorry to hear that.

His "sorry" doesn't upset me much. He didn't do anything wrong, and I appreciate his concern. *It's okay.*

How are you feeling?

Fine, I lie. Given our recent disagreements, I don't feel

comfortable enough to bare my soul to him. Even if I wanted to, I'm not texting my pathetic story. It's too weird.

Wanna go for a drive today? It'll be nice and help you clear your head.

I don't, not really. I'd rather go apartment hunting or just play some piano or maybe sleep. But what Yuna told me earlier in the morning fleets through me—*you'll never feel alive or whole without Tony.* Suddenly, a drive sounds like a great idea, if for no other reason than to prove her wrong. Why *wouldn't* I want to take a nice drive with a friend? He's more real than her or Tony anyway. At least Byron never lied to me about my name! So I text, *That sounds great. When?*

After work?

Traffic's going to suck.

So leave early or leave late…

I check my calendar. I don't have anything to do from two thirty, and I can get all my tasks done by that time. *Two thirty good?*

Perfect. See you then.

I munch on a few crackers at my desk and work through lunch. I also check with Elizabeth at one thirty, and then again at two, to make sure there aren't any emergency items. She says no, her eyes carefully searching my face. She's been doing that a lot recently, and I show her nothing but a serene smile in return. I'm not giving away anything. After a moment, she sighs and dismisses me.

At two thirty, I leave. Bobbi follows, and I tell her, "I'm going on a drive with Byron, so if you want to head home early, that's fine."

"I'll follow in the Escalade. Just in case."

"You don't think he can protect me?" I ask, surprised. Byron's big, competent and probably able to throw a decent punch if he has to.

"I trust nobody with my job."

I should be used to her stubborn pride by now. "If you're sure." I shrug, hoping Byron won't mind. If he's still hung up on that theory about her being Tony's spy… Well, he'll have to just get over that, because I'm not interested in fights or arguments. I just want to have a nice, conflict-free time.

Byron's already waiting at the curb, his Maserati gleaming as usual. He's dressed in a blue V-neck shirt that brings out his eyes, and slacks that fit him just so to emphasize the lean strength of his legs. He gives me a hug. "Good to see you."

"Same here." I squeeze him back. It's a huge relief to see a friendly face who just wants to help me cheer up, especially after back-to-back visits from Tony and Yuna. "I heard from Julie you were away on business. Hope it all went well?"

"Yup. Let's go." He opens the door to his car, then squints. "Is that...that woman?"

Guess he spotted Bobbi. "Go ahead and get in. I'll explain."

He does and pulls into the traffic. Bobbi follows. He isn't exactly a slow driver—hello, he's got a Maserati—but she keeps up. So. *She* can *speed*. Just not when I'm late. Figures.

"Why is she tailing us?" he asks.

"Her contract with Tony isn't over yet, and she insists on finishing the job," I say, glossing over the fact that Bobbi's month was up two days ago. But if I say that, Byron might jump to conclusions, and I'd rather not deal with that. Not right now.

"That's...very professional of her." His tone makes it clear that "professional" isn't really the word he wants to use.

I ignore it, not wanting to argue. I just want to spend some time with a friend and forget about Tony and everything else for a while.

Byron drives along the coastline. It's the same route Tony took when we were first seeing each other. It's still beautiful, just like before, but something about it feels flat. Not as sparkling or vivid, as though I'm seeing the view through an unclean window.

The hole in my heart grows a little bigger.

It infuriates me that Yuna might be right after all, because she should be dead wrong. She doesn't get to call Tony my soul mate, the man who I'll love through a thousand lives and beyond. If he were, he wouldn't have hurt me. There's no way I'm going to go through this pain again if I actually am reborn.

"What are you thinking about?" Byron asks.

"Soul mates." The answer slips out before I can catch myself. I force a smile. "And that it's really pretty here." I turn my gaze to the view.

"You believe in soul mates?" He sounds half surprised, half amused.

I tilt my head. "Don't you?"

"Nope. Too fanciful for my taste. I only believe what I can see and feel now. There are billions of people in the world. How can there be only one person for you? What if you never meet that person? Then you just...die? Alone and pathetic and sad?" He looks out over the landscape. "Hard to swallow."

His practical outlook should be a comfort, especially after Yuna's ridiculously over-the-top romanticism. But it isn't. It makes me sadder. Out of billions of people, and the thousands of men I ran across during my travels around the globe, I couldn't have fallen for one of them. It had to be Tony. I shed tears at the sight of him. Then he rescued me from Jamie Thornton and took me home, took care of me. It doesn't matter what lies Tony told everyone, I know he's the one who beat Jamie almost to a literal pulp. I could've avoided Tony, especially after Marty's warnings. A polite "thank you" would've been enough. But I let myself be curious and open. He pulled me closer, slowly and carefully, never rushing, always making sure I was emotionally and physically okay every step of the way.

"Rizzy..." Byron's voice jerks me out of my reveries.

I realize he's stopped the car on a lookout over the Pacific shore.

"May I still call you that?" he asks.

"Of course." He always said "Iris" was too ordinary, and I honestly don't mind. At least it isn't a fake name people slapped on me for their own amusement and fun.

He reaches out and touches my hand, just our fingertips connecting. "I know it's probably too soon, and it's going to be a sort of rebound if I'm not careful. But I don't want to bide my time and have someone else pluck you away."

I inhale sharply, my throat going dry. *What?*

"I liked you from the moment we met. The only reason I held

back is you're Julie's friend, and she would have be upset if I'd made a move. So I was taking my time to be sure what I was—*am* —feeling for you wasn't just some passing attraction."

Holy shit. Tony was right about Byron all along. "And...?" *Say you decided it was a temporary crush. Say it was nothing.*

Byron looks deeply into my eyes, then smoothly leans over and in for a kiss, his large palm on my cheek.

Oh. My. God. I freeze, unsure what to do. His lips are firm and coaxing. His tongue moves over my closed lips. I'm not repulsed...but I'm not burning up with lust, either. I'm not sure why. He's a good kisser. There's nothing wrong with his technique. Actually...he could probably hold classes.

Come on. Feel something. Anything.

But I can't. Not even a tinge of warmth rises. Instead, I get frustration. Kissing Byron is like trying to fit together puzzle pieces that are obviously wrong. My mind brings up all the ways Byron's kiss is off, how he isn't Tony. And I feel worse—more alone and detached.

Placing a hand on his shoulder, I gently push him back. His eyes are dark. The slight frown on his face says he already knows.

"I'm sorry, Byron. I'm really flattered, but we can't have anything more than friendship. That's all I feel, and it wouldn't be fair for me to make you think it would ever become more." I wish he hadn't tried, because now things are different. I know how he really feels about me, and he knows I know.

Confusion twists his face. "Because of Blackwood?"

An immediate, defensive "no" springs to my lips, but I catch myself in time. If I hadn't met Tony, would I have reacted differently to the kiss? My gaze roams over Byron's classically handsome face, the gorgeous blue eyes women sigh over. I don't think I would have. I've never felt an ounce of possessiveness or vulnerability with him. He's just my friend. That's all. "No."

Byron doesn't pull away; he stays in position, partially suspended, his hand still on my jaw. For the first time, awkwardness permeates the air around us. I can't help but wonder if I'm losing him too. Inhaling slowly, I gather my thoughts and settle my nerves. "It isn't always easy to go back to the way things were, so if you'd rather not be friends, I understand."

Finally, he pulls back, straightening in his seat. "Well, let's not go overboard." He clears his throat, but it doesn't smooth the rough edge of his voice. "Of course we can still be friends."

"Okay," I say, although I'm not one hundred percent sure it's possible now. But I'm willing to try if he is. Otherwise I'm left with only one friend—Julie.

We sit for a time, not speaking, watching the ocean. I'd rather go home, but I don't want to say anything, lest he think I don't even want to spend time with him anymore. But eventually he starts the car, turns it around and drives me back to Julie's.

"Thanks, Byron," I say. "The drive really cheered me up." I lie because I feel like he deserves something after the rejection.

He laughs. "Well, I can't exactly say the same. But I appreciate your being honest."

"Oh, Byron... I'm really sorry."

He smiles. "It's fine. Really. Call me the next time you have a day off and we'll go do something fun together. As friends."

I shoot him a smile as I climb out of the car...and spot Bobbi snapping a photo in our direction.

What the hell? I want to yell at her to stop, but can't. That'll only get Byron's attention, and he already doesn't like her that much. I don't need a public brawl. "Okay. I will," I say, and shut the door.

As soon as Byron pulls away, I march toward her. "Were you talking a picture of me?"

"I was taking a picture of that Maserati. Nice ride. I might get one someday, when my bakery takes off."

Unbelievable. She's not even trying to give me a plausible lie. "You don't have the decency to tell me the truth even when you're caught red-handed?"

"What do you want me to say, Ivy?" Her voice is clipped, like I'm the one being unreasonable and insulting. "I took the photo for my vision board. I'm making one on Pinterest." She purses her lips, a frown pulling her eyebrows together. "I'm taking a course on charting my destiny, and it's this week's homework."

"Okay, straight up. Are you spying on me for Tony?" I never thought she was, but now? The whole excuse about homework sounds so flimsy. Just like Tony's repeated crap about the "danger to my life."

She cocks an eyebrow. "All right, if you want to know that bad." She unlocks her phone and taps and scrolls her screen a few times. "Here. Texts between me and Tony since you moved in with Julie." She hands me her gadget.

I read the one from Tony.

I know how you feel about spying. I'm not asking you to do that. I just want to know if she's safe. Just yes/no is fine.

Since that time, Bobbi's been texting nothing but *Yes* to him every evening. And he always responds, *Thank you.* No matter how liberal a definition you use, that's hardly spying. But I don't know why he's going this far to check up on me. He knows we're done. And he never did this with Audrey. He reacted with annoyance and contempt to her clingy and jealous antics. I always thought if he and I ever broke up, he'd be the same way with me, too, no matter who left whom.

Suddenly, my head is full of conflicting emotions. I give the phone back to Bobbi, who puts it into her pocket.

"Why does he even care?" I say more to myself than to her, looking at my ring-less left hand.

She answers anyway. "I'm not judging you for leaving him. He lied to you, and that's a shitty thing to do. But he didn't lie about the danger you're in."

Her tone is oddly matter-of-fact. It's the same one she used when she spoke about taking a bullet, and a shiver runs through me. "So Tony wasn't just...exaggerating or something? I'm really in danger?"

"Based on what I know? I'd say it's likely. Somebody tried to kill you before. They could try again."

"The other girl could've been the real person they wanted to get."

"And? That makes you a witness. If I were the killer, I'd want you dead for sure."

Tony said something similar, but back then I was so angry

that I rejected it outright. But now, it's really sinking in. I stare, incredulous that I'd be considered a witness to something I only recall bits and pieces of. "But I don't remember anything."

"Uh-huh. And of course the killer will believe that."

The comment puts a hard stop on my denial. If I were the killer... Bobbi's right. I would want the sole witness to the crime permanently silenced.

So whether I was the real target or not, it doesn't matter. Somebody out there wants me dead.

My blood runs cold.

"Now do you get why Tony's still keeping me on the payroll?" Bobbi asks.

I nod jerkily, then go into Julie's apartment, half dazed. Bobbi follows me to the entrance without saying a word, as though she knows exactly the kind of confused fear I'm feeling right now. She nods goodbye as I close the door.

Julie isn't in. Probably running errands or shopping. I fall on the couch and bury my face in my hands. The more I learn, the more I realize Tony's deception wasn't some simple game. And it's only leaving me more conflicted and confused.

I look at my barren ring finger and the scar on my left wrist. Although Sam said it was from an injury sustained from the car accident, was it really? He's the one who made me into Iris Smith. He could've erased the tattoo while I was asleep. The fewer identifying marks I have, the easier it would be for him to lie. Sam said he pulled me out of the water and left the girl in the blue dress behind.

But why? What about me that was so special that he went to such an extreme length? Blackmail, because I was dating Tony? No. Sam would've contacted him and tried to get something going there.

Tony's tormented face from last night pops into my head. I'm not even angry. Just sad and confused and hurt. I close my eyes, imagining how I would've behaved if I were him. What would I have done if I'd lost Tony because he died? Just the thought sends such sharp pain through me that I put a hand over my heart.

And what would I do if he came back from the dead? I would

be incoherent with joy, wouldn't I? I'd hold on to him and never let him go...

But what if he didn't remember me? Or if he was surrounded by people like Sam and Marty? What if he didn't know who he was and was being used?

Would I tell him the truth? Who he is? What we used to be? That we were in love? That I grieved for him? Wouldn't he think I was crazy, especially if his "relatives" told him so? To get him back, I'd have to go along with the bullshit and wait for a good opportunity to pry him away from those who were using him.

And what if I learned Tony could be ripped from me again through death? Wouldn't I do everything in my power to prevent that?

Yes. Yes, I would.

But I still don't truly understand why he didn't tell me the truth when Sam showed his true colors. Didn't Tony know I would've trusted him? Unless I'm mistaken, a lot of his motivation stemmed from a fear of losing me. Did he think so little of me—of us—that he thought he couldn't risk testing my love that way?

I close my eyes as grief ripples through me. He should've trusted me. He should've told me. He should've—

Just like the way you told him about what Sam said about the girl...how you were responsible for her death?

Flinching, I open my eyes. I...I did that, didn't I? I hid it, then ran to Yuna because I couldn't bear to face him out of shame and fear. If I had told him, would that have been a perfect opening for him to tell me my true past?

I hug my legs. Then, resting my chin on my knees, I try to sort through questions I'll never know the real answers to. But mainly I want to know if I would've acted differently from Tony.

It is easy to say that I would've, but I do my best to be honest with myself. I also consider whether Tony deserves a second chance. Yes, he hurt me like hell, but it wasn't like it was all pain between us. He protected me—saved me from Jamie Thornton, from Sam, from everyone else he thought might hurt me. He held me when I needed his strength, dried my tears when I was grieving, and always pleasured me like it was our last night together.

The patient tenderness he showed... It was only for me, no one else. Isn't that why I was so afraid to tell him my fears about what kind of horrible person I might've been in my past? I didn't want him to turn his back on me.

Even if you remember nothing of your soul mate, when you're reborn, you seek out and love the same soul through a thousand lives and beyond. That's you and Tony... You'll never find another like him, and you'll never feel alive and whole without him.

If I hold on to my anger and hurt, I can never give him another chance. But if I don't...I'll have to make myself vulnerable again, open myself to more potential pain. Fear and a smidgeon of helpless longing tighten in my belly until it makes me hunch over.

Self-preservation says I should cut my losses and move on. Surely, there's another man like him somewhere in the world. But another part of me says I'm being chicken again. Can I really let what's between Tony and me end this way and never have a bit of regret? When I'm on my deathbed, won't I wonder what could've been?

I can't answer with any kind of conviction. Then I know... I'm always going to wonder for the rest of my life.

When I woke up from the coma, I promised myself I wouldn't live my life frivolously. And right now, I'm spending my precious time poorly. Every day without Tony creates a bigger and more aching hollowness inside. I'm going to work through the pain, try to salvage what we can. If it really is beyond our ability to fix, then at least I'll know I tried and I won't torture myself with *what-could've-been*s for the rest of my life.

67

IVY

THE NEXT DAY, I CHOOSE MY OUTFIT WITH CARE. A sleeveless carmine dress and sunny yellow sandals. My hair hangs loose around my lightly made-up face. I want to look serious but also somewhat soft and gentle, so Tony knows I'm not seeing him out of anger or some other negative, vindictive feeling.

A clean slate. A fresh new start. Our last try. That's what I'm going to offer.

"Looking fancy. Where are you going?" Julie says, dumping extra sugar into her coffee. She's in a magenta nightshirt that says, "The person wearing this shirt is too hot for any man to handle," in glittery silver and gold across the chest. It reminds me of a disco mirror-ball.

"I have some things to work out with Tony."

Her eyebrows rise. "You've decided to forgive him?"

"I have no clue how it's going to turn out." It's easy to say we're going to start clean, but I don't know what that even entails.

One note at a time, Ivy.

She puts a hand on my arm. "Whatever you want, I'm behind you a hundred percent."

"You are? I thought you didn't like Tony."

"I'm still not crazy about him, but I really don't like how gloomy you've been. Whatever you're going to do, if it'll make you smile again, I'm all for it."

I flush. I had no idea I was that obvious.

"How about some coffee before you go?"

"Thanks." I take a mug and sip it.

When Bobbi shows up, I ask her to check to make sure Tony's home. She nods with a faint grunt, reminding me a little of TJ, and texts him to confirm. "He's home."

"Great." I put my empty cup in the dishwasher. "Let's get going, then."

She drives quietly, not trying to second-guess what I'm doing or offer any advice, for which I'm grateful. I'm already nervous as it is. I told Tony I don't trust him anymore. Will he wonder why I'm doing this now? Will he be suspicious that I'm doing this half-heartedly?

Or maybe he'll be happy I changed my mind. *Come on, Ivy. Think positive.*

Bobbi stops the car and walks with me into the lobby. The concierge smiles from his desk. "Good morning, Miss Smith."

"Hello." I smile back.

Then I notice a blond woman in a royal-blue jumpsuit. Her hair's swirled into a chic French twist, and her makeup is flawless. She's extremely slim, her body small-boned and frail. I tilt my head. Something about her feels familiar, but I can't quite place...

Wait, she's the woman at Sam's funeral. The one who had the "good riddance" smirk. What is she doing here? It seems like too much of a coincidence that she was at the funeral and now is here in Tony's building. I take a closer look at her, trying not to be too obvious. She's beautiful, her nose small and straight, her mouth full and now set in a gracious line. But the most extraordinary features are her eyes—one blue and one green.

She stares at me, meeting my gaze squarely. I feel my cheeks heat.

"So. You're Iris," she says.

She knows who I am? I could swear we've never met. Did I know her before the coma? Or maybe she heard about me from Sam. "Long story, but my name is really Ivy," I say finally.

Her perfectly shaped eyebrows twitch. "Is that so? How very interesting."

Something about her really bothers me. She isn't exactly rude, but she's too coldly controlled...and there's a hint of superiority in her attitude. "I'm sorry, but you are...?"

She smiles, her eyes cool. "I'm Margot Blackwood."

ANTHONY AND IVY'S STORY CONTINUES IN *MERCY*.

TITLES BY NADIA LEE

The Sins Trilogy

Sins

Secrets

Mercy

The Billionaire's Claim Duet

Obsession

Redemption

Sweet Darlings Inc.

That Man Next Door

That Sexy Stranger

That Wild Player

Billionaires' Brides of Convenience

A Hollywood Deal

A Hollywood Bride

An Improper Deal

An Improper Bride

An Improper Ever After

An Unlikely Deal

An Unlikely Bride

A Final Deal

∾

The Pryce Family

The Billionaire's Counterfeit Girlfriend
The Billionaire's Inconvenient Obsession
The Billionaire's Secret Wife
The Billionaire's Forgotten Fiancée
The Billionaire's Forbidden Desire
The Billionaire's Holiday Bride

∾

Seduced by the Billionaire

Taken by Her Unforgiving Billionaire Boss
Pursued by Her Billionaire Hook-Up
Pregnant with Her Billionaire Ex's Baby
Romanced by Her Illicit Millionaire Crush
Wanted by Her Scandalous Billionaire
Loving Her Best Friend's Billionaire Brother

ABOUT NADIA LEE

New York Times and *USA Today* bestselling author Nadia Lee writes sexy contemporary romance. Born with a love for excellent food, travel and adventure, she has lived in four different countries, kissed stingrays, been bitten by a shark, ridden an elephant and petted tigers.

Currently, she shares a condo overlooking a small river and sakura trees in Japan with her husband and son. When she's not writing, she can be found reading books by her favorite authors or planning another trip.

To learn more about Nadia and her projects, please visit http://www.nadialee.net. To receive updates about upcoming works, sneak peeks and bonus epilogues featuring some of your favorite couples from Nadia, please visit http://www.nadialee.net/vip to join her VIP List.